PER⚡L

By

BARBARA LAMB

July 2021

PERIL First Published: July 2021

Author: Barbara Lamb, Toronto, Canada

COPYRIGHT © Barbara Lamb
ISBN Number 978-1-7778099-1-1

All Rights Reserved

Printed in Canada

This book is a work of fiction. Names, characters, places and incidents are the product of the author's imagination. Any resemblance to actual persons, living or dead, is entirely coincidental.

COMPENDIUM OF ACROYNMS

BBC: British Broadcasting Corporation

COMINT: Communications Intelligence

ERR: Einsatzstab Reichsleiter Rosenberg: The Nazi `Special Task Force' which looted art and other cultural assets from victims across Europe

GCHQ: Government Communications Headquarters, responsible for the United Kingdom's cybersecurity, among others;

FRA: Försvarets Radioanstalt, the National Defense Radio Establishment of Sweden, responsible for the country's cybersecurity;

MI5: Military Intelligence, Section 5, the United Kingdom's internal, domestic counter-intelligence agency

MI6: Military Intelligence, Section 6, the United Kingdom's foreign intelligence service

Mossad: Israel's Institute for Intelligence and Special Operations

NATO: North Atlantic Treaty Organization

NSA: National Security Agency of the United States

OSCE: Organization for Security and Cooperation in Europe

UNDP: United Nations Development Programme

London, England	Edinburgh, Scotland	Ungheni, Moldova
Berlin, Germany	Geneva, Switzerland	Sarajevo, Bosnia
Munich, Germany	Chisinau, Moldova	Durres, Albania
Belfast, North Ireland	Transnistria, Moldova	Tirana, Albania
Ostrava, Czechoslakia	Cahul, Moldova	Novi Pasar, Serbia
Belgrade, Serbia	Gaza, Israel	The Hague, Netherlands
Novi Sad, Serbia	Jerusalem, Israel	Odessa, Ukraine
Stockholm, Sweden	Varna, Bulgaria	
Kleipetos, Lithuania	Sanjak, Serbia	
Kaliningrad, Lithuania	Utrecht, Netherlands	

ii

PROLOGUE

March 9, 2019, Kleipedos Port, Lithuania

Lieutenant Jonas Gerulaitis of Lithuania's military took his security job very seriously. He'd almost lost his marriage over his prolonged stint of unemployment. He was not going to go through the pain of separation like that ever again. His new job as a guard of the Light Natural Gas (LNG) Terminal was a stroke of great fortune. To his wife's delight, it had snagged them free housing that just happened to look out over the Baltic Sea. As an added bonus, every day he and the rest of the country could give the Russians the finger now that Lithuania could buy its gas from Norway and store it here at Kleipetos. The Russkis would retaliate, of course, estimating that the bloody Americans, EU and NATO, curse them all, would be too cowardly, too divided, to come to the aid of his little country. He'd spent twenty years of his life under Soviet occupation afraid to speak or even think lest someone hear his real thoughts and disappear him to the camps. May he be spared a return to such a fate. He crossed himself.

Enough! Over the next hour, he must do his part to make sure that Russia's visiting Minister of Energy survived his visit to Kleipetos. Why the idiot politicians were letting a Russian get anywhere near this place... He looked up to the sky asking God this very question. He made a quick prayer that his service to his country would earn him a place in heaven, which he also prayed had an infinite supply of vodka.

There must be two hundred guards on site, many of them hired just for this occasion, most of them bumbling around. To enable him to scan for any sign of trouble, he stationed himself at the back left, below the makeshift elevated podium where meaningless speeches would shortly begin.

As Lithuania's Minister of Foreign Affairs shook hands on stage with Victor Tolstoi, Russia's charismatic Energy Minister, Jonas sensed more than saw a commotion fifty meters away in front of the speakers. Turning slightly to his left to get a better view, Jonas felt a prick in his neck, and then, still facing forward, eyes wide open, took his last breath.

The killer, dressed like Gerulaitis and carrying impeccable military credentials, knew his job. Wait for the diversion. Take forty seconds to kill Gerulaitis while he's still standing. Shoot Tolstoi while holding Gerulaitis' firearm close to his body. Appear to wrestle Gerulaitis to the ground. Make sure Gerulaitis is still holding the weapon. Shoot him with the sod's own rifle. Finally, take credit for bringing him down.

He prepared for the investigation that would undoubtedly follow, happily thinking of the bonus he always received for a job well done.

April 5, 2019, Belgrade, Serbia

Milan Marić, Serbia's dynamic young President, lit a Marlboro and settled back to enjoy the ride in the powerful

Mercedes as it sped south past the rich agricultural lands of Vojvodina to Belgrade. Articulate and charismatic, he was able to share with his people a vision of where Serbia could be and what it could achieve, even if the road was going to be a bumpy one.

With four days to go, his win was a virtual certainty. Still, his nationalist opponent was making late inroads south of Belgrade where he was attracting votes through fear mongering on steroids. Those rural Neanderthals were backwards, always had been, always would be. If they were to vote for the opposition, Serbia would likely split into two, the rich Europe-leaning north leaving the poor south, by force if necessary. Such an outcome was unthinkable. The only people who would benefit from that were the Russians who were overtly courting Serbia, most recently offering to sell military equipment and training. Milan's opponent had seized on the opportunity, arguing that Serbia needed to re-establish itself as a regional power. Milan had no intention of letting his country slide back into the Russian orbit, which could only reignite regional tensions and sink Serbia's bid to join the European Union. Most Serbs knew what they needed and it was freedom and stability.

As his driver pulled to the front of Milan's campaign office in Novi Beograd, Milan sat up abruptly. A phalanx of police was blocking the door to his storefront office. A bomb scare? A threat against his life? Cautiously, he climbed out of the car. Before he could demand an explanation, he was seized and thrown into the back of an armoured car.

Hours of painful interrogation followed in a dark room of Belgrade District Prison. "Write your confession and you'll serve only eight years. You have thirty minutes to accept this generous offer. If you do not, evidence will be presented to the public showing you hired thugs to kill your opponent."

"There is no such evidence!" He could hardly speak through split lips and broken cheekbones.

As the interrogator walked him through a detailed paper trail that demonstrated his guilt, he knew that even the best lawyer could not prove his innocence, though innocent he was.

PART I

JEOPARDY

*The devil can cite scripture
for his purpose…*

William Shakespeare

CHAPTER 1

Morning, April 10, 2019, London, England

"Rik, dear boy. Come. Sit. How long do we have?" Neal slapped him heartily on the back and waved him to the round table. As usual, it was covered with teetering stacks of folders, a laptop, assorted candy wrappers and a stained teacup of Queen Victoria that hadn't been washed for days.

Rik Whitford smiled. Neal was the same as ever, bald with a ring of grey tufty hair and a ragged, multi-coloured beard. He was most at home in his working office, as he called it. The other one, upstairs, was the `bullshit' place where he met assorted pols and dignitaries. His white shirt was stained with coffee, his pants creased and his shoes scuffed. His skin was so pale that Rik wondered if he ever saw the light of day.

Far from the jolly uncle he projected, Rik's boss was the Chief of MI6. Tempered like steel as a double agent in Russia during the late seventies, Neal could be as ruthless as the job demanded. There was no one Rik trusted or respected more. If Neal sent you out, he had your back.

"We've got two hours," said Rik. "I'm catching my ride at one. Gets me into Moldova around three pm. If everything goes according to schedule, I should be back here tomorrow morning with new Intel on the link between the Russians and the funding of terrorism."

"Good, good. But first things first. I'll brew us some coffee."

"No. Decaf!"

"Decaf," he scoffed. "A waste of time in a cup if you ask me," he said laughing at his joke, the one he told every time they were together.

Rik smiled and completed their ritual. "You know bloody well you wouldn't get a word in edgewise if I drank caffeine. Just imagine. I'd divulge all the secrets of the Crown within ten minutes if my interrogators were to ply me with real coffee."

Neal eyed his favourite agent, a frown beginning to appear. Rik looked haggard, older than his thirty-eight years. The worry lines across his forehead were more pronounced, the circles under his eyes darker than Neal had seen before. "What's bothering you? You've something on your mind, and don't tell me I'm wrong."

There were times that Rik appreciated Neal's role as a surrogate father, but today was not one of them. "I'm just..." He restarted. "When you recruited me, you promised me travel and intrigue. Over our fourteen years together, you've delivered that and more. I still feel a high every time I'm about to go on an Op. I know what we're doing is important. But this fight against terrorism is going to go on for generations. Does this mean that I'll never be able to live a real life?"

"Have you met someone? Is that what this is about?"

"How is that even possible? I'm an agent masquerading as a diplomat. As long as I'm under deep cover, no one, not even my family, can know who I really am. I can't be honest with anyone. It's getting..." He trailed off. "Bloody hell. This is complete drivel. Let's just move on."

Neal remained silent for a moment, considering his response. "Do you know what you'd want to do, if not this? Where you'd want to be?"

His elbows on his knees, Rik looked up at Neal and then down at the dark blue carpet. "I know how fortunate I am to have—" and Rik waved his arm at the room. "Frankly, I can't imagine not working for you. But London no longer feels like home. So, probably somewhere in Europe, doing a job that has relevance but isn't top secret."

"Why don't we leave it that you spend some time mulling over where you might like to land? If and when you tell me you absolutely must move on to a less sensitive position, we'll explore options."

Rik nodded. "Let's change the subject."

"Right. I did want to raise the Milan Marić issue with you. I know you became friends with him and his wife when you were stationed in Belgrade. Could these corruption charges be true?"

"No. Not for a moment. For one thing, Milan inherited considerable wealth from his father. He doesn't need money. And his wife's father, organised crime? When I was in Belgrade exploring criminal groups' ties with the funding of terrorism, if Zoritza's father had been involved in underworld activities I would have heard about it. I know Milan, the man, and I'm certain he'd do nothing to harm the Serbia he wants to bring into the European Union. The question I've been asking myself is who benefits from Milan's departure from the political scene?"

Absently, Neal pawed his beard. "I've been tilling that same ground with our Interpol friends who believe he's been set up. I have my thoughts but before sharing them I'd like to hear yours."

"Milan has launched a full-out attack on populist leaders in Britain, Hungary, Poland and Germany. When he labelled his opposition in Serbia as Hungary Light, I think he hit a nerve."

"You mean –."

"Yes. Milan's polls surged, overnight. Many Serbians, particularly those in the more cosmopolitan north, are afraid of what's been happening over the border in Hungary. Its president mocks anyone, any institution who questions him, however experienced, as corrupt or in some other way, delegitimized. For almost a decade, he's managed to use his power to become a dictator by inciting fear among the population."

Neal nodded. "It seems he's managed to make himself the model for the populists across Europe, in the U.S., and now here for that matter."

"That he has. He says he represents `the people' against `the others'. And you can fill in the blank about who the others are:

immigrants, black people, homosexuals, the elite, the media, Jews, take your pick. He's made the ethnic majority in Hungary believe *they're* the downtrodden minority. Violence between groups is on the rise. The influx of Syrian refugees hasn't helped matters."

"Have you been following our news here?" Neal asked.

Rik looked questioningly at his boss.

"Something strange is going on. Over the past six months, there's been an exponential increase across social media of concocted stories about rapes and murders committed by Muslims in particular, as well as by other minorities. However false, these stories have gone viral."

"Who's responsible?"

"MI5 and GCHQ have been working day and night to identify the source or sources, but without much success. In the meantime, new alt-right, neo-Nazi and skinhead groups are springing up every day and growing their memberships apace. In response, Muslims and other minorities are becoming more active and militant, calling Britain racist."

Rik's eyebrows rose. "I'm surprised GCHQ can't figure out who's spreading this fake news." Government Communications Headquarters or GCHQ was most famous for its work at Bletchley Park during the war, when it broke the Germans' Enigma code. Now, it was among the world's foremost combatants against cyber warfare.

"It's happening too fast. What's just as worrying is that the planted reports are having an alarming impact on our police. It's as if they've been given permission to use force against anyone who's a shade darker than they are, especially in the north of the country and here in parts of London. And now we have a senior military ass beating the drums for military intervention against, as he puts it, the scourge of Islam. MI5 is tearing its hair out."

"Has MI5 brought up these concerns with the Minister?"

"Yes. But he's afraid to seem dovish, particularly since Brexit. When this kind of incendiary rhetoric comes from our law enforcement and military, we're entering a new realm. If this cyber attack continues to ratchet up tensions, I wouldn't be surprised to see an authoritarian alt-right demagogue, well beyond what we have now, win the next election."

Rik frowned. "Milan in Serbia may be a victim of a similar phenomenon. Now that he's gone, his opponent, Branko Grbić a populist hyper-nationalist, will be the biggest winner. It wouldn't surprise me to see the north try to split off. That, I fear, could spark a new war in the Balkans. Grbić is being wooed by the Russians, who want to sell military equipment to Serbia. If it becomes southern Serbia and Russia on one side and northern Serbia and the EU on the other, things could get ugly very fast."

"Bloody hell." Neal waved his hand at Rik. "After tonight, head to Belgrade. See if there's any chance of getting in to see Milan. Perhaps his wife will talk to you. A new war could fatally weaken the EU. And wouldn't Russia just love that. Not to mention far right parties on our Island."

Rik nodded. "I'd better get going. I'll let you know how the Op goes tonight."

Neal walked his best agent to the door. "Good luck," he whispered to himself.

CHAPTER 2

Night, April 10, 2019, The Hague, Netherlands

After years of dangerous fieldwork, everything came down to a rain-soaked night in the village of Cahul in southern Moldova. Yet, here Sofie was stuck in The Hague in the Netherlands, 2000 kilometres away, observing. In the process of putting the whole Op together, she'd somehow gone from its major player to a minor one - if not wholly superfluous.

She stood at the large window looking out over the fast-darkening scene below her until she caught her reflection. She looked away quickly.

Logically, she knew she wasn't ugly, judging from the numerous men who'd had made passes at her. But logic and evidence were weak defences against the wealth of proof she'd accumulated with the help of her parents. "Don't look in the mirror! Only vain people do that and you have nothing to be vain about," her mother had drilled into her.

Whether it was school, piano or sports, she had to be perfect so that she could defend herself against her father's sneak attacks. "Those clothes don't suit you. Your friends have style. Learn from them." The only time she remembered receiving her father's approval was the day she showed up a detested colleague of his in an impromptu skeet-shooting competition.

She wore her thick, wavy ink-black hair jagged and flicked out at the ends. It may look tousled, but it was easy to care for. On the rare occasions that she really looked at herself, she saw intense green-hazel eyes staring back at her, highlighted by strong eyebrows and a pale complexion.

Though she came from money, her furnishings were Spartan and her dress code minimalist: Lace-up black boots, a black leather jacket over a white top and black jeans. She knew she was intense about her work and that others found her exhausting. While she had perfect recall and a photographic memory, she often forgot where she'd put her sunglasses or what day it was. One of her friends got used to saying, sympathetically, "It must be hard to be you!"

"What I observe is a striking woman. That's what I see," her sympathetic physician had once said. "The anxiety attacks you experience are your body's way of dealing with the feelings of insecurity and inadequacy that you acquired in your childhood. You need to learn to be kinder to yourself, to see yourself as the beautiful person you are." Instead, she'd invested herself in her work.

Damn. Her espresso was cold. She drank it anyway. She pushed her hair back from her forehead and, for the umpteenth time, wondered if there was anything more she could have done.

Five years ago, she'd asked to be transferred from the United Nations Development Programme in Belgrade, Serbia to Chisinau, Moldova. Her closest female associates were horrified. Was she insane? Was it a man? Was any man worth it? Why, of all places, Moldova?

It was obvious to her. Moldova, increasingly under Russia's thumb, was tilting towards a pro-Russian government, which could make it ripe for a takeover. It also hosted many international (mainly Russian) criminal organizations operating out of Transnistria, Moldova's lawless Russia-controlled outlier. And it was the epicentre of human trafficking. Moldova would soon make its presence known on the international map, and she was going to be there when it did.

Over her four and half years in Moldova, she'd tracked RussTech, a cover she'd discovered for a branch of the Russian mafia that was trafficking women, arms and drugs using Transnistria as its hub. What made RussTech different was the sheer scale of its operations, especially in its trafficking of humans. Every year, thousands of women were mysteriously disappearing from Moldova, many through the promise of lucrative jobs as nannies and hostesses, or through kidnappings often facilitated by local mayors of small towns. At any one time, up to half of the women in Moldova's rural communities were missing, either having voluntarily trafficked themselves for economic reasons or having been forced into slavery.

Her fieldwork first uncovered Artem Gabori, a drug-smuggling Roma who had deep ties with criminal organizations up and down the Balkans. He, in turn, led her to Evgeny Sokolov, a shadowy Russian oligarch who was the mastermind of crime in Transnistria. Over time, she was able to verify not only that he existed but also that he was the kingpin behind RussTech, the corporate front for a multi-billion dollar international criminal network.

Shortly after, fate intervened in a kick-ass way. An undercover source she'd recruited in Transnistria at no small risk to his own safety presented Sofie with proof of a straight line between RussTech and the funding of global jihadist terrorism. At once triumphant and terrified, she knew she needed to get this information to the right people, fast, namely the Organization for Security and Cooperation in Europe's Hague regional office in the Netherlands, which dealt almost exclusively with trafficking and terrorism.

Afraid that her junior position wouldn't carry the influence necessary to get the attention of the right people, she decided to approach Philippe Lapointe, a seasoned OSCE colleague she'd worked with in Belgrade. She asked him if he would make the overture to an OSCE colleague of his, Marc Jansen in The Hague. Philippe jumped at the opportunity to present her Intel as his own and arranged a confidential get-together with Jansen that would include him and his `assistant', Sofie McAdam.

The meeting got off to a rocky start. While Jansen was obviously interested, Friderik Whitford, a Brit, impatiently shifted in his chair, taking no notes, saying nothing. Marc Jansen neglected to mention why this guy was even at the meeting. Meanwhile, Philippe strutted back and forth like a peacock, presenting her findings. She'd kept her head down, steaming. At least at the end, she was able to field a number of questions that Philippe couldn't answer. She caught Whitford staring at her more than once, which made her increasingly uncomfortable. Just before the end, he disappeared. She was singularly unimpressed.

"Please stay until the end of the day." That was all that Jansen had said. She'd waited for hours, preparing herself to be disappointed and pondering what she was going to do with the rest of her life. She couldn't contain her surprise when Marc indicated that she and Philippe would be seconded to OSCE, The Hague, effective immediately.

Over the following six months, the small team consisting of Marc, Philippe, Sofie and two other colleagues conceived Operation Bessarabia, a complex plan to intercept the traffickers.

Philippe not only seemed to forget who had generated the Intel in the first place, but regularly belittled her in front of their peers. Perhaps, she speculated, he regretted leaving Belgrade, now such a hotbed as the recent arrest of Milan Marić demonstrated. She found it unbelievable that of all people, Marić turned out to be corrupt.

Tonight, assuming all went well, Artem Gabori would be captured and many young girls stolen from Moldovan villages, saved. Based on intelligence gathered by the team, Gabori would be carrying documentation too sensitive to put on the internet, including flash drives with names of jihadi organizations, funding amounts and, ideally, bank account numbers. The hope was that they could deal RussTech a major, if not fatal, blow. At the very least these documents would open up important avenues to undermine the funding of terrorism, not to mention drug running and human trafficking. Failure on the other hand could undermine months of the team's work and could drive RussTech underground.

Friderik Whitford, or, as he preferred to be called, Rik, had been an intermittent presence on the team, never clarifying his role or his position within the OSCE. "He's a rising star in peacekeeping. We're lucky to have him." So went the office chatter. The rising star didn't bother to talk to her, didn't give her the time of day. No problem — but irritating. Though no more than six feet, those who towered over him deferred to him. His solemnity conveyed the impression that he was carrying the weight of the world on his shoulders. Even on those rare occasions when he smiled, it was with a sardonic twist. She'd never seen him laugh. He must be a few years older than her thirty-four. Good-looking, she had to acknowledge. He had thick dark mahogany hair with a few strands of grey. His blue-violet eyes, framed by long dark lashes could have made him pretty if it weren't for a jagged scar that cut through his left eyebrow and the worry lines that so often creased his forehead.

The team assembled, voices muted and strained. At 9:45 pm, the monitor was switched on. Action was about to begin.

Anxiously, she applied her lip balm. Philippe would be in the OSCE's office in Chisinau, and Rik, one hour south at Cahul in a hidden shelter where he'd monitor the intercept as it unfolded. After weeks of drought, the lashing rain out there was an unwelcome surprise. Visibility was almost nil. What if the roads to Cahul became impassable? This operation couldn't fail. Too much depended on it.

The military speak between team members in the armed vehicles became a quiet drone over the drum of the raindrops. Sofie leaned in, frowning. Were those headlights? Was that the convey arriving? Suddenly, the feed turned to static. Then silence.

Night, April 10, 2019, Cahul, Southern Moldova

Rik was getting colder and tenser by the minute in a small dank hut just a few meters from the road. The pelting rain made such a deafening din on the tin roof that he could scarcely hear himself think, let alone communicate with the military unit outside.

The next hour could produce the breakthrough he and Neal had sought for almost fifteen years. Rik remembered that first meeting as if it were yesterday. He'd been a month away from graduation from Oxford when a professor had informed him that a colleague wanted to meet him the next day in a private room on campus.

"We've had you in our sights for quite some time. Your facility with languages, particularly the Slavic ones, and your top marks in economics and European politics are of interest to us." Whatever Rik had responded had gotten him a second interview with, as it turned out, Neal. "We need someone of your skills rather desperately at the moment. The life we're offering won't be easy. But it will be rewarding. What we want you to do is to help us identify and eliminate new sources of funding for terrorism on European soil."

Six months later, he'd completed training in agent running, surveillance, counter-surveillance, arms and explosives, infiltration and exfiltration, many of which he'd had to put to use. Then it was on to money laundering techniques, building on his academic interests in finance and economics.

As it was explained to him, after 9/11, the West's intelligence community had managed to gather irrefutable proof that the House of Saud was complicit in the funding of attacks on U.S. and European soil, and in the spread of terrorism throughout the Arabian Peninsula, Africa and many Asian countries. Yet, despite largely successful efforts to shut down the Saudis' funding of Islamic terrorism, extreme Islam, far from dying off, was exploding. "Find out who this new actor is. That's your brief."

What he *had* uncovered was extremely worrying. Rik now knew where the money wasn't coming from. Not Saudi Arabia. Russia? Not so much. It was terrified as it was of the threat of Islam from Chechnya and many other former Soviet Republics that were predominantly

Muslim. And not Iran. Its leaders were Persian and Shia who hated the Sunni more than they detested the West. Their chosen purveyor of terror was Hezbollah and it focused its brand of evil on Sunnis, the Kurds and Israel.

Rik was forced to conclude that some unknown group or groups were using their criminal spoils to fund new radical Islamic organizations. Whoever it was, the enormity of the funding represented a ticking time bomb for the entire intelligence community throughout Europe and North America, not to mention Israel. Unfortunately, these days, each country's secret service was focused on its own internal problems. The sharing of information was spectacularly absent. Brexit and bellicose rhetoric from the American President had pierced arteries and most intelligence agencies were bleeding.

Six months ago, when Rik caught wind of a meeting about Moldovan criminal organizations and their possible links to terrorism funding, he'd invited himself to attend. He was impressed by the quality of the Intel, clearly not sourced by Philippe Lapointe, who seemed to be acting as a front for Sofie McAdam. He wondered why. He enjoyed observing her when she wasn't looking, the way she carried herself, erect and with attitude. She didn't mar her face with makeup of any kind, thank god. Her translucent complexion set off her eyes, at times vivid green, at others, hazel. Her low voice was quiet and reassuring, except, he mused, when she rushed her sentences as if afraid she might be cut off. She was intense. Well, goddamn it, so was he. She drew him like no one else had in so long. He was going to talk to Neal again about making some cha...

Through the torrential rain, he heard the enemy convoy even before he saw it. He knew what would happen next. The border guards would stop the trucks and ask a few innocuous questions and all the while, soldiers would surround the convoy. With guns to their heads, the interdiction would go smoothly.

Gunfire erupted from the three trucks. The sound ripped through the rain.

Rik sprinted from his shelter. Young girls tumbled from the trucks, pushed out of the panel doors. The gunfire and drumming of rain on the metal vehicles drowned their screams. Their captors were using them as human shields.

"Cease fire! Stop!" Rik yelled into his mike. But Interpol's secret Ops team, OSCE's muscle, kept firing back. He raced to the trucks, the rain blinding him. Frantic, he searched for the commanding officer. He grabbed someone of rank. "You're murdering the girls. Stop your men!" he screamed above the rattling of rain and bullets.

Minutes later, the traffickers were outnumbered and subdued.

No Gabori, no documents. Every single detainee appeared to have been hired for the first time. Worst of all, fourteen girls were killed and ten others injured in the crossfire. Sick and furious, all Rik could do was to order medical back-up to ensure that the surviving girls were properly looked after.

This was the second time in as many months that one of his OSCE missions had gone sideways despite precise planning. He didn't believe in coincidences. There was a mole and whoever it was, it was someone senior in either MI6 or OSCE.

Night, April 10, 2019 Chisinau, Moldova

Philippe called Marc Jansen in The Hague to discuss the disaster unfolding in Cahul. Damn it all to hell. He'd been so close to his first big win. This could kill his career rather than boost it. Needing a good stiff drink, he decided to walk back to his hotel and wait for Rik. It was raining hard. As he unfurled his umbrella, he was blinded by headlights bearing down on him.

Early Morning, April 11, 2019, Ungheni, Moldova

A convoy of trucks three and half hours' drive north of Cahul quietly crossed Moldova's eastern border into Romania leaving two border guards happy with the night's transaction.

CHAPTER 3

Morning, April 11, 2019, The Hague

Her back to the door, Sofie heard Rik enter the room. Still profoundly upset about the previous night, she took her own sweet time to prepare a cup of espresso.

"Sofie."

She turned. He looked dishevelled, defeated. Her annoyance immediately evaporated.

"I assume you understand why I had my colleague, Miriam, set you up here at our safe house last night. Did she explain?" Rik leaned heavily against the window ledge and gazed at the dreary sky.

"No. She only said you'd ordered that I come with her, and that I mustn't speak to anyone else on the team. Suffice it to say, I'm all ears."

He ran his hand back and forth over the top of his head, causing strands to tuft up in spikes. "Someone betrayed us last night. As a result," Rik shook his head back in forth, "as a result, fourteen girls died in the crossfire during our intercept."

"Oh, dear god."

"Some of them looked twelve years old."

"Those animals! For them, these girls are worth less than cattle. I've interviewed dozens of them, many who risked their lives to get their stories out. Another victory for Sokolov," she said bitterly, fighting back tears.

"You're the only person I can be sure had no motive to undermine this operation."

"Me?" She fumbled in the pocket of her black leather jacket for her lip balm.

"Let's end the pretence. It was obvious from that first meeting that you were the real source of the Intel Lapointe presented as his own. I'm sad to say he paid the ultimate price for taking credit for it." Rik moved towards a chair and gestured for her to sit on the sofa.

"What do you mean, the ultimate price?"

"Within minutes of the debacle last night, he was killed. A hit-and-run."

"Philippe's...?"

"I'm afraid so."

Her espresso hit the coffee table. She ran to the counter and returned with a cloth. Methodically, she wiped the drips, focusing on her breathing.

"Based on eyewitness accounts, it wasn't an accident."

"What? Oh, no." Breathe in. Breathe out. In. Out. "I...Why am I in danger?"

She's missing the point. "It seems reasonable to assume that RussTech killed Philippe. Someone in our inner circle sold us out."

"Who? Who would do that?"

"Since it was you who uncovered RussTech, I'm confident you'd do anything to ensure the Op's success. I only hope that your real role hasn't been discovered. But I propose we put you in a safe house in London while we figure out who the traitor is and whether or not he or she knew that it was you who discovered Sokolov and Gabori."

Her eyes grew unfocused.

"Stay with me, Sofie. I've already set the plan in motion to protect you. Until we're certain you're not their next target, you mustn't talk to anyone. Not your colleagues, not your friends, not your family."

Rik's words still weren't making sense. "But what..."

He leaned towards her. "I hope you know you can place your trust in me."

Her mouth pursed creating a little dimple he found distracting.

He continued. "I'm going to share information with you that not even my closest friends or family knows. My boss is not the OSCE although the OSCE believes it is and must continue to do so. You came onto my radar because of the Intel you uncovered linking trafficking to the funding of terrorism."

She looked at him as if seeing him for the first time.

"Only a handful of people are aware of my non-OSCE status. Now you're one of them. I'm trusting you with this information because I fear that your life depends on taking me seriously."

"What do you think happened last night? And how can you be absolutely positive that there was a traitor?"

How lovely you are when your guard comes down, he thought. "I got word this morning that a convoy of trucks, in all likelihood carrying Gabori, went through Ungheni into Romania last night just after our Op began. It's pretty clear that the trucks we intercepted at Cahul were meant as a decoy. All of the drivers and shooters were hired just for the night. You know we kept operational details tight and limited to a very small group. So how did RussTech find out we'd be waiting for them? While I can't provide any details, I had a similar failure occur a number of months ago with an important operation I ran out of Hamburg. If one of our OSCE team is our mole, I'm going to nail him. He cost those girls and Philippe their lives." Rik closed his eyes and rubbed his fingers over his left temple, unable to block the image of a young woman who'd died in his arms. He fought down his nausea.

Sofie was stunned. "Those girls…Oh god, I feel sick for them, for their families, for… But if RussTech knew we were coming, why would anyone even show up, especially with the girls? Why not just leave us there, waiting for the whole night?"

"You're right. It's illogical. It's almost as if they wanted us to confirm that they're into trafficking. You've studied them. What do you think?"

This was the first time Rik had asked her opinion about anything.

She appreciated it more than he could possibly know. "What I've learned during my time in Moldova and Transnistria is that what you see is not what you get. There's always a deeper game. I think they chose to be caught to confirm to us that they know we're on to them. It suggests that they want us to focus on their trafficking rather than whatever else they're planning." She paused for a moment. "I really think that's it. Since no one you captured is part of their trafficking outfit, they must really think we're all marks to buy it as a bona fide intercept. Maybe we should get something published that confirms what they want us to believe. Let poor Philippe be the martyr for uncovering the trafficking racket."

"Makes sense. But it was you, not Philippe, who uncovered the Intel about RussTech's link to terrorism. Who knew that it was your work? Did you tell anyone at the OSCE? Think! I can totally understand if you resented Philippe for taking credit and told someone else about your work. Marc? One of your friends?"

She ran through the events of the last several months and shook her head. "Only my undercover source in Transnistria. As far as I know, he's still alive. He wouldn't be if he ever disclosed his connection to me. But even though I made Philippe commit to total confidentiality, I have no way of knowing if he broke rank. I just don't think he would have," she mused, "because he wanted to be the kingpin. I can't imagine he'd undermine the perception that the operation was based on his Intel. No. I think I'm safe. But obviously, you don't."

"I can't be sure and neither can you."

"No, but I don't think anyone really notices me. I...I find it hard to believe that I'm on anyone's radar."

"Let me explain further. My main job is to identify where terrorist organizations are getting funding for their European operations. Since my work has led me to believe that much of it is coming out of Eastern Europe or Russia, you may imagine my interest when I heard of Philippe's request to meet with Jansen."

"But at that first meeting, you were so obviously uninterested, and since then, only half-heartedly involved."

"So, I was successful." Rik smiled, his lips turning upward in satisfaction. "Hopefully everyone on the team thinks the same, because your life and mine may rely on it." Absently he rubbed his right hand across the dark stubble that revealed he hadn't had time to shave. "While I couldn't show deference to your work, I did steer Marc to take on the mission. I can finally say that I was very impressed that you were able to uncover the link between RussTech and terrorism. But that also leaves you in a vulnerable position, which gets us back to your need to accept our protection."

For an instant, she swelled at his praise and then became agitated. "Actually, what I want to do is to take leave and go home. I'm not sure how much you know about me, about where I grew up. But I do think I'd be safe there."

"I did a little checking on you before and after that first meeting." He ignored her frown. "I know you'll soon turn thirty-five, you're from Canada and speak French and German. You also picked up some Russian for your work. Your family seems to have been affluent, so you don't have to work. You studied in Canada, transferred to Lund in Sweden for your undergrad work. Then you went on to Utrecht, where you did an international development masters focusing on the rebuilding of democracy in Eastern Europe. You have some martial arts training and are a champion marksman. So, perhaps, despite your mild comportment, you're not a soft touch." He smiled. "From what I've observed, you're a workaholic, not so much because you're climbing the career ladder but because you care, maybe too much, about trying to save the world. How am I doing so far?"

Her frown had turned into a glare.

He continued quickly, "I also know that you worked in Belgrade before you went to Moldova. Depending on how you look at it, you were either very fortunate or very unlucky to find out that your work on human trafficking was linked with international terrorism. Oh, and I understand you're somewhat of a musician," he finished.

"How nice, how reassuring to know that I can be summed up so succinctly. Isn't it a shame I can't return the favour with a rundown of your life, since I haven't had the luxury of excavating your past. What you think you know about me is just someone's judgment. And by the way, it wasn't luck that generated the information about RussTech." Now she was positive she didn't want the safe house option. "My family has an isolated summer home in southern Quebec near the U.S. border. I'll fly there today, or tomorrow at the latest. The guys at the office, including Marc, see me as junior. I think the plan always was that my stint at The Hague would end when the mission did. It would be natural for me to call in and tell them I'm taking time off before supposedly returning to my old job in Chisinau, Moldova, which, by the way, I don't want to do. No one will even care if I miss the debrief since I'm such a minor cog." As if talking to herself, she added, "I wonder how long I'm going to have to bury myself..."

He stood up looking troubled but resigned. "I can't force you to choose the London option. And no one thinks of you as a minor cog. Marc's going to see your absence from the debrief as unprofessional. He won't be pleased. Since it's your safety that's at stake, I'll do whatever I can to support your story about taking leave. But your Quebec plan is only going to make it harder for me to protect you."

He took out his pen and wrote something on a scrap of paper. "Here's a telephone number. Memorize it. Use it to reach me once a week no matter what, so that I know you're safe." After a moment, he added, "You'll need to fly covertly. I'll arrange for your passage on a military plane so that it'll be harder to trace where you've gone. I'll make sure passport control is handled at the other end. I'll also have a rental car waiting. Is Montreal where you want to land?"

She nodded.

"I'm going to ask Miriam to go to your place and pack for you. I'll get back to you as to when you can leave, which could be as soon as this afternoon. I'll arrange for you to use a separate mobile phone from now on. Transfer your data and don't use the other one. Tell no one, not even Miriam, what your plans are. And whatever you do, don't tell anyone about my status. Do you understand?"

"Okay. Yes. But Miriam didn't seem very happy to bring me here. She's…"

"She'll do what I tell her to. She has a way of winkling out information. Don't go for it."

"I can't believe this. I feel like I'm in witness protection for god's sake."

"If it's any consolation, we're going to go after RussTech until they're out of business. In the meantime, we're going to identify the terrorist groups they're funding. All the work you've put in will not be in vain, I promise you that." He took her hand in both of his. He looked at her intently for a moment and then issued one of his rare smiles that somehow brightened the entire room. "The next time we meet, maybe, just maybe, I'll give you a chance to dig into my past. For now, stay safe."

Afternoon, April 11, 2019, The Hague, Netherlands

Rik was writing a mission brief when Neal called. "There's more trouble since I last talked to you. We now know Russia's response to Victor Tolstoi's assassination. Russian troops are gathering at the Lithuanian border. We're also detecting unusually high Russian submarine activity in the Baltic."

"What are we and our allies doing?"

"We're trying to wake up NATO, the European Union and the U.S. But, as usual, we're getting little action. Post-Brexit, anything coming out of our sceptred Isle tends to be ignored. I won't keep you. Let me know what you find out about Marić."

CHAPTER 4

Midnight, April 11, 2019, Memphremagog, Quebec, Canada

The Canadian Forces plane landed at 10:30 pm. at a base outside of Montreal. After a smooth passage through military customs, Sofie walked outside and found a rental car waiting for her. It would take ninety minutes to arrive at Magog and then another thirty minutes to reach what had been, throughout her childhood and teenage years, her beloved Fitch Bay retreat. Tomorrow she'd go into Stanstead to get supplies and reacquaint herself.

The cottage, actually more of a mansion, wasn't technically hers, but rather, her Uncle s. He'd inherited it fifteen years ago with the unexpected passing of Sofie's mother and father. Their wills gave use of Fitch to Karl though Sofie assumed she should be welcome to use it from time to time. After all, the will also specified that, when Uncle Karl died, it would revert to her.

As she turned onto Highway 10, it was impossible to prevent that horrifying memory from resurfacing: June 30th, 2004. She'd just completed her second year of university in Montreal. Though she loved McGill University, she was anxious to escape this sheltered world for a life of adventure and meaning. Inspired by Golda Meir's autobiography, she'd arranged to spend her summer on a kibbutz not far from Tel Aviv. She'd announced her plan to her parents, who, as usual, were having cocktails before departing for some social dinner. "Can't you ever be normal?" her mother had railed at her. Sofie had already devoted her life to do the opposite of normal, taking up scuba diving, skydiving and rock climbing while the daughters of her parents' friends were planning to be lawyers or doctors. This summer she was headed for

Israel, period.

"You know full well how I feel about *them*," her father had ranted. "Let me tell you. You won't get a penny of my money to get there. And you can kiss your university tuition goodbye if you go through with this juvenile little excursion."

She'd stood up to them, yelling as they departed, "You shouldn't drink and drive!" Three hours later, the police had arrived and informed her that both her parents had died in a collision with a guardrail.

Their deaths had made her a wealthy, but subdued young woman. To this day, Sofie felt sick with guilt, feeling she could have tried to stop them from driving under the influence that night. Soon, she would pass the cemetery where they were buried. It had been a dark, rainy afternoon that she'd stood by their graves. She hadn't heard the Minister, felt the rain or noticed who stood around her. "I'm going to make something of my life," she'd vowed to herself. "I can't bring either of them back. But I can devote my life from this day forward to making a difference in the world."

She'd loved them. They were her parents, after all. But her father could be a bully when anyone dared disagree with him. When he and her Uncle Karl got together, they fed off each other pushing each other into outrageously extreme statements. "The average person is so ignorant. There are no greater asses than those of the masses. They need someone to tell them what to do. Democracy is just a sham anyway. Those spineless politicians and bureaucrats are ruining the civilized world by polluting us with immigrants." Sofie had heard versions of it her entire life: the interlocking complaints about the failure of democracy; the threat of Islam or the Chinese or the blacks or the Latinos; the destructiveness of feminism or homosexuality or multiculturalism; the hollowing out of the greatness that was Canada due to immigration, and so on.

As she neared the exit ramp off Highway 10, she felt increasingly uncomfortable that she hadn't called Uncle Karl for permission to stay at Fitch. He was hard to understand. When her parents had died, he'd been very caring, encouraging her to realize her dream of studying and then working in Europe. He'd also helped her negotiate the mid-year move from McGill University in Montreal to the international development programme in Sweden. But his attitude about Fitch baffled her. Five years ago, at the end of her stint in Belgrade, just before her transfer to Moldova, she'd felt driven to revisit her once-beloved cottage, to overcome its association with her parents' death. It was one of her more spontaneous decisions. As soon as she'd arrived in Montreal, she'd called Uncle Karl in Washington to tell him she'd be arriving at the property shortly and would like to stay for a week. His response had been extreme. She thought he was going to have a heart attack, he'd yelled so loud. "You will not!"

Shocked, she'd said, "But it's only for a few days, and I've come all this way…"

"No, it's not possible. I have friends who are arriving there tonight."

"Oh. Sorry. No problem. I'll make alternative arrangements," she'd said attempting a conciliatory tone.

"Until my death, I'm the owner of the property. Please do not assume that you can use it. Am I clear?" he'd finished.

Despite her anger, she'd tried to heal the rift, sending Christmas and birthday cards and emailing him from time to time, desperate for some connection to her only remaining family member. She'd gotten no response, leaving her with little choice but to accept that she was on her own.

April was the rainiest and muddiest time of the year, the worst month to be here. Surely, she reassured herself, he won't be using it or care if I stay for a while. He's so busy with his work in Washington, that he probably doesn't visit the cottage much anyway. Even though Rik insisted that I tell no one where I am, I'm going to have to tell Uncle Karl something that makes him understand how important it is that he let me stay. I'll beg if I have to. Too late to call him tonight. First thing tomorrow.

At Magog, she merged onto 141 South. Happy memories from childhood rushed at her as she passed along the dark, ghostly shores of Lake Memphremagog. Almost there! She turned right onto a gravel road that led her up a long driveway lined by pine and spruce. It was pitch black but she knew her way.

As she rounded the bend, her heart skipped a beat. There was a car in the drive and some lights on in the house. Her uncle, judging from the D.C. plates. Damn, damn, damn. How strange that, of all days, he'd be here. She was exhausted and didn't want to have to deal with explanations. Just a nice glass of wine and then, bed. I'll just say I'm staying for a couple of days and then tomorrow, I'll think of a Plan B, she reasoned.

Early Morning, April 12, 2019, Fitch Bay, Quebec

She turned the doorknob. It was locked. Not surprising. It was after 1:00 a.m. She sang out a hello. Getting no answer, she went to the shed and was relieved to find her secret key still there. She entered, calling tentatively, "Uncle Karl? Uncle Karl!" She headed through the large kitchen and across the spacious living room and dining room. Odd. The basement had always been too cold and dark to use. Yet, sounds were coming from below.

Tentatively, she headed down the plush, carpeted stairs, mentally preparing for a possible tirade from her uncle about arriving unannounced. As she reached the bottom step, she could hear more clearly. Her uncle was talking in German. His voice was clipped and angry. She peeked around the corner, but whipped her head back once she registered what she saw. Dear god, she breathed to herself. The enormous room had been fully renovated, and her uncle, with his back to her, was shouting into his laptop. Slowly, she craned her neck to look again. At first, her mind didn't translate what was being said. Instead, her eyes were drawn to papers with a funny logo or symbol sitting on a table directly in her line of sight. Then, she made the automatic switch to German.

"The last two nights, you've been late calling," her uncle said angrily. "Has Geist been paid?"

"Yesterday, I transferred 2.5 million Euros to his account, the final instalment of this sanction. The operation was a success. Even the Lithuanians believe it was one of theirs who killed Tolstoi and our *bruder* in Moscow is very happy. Two hares killed with one shot, he says. It will be easier for him to justify his invasion. Geist has just arrived in England ready to complete his next duties. The 50,000 will be distributed as planned."

"Serbia," he said impatiently.

"It's proceeding as planned. Yes, the election has been put off for a few weeks, but we're working to make sure that nothing affects the outcome."

"You'd better. The most important phase of *Recht und Macht* starts now."

"Yes, *Hochmeister*. But is this not a moment for celebration?"

"No. Not until our goal is realized."

"Shall I invoke the next step?"

"Yes, immediately."

"Very well. Five million Euros to the Arab, in the usual way. I'm closely monitoring all our *bruders'* preparations to ensure our next *putsch* is completed on or before the target date."

"And our diversion?"

"The funds have reached Durres from our Russian partner."

"Take measures to ensure the Arab doesn't cause problems. With less than two months left everything must go as planned."

"Yes, of course."

"Speak to our Banker *bruder*. I want a comprehensive update on all three prongs of our attack. Tell me your schedule for the next few..."

Sofie froze in place, her muscles seizing, her limbs lead-heavy. There was a buzzing in her head, growing louder. Not a panic attack, not now. Breathe. In. Out. Step by agonizing step she tiptoed up the stairs, freezing every time there was the slightest creak. Reaching the top, she ripped off her shoes and tore through the dining room, across the living room into the kitchen. Her heart was pounding like she'd just sprinted a mile. Sweat flooded her body. Don't let the door slam! Frantically she put her shoes back on and hurtled down the verandah steps.

As she reached the car, she realized she hadn't replaced the house key. Put it back. PUT IT BACK. Her mind was screaming at her. Her chest was closing from lack of air. No! No time! She was silently screaming back at herself. She fumbled for the car keys. *Fuck!* She dumped her purse out on the ground. Her hands were shaking. It was so dark. Finally, she felt them. She opened the car and the interior lights came on but thankfully went off as soon as the door closed. She'd have to back out at least sixty feet in the dark. Then, half way to the road, she froze. Had she left anything from her purse on the ground? Should she go back? Would he think of her if he discovered someone had gotten in? Just get the fuck out, now, right now.

Without conscious thought, she reached 141. Her heart still pounded. But she was beginning to get her first real breaths. Slow down. SLOW DOWN! You want to die like Mother and Dad? She jammed on the brakes. The wheels of the car squealed. The panic grew again. Had she mistaken what she'd heard? What should she do? Call Rik. No. Yes. Who else could she call? What time would it be where he was? What if he didn't answer? What was his number? God, I've already forgotten. Where should I go? Breathe in. Breathe out. Her hands felt numb and she feared she was hyperventilating.

And then, in one miraculous moment, a preternatural calm settled over her. Her breath slowed. She felt more cold and deliberate than she ever had in her life. Rik's number came to her perfectly.

She pulled onto a side road. She dialled him knowing that it would be around 8:00 in the morning his time.

"Whitford."

"Rik, it's me. Can you just listen for a moment?"

"Sofie? What the—"

"Please, just listen," she said fiercely. "I'm in danger. I need your help. I can't say more over this line. Can you arrange transport for me where I originally landed? I'll be there in about one hour. Can you meet me when I arrive?" Her calm abandoned her. "If anyone checks it has to seem like I never left The Hague."

"Okay." This was an unwelcome diversion. Milan was surely in more need of his help than she was. "Stay calm. I'll call you back in a few minutes with confirmation."

"It's you I've got to see and no one else." After hanging up, she took a moment to regain her equilibrium. It was beginning to pour as she made her way back onto 141 and shortly, onto Highway 10.

Early Morning April 12, 2019, mid-Atlantic

From the moment she'd boarded the military transport about three hours ago, her calm had abandoned her. Makeshift seats lined the cavernous plane. She was the only person on it apart from the crew who periodically glanced at her with curiosity but otherwise left her alone. She took half a clonazepam. They'd been prescribed for the panic attacks that could come on without warning turning her into a breathless, hyperventilating basket case. The attacks were not, her G.P. had assured her, uncommon in perfectionists, people who were exceptionally hard on themselves. In this case, she thought, she'd earned the panic. She closed her eyes and tried to slow her breathing.

The pill was having its settling effect. She pulled out her laptop and a pad of paper. First, she dictated, word for word in German, what she'd heard. Her perfect recall and photographic memory might have won her the status of freak growing up, but she had long since come to know that they gave her tremendous advantages in her work life. Next, as best she could, she drew a few versions of the strange symbol she'd seen.

As she heard the monotonous drone of the engines, she let herself feel her exhaustion. She knew she couldn't delay those terrible questions a moment longer. Who was her Uncle? What did she really know about him? Could her mother have been aware of what he was? Sofie had rarely seen him interact with her although, when he had, he'd been dismissive. And what about her father? She knew Uncle Karl was internationally respected as a powerful influence broker in D.C. Beyond that, god, she knew so little.

She was terrified of putting herself in the position of having to trust a man to actually come through for her. In her experience, men were weak. She'd had relationships, of course, but she'd made sure that they didn't go beyond the purely physical. Any reliance on Rik, someone she didn't really know, left her feeling small and vulnerable. She tightened her buckle, closed her eyes and let her head fall back.

CHAPTER 5

Morning, April 12, 2019, Fitch Bay, Memphremagog, Quebec, Canada

Karl Mueller lay in his bed waiting for the sun to rise. Three weeks ago, he'd told his underlings in Washington that he was retiring because of undisclosed health issues, effective immediately. He'd spent the last twenty days in Fitch overseeing the essential details that would guarantee the outcome of years of work. If he'd learned anything, it was to trust his intuition. This morning, something didn't feel right. Hadn't there been a fleeting flash of light last night? At the time, he'd dismissed it as being the moon coming out from behind a cloud. But if the rain had started, there would have been no moon.

He pulled on his sweatpants and top and began a check around the house. No signs of disturbance. Out of discipline he walked along the driveway, though he knew the heavy rain would have washed away even a trace of an intruder. He turned toward the boathouse where the foamy waves of Lake Memphremagog were rhythmically slurping over the dock. Nothing appeared out of place.

Fitch, his precious Fitch. He'd turned it into his main base of operations shortly after his sister and brother-in-law had died, seeing to it that his niece, such an annoying creature, moved to Europe and stayed there. He'd also made it clear to her that Fitch was off limits to her until his passing. As far as he knew, no one except her and two *bruders* were aware of the existence of this place and its connection to him – and he'd talked to one of them last night.

Unable to shake his discomfort, he dialled a number on his secure virtual private network. "Verify the whereabouts of the other *bruder* and my niece over the past twenty-four hours and get back to me."

"What's wrong?"

"Just do as I ask, and quickly."

His next call was to the caretaker who lived in a cottage down the next lane. "Were you over here last evening?" he asked.

"No sir."

"Has there been any unusual activity in the vicinity in recent days?"

"What kinds of activity?"

"Strangers in the area, burglaries, that sort of thing."

"No, sir," he repeated, and the call ended.

One of the *bruders*, Karl knew, coveted his position. His extreme caution was not only appropriate but also exemplary. He could think of no one in the world who had more right to hold the power that he did. In due course, he would be recognized for his sublime accomplishments. For now, he held the respect of, and command over, the members of *Der Kreis*, who, under his guidance, were changing the course of history. He owed it to himself and the *bruders* to take every conceivable precaution now.

Born in 1940 to German parents who had moved to Montreal in the 1920s and who had literally struck gold investing in the Noranda mines, Karl could still feel fury rising in him as he recalled growing up as a German. He'd been bullied and ostracized in school and had come to detest Montreal and Canada. His father, who would be so proud, had taken him under his wing those many years ago. "Appreciate your superior intellect as a German. Someday," his father promised, "you'll gain the upper hand over your oppressors if you chart your future wisely."

Accordingly, he studied business and then law at Yale where he met people who changed his life forever. At twenty-three, he began the process to become an American citizen. He worked his way up the ladder as special assistant and then advisor to senators whom he had been judged to be among the up-and-comers. "Money is power, not laws, not politicians, all of whom are controlled by money," his father had drilled into him. Karl had had a front-row seat to the manipulation of senators by lobbyists and their financial backers.

During his 30s and early 40s, he'd made himself a name as a K Street kingpin, seeking out the most powerful money interests, be it the NRA, the Saudis, Turkey, the arms industry or tobacco, helping them to pedal influence with politicians across the country. It hadn't hurt that he was extremely attractive. He towered over most people. With his head of prematurely grey hair, he projected charisma and power.

In time, he'd come to hold sway over both the politicians and the money groups who'd needed his services. He was the *eminence gris*, the puppeteer, as he liked to think of himself. He'd parlayed his substantial inheritance and his Washington skills into a fortune.

Divorced at forty after ten years of a childless, bloodless marriage, he had no real ties to anyone or anything. Meredith had served her purpose as an ornament on his arm at all the obligatory functions. Beyond that, she'd had little to offer. Neither had any other woman.

At some point, he realized he'd mastered Washington. He was bored and ready for something new, something bigger.

That seminal moment arrived on November 11, 1985 in the person of Werner Richthoven, whom his close friend at Yale had introduced him to when he was in his early twenties. Werner had, as it turned out, tracked Karl's education and his subsequent career, eventually identifying Karl as a potential successor. Karl's involvement with one of Yale's secret societies and his apparent support of the society's dark goals had made him Werner's only real candidate. Slowly, over a period of months, the *Hochmeister* had entrusted Karl with the secret history and activities of *Der Kreis*.

Created by Richthoven in 1945 in the aftermath of the disastrous loss, *Der Kreis Im Quadrat* could boast a few significant successes interspersed, Karl thought but had never said, with too many failures.

Karl knew that he would be its saviour. His strategy as the new *Hochmeister* fortuitously began in 1989. Shortly after Werner's sad passing, the fall of the Berlin wall created a vacuum of power that made Bulgaria, Moldova, Albania, Romania, Azerbaijan and others ripe for takeover. Under Karl's leadership, *Der Kreis* had assisted, connived and manoeuvred the KGB and the other secret police into a kind of kleptocracy, part tycoon part organised crime. They filled the power vacuum left by the implosion of the Soviet states. They were grateful for the help of this skilled and knowledgeable American. Mueller infused *Der Kreis* with new members from Russian government, industry and media. His biggest coup was recruiting the Russian. So young in 1989, he'd had been in a perfect position as a rising star of the KGB to support the secret aims of *Der Kreis*. In return, the organization had guaranteed him Russia's presidency and had kept him there. He was, had been, by far their most important partner. After so many years, *the* Russian would finally realize an incalculable return on his long-term investment: The undermining of NATO, the destruction of the European Union, and free-and-clear access to the fortune he had sequestered around the world.

Karl kept *Der Kreis* small enough to control, large enough to be powerful and sophisticated enough to keep hidden. They were roughly sixty men in number, all in powerful positions throughout Europe and North America.

Then, in 2001 came what Karl thought of as his crowning glory thus far: 9/11. That operation would forever change the direction of world history. *Der Kreis* had handpicked the 9/11 jihadists, ensuring that they were bankrolled, given necessary visas, and directed at the right targets. Eleven was the eternal, powerful symbol in Illuminati lore, which Werner Richthoven and the founders of *Der Kreis* had chosen. As for 9/11, September was the 9th month, and when you added 1+1, the number 11 was reached. September 11th was the 254th day of the year, and when totalled together, 2+5+4 equalled eleven. After Sept 11, there were 111 days remaining in the year. One of the planes selected to crash was AA Flight #11.

Der Kreis, under Karl's oversight, had funded many Islamic terrorist acts over the past eighteen years since 9/11, using its media bruders to systematically stoke populist fear and anger and spread nationalistic rhetoric. As planned, unstable times created ideal conditions for *Der Kreis'* strong men to gain political and military influence as heads of state and behind the scenes across Europe.

Under Karl's guidance, *Der Kreis'* Russian `tsar' was happy to routinely test and undermine confidence in NATO. And then there was Sumner Hayes, a dedicated *bruder* who *Der Kreis* had guided to the highest levels of power in America. Reluctantly, Karl admitted, Hayes was doing an excellent job to promote anti-Muslim and anti-NATO, populist messages, although he seemed to believe that he, and not Karl, should be *Der Kreis'* leader.

Karl scoffed to himself and turned his mind to the matters before him. *Recht Und Macht*, Right and Might, was, at long last, only weeks away. His only regret was that Werner was not here to witness the fulfilment of his vision.

Morning, April 12, 2019, London, England

Geist – he smiled at his ghostly moniker – was tired and relieved to arrive back at his seedy little bedsit in High Holborn. It was never too early he said to himself as he took his nicely chilled Stoli out of the freezer and downed a shot. Absently, he turned on the telly to the BBC.

A couple of days ago, his instructions had taken him to a *hawala*, an informal money transfer hole in the wall on the third floor of a sooty old building in East London. After providing a code number he was provided with £50,000 authorized by *Der Kreis' hawalandar* in Dubai.

Such an ingenious scheme to launder money. No wired funds, just an arrangement between *hawalandars*, who would help their clients send and pick up money, a healthy commission taken by each.

The next day he'd taken £40,000 to a specified location where he picked up a van full of Russian and American semi-automatics. He'd divided the cache into eight bundles of arms and delivered them to some of Britain's most active hate groups, along with instructions for each: Brighton White Power Alliance; Brighton Madrassa Jalal; Oldham's Crater Boys; Manchester Shah Mashjid Cultural Centre; Springfield Ward Knights; Handsworth Islamic Friendship Centre, Birmingham; Knowlton Biker Gang and Warriors of Jenin, Luton. If successful with their missions, he told them, there'd be more to come in the future. The remaining £10,000 he'd distributed to numerous media outlets and dark web actors in England who would spread accounts, both accurate and false, of immigrant and alt-right atrocities.

He worked his way through the pile of newspapers he'd picked up, among them the *Daily Standard*, one of England's rags that could be bought in any small town throughout the country, not to mention London. He sat up straight as he leafed through the headlines:

"Birmingham: Four young girls gunned down in their schoolyards... Islamic links..."

"Gun battle at Birmingham mosque kills 25...Police considering curfews..."

"Islamic terrorists raping our women";

"Innocent victims of Brighton shooting in wrong place at wrong time."

"We are at war. Violence surges across the country."

"Our country under siege: Radical Islamic terrorists rule our streets."

"Police arrive late to slaughter of elderly."

"Wanda Pierce, Leader of the Opposition says it's time to rethink

our approach to terrorists…"

"We take you now to our correspondent who is live at the scene."

Early this morning, two mosques were bombed, one in Manchester, and the other in London. Early estimates are that sixty people died and an additional one hundred and fifty, injured. Among those dead is Imam Al Tahtawi, considered a moderate voice in an increasingly militant part of the city. Notes were left by the perpetrators indicating that a Christian crusade is being waged to avenge recent attacks against British citizens.

A senior Scotland Yard official expressed fear that any further escalation of violence on British soil could result in the need for curfews and troops on the street to prevent an outbreak of what he termed a war between Muslim and non-Muslim factions.

He switched on his laptop and scanned social media. Facebook was full of video of the violent events he'd seeded. Tweets by politicians and police were going viral. It appeared the money he'd spread was being put to good use. He would be rewarded handsomely.

He poured himself another shot of Stoli and switched to the sports channel.

CHAPTER 6

Afternoon, April 12, 2019, The Hague, Netherlands

From the moment he'd heard from Sofie, Rik had acted fast to cover her tracks. Yesterday, he'd instructed Miriam to call Jansen's secretary to let the office know that Sofie was taking some leave effective immediately and that she wasn't sure what her future plans were.

Immediately after Sofie's urgent call early this morning, Rik had returned from Belgrade to The Hague, putting in an appearance at the OSCE.

He poked his head into Marc's office. "Hi. Sorry I couldn't meet for a debrief yesterday. I have some time now if you're free."

"Grab a coffee and a chair." Marc eyed him and said, "You look terrible! I guess you didn't get much sleep after the disaster the other night. God! It's just unbelievable about Philippe, about the whole fucking disaster."

"It was rough. Those young girls died right in front of me. It isn't something I'll forget any time soon. And then Philippe."

"Rik, do you happen to know where Sofie is?" asked Marc. "I was surprised that she didn't show up yesterday since she'd been so involved all this time. For her to go AWOL, given what happened..."

"That's odd," said Rik. "I thought she was going to let you know. She called me yesterday and was practically crying. Said she needed to meet with me in a neutral place yesterday so that she could hear what exactly happened. Since I was out of town, I postponed it. We're getting together later. She seems to be blaming me for what went down. I'll tell her she should have called you."

"No, don't bother. Someone did call my secretary to tell me she wasn't coming in. I just wondered what was going on. We're all going to have to do a post-mortem. I've scheduled a meeting for late this afternoon. Whether or not Sofie shows up, I'm relieved you're available."

"Yes, absolutely. By the way, I haven't seen anything in the press. Our efforts to keep the whole damn mess quiet seem to have worked. I've prepared an end-of-mission report. Maybe we can use that as our basis for discussions. Obviously we were set up and I want to know how! God damn it, Marc! This is the second time in just a few months our Op has been breached."

Marc nodded. "I've already started to look into it. So far, nothing." He looked intently at Rik and added, "What about Sofie? Could she have let something slip with one of her Moldova contacts?"

Rik smoothly hid his dismay. "Not a chance. She was just a junior and didn't have the contacts that Philippe did. We'll all have to go over every move we've each made to figure out where it got eff'd up."

Three hours later, Rik was relieved to see Sofie in the appointed spot on the military base. She slid into the back seat of the car and, as prearranged, ducked down. He headed for the same safe house in The Hague they'd used a little more than twenty-four hours ago. Not a word was spoken as they walked up the backstairs to the second floor room.

This time, there was espresso and some syrupy sweet stroopwafels sitting on the side table. They sat across from each other, Sofie hunched, her hands shaking as she tried to pick up her coffee.

"Are you all right?" asked Rik.

After a lengthy silence, she began. "Are you sure that there is no bug in here, that we can talk freely?"

He nodded.

"I need to know that you're the right person. It has to be someone who has the highest security clearance and who...I think it just has to be you." Her voice rose in panic. "I don't know who else to tell."

Rik brought over a sweet and commanded her to eat. He gave them both a moment as he pondered what to say. "Yes, I do have reach, and people whom I trust, literally with my life. They'll all be on board if it relates to the RussTech terrorism ties."

"No! No, it's not about that at all. It's way beyond that."

Rik shook his head, his brow furrowing into a frown. She seemed to shrink and age before him. He schooled his face to be neutral. "You've obviously put some level of trust in me, and I've come through with the support you asked for. So, yes, for better or worse, I'm it. What's going on?"

"The story begins with my Uncle Karl, Karl Mueller." She looked at Rik for some sign of recognition. "You must have heard of him. He's been a huge power player, a big lobbyist in Washington over the years."

Uncle Karl? He'd abandoned Milan Marić for a family problem? Relief battled with fury.

"He's my mother's brother. When my parents died, our summerhouse passed on to him with the understanding that when he dies it comes to me. Growing up, I spent all my summers there. It felt like my real home. Uncle Karl rarely came to Fitch during my childhood. He spent most of his time in Washington doing his power politics and might only come once or twice a year to the cottage."

"What the hell does this have to do with anything?"

Sofie stared at the wall, as if in a trance. "I knew I'd have to call him in the next couple of days about staying at Fitch. That's where I headed last night. My god. It was only last night! It feels like a lifetime ago. Since you looked into me, you must know that my grandparents were German, though they made their fortune in Quebec." Before Rik could interrupt, she rushed on. "Uncle Karl and my mother grew up speaking German, and he was proud of his German heritage. Anyway, April is muddy and cold at Fitch, really a miserable time of the year to be there, so I was shocked to find his car in the driveway when I arrived."

Rik grabbed the back of his neck. "You're not making any sense."

"Stop it, Rik. Listen, please," she pleaded. "I overheard something horrifying. God, I was afraid you'd be like this."

"You have my attention. Get to the point."

"I wrote everything down, both in German and in English, to ensure nothing got lost in translation. Can you print this out?" She handed him a flash drive, which he inserted into his laptop.

She remained silent as he read it. He looked up and his mouth opened.

"Finish it."

When he had, he looked at her incredulously and then with a coldness she'd never before seen from him.

"Did your uncle discover you were there," he demanded harshly.

"I don't know. I don't think so. Even if he knew someone had been, how would he know it was me? When I arrived, the lights were on. I let myself in and called his name. No one answered. I heard voices and followed the sound downstairs to the basement. Rik, that part of the house was never used, but he's totally made it into a lair of some sort, with all kinds of equipment and monitors." She shivered as she thought back. "When I'd heard enough to be petrified, I inched back up the stairs and then ran for my life."

"Fuck," he muttered under his breath. "Are you sure you heard correctly? Is your German that good?"

"Oh for god's sake," she said, her voice rising. "Do you think I could make this up?"

"Give me a moment while I process this." After a silence, he began slowly as he formulated his thoughts. "When you called me early this morning I was in Belgrade trying to find out what had happened to Milan Marić, who, apart from being discredited and deposed from power there, is a friend of mine. And now it seems that your uncle was involved in that and in the assassination in Lithuania and god knows what else. Are you certain you heard that a putsch is in the works within the next two months?"

"Yes. I'm positive, Rik. *Putsch* means overthrow. And it appears they've already achieved it in Serbia." She wrapped her arms painfully tight around herself, trying to keep herself from falling apart.

"Everyone I talked to in Belgrade yesterday could not believe that Marić had been corrupt. Now it all makes more sense. And, with the death of Russia's Minister, Tolstoi, in Lithuania, Russia has the excuse it's been looking for to invade. If you heard correctly, then there are other overthrows in the making. Bloody hell."

She nodded and then showed him the symbol. "Read the notes again. Do you see *"Hochmeister?"* In English, that means Grand Master. *"Der Kreis"* means the Circle. It all sounds ridiculous, like a secret handshake."

Rik's immediate inclination to contact Neal fought with recognition of the position that Sofie had put herself in, one that required immediate action. He spoke in a deliberative tone. "What you overheard has the makings of being at once one of the greatest threats we've ever faced, and, I dare say, one of the biggest breakthroughs in intelligence over the past decade. However, we must deal with the immediate situation. Someone is checking on your whereabouts. Marc Jansen was asking me about you and I covered. We can't know for sure, but we must assume that someone wants to determine where you've been over the past couple of days. As tired and scared as you are, you must go to the OSCE in an hour to reinforce the impression that you've been here and not in Quebec."

"What if my uncle and his group are after me?"

"We're going to take extreme measures right now to confirm that you've been here. Also, I'll go with you to the OSCE and confirm your story. I'm going to bring in Miriam Maartens again. She's the person whom you supposedly spent part of yesterday with, and whom I instructed to call into the OSCE yesterday to say that you were taking some time off."

He walked to the door and said something.

A cloying perfume odour accompanied a woman's entry. "Hi again. Let's discuss our `friendship' and what we've been doing with our time together."

"Yes. Go over your stories and make sure they mesh. I need to make some calls." Rik pulled out a special cell phone and left the room.

Late Afternoon, April 12, 2019, Berlin, Germany

Max was deeply absorbed in his work at his plush office off the Ku Damm. He loved a good mystery. The one that Henry Maplethorpe of Barron's Bank in London had called him about was proving to be extremely interesting.

He stretched his arms towards the ceiling and rolled his neck. It was raining out again, he thought absently. He took off the black-framed glasses that he used for reading and rubbed his left hand down the black stubble that, according to more than one woman friend, apparently made him look like some American actor — that and the dimples that he'd been teased about for most of his thirty-nine years.

Former Mossad, Max was one of Israel's top-secret operatives in Europe. His facility with numbers had drawn the attention first of Mossad and then, over a decade ago, an off-the-books division answering solely to the Prime Minister. He'd been trained in banking and high finance. Over the past nine years, he'd developed a roster of elite banking clients across Europe. His ability to help them address money laundering and negotiate the growing number of EU regulatory hurdles had given him access to massive bank databases. To his clients, he was a Houdini who could problem-solve like few others in Europe. What they didn't need to know was that he was drawing on the analytic skills of a set of Jerusalem-based operatives and that his clients' banking information was of paramount importance to Israel in its quest to identify terrorists and their money laundering escapades.

He wondered if he was fooling himself believing that he'd had a breakthrough on the Maplethorpe file. The pattern was there. It was so elaborate, so labyrinthic, that it bordered on impossible to believe. It would have taken years to set up and implement. Nevertheless, if his suspicions were borne out, an unknown agent was targeting Barron's and the other top banks in Britain. Kudos to Maplethorpe, he thought admiringly. He might be an odd duck, but Henry was one of those geniuses who could see beyond a spreadsheet, who could scan the numbers and know that something wasn't right.

Just as Maplethorpe had indicated, eighteen mid-sized banks across Europe and Britain had failed over the last nine months alone. What had first caught Max's attention were some unusual characteristics of the banks themselves, particularly in the ways they operated. There was the odd coincidence that a very large proportion of the failed banks' loans had been made to companies owned by one of their Board of Directors, leaving the European banks vulnerable if these companies' share values should crash. Which, of course, they had. Also troubling was the fact that many of the banks held large investments in the *same* few failed second mortgage companies. The interconnectedness of banking these days was one thing. But the fact that these failed banks were all linked by their high exposure to the implosion of this prominent secondary mortgage company was striking. Max's antennae also went up exponentially when he saw that, in a few other cases, a dangerously high proportion of the failed banks' assets were in the hands of one corporate depositor who stood to affect bank liquidity. In all cases, the failed banks' capital cushions were at the lowest levels permitted under the law. Until they'd failed, the banks had appeared to be performing well above industry averages.

Max walked over to the sideboard and replenished his coffee. Maplethorpe was right, he realized. There was a pattern. The biggest losers were Britain's top four banks, all of which had significantly invested in a number of these failed banks. Someone had deliberately targeted their vulnerabilities and engineered their failures. So simple. A domino effect: The large corporate depositors unexpectedly withdrew their money, leaving the banks scrambling without success to make up for the loss of capital. As a result, share values of the banks themselves *and* of the companies they'd lent so heavily suddenly fell, compounding the devastating impact on the banks. Isn't this interesting, Max thought. The banks might have been able to stabilize themselves if it hadn't been for media reports that came out of nowhere. "Bank X is facing insolvency," read the by-line. Once panic set in and spread, a run on the banks and their bankruptcy were inevitable. It was deliberate, and it was genius.

He sent Maplethorpe a terse note. "I think you're right. Let your bosses know. Let me know how I can help."

Who, Max wondered, would have had the financial resources to make enormous deposits and then withdraw them all of a sudden? Who would engineer this process and why? His first and only thought was the Russian kleptocracy that had looted its own country as well as every state that had existed under the former Soviet Union. It had also mastered the art of money laundering. Yes, Max thought, the sheer magnitude of capital required to pull off these bank failures could only come from the wily neighbours to the north. But why? What possible motive could they have? Why bring down British banks, as it seemed Maplethorpe's original observations were now proving true?

He swivelled his chair towards the window although so deep in thought was he that he didn't register the sun poking through the clouds or the beautiful view to the thrumming shops and restaurants below. He heard music and immediately came back to his surroundings. He fumbled in his jacket pocket for the cell phone reserved for only a handful of people.

"Max Becker."

"Max, It's Rik. I need your help."

"What else is new?"

You're going to want to hear what I have to say, though it isn't good news."

Max was incredulous as he listened to Rik. "Okay. First things first, Rik. We'll need a secure base of operations. I have a safe house here in the Dahlem neighbourhood, complete with high-tech security and communications. It's private. We can come and go without being noticed."

"Thanks, but Berlin? I'm not sure that's the best."

"Berlin's ideal. It's out of the orbit of The Hague, easily reachable and, perhaps, in close proximity to whatever and whoever this *"Der Kreis"* is. Do you have a better alternative?"

Rik thought. "We might have some facility in London, but it would mean justifying our need for it. Right now, confidentiality is paramount. We don't know what or whom we're up against, so yes, your set-up sounds good. Let's get started."

"I'll send you the location in a few minutes." They completed their conversation quickly. Damn! The banking file would have to wait. On the other hand, despite the gravity of what he'd heard and read, Max felt more alive than he had in months.

Rik was a special guy, considering that the first time we met, he saved my career, thought Max with a mental shudder as he remembered how naïve he'd been. His job as an Israeli agent had been to report back to his bosses in Israel on the progress of a war between The Republic of Georgia, backed by the Americans on the one hand, and the breakaway Russian-dominated South Ossetia. Israel had made the surprising move to halt military or any other support to Georgia. Unfortunately, Max had taken bad advice from a Georgian source and gotten too close to the front lines. He was about to be seized by Russian troops when someone shouted a warning and waved at Georgian soldiers to pull Max back. Had Russia caught Max, it would have been a political nightmare for

Israel, not to mention for Max himself.

He'd taken his saviour, Rik, out to the bar two nights later and they'd talked well into the early morning. He chose to divulge a little of what his real position was within Israel. "I owe you a favour if and when you need help at my end." Max's gut was telling him that Rik's OSCE position was a front for deeper intelligence. He'd indicated as much to Rik who just smiled benignly, no denial forthcoming.

Since then, they'd collaborated on several matters of mutual interest, particularly as it related to funding sources for terrorism. They'd also divulged much more about their lives.

Theirs was a strange bond that went deeper than friendship. Only a handful of people in Max's life could understand what his existence was about, the sacrifices he'd made, the perilous situations he'd lived through and the unsung aspect of doing a job that someone had to do but few were able. Rik understood all too well. Their shared experiences and challenges made him one of Max's most trusted and respected colleagues.

Late Afternoon, April 12, 2019, The Hague, Netherlands

Rik returned to collect Sofie and headed for the OSCE. "Present yourself as overwrought about the death of the girls and Philippe and over the failure of the mission. If it seems right, blame me for the failure. Say you're going to take leave from your job to consider your future."

Sofie entered the building first, Rik's instructions ringing in her ears. The boardroom was already full, Marc at the head of the table. Sofie took an empty seat on one side. Rik, arriving a few minutes later, sat on the other side. She sent him a furious glare, which others could not help but notice.

"Before we get started," Marc began, "let's all take a minute to recognise the loss of our colleague, Philippe. He was a good man who gave his life for his nation and for Europe. Because of his bravery in bringing RussTech to our attention in the first place, he was targeted." Sofie gritted her teeth and reached for her lip balm. Marc continued. "Sofie, we missed you yesterday. The team was surprised you didn't come in."

"I know. I had a sleepless night and just felt sick and exhausted. I didn't think there'd be a meeting so soon after...after..." Her voice shook. "I did call Rik yesterday to find out what had happened on the ground. Rik," she frowned darkly at him, "didn't you tell anyone I was staying at home?" Before he could respond, she looked at Marc. "I asked my friend, Miriam, to call you to let you know I wasn't going to make it. I'm...I...I'm going to take leave." She felt real tears come to her eyes as she shook her head back and forth. "Philippe...I just can't believe he's gone."

The men in the room shuffled in their chairs and cleared their throats.

Rik broke the silence. "Marc, how do you want to handle this? Shall I start with what I know?" As the meeting progressed it was clear that no one was ready to consider the possibility of a mole.

Marc concluded. "It looks as if RussTech caught wind of something and created the decoy convoy. Any number of things could have tipped them off. Maybe, if Philippe were alive today he'd be able to shed light since he knew the most. Just so you know, staff and Interpol in Moldova are doing what they can to track down his killer. In the meantime, I'll finalize a report and you can all contribute your comments and inputs before I submit it upwards."

As team members filed out of the room, Jansen asked Sofie to come to his office. She glanced quickly back at Rik who cast a faint look of warning. She entered and sat down. Marc stared at her for a moment and then asked, "What's really going on?" She turned red.

"What? How do you mean?"

"You're acting strangely, like you're nervous. Is there something you haven't told us?" he asked brusquely.

She thought quickly. "No, no, well, not exactly…"

Marc's eyes bore into hers, his eyebrows raised.

"It's, you know, just an emotional time for me. Umm. Maybe you didn't know, but, well, Philippe and I, well, he and I," she rubbed her brow, cleared her throat. "It's just that," she swallowed, "his death hit me very hard. I just, I just…." Her voice grew reedy.

Jansen looked mollified. "I'm sorry for your loss. As you know, your secondment here is ended, though I'll want your comments on my report. I assume you'll deal with your UNDP bosses regarding the leave you talked about. I guess this is it. Good luck with your future endeavours." He stood. She shook hands and walked out.

After, she called Rik and gave him the gist of the conversation.

Well done, he thought, and told her that his team had moved her belongings to a flat that she'd be sharing with Miriam for the next day or two. She'd be picked up shortly and taken there.

Jansen watched Sofie exit. He wouldn't have taken Philippe as being her type, but you just never knew. He turned to the email he'd been waiting for.

CHAPTER 7

Evening, April 14, 2019, Berlin, Germany

When Rik arrived at the safe house, Max was there to greet him with a bone-crushing handshake. One might reasonably expect someone in his business to be invisible. Max was larger than life in build and personality. Tall and burly, he had a square face that was chiselled and included a few days' stubble to match his black hair, his penetrating dark eyes and a downturned mouth. On a good day, he was a jokester and raconteur, keeping an entire room in thrall. On a bad day, he was an angry grizzly bear. Today was a bad day, thought Rik, as Max surveyed him with eyebrows raised and an intense stare that would intimidate most. Sarcastically, he bowed and swung his right hand away from his body as if welcoming royalty to enter.

Perfect spot, thought Rik, as they toured the property. A lane running along the east side of the house led to a parking area at the back that would be invisible from any direction. A large chain-link fence with barbwire atop it defined the southern border of the lot. Beyond it were a heavy forest and a deep valley with a creek at its base. Any attempt to access the lot from the back would be extremely difficult.

The house, early 1950s, had two floors and a finished basement. On the main level, the front door opened onto a large living room facing north that had been converted into a boardroom. Off it was a kitchen and a dining room, each with heavily curtained windows looking to the south and east side of the lot. There was a bathroom and two bedrooms, the larger of which now served as a high-tech communications site complete with monitors and terminals, a hacker's nirvana.

The musty smell signalled that the house had not been used for some time. However, Max had put on some coffee, which was effectively masking the odour by the minute. Rik opened the refrigerator and was pleased to see it fully stocked.

The large armchairs, chintz sofas and the thick Oriental carpet gave an air of old-world comfort, as did the carved high ceilings all of which, together, evoked pre-war Berlin. There was a fireplace, though it would not be used lest it draw attention. On the long wall was a large whiteboard and wet bar, and on another, a wall-mounted television that was silently showing the BBC, a nice touch thought Rik. In the middle of the room was a large boardroom table capable of seating at least a dozen people. Electric outlets on the wooden floor below enabled around-the-clock work on laptops. With some light faintly filtering through the dark orange curtains, the living room reminded Rik of one of those seventeenth century Dutch paintings.

The second floor included four small bedrooms each with two single beds and two bathrooms, all very Spartan but sufficient to accommodate a sizeable team. The basement held laundry facilities, a workout room, a library, an upright piano and television along with a selection of DVDs. A queen-size sleeper sofa sat at the far wall. The entire house was wired to prevent interception of communications. The security system would provide immediate surveillance of visitors. Perfect.

The next arrival was Noah Sindegard, a navy seal who'd eventually found his way to the CIA where he'd been in counterintelligence for almost sixteen years, operating undercover in some tight spots in the Middle East. From there, he'd gone on to the National Security Agency. Four years ago, he'd accepted a new post with NATO in Brussels in cyber warfare. "Anything to escape the toxic politics of D.C.," he'd told Rik.

Despite his sixty-five years, Noah looked at least ten years younger. His hair was still dark, though sprinkled with grey. His erect posture and crew cut shouted military. He was a straight shooter who had manoeuvred his career to encompass most of the important issues of the day, whether terrorism, strengthening of NATO or cyber warfare. The current government in Washington may not have valued him enough to keep him there, but others did. Rik felt a kinship with Noah and looked up to him as a combat-worn veteran. Like Rik and Max, Noah lived a lonely life in the service of his nation.

Over the past decade, Rik, Max and Noah had, through trials by fire, disclosed that each of them was not who they said they were. Rik was not OSCE. Max was not a banker and Noah was more than just a NATO appointee. Their mutual interests and superior intelligence skills had forged an exceptional bond on some high-octane missions. Their skills complimented each other's and there was considerable mutual respect. Together they'd prevented terrorism-related disasters in Istanbul, Jerusalem and Munich. Having penetrated each other's cover stories, they agreed that their missions were sufficiently similar to share Intel on a regular basis.

About eight years ago, Max, Noah and Rik had developed an off-book protocol regarding how to deal with an intelligence leak. Today, Rik was invoking it in view of the danger of betrayal trumped the sharing of information with their intelligence respective agencies.

Off-book, by definition, limited, if not eliminated, the resources one could muster. The scale of what Sofie had recounted meant that whoever, whatever, this Der Kreis was, and whoever Mueller was, the organization must have people in high places.

Ten minutes into Rik's detailed description of Sofie's Memphremagog experience, Max got up and made a call.

Afternoon, April 15, 2019, Jerusalem, Israel

Adina Kagan was furious. This time yesterday she'd been out on a regular date with Joshua at the beach. He was attentive and kind. Life was good. Then, that sneak attack last night. One call after six years. Correction: One call too many after six years that threatened to send up in flames the walls she'd thought were indestructible.

She stretched to her full 5' 3" and rolled her neck in pain realizing that she'd worked non-stop through the night. She felt jumpy and sick. No way Max would have contacted her unless he was desperate.

She sat down, pushed up her glasses and prepared to synthesize her findings into a report. Very interesting though somewhat obscure, this *Der Kreis*. She wondered what it all meant, where it would lead. She called her boss to tell him she was taking a few days' leave.

Caution dictated that she take a roundabout route, this time via Prague, where she'd be picked up and driven to Berlin. She'd rather be sent undercover to Iran than see him again. And to make things worse, she absolutely hated being driven by anyone. After numerous narrow escapes, she'd concluded that most people were terrible drivers. She'd persuade her Mossad chauffeur to let her drive.

God. How was she going to control her reactions to him, to being near him after all these years? Painful memories flooded her senses. Adina was a true Sabra, prickly on the outside and mush on the inside. It was hard to break through her fiercely protected exterior. But once she let someone in, she gave everything, leaving herself utterly defenceless. After months of covert dating, she hadn't been able to hold back her need for Max. They'd first made love for two days in the privacy of his little place on the kibbutz where he'd grown up. He was gentle at times, funny and passionate. Her wall had come down. And then he'd betrayed her, leaving early that fateful morning on a dangerous mission to Egypt that was to have included her. God damn him, she'd done more dangerous work than he had, including in Iraq and Gaza. Apparently, he'd thought nothing of replacing her with a friend of theirs. They must have planned it well ahead of time. By the time he'd returned, she made sure she was on an undercover assignment in Syria. She hadn't seen or talked to him since. Her prickly Sabra skin was thicker now than it had ever been.

CHAPTER 8

Early Morning, April 16, 2019, The Hague, Netherlands

Miriam screeched to a halt in front of the safe house. The moment she saw the *prima donna* exit, she opened the trunk, or boot, as her boss called it. God damn it, she hated being treated like a lackey, a chauffeur, some kind of babysitter. And she'd had to cut short her early morning sojourn with her lover, just when he'd seemed to be into her.

"Good morning, or should I say, good night," said Sofie, smiling.

"*Morgen*," she replied. "We've got a long drive ahead, so you'd better get settled."

Miriam was soon careening down the highway at what looked like over 140 km. Sofie reached for her lip balm. "Could you slow down please?"

"Don't worry. I'll get you there safely."

Sofie rolled down the window, overcome by the powerful perfume that permeated the car. "Where are we going?"

"Berlin," Miriam acknowledged.

"Why there, I wonder?"

"We'll all find out, soon enough."

"Did Rik...he just told me to be ready..."

"Yes, Rik."

"I need to go to the bathroom. Can we stop, please?"

"Now? There's no place. Can't you hold it in?" Miriam responded.

Sofie's tension was mounting. "I need a break." She felt for her mobile.

Ten long minutes later they pulled into a stop. It was 8:00 a.m.

"Hello."

"Rik. It's me. I'm with Miriam. Am I supposed to be with her?"

"Yes. Why?"

"She's…Okay. Never mind. We're supposed to be going to Berlin, right?"

"Yes."

"Sorry. I'm…"

"Miriam can be abrupt. Don't let her push you around. See you soon."

Morning, April 16, 2019, Berlin, Germany

Rik, Max and Noah had worked tirelessly through the past day and night in preparation for the arrival of the group they'd instructed Miriam Maartens to invite. It was just before 11:00 a.m. Miriam and Sofie were the first to arrive, Sofie looking haggard.

Rik beckoned Max to the door. "Max, I want you to meet Sofie McAdam. Sofie, Max is a long-time colleague of mine and our host."

Sofie felt dwarfed by this larger-than-life presence who took her hand in both of his. He was training his dark eyes on hers as if trying to see into her soul. She stared back and then smiled. She felt an inexplicable bond with him. What was it with him and Miriam? She'd all but draped herself over Max, who, in turn, had forcibly brushed her arm off and scowled some sort of warning before turning on his heels.

Rik was over by the entrance to what looked like a dining room. He was brushing the stubble of beard that, Sofie mused, gave him an edge that would attract women in hordes. Today, however, the worry lines across his forehead made him look much older.

Sofie surveyed her surroundings. The living room gave off a welcoming ambiance despite the efforts that had been made to turn it into a place to work. As she entered the kitchen, she walked across to the window and peeked out to the backyard, which was more of a parking lot.

Because the coffee needed replenishing, she prepared a new pot. She was hungry and suspected others would be as well. Once they sat down for the meeting, they might not want to take time to prepare food. So, it was now or never. Her female colleagues in Moldova had chided her for serving coffee, believing, they said, that it fed into stereotypes. Having been raised with the proverbial silver spoon, Sofie had always felt uncomfortable accepting the service of others. At any rate, preparation of food beat making small talk with people she didn't know. She washed her hands in the sink, pulled out two large platters and laid out the standard German fare - cheeses, sliced salamis and fresh breads of various dark varieties, grapes and some nasty looking apple quarters. She saw that there were soft drinks and mineral water. Quietly, she took several trips from the kitchen to the living room. Max smiled his thanks and helped her with the arrangement of glasses, mugs, plates and cutlery in the middle of the long boardroom table.

Next to arrive was a small man with a heavy black beard who looked very tired and creased, as if he'd travelled a great distance, which, she supposed, he may well have. Rik greeted him with a bear hug. "Aslan, how long has it been?"

"Two years."

"How's Baku been treating you?"

Ah, so he was from Azerbaijan. Why was he here? Rik introduced him to her. He spoke excellent English with a pronounced Russian accent.

Max was taking people's luggage upstairs. It appeared that she and Miriam were to bunk together. Was there an option, she wondered?

The food she'd laid out was drawing people to the boardroom table. Sofie assumed the gang was all here. She took an inconspicuous seat near the end of the table awaiting opening remarks.

Max stood up, hurried to the vestibule and opened the door. Sofie heard murmurs. In walked a thin, elegant sixty-ish woman. Her long slate-grey hair was arranged in a chignon parted in the centre such that strands fell to each side of her face, framing light blue eyes, a patrician nose and lips that were, at the moment, pressed tightly together in a grimace.

Max took her over to Rik and made quiet introductions. Noah drew out her chair. He helped her take off her tailored black and white coat.

She nodded her thanks and rearranged a multi-coloured scarf that draped around her neck and across her left shoulder. Once seated, she opened a briefcase to extract a thick, obviously work-worn file.

"People, I'd like to introduce you to Hélène Lévy, who has come from Paris at my request," said Max.

Hélène's hands were shaking.

She's afraid or wary of us all, concluded Sofie, who sent her what she hoped was a reassuring smile.

Hélène nodded and said hello with a strong though intelligible French accent.

"Thank you for agreeing to come here, some of you from a very long way, and others without having a full reason for the necessity of your presence." Rik paused, gathering his thoughts. "I must begin by asking each of you, one by one, to swear your commitment to absolute confidentiality regarding each and every aspect of what we are to discuss here, and who we are. If you even hold a shred of doubt you must say so now." As each person pledged their agreement, a solemnity infused the room.

"I'll start the introductions. I'm Rik Whitford. For many years, I've been working for the OSCE, stationed, over time, in Baku, Tirana, and Belgrade and, for the last few years, Sarajevo."

Interesting, thought Sofie. He'd confided in her that he was not OSCE but this fact was apparently not for consumption here. How many – how few – were privy to who he really was?

"My work," he continued, "has been focused on the prevention of the spread of terrorism on European soil. In recent years, I've been fortunate enough to develop special relationships with a select few colleagues whom I've come to trust. That would include some of you here today. What we have before us may be the most challenging and important work that any of us has ever, or will ever, take on. I want to thank each of you in advance for having expressed your willingness to be a part of this top-secret team."

Top-secret team? Secret from whom, Hélène wondered. Please god, may my agreement to attend not be a mistake.

Rik also noticed her discomfort but continued. "Why are we here today? Simply put, Sofie McAdam, who will introduce herself shortly, came to me with a story she overheard less than a week ago that indicates there is an imminent threat to the very future of Europe as we know it."

The silence in the room was profound.

"I've worked with Sofie for the past six months. Lest any of you hope that her information is faulty, I must emphasize that we are confident of its veracity. When I say we, I refer to myself, and two colleagues who represent the most senior levels of intelligence in Europe. Over the past two days, we've drafted a plan that involves all of you. Noah, Max, will you introduce yourselves please?"

Noah began. "I'll be brief. When I first met Rik, I was with the CIA. We cooperated on a number of Ops together. It's he I blame for forcing me to work with Max, a task not to be taken lightly, I warn you all now!" prompting Max to produce a faint, mocking smile and others to laugh.

Noah sensed Hélène relax slightly just as he'd intended. He continued. "Of late, I've been working with a special northern European intelligence service as well as with NATO. The safety of Europe and the U.S. is what I spend every day worrying about. We'll talk about the threats we're facing shortly. Based on what I've heard from Rik, there's nothing more important than what we're here to do and I promise my unlimited support. With trepidation, I pass you onto Max."

"Absolutely a false portrayal of me," Max boomed. "I'm a delight to work with, as Rik will attest."

Rik gave him the finger. Again, there were snorts and laughs around the table.

"While I'm based here in Germany, my home is a small country bordering the Mediterranean that is hemmed in on all sides by states that hate it. What we're about to discuss, based on what Rik has told me, is highly relevant not just to Europe but also to Israel. I assist banks to defend against money laundering, which, fortunately, often gives me access to money transfers across Europe and beyond." Max's dark eyes became ice-cold.

Do not underestimate him, shivered Sofie.

"What we're taking on is existential. The principal person in power who backs me has given me direction to be a full partner with Rik and Noah, and to be an active participant, particularly as it involves, as they say, following the money. After Rik's briefing two days ago, I immediately knew I must invite an important ally of Israel, Hélène, who has spent decades helping us to combat anti-Semitism in France. When you hear her story, her commitment and contribution to our group will become clear."

Noah turned once again to look at Hélène, this time through new eyes. She seemed so frozen that he touched her arm and then, when she turned to look him, began subtly and gently to massage her hands and wrists, to warm them. His protectiveness warred with a concern that she seemed to be unravelling.

"In addition," continued Max, "I've asked another Israeli contact, Adina Kagan, to contribute her research to our team. She'll arrive shortly."

Sofie felt herself growing breathless with fear. She was just a researcher, not an espionage agent. She bit her lip. She closed her eyes and visualized a calming scene that usually helped dispel signs of an impending panic attack. As her heart rate slowed, she began to refocus on what was happening in the room.

Hélène would have been next to speak. However, Rik intervened. "If you don't mind, let's save your introduction until last. Your particular knowledge relates to a subject that has not yet been divulged to many here." Hélène nodded, visibly relieved. She looked to her right.

"I'm Miriam Maartens. My boss for many years has been Rik. To do my work, I own a network of three travel agencies in Netherlands. The travel industry has given me the freedom, the cover, shall we say, to help Rik and, on occasion, Max. I keep my eye on the comings and goings in and out of Amsterdam of various actors who have known terrorism ties. I must also say that I've acquired other specialized skills that, I hope, will not be required."

Sofie felt chilled.

Rik interjected. "Miriam has great organizational skills and will be a useful part of the team."

Miriam shrugged, clearly unimpressed with Rik's prosaic endorsement of her.

A discrete knock came at the back door. Max rose and moved swiftly to meet the new arrival. The entrance was not visible from the living room table. Sofie thought she might have heard a quiet greeting but was unsure.

Everyone turned around to see a woman enter, followed by Max. She left her bag near the door and took off her oilskin coat. It was clear to Sofie that she was no-nonsense and guarded. Whoever this was, she made no eye contact and, from her brisk entrance, was not thrilled to be here. Small and pretty, with dark hair and features, she strode confidently to her seat and put down her briefcase.

Rik stood up to shake hands. "You must be Adina. Welcome."

"Hello." She nodded and sat next to Aslan.

Others murmured their greetings.

Sofie, next to speak, took a deep breath, collected her thoughts and began. "I'm Sofie McAdam. I grew up in Canada, Quebec to be specific. After my studies in Sweden and Netherlands, I went to the United Nations Development Programme. Over the past ten years, I've specialized in the promotion of economic development in post-Soviet countries, particularly related to women. Because my family has German and French heritage, I speak those languages fluently and have picked up Russian and some Hebrew." When the Israelis looked questioningly at her, she responded, "I spent two months on a kibbutz, and absolutely loved it."

"Which one?" asked Max.

"Ramat Hakovesh, near Kvar Saba."

"Ken. I know it," smiled Max.

"So do I," exclaimed Adina, spontaneously. "Many kibbutzim have disappeared, but yes, to my knowledge, Ramat Hakovesh still thrives."

Rik's intense stare quelled Sofie's enthusiasm and revived her nervousness. "Anyway, I spent the first five years of my working life in Belgrade. Then, I requested a move to Moldova. For the past five years, I worked on the trafficking of women. Recently, my work led me to a group called RussTech operating out of Transnistria which, I discovered through covert sources, is an international criminal network dealing in human and drug trafficking from Eastern Europe down through the Balkans. Through my sources, I also identified its two leaders, one a Russian, the other, a Moldovan Roma."

"I'm surprised the UNDP would allow one of its local staff to get mixed up in such serious matters," said Max without thinking.

As Adina shook her head in disgust, he winced.

Max's challenge helped Sofie to steady herself. "My bosses all but patted me on the head. My reports to them regarding trafficking satisfied them that I was producing something but didn't seem to interest them as much as various social projects they were managing. I was fortunate to recruit an informant living in Transnistria."

Responding to Hélène's look of confusion, Sofie clarified. "It's a lawless self-proclaimed independent sliver of Moldova that also happens to be the European epicentre for trafficking controlled by Russia. About six months ago, with the help of my confidant, I made a definitive link between RussTech and the funding, beyond drugs and trafficking, to terrorism. For a number of reasons I chose to sidestep my immediate bosses and share this intelligence with a colleague in Belgrade who, I thought, would take my findings more seriously. After some research, he and I agreed to approach the OSCE in The Hague. Six months ago, a small team was formed. It included Rik. My colleague, Philippe, took the lead. We planned an operation to capture one of RussTech's leaders in order to obtain proof of the organization's tie to terrorism. Long story short, it was a disaster. A few days ago, Philippe was murdered, likely by RussTech, and there was some fear they might come after me if they knew my role."

Miriam interrupted. "At that point, Rik asked me to help keep her safe."

Safe, scoffed Sofie. More like terrified. She took a moment to sip from her glass of water. "Less than a week ago, I left for Quebec, intending to disappear until I could be sure I wasn't a target as Philippe had been. Within three hours of landing in Montreal, I found myself in even greater danger. Rik, is now the time to share what I overheard? Or, should we wait until after the introductions?"

"Let's complete the introductions. I've invited Aslan Aliyev with whom I first worked in Baku, and on several occasions since then. He's excellent at what he does and I think he'll be an important asset to us all." Rik smiled at his friend.

Nodding respectfully in return, Aslan began: "I am Azeri - from Azerbaijan. My father was a great physicist during the time of the Soviet Union. The first seven years of my life, we lived in Cairo. Father was teaching at the university there. Of course, we spoke Russian at the house, but I became fluent in Arabic and learned some English. Then, we returned home to Mingachevir in the interior of Azerbaijan. There, he resumed his work at a big hydro dam and power plant. Life was good for us. But, on April 26, 1986, when I was ten, my family's life was destroyed. Can you guess?" He paused, looking around the table. "On that day, my father was picked up by the Russians and taken to Chernobyl as one of the first responders. He did not know – we did not know – where he was going. He was given no choice. When he came home, he was very sick. Six months later, cancer killed him. He was not made a hero for his sacrifice. We had little money, but education was free. I became a translator and language specialist. And then, we Azeris were attacked by the Armenians who stole Ngorno Karabakh from us. Since then, Russia and the puppet Baku government have continued to do nothing to help our people." Aslan cleared his throat. "If we are speaking confidentially here, I can say, I have worked with Rik and a little with Noah and Max, first in Baku as a translator. Then, Rik convinced me I could work with him against Russians and the terrorism. So, after this training, I went to Cairo to infiltrate the Muslim Brotherhood. Later, Rik asked me to go to Syria to do the same with D'a-ash. I was there for eight months. It was a terrible time. That's me."

There were murmurs around the table at the humility of this courageous man.

"Perhaps, Adina, you could say a few words about yourself before we move on," Rik suggested.

Max interrupted. "When Rik told me what Sofie had overheard, I immediately called my boss to arrange for the best intelligence analyst we have in Israel to do some research and to join us."

Adina, ignoring Max's praise, projected a business-like demeanour and began without any personal introduction. "I've spent the last twenty-four hours undertaking a rapid appraisal of information that might be relevant to our enquiry based on what Max was able to convey. I think it best if I say little more until I understand the larger picture."

"Thanks, Adina, and to you all. I think we should take a brief break. When we reconvene, Sofie, you can tell the group what you overheard, which then leads directly to Hélène and Adina."

It had taken almost two hours for the introductions to be completed. Rik knew it was time well spent. If the team failed to jell, the consequences could be disastrous. He went out to the back and enjoyed several deep breaths of fresh air. He was well aware that he'd need all of his faculties and abilities to enrol every member in the mission. Failure was unthinkable, but it loomed like the enormous blackened sky in front of him.

Afternoon, April 16, 2019, Berlin, Germany

Max offered to take Adina down to her room in the basement. Without even glancing at him, Adina said, "Thank you, but I can find it myself." As she left the room, Sofie caught Max's look of frustration.

The team reassembled. At last, it was time to discover why they were all here.

Sofie's throat constricted as she began to recount her time at Fitch Bay. Unconsciously, Sofie spoke in German, repeating word for word, what she'd heard, without once consulting her notes. "No one will know it's *Der Kreis*. As instructed, *Hochmeister*...the final phase of *Recht und Macht*..."

As she finished, there was a clamour by all who did not speak German for her to restate it in English. Rik hastily pointed at the transcript he'd passed around.

Hélène gasped and almost shouted, "Are you sure he said *Der Kreis*?"

Sofie replied, "Yes. *Der Kreis*."

"And *Hochmeister*?" Hélène demanded.

"Yes, yes. I've been cursed with both a photographic and auditory memory. Why do you ask?"

Hélène grasped her hands tightly together. "Please, continue."

Sofie completed what she'd overheard and described her traumatic return to The Hague. "Oh, and the other thing is that I recreated a funny symbol I saw on the basement wall."

Rik projected it onto the television screen.

"*Mon Dieu ...*" moaned Hélène.

Several members of the team began to talk at once.

"Quiet, please," Rik instructed.

Max asked in German, "What can you tell us about the other voice on the call with your uncle?"

She responded in English. "I know he's German, Austrian or perhaps Swiss. His voice wasn't a young one. He spoke correct German. So, he might be well educated."

"Would you recognize it again if you heard it?"

"I can hear him in my head. I think I would but I can't be sure."

"I must speak. I must!" asserted Hélène,

Chairs scraped as people around the table reacted.

CHAPTER 9

Evening, April 16, 2019, Berlin, Germany

"My mother would be so ashamed." Why had she waited so long? "Shame! Shame!" Tears erupted, streaming down Hélène's face.

Noah, sitting beside Rik, turned to him and whispered. "She seems to be falling apart. Something about her mother."

Rik leaned over the table and said quietly, "Sofie, can you help with Hélène? We need to hear her story."

She nodded.. "Let's get some air, shall we?" Taking Hélène by the arm, she walked her back and forth along the edge of the house. "What can I do to help?"

Choked with tears, Hélène couldn't respond.

"Are you afraid you can't trust us? Do you feel unsafe here?"

Non, non, pas de tout. Ce n'est pas ça. J'ai tellement honte."

Sofie's patience was replaced by fury. "Listen! We have a crisis, perhaps a calamity. Why are you here? Do you have something to say? If so, say it but do it fast, because we have no time for drama." Damn and blast. What have I done?

Hélène looked shocked. Suddenly her face transformed into a watery smile. "*Merci,*" she said shaking her head back and forth.

Confused, Sofie wondered if she'd pushed her too far.

"*Merci,*" she repeated and pulled Sofie back into the house. "I am ready."

Rik looked at Sofie questioningly. She raised her shoulders and shook her head.

Hélène looked off into the distance. "My story must begin over one hundred years ago. My mother, you see, was a Jew, born in Bonn in 1918 to a wealthy family who was of both German and Czech descent. She was an only child. By 1930, my grandparents, unlike many of their friends, could see the peril that the Nazis posed. Their money, how do you say, talked. They moved the family to Ostrava, a Czechoslovakian coal-mining town with a large German minority where they hoped that they could reinvent themselves. Having changed their name from Goldman to Hegel, they disappeared into daily life. My grandfather, a tailor by trade, was able to set up a small business and prosper. They never ceased celebrating Shabbat, despite the danger," she murmured.

"Why didn't they choose to go somewhere far from Germany?" asked Max.

Adina glared at him. He'd clearly learned little about sensitivity since she'd last seen him.

Hélène appeared to take no offence. Instead, she nodded. "I've wondered the same thing. I do not know, though, I suppose, my grandfather could not have imagined the enormity, the full horror, of the Nazis' ambitions. No one could. In any event, in 1936, my mother, Anna, who was by then eighteen years old, fell in love and married a Czech Ostravian. She'd grown up speaking both German and Czech so she had little trouble making her home there. When the invasion of Czechoslovakia was imminent, my mother and her husband fled to Geneva with the financial help of my grandparents. This was in January of 1939. My grandparents were old and stubborn and, as far as I understand, would not leave Bohemia though it was soon to be under Nazi occupation. Both of them died in the war. While they must have been under constant fear of discovery by the Nazis, they were killed, ironically, when their town was heavily bombed by the Allies who were after the coal mine because it was important to the Nazi war effort and must be destroyed."

She frowned in concentration. "During the war, my mother and her first husband struggled terribly, though they were fortunate to gain entry to Switzerland. Swiss neutrality was carried to an extreme, and thousands and thousands of Jews running for their lives were turned away. Fortunately, my mother and her husband were helped by a remote family connection he had in Geneva, and by the money my grandparents provided. I do not believe that even my mother's husband knew that he had married a Jewish girl. They survived by taking any kind of work they could find, delivering newspapers, cleaning homes, and in her case, teaching German. Then, in late 1945, my mother's husband suddenly became ill and died. Mother was destitute."

December, 1945 - July 1946, Geneva, Switzerland

Anna's grief was surpassed only by her desperation. Every last franc had gone to the burial of her husband. If she could not find work over the next two days, she would be out on the street with nowhere to go, with no family in the world. Life here, she thought bitterly, ticked on like a Swiss watch. Even amid the unfolding stories of the horrors that the Nazis had perpetrated on millions, Switzerland had remained steadfastly neutral and seemed determined to continue as normal. How was this humanly possible? It seemed there was no capacity among these people for even the smallest gesture of compassion.

Near the entrance of the city's largest post office was a bulletin board that sometimes listed jobs. She went there first. Nothing. After that, she walked miles to a Czech cultural centre, praying that she might be able to find a place to stay while she scrounged for work. Her heart leapt as she saw the notice:

"Immediate need for a maid and cleaning lady. Must speak Czech, and Czech only. Must apply in person between the hours of 10:00 a.m. and 1:00 pm. References required."

Ashamed, Anna nevertheless could not prevent herself from

removing the notice. She went to the bus depot, waiting in line for what seemed like an eternity before finally reaching the attendant to ask directions to the address. One hour later, at 10:30 a.m., she arrived at what seemed a fortress in the Russian Church district. A wrought iron fence about four meters tall surrounded the imposing property. She walked and walked until she found only a gate wide enough to permit one car to enter, and a guardhouse.

She was intimidated. Who wouldn't be? In Czech, she introduced herself as Anna Novak to the rifle-toting guard. He made a call and waved her through. Marshalling every ounce of bravery she possessed, she strode across a large circular car park to the mansion and firmly used the knocker on the front door. After a moment, a maid appeared and ordered Anna to follow her into an elegant drawing room located off the hall entrance. She left Anna standing, gazing at the ornate, gilded table and chairs and then at her own image reflected back from a mirror sitting over a china cabinet that housed what was surely Meissen china.

"Please be seated," said a severe looking woman who entered the room from behind Anna. She spoke in German. Anna remained standing, having prepared herself for the language test. Visibly relieved, the woman repeated her instruction in Czech. When Anna sat, the lady remained on her feet, asserting her superiority, or so it felt to Anna.

"I am Mrs. Richthoven. We require someone immediately to work six-and-a-half days a week with one half-day off on Sundays. My husband and I receive many important visitors. While we have a cleaning staff for part of the house, we require a maid to serve food and drinks to our guests during the day. Whomever we hire may be asked to extend their hours into the evening upon occasion. In those instances, they would stay in temporary staff quarters overnight. Other duties would be determined by me on a day-to-day basis."

Having said her piece, the woman seemed to take in Anna now as if seeing her for the first time. She frowned, undoubtedly wondering if Anna, small of stature, emaciated from these past hard months and years and dressed in clearly shabby clothes, was up to the job. Anna straightened and stared back firmly.

"Please introduce yourself," the lady instructed.

"My name is Anna Novak. My husband recently passed away." She squeezed her left hand tightly to mask her pain. "He and I moved here five years ago from Czechoslovakia because he had relatives here and we wanted to better ourselves. There were few jobs where we lived, in Ostrava. Since then, I've done many types of work with my husband. I am trustworthy and can promise absolute discretion."

"Do you have experience as a maid?"

Anna paused. What I say next will determine my entire future. "I believe from your comments that you're looking for someone who can promise absolute trustworthiness. That is I. I will tell you the truth at all times, as I do now. I'm not a maid by background. However, I'm capable of running an entire household if necessary. I'm willing to work for my first two days free. If at the end of these two days you decide I am not acceptable then you must let me go. If, however, I am satisfactory, then you will pay me for those two days and, I hope, I will have this job."

There was silence. Despite the ticking of a clock somewhere in the room, Anna felt time stand still. She looked at this rigid, elegant middle-aged woman who seemed under a great deal of stress and who held Anna's future in her hands and waited, holding her breath.

"Very well. You will be given a trial period. Can you start immediately?"

With Anna's affirmation, Mrs. Richthoven warned, "I had to dismiss our previous maid for her lack of judgement. No one will remain in our employ if they discuss any aspect of our household or our personal business."

The woman mentioned a wage well above anything she could ever have dreamed. Better than selling stockings at the hoity-toity stores.

Better than working in a nice hotel. She would be the best maid that they had ever had.

By the end of the first week, Anna was exhausted but victorious having worked long hours and having received her first paycheque, enough to afford a small room near the Czech cultural centre. There had been no guests thus far. Apart from intense cleaning assignments, she had served two meals each day to Mr. and Mrs. Richthoven. What was odd and kept Anna on her guard was the strange fact that they were speaking German to each other. Why was the whole staff only allowed to be Czech when, clearly, German was the mother tongue of her clients?

She did not like Mr. Richthoven who spoke to Anna contemptuously as if he were Gestapo and she was being interrogated. He treated his wife the same way. Were they even Swiss? Unlikely, she thought. His German accent sounded as if it came from Bohemia or perhaps Moravia. Certainly not Austria or the Germany she had known during the early years of her life. She must keep her guard up to think only in Czech, she scolded herself.

Ten days after she'd started, Mrs. Richthoven, or Madame as she was instructed to address her, summoned her to the parlour.

"Tomorrow night important guests will be hosted by my husband. You will ensure that they have the food and drinks they request, that ashtrays are emptied and that they are able to do their work in comfort. You will also lay out paper and pens for a dozen people in advance and clean up afterwards. You must not draw attention to yourself, but simply sit quietly and respond to requests. Is that clear?"

"Yes, Madame."

"You and I will go now and plan for it. There are likely to be many such evenings that will be held in a private room off the main dining room. My husband takes his business very seriously and perfection is what he demands. If you provide it, your salary will be increased. If he is not satisfied, you will be dismissed."

The next night, Anna stood to attention as Werner Richthoven strode into the study where she had been told to wait. Think in Czech she silently repeated, as if reciting a prayer. At first, he didn't appear to notice her, but instead marched around the big oval table, inspecting it to ensure that everything was in meticulous order for his guests.

He fixed his falcon-like gaze on Anna and moved towards her. Standing above her he barked at her in German, "Is everything ready?" She coloured and looked troubled and, she hoped, vacant. Apparently satisfied, he repeated what he had said in Czech. She nodded.

He said, "You shall say nothing to anyone but me. Do you understand?" Again, she nodded. With that, he turned on his heel as if he were in the military and marched out of the room leaving her shaken. If it weren't for the salary, she would never stay here. The war may be over but Jews like her could be found out and killed at any moment. She knew, of course, through personal messages passed on from her family and friends in Ostrava and Bonn, what had been done to Jews like her before and during the war. So many had been sent to work camps and had not come back. Now, other stories were being printed in the newspapers that must surely be false, for there could not be such evil. And yet, standing in this room, awaiting guests, she had not felt this chilled and terrified since saying goodbye to her parents those six long years ago.

Eight men arrived clearly deferential to Mr. Richthoven who sat at the head of the table. The meeting began and she was quickly called to serve coffee and a variety of sweets.

When she was finished she sat in a corner adjacent to the food and drinks cart and, for the first time, looked around her at the beautiful art adorning the pale gold walls. The one closest to her was one of a young man, or perhaps it was a woman, but she didn't think so, with long flowing hair from medieval times sitting and turning his head to look out at the observer. The signature at the bottom was Raphael Sant.

Speak Czech she scolded herself, trying, without success, to screen out the German that everyone in the room was speaking.

The Present, Evening, April 16, 2019, Berlin, Germany

"After my mother left the Richthovens, she knew, as I shall explain to you all, that she must get away from Switzerland, away from that evil house. Fortunately, she'd met my father, Jaime Lévy, a Swiss-French man at the cultural centre in Geneva. Since it was post-war, borders were quite fluid. They chose to head for France and eventually reached Paris. They married in 1946. I was an only child, born in 1955."

Hélène smiled, wryly, seeing mental calculations being undertaken around the room. "I'm sixty-three years of age, soon to be sixty-four. It was not until mid-September, 1972 that my mother told me about the Richthovens. After the massacre of the Israeli athletes in Munich, a resurgence of anti-Semitic acts was occurring in France, including one that I experienced during my first year at the Sorbonne. I'm almost certain that the Munich tragedy and my own trauma helped my mother to overcome her reluctance to share her story with me after all those years. Also, she'd become very sick quite suddenly and, as it turned out, would only live another three months."

Noah touched her shoulder and she turned her head as if to acknowledge his presence.

She closed her eyes struggling to remember every detail. "That evening, she called me into her room where she lay bedridden. She asked me to bring to her a small thin bag that she had pinned to the inside of an old dress hanging in her clothes closet. This, I thought to be very strange." Hélène reached into her briefcase. "I've brought with me this evening those original documents that my mother had hidden for so many years, and that she read to me that night. Here are copies for each of you though I'll read them to you now."

December 18, 1945. Yesterday, on December 17th, I was asked to serve coffee and food in the large study. Exactly eight men, including Mr. R., attended. Mr. R. said, in German, "Now begins the second meeting of Der Kreis Im Quadrat with all founding members present."

There were audible gasps around the table.

"Der Kreis?" Sofie paled and stared, aghast at Rik. Any miniscule hope that she'd overheard her uncle incorrectly died and the terror of the moment flooded back.

Hélène seemed not to notice.

> *"The minutes of the first meeting may now be reviewed but will be left behind here and destroyed to maintain security." Then he said, "We have agreed to accept the insignia I have prepared as that of our organization. We have also agreed that the consequences of revealing our existence to anyone beyond our circle will be met with the harshest of sanctions as our doctrine sets out."*
>
> *As the meeting ended, Mr. R. walked out with everyone. A paper had fallen under the table. I picked it up. It had a strange symbol on it. I couldn't stop myself from skimming the first sentence and then the next... "... Restore Europe to racial purity..." Then, something like, "Allowing only the most powerful and superior beings into our Circle, we, together, will take control over all of Europe..." It also said something about a military industrial dominance? Terrified that Mr. R. might return, I put the paper back under the table and began clearing the dishes. The symbol had an owl on it and a circle in the square. Maybe these men are just playing, like at some secret men's club, but I do not think so.*

Jan. 18, 1946. I was in the study when the first five men arrived. One was obviously new and was introduced as the head of the Banque Cantonarde de Genève. I did not hear his name. The others I had seen before but did not know. "Girl, get me some water," someone said in German. I jerked, but did not look up. "Girl!" and then, Mr. R. interrupted and said I didn't speak German. He then directed me in Czech. My heart was pounding so hard. I feel evil coming from this room. If they knew I was Jewish, I think I would be killed.

April 10, 1946. Mr. R told the banker. "Heinrich has opened five accounts each of which now has a balance of $50 million. (!) Only he and I can authorize its use." He also talked about a vault where art and other valuables contributed by the members were stored. The meeting continued and seemed to be about planning their first operation, as they called it. I must try to describe these men, but it is hard. Most are over fifty. All seem very rich. Next to Mr. R., the banker, this Heinrich, seems to be very important.

June 14, 1946. There were nine men in attendance, one new to the group. I have seen him on newsreels. I'm sure he is Germany's Foreign Minister or whatever they call that position. Another, it was mentioned, was at the Nuremberg hearings that have been so shocking. Last night, they talked about Jews and finishing the job, and then, about how a Russian will join the circle. The strangest thing. Now they call Mr. R. `Hochmeister', and each other, `bruder'. They are doing something terrible. I will ask for a day off and must find another job. I am scared.

July 12, 1946. When I arrived, I gave Mrs. R. my notice. She was very upset and asked me to stay at least for a week until she could find a replacement. I didn't want to but was afraid of them, that they might be suspicious. I was up in the bedroom cleaning when people started to arrive. I was prepared. Today I used my camera from my purse to take pictures through the crack in the curtains. Mrs. R. was downstairs so I knew I would hear her if she came up. I hid the camera in my bag when I heard her calling me. She told me to go to the study. Again, there were eight men. This time, the one called Bruder Wilhelm seemed to be reading minutes. He was driving one of the cars, I'm sure. He said that the next meeting would be in Paris. There are new members from Russia, America and someone from Connetic University? Or some other place? They said the name but I did not recognize it. This seemed to please the group. Mr. R. said they will have a member in a new organization called international money group, or something like that. This seems to be very important.

July 18, 1946. "I had my last day today. I did not see Mr. R., thank god. I have no new job, but have saved money. Last month, I met Mr. Jaime Lévy and I think he wants to marry me. He's older, but he's kind. I met at a cultural centre social. He may be the answer to my prayers. If for no other reason, I need to have a new identity so that they can never find me.

Miriam opened her mouth as if to say something but Rik held up his hand to pre-empt interruptions. "Is there anything more you would like to say, Hélène?"

Hélène, looking as if a great burden had been lifted, indicated her desire to complete her story. "My mother did try to let people know. She said that once she'd entered France she sought out a Jewish relief group. But at that time, their focus was almost entirely on getting Jews to Israel or reuniting loved ones. They said that they did not have the capacity to hunt down such a group. They already had too much that they were attempting to do with not enough resources."

Max growled something under his breath. Adina, too, was shaking her head.

Hélène continued. "When I asked my mother if she could possibly believe that this *Der Kreis* was real, she said, "Yes I told Jaime so long ago, but he said they were a bunch of cranks and that after the horrors of the war, we must get on with life. You were on the way to being born, but I always knew those men were evil and planning many bad things."

"My mother also said that, about ten years before she revealed her story to me, around 1960 or so, President Eisenhower made a speech about a military industrial establishment and a munitions industry, a hidden power in the U.S. Eisenhower used almost the exact same expression as my mother had heard in that room in 1945. Also, just as Richthoven said, an International Monetary Fund was about to be announced at that time. I asked if my mother ever saw any of those men again. She said she hadn't but then she reached into the bag and held out several photographs that she had taken from the upstairs window."

Noah reached across the table and refilled her glass.

Buoyed by this gesture, Hélène resumed. "She told me that with these papers and photos someone might be able to identify them. I'll never forget her final words to me that night: "After what happened to us in the war, I vowed to bear witness before I died. But that witness must now become you."

Hélène shook her head back and forth. Silent tears fell onto her mother's papers, forcing Noah to rescue them.

The room remained silent.

"Such shame, such dreadful shame." Wiping her tears, she looked sightlessly at the wall, lost in the past. "I was so young when my mother revealed her secret to me. It had been over twenty-five years since she'd seen these men. Maybe they'd all died, I thought. Perhaps my mother was somehow mistaken."

"The past is the past. Nothing can be done to change it," Adina said crisply, looking at Max who felt, but would not return, her gaze.

Adina's admonishment had the desired effect. Hélène straightened up and nodded to Adina. "*Oui*. Though I was not sure what to do with the papers, I was intrigued with the symbol and went to the library to see what I could find. There are books that are devoted to such things. *Der Kreis Im Quadrat*, translated, means The Circle in the Square. I found no record of that name. But without too much trouble, I discovered the freemason symbol, which is both similar and different. In fact, it almost seems as if whoever drew the symbol was trying to turn the freemason symbol upside down."

The group stirred. This was an interesting twist.

"When I was in my mid-thirties, I was working for a French organization that was allied with an Israeli agency combatting anti-Semitism in France. I received an invitation to visit Jerusalem. I decided that now was the time to satisfy the request that my mother had made, that I bear witness. There, I met with someone recommended by my Israeli counterpart. He was polite and made copies of everything, though he didn't appear terribly interested. I never heard anything more until, after all these years, I was contacted by Mr. Becker who asked if I would meet with one of his colleagues in Paris. I must admit that I was astonished. And intrigued."

Looking at Miriam, she smiled. "I met Ms. Maartens in the Tuileries. She told me that my name had come up in a database kept by Israel in relation to *Der Kreis Im Quadrat*. She convinced me that it was important that I come to you. There is one final folder I must share with you." With that, she pulled out a series of black and white photographs, wilted with age.

As they were passed around the table, Hélène looked exhausted but somehow cleansed, thought Sofie.

"Hélène, you've given us many avenues of enquiry to determine who and what this group is. Your mother had great courage to do what she did. And you, by coming here not even knowing who we were, demonstrated your own."

Well done, thought Sofie.

Rik pushed his chair away from the table. "There are some matters I need to take care of tonight. Let's convene tomorrow morning at 8:00 a.m. when Adina can describe what she's found in Israel's database."

Max looked around at the tired faces around the table and knew what he needed to do. He slipped out of the room, unnoticed.

CHAPTER 10

Morning, April 17, 2019, Berlin, Germany

Despite her exhaustion, Sofie suffered a jagged sleep she attributed to the suffocating cloud of perfume that emanated from Miriam's side of the room. At 6:00 a.m., she crept downstairs in her sweats and headed directly for the coffee. Her nervous energy pushed her to set out a German breakfast while she waited for two pots' worth to drip. She would like to have gone on a run but felt unsure as to whether she would be upsetting any security protocol.

As she stood at the window looking out over the back of the property, a voice behind her made her jump and spill her coffee all over herself and the floor. Her heart thumping, she put the cup down and whirled around only to have Rik catch her arms and prevent her from doing further damage. Wrenching back from him, she glared at him. "Could you be any quieter for god's sake? Next time, ninja boy, make some noise!"

"Not a morning person, I see," he replied in defence.

She headed for a mop and paper towels to clean up the mess. Without giving him another look, she replaced her coffee. Leaning against the counter, she turned to eye him suspiciously. He edged towards the jar of instant decaf coffee careful not to get any closer to her than necessary.

Damn! Her left hand and wrist were on the way to blistering.

He went to the refrigerator and extracted an ice cube from the freezer. He held out his hand as if to ask her to give him hers, which, with reluctance, she did. Without any words, he focused on soothing the injuries, aware of the quickening pulse he could feel and of the extreme mutual consciousness of the moment.

Both were saved from further awkwardness by the greeting of Hélène who came from the small room off the kitchen. *"Bonjour,"* she said, looking questioningly at them both.

Sofie blushed. *"Bonjour,"* she stammered and explained the accident.

Adina came in looking as if she hadn't slept, which as it turned out, she hadn't.

Max suddenly loomed over Adina's shoulder like a dazed bear that had just come out of hibernation, dishevelled and hungry. Moving to create a distance, Adina casually nodded to him. She seized her tea and headed to her room, feeling, rather than seeing, Max follow her. As she reached the stairs going down to the basement she glimpsed Miriam coming down the stairs, her gaze trained on Max. All good luck to her if she had her sights set on him. Adina quietly closed the door to the basement behind her.

Half an hour later, the team assembled at the table.

Adina took a series of papers out of her briefcase and signalled to Rik that she was ready. Pushing her glasses up, she began. "As you may know, two days ago, I was asked to find anything I could in such a short time about something called *Der Kreis*. I was unaware of Sofie's account about her uncle, Karl Mueller, so conducted no search on him. After hearing Hélène's account of her mother's experience, certain avenues of enquiry occurred to me. I pursued these last night. If you'll indulge me, I will tell you why I think our story begins in the late 1800s, though indirectly, it dates back to the 1200s."

Noah looked sideways at Hélène whose hands were clasped tightly, her gaze riveted on Adina. Rik and Max, who had been speaking quietly to one another looked up with surprise.

"I feel it's critically important for us to understand the historical context for the creation of a group such as *Der Kreis Im Quadrat*, The Circle in the Square. Over the final decade of the 19th Century and the first three decades of the 20th Century, considerable angst existed among Germans who thought their country's status as a world power had come to an end. From the death of Bismarck in 1898, through implementation of the Versailles Treaty in the 1920s, Germans suffered severe economic hardship and social discord. Between 1900 and 1930, that malaise led to the resurgence in Germany of memberships in secret societies. Secret societies were also enjoying a renaissance in other parts of Europe, particularly the Balkans where the policies of nationalist messages took an ugly and extreme form of populism."

"It sounds fantastical, like a bad movie," exclaimed Sofie, as Hélène nodded in agreement.

"However unlikely it may seem to us today, German occult groups had survived for centuries drawing on the beliefs of the Rosicrucians and the Illuminati who had planted powerful roots there starting around 1200. Up until the 1900s, these groups' practices had relied on mysticism. With the turn of the century, mysticism became mixed with a new message that Germans were the master Nordic race, that they were Aryans at the top of a racial hierarchy. To many, these groups' beliefs offered an alternative vision to the hard realities of day-to-day life in Germany."

She looked down at her notes and then across at the wall, blind to their attention. "The popularity of occult groups grew even more with the release of *The Protocols of the Elders of Zion*, written at the direction, it is believed, of the Russian secret police around 1900. Later, it was translated and distributed throughout Europe and North America. This was a truly vile document that accused Jews, particularly from Germany, of trying to take over the world. Despite having been definitively and promptly discredited as false, it nevertheless became a force to rally members of many of the secret societies against the apparent threat of Jews. I must add that it also laid the groundwork for the Nazi message that was soon to come. *The Protocols* attacked Freemasonry, alleging that it had been infiltrated by the Jews who were, according to it, now running Germany."

Once again, Adina paused. *"The Protocols* diatribe was circulated widely as a result of the efforts of the American, Henry Ford, who, it is held, funded the translation, printing and dissemination of an estimated five thousand copies. Years later, he did publish a public apology acknowledging the document's fraudulent nature. It is believed that some of the U.S.'s most powerful politicians and business moguls were at one time or another members of Yale's secret societies. The Skull and Bones Society, for example, was reputedly an independent Freemason or Illuminati-inspired lodge, which may have taken part in the anti-Semitic scourge crossing the ocean from Europe. It became a very important gathering spot for the most powerful in the world over the decades, including a number of presidential hopefuls. Bear this in mind as we draw closer to *Der Kreis.*

"And then, around 1915, along came Rudolf Von Sebottendorf. Once a Freemason, Sebottendorff was horrified at what he believed was a takeover by the Jews of Germany's political structures, including Freemasonry. Around 1916, he came into contact with the occult Teutonic Order, which had survived for centuries, linked as it was, with medieval German Crusades-related Knights. The Teutonic Order or *Germanenorden* was heavily anti-Semitic. It epitomised populism and nationalism. Its symbol was the swastika.

"Sebottendorff quickly rose to become head of its Bavarian chapter. Shortly thereafter, he merged his group with the *Thule Society*. According to the *Thule Society*, its members would be guided by `masters in hiding' who would magically appear and endow these practitioners with superhuman strengths required to create a master race."

"And people actually believed such nonsense?" scoffed Noah.

"Many did, and one man, in particular, saw an opportunity. Hitler was in Munich at this time, although there is conflicting information as to whether Hitler actually was a *Thule* member. To qualify as a member of the *Thule Society*, one must, and I quote,

> *"Swear to the best of my knowledge and belief that no Jewish or coloured blood flows in either my or in my wife's veins, and that among my ancestors are no members of the coloured races."*

"Through the *Thule Society*, Sebottendorf created what would soon become the Nazi Party. From what we know, His *Thule Society* was largely taken over, co-opted by Hitler and reshaped to maintain its core beliefs. You must all be wondering how any of what I've said gets us to *Der Kreis*."

"It'll be worth the wait, I guarantee you," said Max in an uncharacteristically quiet voice.

"Based on the pictures that Anna, Hélène's mother, was able to provide to us, the man she worked for, Werner Richthoven, was, in fact, one Werner Haas, a notorious WW II Nazi war criminal who disappeared in early spring of 1945 despite the best efforts of the Allies to arrest him."

"What? Are you certain of this?" exclaimed Rik.

Hélène pressed her hands to her cheeks and closed her eyes. *Mon Dieu*. Her Jewish mother working so close to a monster.

"I had a facial recognition test run early this morning. Haas had some surgery. But with the new technology we have today, we can be certain, as you can see, they're one and the same. Thanks to Anna and Hélène we now know that Werner Haas managed to change his identity and make his escape to Switzerland just before the war against Germany ended. What I've discovered so far, and it may only be scratching the surface, is that Haas/Richthoven was born in a small town in the German-dominated part of Czechoslovakia. While he spent the first ten years of his life there, we know that he was sent to relatives on his father's side in Munich in 1915 where he completed his schooling, receiving very high marks. He was a loyal foot soldier of the Workers Party and became a rising star within the Munich branch of the Nazi party."

"Why?" Rik asked more belligerently than he'd intended. "Why didn't anyone make the Haas-Richthoven connection after Hélène provided her mother's information to your intelligence service back in the 1990s?"

Outwardly calm, Adina replied, "I can't know for sure, Rik. But I believe it's fair to say that at that time there was no evidence to validate the existence of *Der Kreis*, which would, by then, have been forty-five years old. We didn't have facial recognition capabilities as we do today. And, our attention was on the constant threats from the Arab world as well as the birth around that time of *Al Qaeda*. That's my guess, although I can't be sure."

Max shot Rik a withering glare and was about to say something when Adina continued. "There's more. War films and pictures show Werner Haas standing next to Hitler and Alfred Rosenberg, who was Haas' boss. Rosenberg, a great supporter of the *Protocols of the Elders of Zion* was the infamous author of Aryan theories and a major contributor to the Holocaust. He created the *Einsatzstab Reichsleiter Rosenberg* (ERR), the Special Task Force that looted art and other cultural assets from across Europe. Though I can't yet say for sure, I believe it is very telling that Hélène's mother, Anna, described a piece of art in Richthoven's study that was signed by Raphael Sant. It tweaked my memory. Just as I suspected, Raphael's *Portrait of a Young Man*, one of the world's most valuable paintings, went missing during World War II and remains unaccounted for to this day. This was surely the painting she saw that day. So, Richthoven/Haas, working for Rosenberg and the *ERR*, pilfered the Raphael. Art may have funded his escape. By the way, Rosenberg, unlike Haas, was captured, convicted and hanged as a war criminal at Nuremberg in 1946."

Hélène looked ill. Sofie managed to get Rik's attention. He picked up her signal, rushing his words to interrupt Adina. "Sorry. I need to make a call. Let's come back in fifteen minutes."

Sofie bent down over Hélène. "Can I get you something? It must be stressful to relive your mother's past."

"*Oui, ma chère*, I would be grateful for tea and a biscuit."

Afternoon, April 17, 2019, Berlin, Germany

Max took an empty seat beside Adina before she could take countermeasures. "You haven't lost your touch after all these years," he said quietly. "Still the best. Now's not the time, but we need to clear the air, Dini."

Unprepared and momentarily flustered, she stalled. "There's no way to clear air that's so stale, don't you think? Whatever happened in the past is irrelevant, at least to me. I'm a professional as are you. We can each do our part to deal with whatever this challenge is going to be. *Beseder*?"

At that point, Rik called the room to attention. Max, growling to himself, had no choice but to return to his chair.

Adina resumed. "It makes perfect sense to me that Richthoven/ Haas created *Der Kreis*. He and Rosenberg had already been members of a secret society, *Thule*. Anna's writings confirm that the `racially pure' vision of *Der Kreis* was entirely consistent with that of the *Thule Society* and of Rosenberg for whom he worked. Also, *Hochmeister* was commonly used to address the Grand Master in secret societies. We might also infer from the insignia of *Der Kreis Im Quadrat*, which resembles an upside-down version of the Freemason sign, that Richthoven was contemptuous of Freemasonry. He believed the false *Protocols of the Elders of Zion* message. I realize I'm speculating. I need to have additional time with the insignia before I can be more conclusive."

"Jesus," exclaimed Noah.

"Finally, I think it may be relevant that Sofie's uncle, Karl Mueller, went to Yale. Was he part of one of one of the secret societies on campus? Could it be that Richthoven already identified some of these as being anti-Semitic during the time of Henry Ford and believed, as he aged, that he might find a successor for *Der Kreis* there? I know that my supposition is tenuous. However, I hope there are some useful clues that will arise from my comments." Adina rubbed the back of her neck and pushed her glasses up.

After a profound silence, Rik looked at her and then around the room and said, "We all see why Max made sure you were on our side!" He stood in front of an empty whiteboard. "Let's summarize what we think we know. In 1945, Werner Haas, a Nazi war criminal, escapes to Switzerland and becomes Werner Richthoven. With financial assets stolen during the war, he creates *Der Kreis*. Anna, Hélène's mother, documents information on some of the members of *Der Kreis* and its mission to recreate a racially pure Europe. Nothing is known of the existence of *Der Kreis* for almost seventy-five years until just a few days ago when Sofie overhears what she does in Quebec. Karl Mueller is now the *Hochmeister*. Whether he inherited that role directly from Richthoven, we're not sure. As Adina has intuited, it may be a Yale secret society that links Richthoven with Mueller."

Max took over. "Mueller's communication with an unknown associate, let's refer to him as 'The German', indicates that *Der Kreis* outsourced the assassination of Victor Tolstoi, Russia's Energy minister who was visiting Lithuania. We hear that `our bruder in Moscow' is pleased with the results and that Geist, the assassin, has been instructed to head for England. They've provided the nationalists in Serbia with false evidence to ensure that the moderate, Marić, and his party, are out of the picture. Some Arab, we learn, is receiving massive funding. There's some allusion to this same Arab being upset when he hears about `the diversion'. One event, likely an overthrow, is being planned under a program called *Recht und Macht* — Right and Might — scheduled to occur within two months. Money has arrived in Albania from a Russian `partner'. Durres, Albania is the next destination for the German. And there's something related to banking that's going to happen," added Max.

"Right. Anything else?" Rik waited a moment. "Unless anyone has something to add, it's time to finalize our priorities for action. Who wants to start?"

An obviously exhausted Hélène spoke first, her heavy French accent making it hard to follow. "It is my belief that Werner Richthoven is surely where we must start. He is at the heart of this story of *Der Kreis Im Quadra*t. We should begin our enquiries in 1945. Who was he? How did he meet Mueller? Who were those men my mother captured in her photos?"

"Besides Richthoven, my uncle is our most obvious target." Resolve rang in Sofie's voice. "We know where he is and we know he's the head of *Der Kreis*. As appalled as I am that I'm related, we must arrest him and stop whatever it is that *Der Kreis* is planning."

Noah frowned. "I'm concerned that if we neutralize Mueller we lose our chance to uncover the other members of the organization. Wouldn't we expect him to be prepared to withstand the worst of our interrogations? And if he doesn't give us anything or sends us in the wrong direction, we may not be able to discover what *Der Kreis* has planned. Furthermore, if its members know he's been picked up they'll become invisible and we may never be able to track them down. So, let's place him under a microscope, his movements and his communications, until we have what we need. Then we seize him."

"Can we wiretap him?" asked Sofie. "I guess that would require Canada's approval..."

"Our situation stinks. I think Rik, Max and I are going to need to confer with our bosses to identify the best way to track Mueller's communications, assuming we agree that we're not taking him out of the picture," said Noah. Max and Rik both nodded.

"And I think we need to ask ourselves whom we can trust," Noah continued. "Mueller may well have moles within the U.S. Intelligence establishment. In fact, I'd be astonished if he and *Der Kreis* didn't, given what they've accomplished and are planning. Plus, he's undoubtedly using some sort of VPN network and privacy software for his mobile communications. We might be able to work with that, but our top priority must be not to alert him."

"VPN?" asked Hélène.

"Virtual Private Network," Noah clarified, smiling at her. "When someone doesn't want anyone to know whom he's contacting, what he searches or where he's located, he signs on to a VPN. The VPN service creates what some call a tunnel, a secret encrypted passage between it and its Internet customer. Only a few intelligence agencies have been able to decrypt some of the most dangerous VPNs. We'll have to wait and see if we can break into their communications, assuming, of course, that a VPN is being used by *Der Kreis*."

"Let's all agree. Our top priority must be to keep our eyes on Mueller. If he disappears we lose our main way to crack *Der Kreis*." Max seemed to dare anyone to disagree.

"You're right," said Rik. "And the only people we can trust right now are in this room as well as Neal, my boss. We can't risk bringing others into our investigations at this point, lest we alert this enemy. We'll decide before we finish who is going to go where. I can guarantee you that at least two of us will be on a plane to Montreal tomorrow morning."

"Rik, I believe we'll have to bring my boss into our team. You know he'd been an asset, and is hardly a candidate for *Der Kreis*," said Max.

"Let's talk after."

Before arriving, Adina hadn't known what to expect. What she was hearing was far more urgent that she'd understood, and she felt a surge of adrenalin she'd not experienced in almost five years. "I'd like to add to our plan. I think if we track Haas/Richthoven's contacts, the ones Anna exposed – Richthoven's wife, the banker and the Foreign Minister of Germany – then maybe we can identify the people who started *Der Kreis*. Anna's photographs will help us discover who they were. In this way, we can run down their family to see whether their sons or daughters are carrying on the family tradition. I would like to work on those angles."

Rik looked around the table. "Here's what we'll do. Sofie, Noah and I will take on Mueller, whether it means surveiling or seizing him. Noah, you'll follow the cyber leads. Adina and Hélène, find out as much as you can about Richthoven and *Der Kreis*, including who their present members might be. Max, if Noah's work with his surveillance agency produces leads about the transfer of funds that Sofie described, we need you to delve into the banking world to see if you can identify and match the ones the German was referring to when he referred to `the Arab'. Also, can you take the Serbia angle? See if we can find out who received the false evidence, and, from whom? That should lead us back to *Der Kreis* and its members. Aslan, we need you to map out who the Islamic terrorist groups that *Der Kreis* is funding might be. Miriam, you'll function as our command central at a secure, high-tech space my boss, Neal, has arranged in London. We'll need you to keep us all informed of progress and to do research as required. You'll be our hub and our logistics expert. See if you can trace a Russian or Lithuanian national traveling into England from Vilnius, Kaliningrad or Moscow over the past five days. Were there any photos of the assassination? If so, try to cross-reference faces. Maybe we'll get lucky."

"If we're done," Max said, "I'd like to invite you to the basement for a moment."

Adina, beyond exhausted, could barely suppress her fury at his insensitivity. The others, tired and hungry, along with a reluctant Adina, agreed.

At first, no one understood what was before them, and then, Hélène went to Max and embraced him. She smiled and turned to everyone. "This is our last evening here, and since today is the first day of *Pesach*, Max has made it possible that we can mark the occasion together."

Max followed. "I know you're all tired, but would some of you like to join us?" Everyone replied with enthusiasm. Adina was still for a moment, and then went to the table and sat down.

Max read an abbreviated English version of the *Haggadah*, the story of the exodus of the Israelites from Egypt, lifting, one by one from a plate in the centre of the table, items that he had been able to find to resemble the seven symbolic foods that assist in the telling of the story of Passover.

And then, to the amazement of all but one, he began, in a haunting bass voice to sing *Ma Nishtanah*, the four questions, in Hebrew. Hélène and Adina mouthed the words, lifted by the song. When he finished, clapping erupted. Looking endearingly vulnerable, Max said, "I guess my grandparents would be happy. They insisted that all us kids take part in the special Seder."

With renewed energy, the team, following Max's instructions, brought a feast of meats, soup, and wine down to the table.

As they dispersed to work out travel arrangements with Miriam, Adina slipped out, her throat constricted by those long-buried memories Max's gesture tonight had brought back.

Morning, April 18, 2019, Berlin, Germany

The team milled around coffee and croissants, compliments of Max who'd picked them up on this cold and rainy morning.

Rik ran down the stairs and went directly to Sofie. Taking her elbow, he steered her into Hélène's bedroom, which was empty.

"What's going on?" she asked gruffly, staring at his hand.

He let her go. By now, he knew that she'd not thank him for being gentle. "It's your uncle. He's reported to have died in an explosion at his home in southern Quebec. But," he held up his hand, "they haven't retrieved a body."

She raised her head and stared at him, her hazel eyes almost translucent in the light, her teeth biting her bottom lip.

She was silent for so long that Rik thought she hadn't understood him. He began, "Did you hear wh—?"

"I don't buy it," she said flatly. "An explosion. It's just too convenient, isn't it? How can we find out? Oh, hell. If I'm right, it probably means that he either suspects, or knows, that someone, maybe me, is on to him."

Surprise and a faint hint of relief showed, and then, worry. He said, "Precisely what I was thinking. Let's get back to the group. This isn't good news. But at least we're still together so that we can adjust our plan. We also have to consider what this means for your safety."

Adina and Max were looking expectantly at them as they returned to the kitchen.

"Gather the group. We're going to have to be quick or people will miss their planes."

Some were in their overcoats as they sat down.

"We've got a leak," Rik said flatly. "Days after Sofie overhears him, Mueller disappears."

"It may not be Sofie who was the trigger," Adina said quietly. "The mole could well be someone within our Israeli intelligence. If Mueller had suspected Sofie, he likely would have disappeared sooner or made a move on her. I think it's more likely that someone within our country was ordered to flag queries on words like Richthoven, Haas or *Der Kreis*. I suspect my search could well have induced Mueller to disappear, unless he really did die," she trailed off looking apologetically at Sofie.

"Shit." Max could barely suppress his desire to pick up the table in front of him and throw it against the wall. He'd thought he was so clever, getting Adina involved. Instead, he'd put her in danger. Given her response to his protective instincts five years ago, he could lose her again, whatever he did now.

Rik took charge. "There will be a funeral that Sofie will have to attend. We'll ensure her safety, and monitor whoever shows up. Then, Sofie, under the cover of working for me in Sarajevo, will get as much information about Mueller as possible."

Rik had discussed her move to Sarajevo with her last evening. It made the most sense, so she'd had to agree. A transfer from UNDP to OSCE would raise no flags, particularly since she and Rik had already worked on a file together for six months.

"Adina, if there is a mole or moles, we want them. So, devise a way to identify him or her without spooking them. Be careful! They'll know it's you who is doing the search. Whatever you do, don't underestimate this group. I think we can all agree," said Rik as he looked around the room, "that every one of us, after hearing what we're up against needs to take strong precautions to stay safe."

"I'm going with her," Max said defiantly, receiving no objections, even from Adina, who was too tired to argue.

"Noah and Max, compare notes. Find the best forensics experts. Who can we get into the Fitch house right away to figure out if it was Mueller who died, or not? Miriam, we need to know everything we can about Mueller. Search travel logs. Was anyone fitting the description of Mueller travelling the night of his apparent death? If we can't find him there's even more pressure on all of us to create new leads. My final and most important point: Everyone, work with Miriam to devise a safe communication protocol with each other. Trust no one. This is the extent of our team until further notice."

PART II

PURSUIT

*Never interrupt your enemy when
he is making a mistake…*

Napoleon Bonaparte

CHAPTER 11

Morning, April 18, 2019, London, England

Until the last few days, panic had been a foreign emotion to Karl. His life, when it was recorded for posterity, would highlight his steely calm, his performance under pressure. But when *Der Kreis'* low life Israeli informer had revealed that someone was searching `Der Kreis' and `Richthoven', he'd had to summon all the strength he possessed. At least, he reasoned, `Mueller' was not included in the search. And Werner, who'd died over twenty-five years ago, surely could not be linked to him.

After so many years of planning, nothing must be left to chance. He sent out the urgent call to set the death plan in motion. It worked just as it had been designed. He and his *Der Kreis* helper ensured that the explosion would be attributed to a gas leak. The body, which would be assumed to be Mueller's, was actually that of a local druggie. They'd made sure the body was black-burnt so that whatever was recovered would not yield dental records, DNA or any other identifying feature.

Careful to obliterate their footprints down to the dock, they slipped away in an inflatable boat. Under heavy cloud cover, they followed closely along the shoreline to a deserted logging road where an SUV was awaiting them. From there it was a simple matter of deflating the skiff and slipping over the U.S. border into northern New York State where their private jet awaited them at a small airfield. Six hours later, they'd quietly passed through British customs.

Karl felt deeper sorrow over the destruction of Fitch, far more than for any deceased family member or friend. It had been instrumental to his work. What he'd accomplished there over fifteen years had brought him to the brink of his biggest victory. It didn't deserve its explosive demise.

Such emotional weakness was unacceptable. He must, for now, fully embrace his alias, Alfred Mosely, Alfred, honouring Richthoven's mentor, the great Alfred Rosenberg, and Mosely, a fitting tribute to Mosely Williams, Karl's fellow Yale alumnus who'd risen to become the leader of the American conservatism movement.

Before key members of Der Kreis arrived to finalize plans, he must squash that female Jewish bug who'd made these annoying adjustments in his life necessary.

As he looked at his handcrafted watch, now set to London time, he wondered what type of funeral they would have for him, who would come and what they would say about him.

He prepared his second Canadian rye and sat back thinking of Werner who would only have expected, as a matter of course, the discipline and the strength that Karl had mustered under duress.

1985-1989, Washington, D.C.

Werner Richthoven prided himself on his physical prowess and mental acuity at eighty-five years old. He still hiked and was in better shape than most men years younger than he. The inferiors, as he thought of the masses, lacked the daily discipline it took. This same iron discipline told him it was time to select his successor.

Over the years, he'd identified only two candidates who met his onerous criteria, one American and one Swiss. They must be sympathetic to the Germany of the past, display an unwavering recognition of the existence of a superior race, maintain but not be driven by their own wealth, demonstrate ruthlessness and discretion, and confer upon Werner the respect he deserved.

He couldn't reveal *Der Kreis*, of course, but could float the opportunity of running a global business beyond any scale his pretenders to the throne had touched. Over the decades, he'd become a power broker in energy, a field that had become an increasingly useful cover as he'd accumulated wealth. His was a name that could get him through any door in the world. While he was, he prided himself, anything but vain, he could not choose a candidate who failed to bequeath him with the proper awe he merited. It had been frustrating beyond belief that he must hide *Der Kreis* and its triumphs over the years, its global power network, the OPEC manipulation, Martin Luther King's assassination and Munich, not to mention what was in store.

His favoured candidate was Karl Mueller, the best friend of the son of a founding member of *Der Kreis*. During their years at Yale, the son and Karl had both belonged to a secret society. Karl had quickly risen to the top.

By the time Werner first chose to meet Karl, he was the unchallenged king of D.C. lobbyists. They'd had dinner together. Instead of boasting of his accomplishments, Karl had been closed and protective of his own privacy. Werner had appreciated that. Slowly, through subsequent meetings, it became clear that Karl had not yet achieved the greatness he craved, and they both knew it.

As they became more comfortable together, Karl had asked Werner about his experiences in World War II. Werner, of course, could not divulge his real identify for fear of being exposed for war crimes. However, the cover story for his role in the war was impressive enough and mostly true. He'd known Hitler, Rosenberg, Himmler, Goering and Speer, and had worked with senior staff involved with the Jewish question.

Karl had shown the appropriate enthusiasm and admiration. He'd opened up about his love for Germany and shared the post-war upbringing that had made him feel like a pariah for his German heritage. When he expressed his bitterness that Germany had lost the war and fervently wished that the cleansing of weak and corrupt parts of European society had been completed, Werner knew he had his man.

Werner greatly enjoyed mentoring Karl. All but one of *Der Kreis'* members were supportive. That one had had to be permanently removed. Werner knew he didn't have much time left and asked Karl to meet him at his palatial home outside of Munich. "Before I die, Karl, I want you to know my past. Then, when *Der Kreis* has achieved its goals, you must ensure that my legacy is widely known and properly honoured."

Karl could not restrain himself. "I'm anxious to hear your life story. I've tried so often to find traces of you during the war, but with no success."

Werner smiled, wondering if Karl thought he'd manufactured his Nazi past. "My real name is Werner Haas." His eyes twinkled when Karl sat up abruptly.

"I first encountered Hitler in Munich when I was only eighteen years old, in 1918. I'd become a member of the *Thule* Society.

"What did you think of Hitler? What was he like?" Karl asked, trying without success to control his awe.

Richthoven's eyes blanked. As if in a trance, he began to speak slowly. "Adolf was a contradiction within himself. He was eccentric, at times childlike and at others brilliant, and aged beyond his years. He was arrogant in public rallies and painfully awkward in small groups. When he spoke, it was as if he were mesmerizing himself. His dreams were beyond anything we could imagine. At the beginning, we could see he was already making great strides. Though I could not say I liked him - he was coarse and lacked refinement - we all knew that, in him, we held the future of Germany. But Hitler is not the story here."

"Pardon me. Werner Haas! It is an honour."

"I can say without hubris that Adolph saw me as a leader from the time I was a lad. The turning point for me was in August, 1919, when Adolph introduced me to Alfred Rosenberg. I was only nineteen years old."

"I...I knew about you during the war but..."

"Through the 1920s and early 1930s, I followed Adolph's orders. One of our most important jobs was to get the Jews out of our government and rid them of our country. They were a contamination of good German stock. They held the money, and my job was to master banking and finance. That, I did. But my real boss was Alfred."

Karl nodded, wondering but being unwilling to ask, if Werner believed what Karl did, that someone should have overthrown Hitler and led Germany in victory.

"Alfred knew everything about the infiltration by the Jews of our government and places of power. It was he who ignited a fire under Hitler to arrest and exterminate them. He continued to keep up the heat on the Jews." Werner laughed at his little pun.

"For most of the war I worked with Alfred, with *Der Einsatzstab Reichsleiter Rosenberg*. In 1936, Alfred sent me undercover as `Werner Richthoven' to Switzerland, to make financial arrangements for the war and after. This was a great honour and opportunity. As you know, we at the *ERR* amassed a fortune in art and valuables that we confiscated during our conquests. *Der Kreis* owes its existence to the wealth I was able to secrete during my work for it. Unfortunately, by late 1943, some of us knew defeat was inevitable. So many mistakes..." His mouth tightened with unmistakable bitterness. "I chose to work with Heinrich Friedl of the Banque Cantonarde de Genève. He became a lifelong friend and a founding member of Der Kreis. It was he, of course, who brought you to my attention based on what your friend at Yale, Manfred Friedl, had told his father about you." He took a sip of his drink. "So, you see, I've had my eyes on you for a long time."

Karl nodded, accepting this compliment as his due. "I've wondered about our symbol and its origins."

Werner smiled, delighted at the question. "In 1940, when we invaded Paris, I assisted with the roundup of the Jews. We herded some of them to the *Square du Temple*, a park in the upper Marais. That *Square* held great meaning, as, many centuries ago, it had been a spiritual site for the Knights Templar. I never forgot those days I spent at the *Square*. Later, as I conceived *Der Kreis*, I also remembered those early heady times in Munich when we were purging the Freemasons whose infiltration by the Jews had revealed them to be sanctimonious cowards. *Der Kreis* must be the opposite of Freemasonry and its mystic drivel."

Taking a pen and paper from his desk, he drew their symbols.

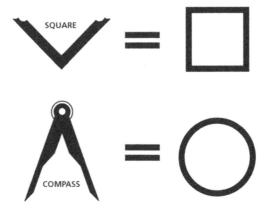

"Euclid's 47th problem is squaring the circle. How does one create a circle that has the same area as any particular square? It's been proven mathematically impossible. For the masons, the circle represented spiritual explorations and the square, material accomplishments. The Freemasons created some nonsense about aspiring to achieve a balance between the two." Werner snorted in derision. "I formed *Der Kreis* to create the results that Hitler failed to — to rid Europe of immigrants and Jews and to assert our superior power as northern Europeans. Over the past forty-five years, I've gathered together like-minded thinkers in powerful places to prepare for the takeover of the weak and insipid so-called democracies that have lost any moral compass. Ultimately, we will eradicate weak regimes, and assume control so that we can restore Europe to what it once was."

"And so, our symbol...?"

"The symbol turns the Freemason symbol upside down. The square and the compass are reversed. The square evokes the Square du Temple and the brave Knights Templar. The inversion of the compass symbolizes our disdain for the Freemasons and the mysticism that the circle was said to represent. The square represents our commitment, above all, to *material* results. I chose the owl as it connotes intelligence. *Der Kreis Im Quadrat*, Circle in the Square, captures our commitment to use our intelligence, not mystic babble, to achieve our vision."

"Werner, may I speak of the future with you now? As I see it, our future is exactly as our insignia reflects."

Werner nodded, cautiously.

"I believe there are opportunities that *Der Kreis* must act on now. I've recently returned from Moscow on business. Gorbachev's *perestroika* will finish the Soviet Union, I'm sure. We must be ready when those countries presently under Moscow's control fall into chaos. Imagine, on the one hand, the financial resources we'll be able to seize and use to our advantage, to establish our own leaders and gain control of all those countries: Czechoslovakia, Poland, Hungary, the Baltics, Ukraine, Bulgaria, Moldova, Azerbaijan — all of them!"

"And," Werner interjected, "there may be an outside chance of gaining influence over whoever takes control of Russia itself. Your comments reassure me. This is exactly the strategy that holds our future."

Afternoon, April 18, 2019, Jerusalem, Israel

She passed through Ben Gurion airport as she had on several occasions and took a taxi to his small flat off Dizengoff Street. She slipped through a back entrance where there were no cameras and walked up one flight.

He opened the door and was surprised to see a woman. All previous contacts had been male. His hands shook as he invited her to enter. "May I offer you something cold to drink? Lemonade, perhaps?"

"Yes, please."

As he turned towards the small kitchen, she calmly took the needle out of her pocket and injected a fatal dose of methadone. He looked back in frozen horror and fell to the ground. She arranged the body as she'd done many times before. Using gloves she scoured the flat for computers, flash drives and documents that could prove problematic. She left the way she came, walked for fifteen minutes and then hailed a cab back to the airport. A medical examiner would conclude death as a suicide resulting from an overdose of an antidepressant. Loneliness perhaps, his neighbours would speculate. After all, life was hard for everyone these days.

CHAPTER 12

Night, April 18, 2019, Jerusalem, Israel.

Adina closed her eyes and slid into semi-consciousness as the engines of the plane back to Israel droned a comforting rhythm. She was beyond exhausted and anxious to get back to her beloved home in a neighbourhood that her great-great-great grandfather and six other families had built around 1870 outside of the walls of the Old City. As an only child, she'd inherited it twelve years ago when her father had died. She never wanted to leave this little refuge from the world, this precious tie to her heritage. They'd been the real pioneers of Israel, those who'd settled in Palestine at least forty years before the influx of American and European Jewry in the early 1900s. As *Bilu'im*, or Palestine Pioneers, they'd emigrated from Kiev, foreseeing the pogroms that were soon to come. Adina, a Sabra, saw the soil of Jerusalem's hills as her soil, felt the sun as a uniquely Israeli sun, tasted Israeli fruit as more succulent than any in the world, heard the bird calls as only native Sabra birds could sound. She would never leave. She must have a child…

Max didn't know what to do. When he tried to make her laugh as he'd so easily done in the past, she'd turned away and closed her eyes. What was wrong with her, he wondered, as he battled insecurity, an emotion that was becoming all too familiar. He'd done what he'd done to protect her because he'd cared deeply for her. That she'd never talked to him, still wouldn't give him a chance to explain his actions, was infuriating. Perhaps she didn't care about him any more. By the time they arrived, he was sullen. "I'll see you tomorrow morning then, at my boss' office."

"I'll be there at 8:00 a.m.," she responded. How was she going to work with him every day, the attraction still overpowering but the trust gone? Her breath caught. She was grateful to see a taxi arrive. *"Nahalat Shiv'a toda."*

She wondered if there was any news. When she heard Mueller was dead, she was virtually certain that someone in her office must have tipped him off about her enquiries into Der Kreis and Werner Richthoven. She felt personally responsible, but goddamn it, she hadn't understood how sensitive it was.

Max arrived at his favourite Jerusalem hotel and grabbed a cold beer. Time for a shower and then sleep.

Early Morning, April 19, 2019

Adina's dreams were interrupted by a disturbing noise. Groggily she realized it was her secure phone. She fumbled for it. "Adina Kagan."

It was Max's boss, Svi Bikovsky.

"What's happened?" Adina asked, coming fully awake.

"Better for me to tell you in person. Get a pen. I'll give you an address."

When she arrived in front of the building, Max was waiting.

"Do you know what's going on?" asked Adina without so much as a hello.

"No clue. Do you know Svi?"

She shook her head.

"He never says anything by phone if he doesn't have to. He works like an animal, but usually draws the line at midnight. It must be something urgent."

Five years ago, Max's boss had created this elite, covert division of Israeli intelligence. Its purpose was to serve this particularly long-reigning Prime Minister, bypassing the country's other intelligence and military agencies, even if – especially if – extraordinarily risky and potentially illegal measures were necessary.

Adina was wired by the time they arrived at a security gate. On the other side was an unimpressive three-storey, T-shaped building complex. Max led the way down the corridor to a stark, deserted office labelled `Logistics and Research'. They passed through an anteroom into a hidden set of offices behind. Adina stopped abruptly, causing Max to take measures to avoid a collision with her.

Svi was painfully thin and sixty or so, she'd guess. His shaven head accentuated the stark lines of his face. He was immaculate in a white shirt and dress pants.

"I don't think we've met. I'm Svi Bikovsky. I've heard good things about you. Happy to have you with us. Let's skip the rest of the niceties. Grab a coffee and I'll tell you what's what." He waited for them to seat themselves. "Based on what Max has told me, I think we may have a lead on this *Der Kreis*."

Adina and Max turned to each other, just as they had in the past when they'd been so close.

Svi continued. "We've been having intelligence leaks, to the point where the Prime Minister asked me to look into them a couple of months ago. We identified three suspects. Within the last two days, the search narrowed down to one in particular. We've had a watch on him at his work and his apartment. At 15:00 hours yesterday, a woman was seen on video entering the back entrance. Our agents said she appeared to be looking for signs of a tail. They didn't know if she was heading to our suspect's flat, but one of our guys saw her exit about twenty minutes later. Our mole habitually meets his friends for a coffee at 16:30. Our agents waited until 20:00, thinking that maybe he was just staying in. They became worried about what to do and called in. We instructed them to see if he was there. When he didn't answer their knocks, they entered and found him dead."

"Here's a photo of the female. We're running facial recognition. We think the woman is tied to the mole. Also, our electronic surveillance picked up sound. Unfortunately, she only said two words." Svi played it as she said, "yes, please."

Adina and Max stared at the photos. She was wearing a hat, despite the heat of the afternoon. She appeared to have dark brown hair, was average in height, trim and athletic, perhaps mid-thirties.

"What do you think?" asked Max, looking at Adina and then at his boss.

"My first response is that we've lost our chance to interrogate him about his ties to *Der Kreis*," Adina responded. "That's a major blow, particularly since Mueller, our best possible source of information, has died or disappeared. I guess we'll soon hear whether the body at Fitch was his. My bet is it's not. This woman may be the best lead we have. If we can identify her or track where's she come from and the name she used going through customs we'll have a lot more than when we arrived."

"Agreed," said Max. "My take is that *Der Kreis* is thorough and sophisticated. Obviously, Adina's search for 'Richthoven' and '*Der Kreis*' spooked Mueller enough to make him disappear. If he staged his own death and killed our traitor, they're not leaving anything to chance. Svi, what do we know about this guy's background?"

Svi handed over two identical thin files with a few pages of notes and photographs. "It's highly likely he was blackmailed. He was gay and had a habit of going to bathhouses. He was into some pretty kinky things. The breaches have been occurring over the last year. We looked at his bank accounts and several small deposits began to appear around that time. He used two banks, suggesting he tried to conceal the payments. The deposits were in cash. There's no way to track where the payments originated. Frankly, until this *Der Kreis* thing, we suspected the Russians. It's their *modus operandi*."

Adina interjected, "If they've had to terminate him, it's reasonable to believe they'll be working on getting another in place. They'll also know that I was doing the search. That means they may still be interested in me. I need to start on some really important research right away. I must have absolute certainty that I'm safe." She took off her glasses and rubbed her eyes.

Max couldn't stop himself. "You'll need to move temporarily. And we'll give you protection. You'll work out of here, of course."

Reddening with a surge of anger, she said, "Thank you, but I have been in danger before and managed to survive by using my head." Not wanting to make a scene in front of Max's boss, she said, "But, yes, of course it makes sense to take some precautions. Svi, may I ask for your thoughts?"

"If they are after you, they'll expect to see you at your old place of work. For the next few days, you need to make things look normal. They mustn't know we're tracking them. We'll have coverage on you and be on the lookout for anything suspicious. I'd suggest you ask for leave and then join us here. We'll have an office waiting for you."

"Are your research facilities as good as we've got at our headquarters?"

Svi said, "They better be, after all the money we spent. You can take a look now if you'd like. Get a feel for what's here."

"Hélène Lévy, who brought the *Der Kreis* file to Israel in the 1990s, will be working with me. We'll need space for the two of us. We're also going to have to pick the brains of some of our experts on the Nazis."

Max said, "I'll work with Svi over the next couple of days to develop a plan to allow you to operate safely."

Svi took Adina through a series of interconnecting doors within which several rooms housed the types of high-tech equipment and communications she needed. "This will do very nicely."

They returned to Svi's office just as his phone rang. "Yes? Good."

Hanging up, he said, "Customs video shows her coming through, using an Austrian passport in the name of Marta Geller. On her way out, she has blond hair, by the way. Bound for Rome, but that may have just been a transit stop."

"I'm going home. I haven't slept in almost three days. I'll return to my old office later this afternoon," said Adina.

Morning, April 19, 2019, Jerusalem, Israel

Dini was in danger. It was his duty, Max reasoned, to ensure the sanctity of the team's work by protecting her. If caught, she knew everything about the team's plans. His focus now was on keeping her safe. He followed her at a discreet distance.

Dina drove her car into her aboveground parking lot at the back. It was a quiet neighbourhood, especially before dawn. Since all the families were descendants of the original pioneers they were like her own family, always there for her when it counted.

She emerged from the car and reached the stairwell at the entrance. A gun pressed against her back. She heard a voice behind her speaking in Hebrew. She froze and waited, considering her options. She must overcome her exhaustion. Desperately she tried to formulate a plan. One thing was sure. She would not be taken or interrogated.

"Follow my directions, exactly. Drop your bag and put your hands behind your back."

She had to delay him. Slowly, she bent to put her purse on the ground. As she did, she let herself fall, twisting so that she lay, half on her side on one of the steps. Roughly, he turned her over, grinding her face into the concrete, cutting her lip. "Try anything like that again and you'll die a more painful death than I had planned, after my little interrogation." He hummed quietly as he pulled her arms to her back and wrapped it painfully tight around her wrists. "We're going to take a walk over to my car. Get up!"

He lifted her by the binding around her hands. Suddenly two gunshots rang out. Released, she fell back down, face first, hitting her chin. She cried out. She heard a snarl, then a groan, and felt a body fall on her. A moment later, the weight was gone. Struggling to turn over, she looked up. The thug looked dead. Max, apparently unharmed, stood over him.

"Are you all right? Did he hurt you?"

Shaking, she felt tears of pain and relief welling. *"Toda rabah,"* she mumbled painfully. "But how did you know?"

He removed the twine from her wrists and then bent down to the attacker. He was dead. Nothing in his pockets to identify him. He took her arms and stood her up as gently as he could. Concern and anger showed on his face. "I didn't. But I figured if they were going to try something it would be soon. And frankly, I couldn't be sure Svi had put someone on you right away. I decided to follow you home and make sure you got here safely. I left my car down the lane. When I walked to the corner of your building, I saw you two. The hard part was getting to you without him knowing. Fortunately, your little stunt worked," he said holding her chin gently. "It looks as if you may need some stitches."

"Aghh!" she bleated, jerking her head away. "Again, thank you, but did you have to kill him?" she asked her voice rising.

Rage surged through him as he looked down at the body. "It obviously wasn't what I wanted to do," he gritted out. "He must have seen me out of the corner of his eye, because he swung around to take a shot at me. Before I even knew if I was hit, I took him down." He looked back up at her. "No choice as far as I'm concerned. He could have gotten another shot off if I hadn't." Had she forgotten how much he loathed, was sickened, by killing?

She sat down on the steps, afraid that her legs were going to give out. Neighbours were beginning to pour out of the apartment door.

"Please, I'm okay. Thanks for your care," she said. "I got mugged and a friend rescued me." As they milled around her, she could only manage a painful half smile. "I guess I'm off to the hospital to get checked out. Meanwhile, some of my police friends are going to take this creep away. I may have to be gone for a few days on business, but I really appreciate your concern." She tried to smile. "I'll let you all know when I return." With that, she lifted her arm to Max who, again, hoisted her up.

Her friends were still hovering, unwilling to leave the scene. Max took charge. "Look, I know this is upsetting, but it would be helpful if you could go back to your homes. This is a crime scene and we need to preserve it. Don't worry. I'll look after Adina."

Gruffly he said to Adina, "I'm going to drive my car back here. Sit in the front seat and wait for me. I'll call this in and make some arrangements."

Meekly, she nodded. She felt shame, remembering what she'd said to him. "Max, I'm sorry."

"Sorry for what?" His tone was abrupt.

"What I said about you killing him." Her mouth was so sore, she was having a hard time forming the words. "I don't even want to think what would have happened if you hadn't…" The salt of the tears leaking down her face deepened her pain.

Three hours later, after a private doctor finished stitching the inside of her mouth, Max delivered Adina to a safe house near his boss' office. She was struggling to stay awake. As he took her arm to lead her through the back door, he felt her sag. He scooped her up, got her to the bedroom and helped her off with her blouse and pants. "Get into bed." She was semi-conscious as Max administered the painkillers the doctor had prescribed. Hélène was arriving in an hour and would keep a close watch on her.

He went into the living room and called Rik. "I'm sending you a photo of Adina's attacker. We also have an image of the woman assassin who killed our mole."

"Fuck. How is she?"

"She's sleeping. It's going to be a painful few days."

"Thank god you had the presence of mind to follow her. We can't do without her and frankly, we all really like her. Tell her we're thinking about her."

"Will do."

"I'll have Miriam run the photos through our system and get back to you if we get any results." Rik added. "It looks like we've gone from guerrilla warfare to outright battle. And that battle is with Mueller. The body at Fitch Bay was burned beyond recognition. According to our guy, the explosion was not an accident and he's one of the best at what he does. He said that if it had been a gas leak, as they wanted everyone to believe, the explosion would have destroyed only a part of the house, not the whole place. There had to be a secondary source of gas or some other explosive at the other end of the house."

"Fast work."

"We're making sure the investigators officially find Mueller's `death' a tragic accident. We don't want him to suspect that we know he's alive. What are the chances that the death of Adina's attacker is going to make them go after Adina again?"

"Good question," said Max. "Unfortunately, neighbours saw the bullet wound. We're going to spin it as a domestic violence complaint that brought the police to her building. A friend interceded to save her from an apparent mugger. That's the best we can do until tomorrow. Adina is going to ask one of the trusted people in her apartment complex to tell every family not to talk to anyone about what happened. They'll let her know if anyone is sniffing around. They're like family to her. I think they'll go along."

"One more thing. A funeral has been announced for Mueller in D.C., in a couple of days. Sofie has to attend or it would look off. I'll be in the background making sure she's safe. It will also give us a chance to observe who attends. I've asked Noah to have some ex-secret service on hand to ensure her safety. Give our best regards to Adina."

Max, unconsciously gnawing on his lower lip, growled, "If Mueller's after Adina, it's because he knows she was searching the database. He's not going to stop until he finds out how much she knows. I'm going to be here until I'm comfortable that Hélène and Adina are safe."

He returned to the bedroom. Dini was asleep. It's too cold with the air conditioning, he thought. He found an extra blanket and laid it over her.

Evening, April 19, 2019

Svi called Max. "I need you to get over here."

"I won't leave Adina on her own."

"Three of my men are outside. Hélène's landed and will be there shortly. Get yourself over here."

Twenty minutes later, Max came in and sat down. "What's happened?"

"Something very interesting. We don't have a name for her yet, but this isn't the first time the woman who killed our mole was here. She entered Gaza on February 1st and left on March 11th. What do we make of that? Is she some kind of Arab terrorist? I thought we were dealing with this *Der Kreis* business, not Gaza."

"Do we know what name she used, what her purpose of business was?"

Svi looked sheepish. "Things were a bit disrupted at the border those days. Computers were down so everything was done by hand. I don't hold out much hope, though I've asked for a search."

"On both days? Do you really think that's a coincidence?"

"You're right. It's not that common, but it does happen. Still…"

Svi trailed off.

Max thought for a moment. "Sofie McAdam overheard her uncle talk about 'the Arab'. If he's from Gaza..."

"Sending terrorists against someone other than us? Against the Europeans? Why would the Gazans do that? And why would *Der Kreis* be working with them? I thought its game was to overthrow a European government or two." Svi shook his head, frowning.

"At this point, we're not sure what *Der Kreis* is doing. I'll talk it over with Rik." However, the moment he left the office, Max focused all of his attention on a plan to protect Dini. She would not be hurt again.

CHAPTER 13

Morning, April 19, 2019, Stockholm, Sweden

Noah Sindegard arrived at *Försvarets Radioanstalt*, better known as the FRA or the National Defense Radio Establishment of Sweden, one of the most respected communication intelligence agencies in the western world.

To some it might seem odd that Sweden had distinguished itself in the cyber warfare arena. There was one very compelling reason for its preeminence. Its close neighbour was Russia. It was connected to the rest of the world by six fiber optic cables, enabling it to capture an estimated 80% of all cable-based communications to and from Russia. Russia was hungry to expand and Sweden feared it or its neighbours could be targets. Helpfully, in 2008, Sweden's government had given the FRA unprecedented power to collect all communications coming in and out of the fiber optic cables, including Russian emails, text messages, telephone or other types of communication. The FRA routinely shared its data with the NSA in Washington, GCHQ in the U.K., and NATO to name a few. And the favour was returned.

Assistant Director Ingrid Gustafsson, an attractive middle-aged woman, entered the room. After pleasantries were exchanged and they were settled around a table, she said in a singsong voice, " So. You tell me what specific information you are looking for and I will tell you how and if, we can assist you. If we cannot, I may be able to refer you to other agencies."

"I've summarized my needs here," he said as he passed two pages to her.

She scanned the list:

1. Transfer of EUR 2.5 million on April 12 or 13 sent from Germany, Switzerland or Austria to an offshore bank account. A communication might also have been sent to Vilnius confirming the transfer:
   a. Who sent the communication?
   b. Who received it?
   c. What banks were used for the money transfer?

2. Transfer of EUR 5 million from the same source to a destination associated with 'an Arab' within the past ten days;

3. Communications between a German/Swiss/Austrian source in Europe and Memphremagog, Quebec over the past five years, but most importantly over the past ten days;

4. Communications to or from Evgeny Sokolov, Artem Gabori and/or RussTech,
   emanating from their base of operations in Transnistria, Moldova;

5. Transfers of funds to/from Sokolov and Gabori over the last twelve months. Who sent and received the funds?

Ingrid scanned the list. "Beyond our own, we have access to the NSA's databases. We can also make use of GCHQ's Edgehill, among others. Without a doubt, those you want to track are using VPNs to mask their Internet usage. Unfortunately, Snowden did us all great harm by exposing our success in decrypting so many VPNs."

Noah made a face of commiseration. Sweden wasn't the

only country furious about Edward Snowden's leaks.

"Again, you must hope that we've been able to decrypt the VPNs being used. If not, we may be unable to help."

"Understood. What about money transfers?"

"The illicit transfer of money remains very difficult to trace, despite all of our efforts here in Europe and in North America. Those who transfer large sums of money have developed highly sophisticated and difficult-to-trace methods such as the use of correspondent accounts and nesting."

Noah raised his eyebrows. "Nesting?"

"Let's say you want to transfer large sums from somewhere in Europe to a terrorist cell that accesses its funds in Dubai. You create an account at your own small European Bank and ask that that money be transferred to a bank in Dubai. To do so, your small European bank likely has to transfer the money to some bigger European bank that happens to have a branch in Dubai. The money goes from your account at the smaller bank to the larger bank and then on to Dubai. The owner of the account in the Dubai bank will then be instructed to transfer the funds to an account at a smaller bank there. Likely, the terrorist cell will have created an account disguised as some type of shell company whose owners are not always easy to identify. Despite all of our efforts to detect and seize terrorist funding, the problem is that banks and countries have not allocated the human and financial resources to implement their own money-laundering laws."

Noah remained silent, wondering if this visit was going to be productive.

"As to whether we can track those sums you've identified, we must hope we get lucky. For the communications to Quebec, we'll use our NSA and GCHQ databases which would better locate this transatlantic communication. Likely, this group you're tracing will be using encryption software to make it more difficult for us to tap into their mobile communications.

"How long until a possible result?" asked Noah.

"The more criteria used to limit our search, the better. Otherwise, we'll have to wade through masses of irrelevant data. Since your request has been given top priority, we'll hope for some results in a week or two. Some data may come in sooner. You must hope that we've already decrypted the VPNs that are being used."

Noah thought for a moment. "We'll want to work with you to review whatever data you obtain."

"Of course," she said.

"One of our biggest concerns is to make sure that the enemy we're tracking doesn't cotton on to the fact that we're doing a search on them."

"Cotton?"

"Sorry!" Noah gave one of his rare smiles, his stubbled cheeks revealing dimples that made him look much younger. "Our enemy may have people within the NSA or some other intelligence agency. We don't want to tip them off that we're tracking them. And if we can't prevent that, we must take measures to hide our identity."

"I see. Yes, this is a problem for many of our searches. Over the years, we did have incidents. However, we managed to apprehend those who leaked information, including some consorting with the Russians. Nowadays, FRA is known for its impenetrability. You'll be happy to know that we do have ways of hiding who's running the search. If anyone is looking, they won't know it's the FRA." A quiet pride radiated from her.

She looked at her watch and stood up. "I'll assign one of my top project managers. He'll need you to guide him. Shall we get started?"

"Right away. My sincere thanks," he said, as he extended his hand to hers.

CHAPTER 14

Evening, April 19, 2019, London, England

She wished this man were her real uncle. She hadn't seen him for months, since she'd had no excuse to be in Washington, or Quebec for that matter.

She took the usual diversionary measures to reach the estate that was now Karl's new home. He opened the door and held out his arms to the only person in the world for whom he felt a bond, a love borne out of recognizing oneself in another. Putting his arm over her shoulders, he drew her towards the giant living room. "Take off your coat and sit over by the fire. England is infernally cold. I'll be very happy when this charade is over. I've been waiting for you with a Kir Royale."

They sat comfortably, smiling at each other, enjoying their reunion. After a while, he asked, "How did it go?"

"As planned. I was in and out of the flat in a minute or two. No word if the body has been discovered yet. I hope you have something more interesting for me to do. I'm not just a pretty face, you know," she joked.

"Come now, dear. You are pretty! I hated the thought of you being in that Jew country."

"I know. I feel like I need a shower."

"I spoke with your father earlier today."

"How was he?"

"Testy, as usual. You know how he loathes going to Albania and being away from home and the company." Karl owed an immeasurable debt to Manfred, his Yale friend and closest confidant, his closest *bruder*. When Heinrich died, Manfred had become *Der Kreis'* second in command. Fortunately, thought Karl, Manfred had never coveted the leadership role. Quite the opposite. He'd been anxious for Karl to take over from the aging Werner.

"Your father wants an update from you. You can do that after we've had dinner."

Karl was her godfather. He was unfailingly proud of her intelligence abilities. At sixteen, she'd come to him, not her father. "What are you doing? I know it's something important. I want to be a part of it."

When Manfred and he had ignored her, she'd made them pay. Karl smiled at the memory. She'd embarked on dangerous forays with her neo-Nazi friends. Karl had had to fly back from Washington when he discovered she was on the verge of acquiring a criminal record.

Ultimately, it was he, not Manfred, she'd sought out. "Most people are weak and stupid. They're sheep. And now we have more and more mongrels. Europe is being ruined. I never want to go to Paris again, it's so polluted with immigrants. I need to do something important. If you give me a chance, I'll be good and do what you tell me to. Just let me work with you."

"I'll consider it, but only when you've proven yourself. First, you'll finish high school. You'll earn the highest marks in your class. Then, you'll enroll in the military and earn your way to the top. While there, you are going to work to get a degree in whatever subject you choose. After that, if you obtain a superior degree, we'll get you special forces training. If and when I know you've earned my trust, we'll talk about what you can do. Agreed?"

"I'll do anything you ask. But what about my father? He treats my mother like a servant, and me, like an annoying child."

"You let me handle him."

At twenty-four, she'd fulfilled his requirements. Only then had Karl and her father introduced her to *Der Kreis*. She'd begun with routine surveillance of their enemies. It was when they asked her to observe and report on the performance of a Russian trafficking group linked to *Der Kreis* that she'd killed her first person, a young woman, girl really, who was attempting to escape. Mueller was struck by her dispassion. At that very moment, he knew she'd be his valued right hand, in some respects closer to him than Manfred. He'd made sure that her military special forces training was amplified, ordering one of *Der Kreis'* enforcers to train and mentor her. Reluctant at first, the trainer soon realized that she was exceptional.

As she sipped her drink, Marta felt a fierce joy and exultation at the exciting, meaningful life she lived, all thanks to the man sitting across from her. She loved him as fiercely as she was disappointed in her bland father. She grudgingly conceded, however, that her father deserved her respect for his hard work.

"I'm so happy that you asked me to come here instead of back to Geneva. But I know you have a reason, too. What are you thinking about?"

"My funeral," he laughed mirthlessly. "It's to be in Washington in two days. All those obsequious congressional fools I owned, all those hypocrites on K Street, will barely be able to contain their relief. Society dames who tried to woo me will be there and, of course, our dear Vice-President." He drifted into silence, contemplating his own wake.

"Hmmm. Sounds fun. Can I go?" she teased him, trying to lighten the mood.

It didn't work. "The fact that I've had to kill myself off is beyond galling. The Israeli vermin have been looking into Der Kreis and Werner. After almost seventy years of secrecy, just two months before we take power, someone discovers us?" His voice rose, spittle flying from his mouth.

"I'm just relieved you're safe."

Karl wiped his mouth with his handkerchief. "I wish I'd asked you to do the other hit while you were there. Instead of seizing the Israeli researcher and interrogating her, the idiot botched the job. At least he died immediately."

Marta shook her head in disgust. "So she survived? Do you think she'll suspect us of being behind it?"

"The Israelis have concluded it was a mugging, that her military boyfriend heroically saved her. We can't know for sure what she suspects."

He's rattled. He looks old, she thought. I've never seen him like this.

"What I'd give to attend my funeral."

"I hope I never ever have to," she replied, her voice replete with emotion.

"I wonder if my niece will show up."

"That bitch?" Marta had always been jealous that Karl had a blood relative her own age.

"She's less than nothing to me. You know you're the daughter I never had."

This was a sentimental Karl she rarely saw. Though she was touched by his expression of love, she began to worry.

They gazed at the flames of the crackly fire.

Karl was the first to break the lengthy silence. "There's something I need you to do for me."

"Anything. Shall I complete the job, grab the Israeli woman and interrogate her?" She relished the thought.

"No. It's not smart to send you back to Israel after your day today."

"But isn't seizing the Israeli our highest priority? She's the most likely to give us the answers we need. Why not let me get her? I'll make sure there are no mistakes this time."

"No, Marta! I have a different assignment for you."

As Karl explained, she frowned. "I still think the Israeli woman is more important," she muttered.

"Just do as I ask," he almost shouted. He rubbed the back of his neck. "Then," he said in a quieter voice, "when you get back in a couple of days, I'll have a very important assignment for you, one you'll appreciate."

"What?"

"You'll finish the work you started in Gaza."

She sighed. "Whatever you want." She looked at her watch. "I'd better give Father a quick call before I pack."

"I'll expect you back here in half an hour. We need to go over what I expect from you over the next couple of days."

April 20, 2019, Durres, Albania

Manfred Friedl drove past the endless row of Durres' cheap coastal hotels that catered to Eastern Europeans. He parked behind a nondescript building and entered through the side door. Artem Gabori, RussTech's moneyman was leaning on the reception desk, smoking and chatting up the dumb girl he'd hired as a pretend secretary for the bogus trading company that Manfred had helped the leader of *Hamas* to set up a few weeks ago.

Gabori may be a greasy gypsy, but he and his group were channeling significant trafficking money into a Palestinian cell here in Albania, at the instruction of Russia's President. At first, the Russian had been extremely reluctant to fund Arabs. Over time, however, Manfred and Karl had convinced him that the terrorism acts of *Der Kreis* he supported would put anti-immigrant authoritarians in power throughout Europe, which would also conveniently undermine the European Union and NATO.

They sat down in a private room. "We've wired one million Euros to the account you specified, as agreed," said Gabori.

"What about the weapons?" asked Manfred.

"They're in a storage space we use not too far from here. We'll want to unload them right away."

"When they're found, they'll be traced to Syria?"

"Yes," replied Gabori. "Give me a couple of days. I think that completes our transaction."

After Gabori left, Manfred used his secure VPN to call the *Hamas* leader in Gaza. "The weapons are here and the money's in your account."

Manfred heard the click of computer keys.

"Good. What is the timing of the mission?"

"I'll let you know, but it will be within the next two weeks. They must follow the instructions I'm going to give you, exactly. Is that understood?"

The *Hamas* leader smiled. With the money stashed in Albania, he'd be able to buy weaponry from RussTech and other criminal organizations passing through Albania and then use a shipping company there to smuggle the product to Gaza. And his Dubai account would let him live the life he deserved.

Manfred headed back to the Nene Teresa Airport. He couldn't wait to return to civilization.

CHAPTER 15

Morning, April 21, 2019, Washington, D.C.

Sofie flew in from Sarajevo via Rome to Dulles. The taxi pulled in front of an old colonial brownstone house on a street off M Street.

Rik met her at the door. "You made it okay? Get any sleep?" as he took her bag into a small bedroom off the foyer.

"Yes, actually I did. I want to be sharp today."

She looked around. The walls and antique furniture were covered with photographs of Noah and his military exploits.

"Are you hungry? Thirsty?"

"Maybe something cold," she said already walking towards the kitchen, not waiting for him to play host. He was her boss, and he would be treated as such.

Rik admired her as he trailed behind her. She was wearing her uniform, black pants and jacket, and a white blouse with a gauzy scarf that, he'd noticed, elevated her hazel eyes to a stunning green.

With glass in hand, she stood leaning against the counter, one hand in her pants pocket and then drew it out to look at a gold Rolex watch that she rarely wore, but which, she had decided, would befit the company she'd keep today. "I've got a couple of hours before I need to head to the church. Anything happen over the past few hours that I should know?"

"Let's go into the living room and I'll bring you up to date." They sat down across from each other, she on a plush sofa and he on a reclining chair. "*Der Kreis* got to the Israeli mole before we could. He was killed yesterday afternoon in Tel Aviv. A professional hit."

"Oh no."

"Actually, we got a big break. The Israelis had a watch on him, had suspected him for weeks of a number of leaks. They caught the woman."

"A woman?" she interrupted. "Fantastic. Has she been interrogated?"

"No, no! I mean they caught a few photos of her. Unfortunately, she went back through Customs. At that point, they had no reason to track her, so she's in the wind. Max ran her through facial recognition."

"Anything?"

"Yes, but I'm not sure what to make of it. Max just called to say that this same woman was caught by Customs entering Gaza two months ago. She stayed until mid-March." Rik passed over the grainy photo. "What would she be doing there?"

Sofie raised her eyebrows, her teeth gnawing on her lips. "Isn't that interesting. I wonder if her entry into Gaza could have anything to do with 'the Arab' my uncle and the German referenced."

"Same thing occurred to us. I guess it's possible that Gaza could be *Der Kreis'* source of manpower for these so-called *putsches*. But the Palestinians would be a very odd choice. They usually confine their fights to Israel, not Europe."

"Could this assassin have been hired by *Der Kreis* as a one-off? In that case, her entry to Gaza could be for an entirely different client."

Rik nodded. "Possibly." And then he leaned forward. "Adina was attacked. She only survived because Max intercepted what looks to have been a kidnapping attempt. Unfortunately, Max had no choice but to kill the man. We're putting extra protection on her for the foreseeable future. I think it's fair to conclude that *Der Kreis* targeted her because their mole revealed her as the source of the search on Richthoven and *Der Kreis*."

"Oh no. Is she alright?"

"She got banged up. Nasty bruises and deep cuts. Max says they're painful enough that they'll keep her out of commission for a couple of days. The only good thing is that *Der Kreis* has hopefully concluded that she's the leak, not you."

"God. I hope she's going to be okay. I like her, so much, and we need her..."

"Let's switch our focus. Are you nervous about this afternoon?"

"I'm not sure what to expect."

You won't see me but I'll be close, and you'll be wired, speaking of which..."

"Yes?"

"Can you stand up?"

Sofie raised her eyebrows, but did so, slowly.

Turn around." Rik was behind her.

She saw a gold chain appear above her and felt it come up against her throat. She felt his hands warm against the back of her neck. He took his time to fasten it and then came around to admire his work. His hand brushed her breast as he took hold of a small attractive pendant.

She reddened and jerked. "What's this?"

"One part of your wire. The wonders of modern technology. Here's the other." He handed her a small metal piece to put in her ear. "Let's test it out." Rik walked to the door. "As soon as I'm outside, say something."

"Like, how you must get told you're a ..." she muttered something under her breath... "At least once a day?"

Rik laughed. The wire was working.

He came back in. "Just remember. We'll have protection on you today."

"I do have some martial arts training, Rik. But yes, that's good. I never dreamed I'd have to wear a wire. It's surreal."

After he went over the arrangements, they both went to change into dress clothes. She reappeared in a black skirt and chequered black jacket over a white blouse. He was wearing a dark leather jacket and black jeans.

He reminds me of a football coach with that athletic build and coiled up power, she thought idly.

"You look very nice, all dressed up," he smiled, feeling pleasure rush through him at seeing her in this feminine garb.

Again, he'd made her blush. "Don't get used to it," she called, as she exited the house.

She arrived thirty minutes ahead of time. Once she'd identified herself as Karl Mueller's niece, she was ushered to the front pew of the beautifully appointed St. John's Episcopal Church. The solemnity of the occasion was augmented by sonorous organ music. Already, the church was quite full. She felt awkward being the only family member when she hadn't been as close to him as most of the people here. She looked sideways across the aisle and noticed a few senators and House members she'd seen on the news. According to Rik, some ex-secret service guys would be here, too. The thought comforted her and she settled into the pew, looking at the programme that exhorted her uncle for his patriotism.

She raised her head as she felt someone approach. She immediately recognized him. Sumner Hayes took her arm and grasped her hand in his. "May I sit here beside you?"

"Of course, Mr. Vice-President," she replied.

He turned towards her, smiling. "It's a turnout worthy of the man."

"Yes, he'd be very pleased, I imagine."

"I'm so sorry that he died in such a tragic way. Washington won't be the same without him. Did you see him often?"

"Unfortunately, no. I live in Europe and he has, I mean had, such a busy schedule that it was hard."

"When did you last get to spend time with him?"

"I've been asking myself the same question. About two years ago. We may not have been close, but he did help me with my career in the early days."

"I understand you had some connection with this Fitch place…"

"Yes, I spent my summers there until I went to college. It's hard to lose him, my only family member. And the cottage, the last real connection I had to my parents."

He nodded sympathetically and they lapsed into silence.

Karl had requested a straightforward church service with no fuss, and so it was.

At the end, she shook hands with many who came up to her, all curious and sympathetic. Finally, she was able to leave. She walked along the sidewalk trailing behind the others, her feet hurting from the damn high heels.

Suddenly, with no warning, she flew off the curb into the path of a bus hurtling towards her. Before she could even summon a scream, she was pulled back with a bruising yank on her arm that saved her life. She was deaf for a moment and then was brought back from her shock by the blaring of horns.

"Sofie!" she heard Rik yell into her ear. "Tell me you're okay." Her muscles seized in horror at what might have been.

Before she could respond, she heard "My god! Are you all right?" An attractive dark-haired woman about her own age was holding her.

"Thank you!" Sofie tried to catch her breath and leaned into her saviour, her arm hurting from being handled so roughly. She straightened and rubbed her shoulder. "Thank you," she said again with feeling. "Did you see what happened, who bumped me?"

"No. It all happened so fast," said her companion. "Do you need to sit down?"

"Umm. No, just give me a minute to catch my breath." Her shoulder really hurt, but at least she was alive.

"Are you on the way to Karl Mueller's reception?" the woman inquired, bringing Sofie back to the present.

"Yes. Yes. Yes, I am."

"So am I."

Sofie took some shaky steps, making sure to create distance

between herself and the curb.

"I was a business colleague of Karl's," said her companion. "He was very kind to me."

Suddenly, Rik's voice came on softly. "Do not react to what I'm going to say. Look down at the ground or stop to adjust your skirt or something."

Obediently, Sofie paused and reached down as if to fix one of her shoes.

Rik continued, "The bump and rescue were deliberate. You're talking to the woman whose picture I showed you earlier today. Just keep walking for a moment until we figure out what to do. You've got protection right behind you."

Some protection. It hadn't prevented her from being tossed in front of a bus. She did as Rik had instructed, reaching down to adjust her high heels, and then felt lightheaded. This woman was the assassin?

"You're looking awfully pale. Are you sure you're up to attending?"

Sofie thought of the team and drew upon their strength, and Rik's. She rose to her full height, regained her composure and forced herself to look down into the eyes of this evil woman. "Yes, thank you again for being there at the right time."

As they walked into the huge room that had been arranged for the reception, the woman asked, "Were you close to Karl?"

"Oh! We must introduce ourselves. I'm Sofie McAdam, Karl's niece. My mother was his sister."

"His death must be a terrible shock for you."

"Yes. It's sad. He was my only remaining family. I can see from those who attended the service that he was a much greater presence than I'd ever imagined. I'm just about to start a new job, so I was glad that I could get away to be here, even though, really, it would be a lie to say we were close."

"Why not? Didn't you like him? Did he not like you?"

Raising her eyebrows, Sofie replied. "It's more a case that I only saw him a couple of times over the past five years and even growing up, not very much. For over a decade I've lived in Europe. I haven't had much chance to come to Washington and, when I did, he was always so busy. But, like you, I'm grateful to him. He comforted me when my parents died. And I suspect, though he never said a word, that he helped behind the scenes to get me my first job in Europe. I'm only sorry that I didn't make more of an effort to see him. But I thought I'd have years..."

At least two hundred people circulated, doing business, and, by the looks of it, were enjoying their afternoon off. Sofie couldn't detect any sign of real grief.

"Surprising that he died away from Washington. I never knew he had a connection to Canada," said the woman, taking hold of her arm and steering her towards the food.

"Yes. He was at Fitch when it happened and now Fitch is gone, too."

"So you've been to this place?"

"Oh, yes. Growing up, I spent many a happy summer there."

"When was the last time you were there?" the woman asked, taking a glass of wine, as did Sofie, for purely medicinal purposes, she thought wryly.

"It's got to have been five years ago," Sofie said softly looking off into space. And then, as if it had just come to here, "Gosh. I don't even know the name of the person who saved me!"

"Greta. I worked for a lobbying firm for a while and got to know Karl. We weren't what you'd call close, but he mentored me and I owe him for what I am today."

"Good, Sofie," said Rik. "You're doing great. Keep her talking while we prepare a plan to deal with this."

"You're not from the States. Is that a German accent I'm hearing?"

"I spent time in Austria when I was very young."

A strange response, thought Sofie.

"By the way, where are you staying?" Greta asked.

"At a friend's and then I may go to Fitch, just to see it. I guess whatever is left of it will be mine. No doubt, there are going to be all kinds of questions about insurance. How about you? What kind of lobbying work do you do?"

"All different kinds over the course of my career. And you? Where were you working before you got this new job?" she said, ignoring Sofie's question.

"I've been in The Hague for the last several months, and before that, Moldova." answered Sofie.

"Moldova! Where is that?" she asked, her trilling laugh at odds with her eyes.

"It's just south of Ukraine. A real backwater. I'm glad to get out of there, and this new job is a bit of a promotion. Please give me your card so that I can contact you and thank you again for saving my life!"

"Sorry, I didn't bring my usual purse. Why don't you give me your card?"

"I don't have one yet."

"Try to look after yourself." With that, the woman walked away. Rik broke in. "Well done. We're going to keep an eye on her. But we can't afford to alert her or she'll get suspicious of you. If you feel up to it, circulate and see if there are any more strange occurrences."

After an hour, she knew it was time to get out of there. No one else had seemed particularly interested in her. Most had general comments about him, but she sensed that he hadn't been particularly well liked. She hadn't seen Greta since they'd said goodbye.

As instructed by Rik, she entered a quiet bar off the reception area of a nearby hotel and sat, looking as if she were dejected, until an attractive man sat beside her.

"Hi!" he said, and talked to her for a few minutes. "Let's go somewhere else for a drink." She smiled in agreement, taking the arm he offered. They exited the hotel and got into a nondescript car. After making a sudden turn onto a side street, the car suddenly pulled into a garage. The garage door quickly closed behind them.

Rik helped her out and, before she could stop him, pulled her tightly into his arms. She could feel his chin resting on the top of her head. For a fraction of a second, she let herself melt. Then, she pulled back, unable to hide the pain that was shooting down her arm.

"Did she hurt you? Did I?" Rik looked horrified.

"I'm fine. I'm fine," she repeated holding her arm. "Are we following Greta, Marta or whatever her name is?"

He stared hard at her, two vertical lines appearing between his eyebrows. "How badly are you hurt?"

"No, I'm okay. When she yanked me back onto the sidewalk, let's just say that she took pleasure in it. What about her? Are we following her?"

"One moment she was talking to the Vice-President over in a corner of the room. Then, according to our guy, she was allowed by the Vice-President's Secret Service agents to pass through a door that gave her a quick exit to the street." Rik added, "How she got through the Secret Service without requiring any I.D. is the question. Let's sit down." He led her over to a couch and sat sideways, close to her.

"At the risk of sounding idiotic," said Sofie, "it occurred to me that the Vice- President was asking rather odd questions, considering he'd never met me before. Is paranoia part of being in this espionage world? Because, I seem to have acquired it. For a moment I actually wondered if he could be part of this whole mess," she laughed ruefully.

Rik didn't even smile. "Suspicion is our best friend in this business. Frankly, at this point, we can't rule out anything. Trust your instincts, and, on this occasion, I will too." Rik found it hard to imagine that the Vice-President of the United States could be *Der Kreis*. "I'm going to ask Noah and Miriam to do some background research on Sumner Hayes and Mueller. Let's see if their paths ever crossed."

Evening, April 21, 2019, Dulles Airport, Virginia

What a waste of my time, thought Marta. The woman lets herself be picked up at a bar on the night of her Uncle's funeral? There was no way that this insipid excuse for Karl's niece had any knowledge of *Der Kreis* or her Uncle's faked death, especially the way she babbled endlessly after Marta 'saved her life'. Hard to believe that Karl and his niece shared the same genetic stock.

Wasn't Karl going to be interested in Sumner Hayes and his outright fury at the leak and the need for Mueller to disappear! "Does he realize the position he's put me in? I'm one election away from realizing our takeover here. And how could he allow this to happen so close to the conclusion of our biggest success yet in Europe? You can tell him for me that the leak came from him and he'd better plug it."

Marta had stood up and glared at him, biting back a reply. This Clooney look-alike seemed to have forgotten that, if not for Karl and her father, he'd never have risen as far as he had. And how dare he treat her as if she were a messenger girl. *Der Kreis* depended on loyalty. Hayes' comments bordered on breaking its code of conduct.

Marta looked at the departure board, turning her mind to the next assignment. Karl was counting on her and she'd not disappoint.

CHAPTER 16

Morning, April 24, 2019, Stockholm, Sweden

As soon as he got the call, Noah caught the next flight to Stockholm.

"Good morning," said Ingrid. "Please, sit down and I'll review our results. They relate to your RussTech enquiries. Our agency's focus on the Russians helped, as did your provision of specific names. We were able to identify the destinations of many, though not all, of their communications. May I suggest that you review the transactions that we have here? It would be imprudent to let them outside of our secure building."

Two hours in, Noah blinked and blinked again. Now this was interesting. RussTech transferred twelve million Euros from a Transnistria account to a numbered Swiss account at the *Banque Cantonarde de Genève* four days ago. Hadn't Anna, so many decades ago, written that one of the founders of *Der Kreis* had been the head of the this same bank? He could feel his heart rate increase. The data was also showing that RussTech had sent a separate wired instruction to the *Cantonarde* to send nine million Euros to a bank account in Tirana, Albania. Noah checked the transcript Sofie had written of the Fitch conversation: "The funds have reached Albania from our Russian partner." And, then there was a transfer of five million Euros from the *Cantonarde* account to Dubai. Again, he read Sofie's transcript. "As instructed, *Hochmeister*, I've just transferred five million to the Arab, in the usual way."

That's odd, he thought. Why was Russ Tech making dozens of calls over a period of years to a Geneva-based business called Decorative Arts International? What possible link would RussTech have with such a company?

He arrived back at the airport and boarded his plane. As he sat nursing a Scotch on his way back to Brussels, Noah felt encouraged for the first time since becoming involved with this *Der Kreis* business. In a few short hours, he'd established a connection between RussTech and *Der Kreis* through the *Banque Cantonarde*, which must surely become a focus of the team's attention.

He pushed his seat back and closed his eyes. His tired mind was whirling back to the others. Rik and Sofie would be back from Fitch by now. It was time for Noah to bring people up-to-date on his findings, which also happened to encompass Sumner Hayes.

Morning, April 24, 2019, Jerusalem, Israel

Adina was still in pain, her face so bruised and cut that she couldn't apply makeup to mask her wounds. The word had been put out to her usual office that she was more injured than originally thought and was taking time off. She'd headed to Svi's office this morning with Hélène, but was struggling now. She took another painkiller and kept her head down hoping that Max would stop staring at her.

"You shouldn't be here after what you've been through. I heard from Rik and Sofie."

"What?" she mumbled.

"It's significant. Our mole's assassin showed up at the funeral, pretending to be a work colleague of Mueller. Sofie was pushed off the curb, and the assassin `saved' her," Max said, shaking his head. "Apparently, she pulled her back from traffic and then proceeded to ask Sofie about her ties to Mueller and Fitch."

"Is she okay?"

"Rik says she was shaken. Apparently, the woman has a slight German accent. She somehow slipped Rik's surveillance, so we don't know where she went."

Adina unconsciously touching a bruise under her eye, said, "Maybe she didn't have to follow her because she knows Sofie's headed for Fitch. They'd better be careful." As she moved to take a sip of water, she winced, and then wished she hadn't when she saw the look on Max's face.

He couldn't help himself. "Dini, you should go back to the house. You still aren't well enough to be here."

"Stop fussing," she said, forgetting to correct his affectionate name for her. "I need to be here."

He left without saying where he was going. Adina watched him leave, knowing that she shouldn't have been so bitchy. It wasn't her style and he didn't deserve it. He'd saved her life, and he'd had to kill to do it. She'd loved him for his hatred of taking another life. Could she let her guard down again? Let him in?

Hélène had arrived earlier and had been talking to Svi. She entered the small room looking regal as always, and, Adina thought, happy. "You seem to be in a good mood. I'm glad."

"How are you feeling?"

Adina shrugged.

"I'm so sorry for what you've gone through. But yes, I am happy. I'm so grateful to be able to perhaps help finish what my mother started. I was nervous with you all in Berlin, but here in Jerusalem I feel as if I've come home. It's been a long time since I felt I was doing something worthwhile. Do I sound foolish to be excited, even though this *Der Kreis* is planning something terrible?"

"I'm a *Sabra*. But this is home, not just for those of us who were born here, but for all of us. There is no place I've found in the world that I would rather be than Israel and, in particular, Jerusalem. I love walking the narrow lanes of the Old City and picturing what it was like a thousand years ago. I never tire of it. When we can grab some time away from all of this, I'd like to show you some of my favourite sites."

"I would love to see Jerusalem with you. I only wish Mother could have experienced it. I know she yearned to visit, but it just wasn't to be." Hélène felt a familiar sadness come over her. "I want to discover everything I can about this evil man that my mother worked for. Perhaps Haas' history will link him to the present danger we face."

"If you do that, I'll focus on those photos your mother took."

Late Afternoon, April 24, 2019, Sarajevo, Bosnia and Herzegovina

Rik and Sofie had flown from Montreal to Sarajevo overnight. The scene at Fitch had been heartbreaking. Her childhood haven was reduced to a pile of ash and melted metal. They'd detected no tail either at Fitch or in Montreal where she'd met with the insurance company. An investigation would begin to determine its cause and who was at fault.

After a few hours of rest at an apartment arranged for her, she met Rik at the OSCE office, housed in a modern office tower a long walking distance from Sarajevo's historical old centre. Rik introduced her to his office colleagues and then got her settled in an empty office. A few minutes later, he looked in on her. "Can you come to my office?"

At Rik's instruction, Miriam had arranged a conference call with the entire team. Rik began. "I know you've all heard about Sofie and her adventures in Washington with Greta, or whatever her name is. We're hoping she decided Sofie was an innocent bystander. Sofie was also grilled by Sumner Hayes. I asked Noah to gather what he could on him without raising any eyebrows. So, let's start with you first."

"I thought you were crazy to ask about him, but now I'm not so sure," Noah said slowly. "He's seventy-one years old, born in 1948 in a small Mississippi town. Hayes first surfaces when he's twenty-one, fighting in Vietnam. He's accused of being a part of a civilian massacre. But everyone is exonerated. He returns to Mississippi as a military hero after a rescue mission. He draws the eye of the daughter of the future Governor of the State. In 1977, he's in Washington, working for his father-in-law, the ex-Governor who's become a Senator. At thirty, Hayes, wanting to establish himself, obtains a position with Megathon, a company that sells a variety of items, including weaponry, worldwide. Hayes rises to a position of power in that organization. It would seem quite possible, even likely, that he met Karl Mueller in Washington."

"Why do you say that?" asked Rik.

"Because Mueller was a lobbyist working on Megathon's behalf. And when Hayes decided to fill the Senate seat previously held by his late father-in-law, guess who bankrolled his run? Nothing hidden about it. Mueller, by then the head of a big Washington lobbying company, was *the* major campaign contributor. After Hayes became Senator, he joined the Foreign Relations Committee, before 9/11. His rhetoric then and since has been what we're now calling populist. He's also virulently anti-Muslim. I'm still looking into how Hayes was chosen by the current President to be his Vice-President. We can't rule out a connection between *Der Kreis* and the President, either."

Horrified, Adina said, "If what you're suggesting is true, then, at the very least, *Der Kreis* is one step away from having control of the Presidency of the United States!"

"Let's not get ahead of ourselves. We can't be absolutely certain that Hayes is linked to the organization," cautioned Rik. "Any research on him will have to be done very carefully."

"We need to keep an eye on Hayes, in case he's in contact with my uncle." Each day they were uncovering something even more horrific than the day before about *Der Kreis*.

"We're walking a fine line here," warned Rik. "Noah, can you consult your FRA contact again about how to surreal a senior figure in the U.S., without alerting him? Don't get more specific than that. In the meantime, I'm hoping that we can unearth some paths of enquiry that get us to Mueller and *Der Kreis*."

"As a matter of fact, I can offer just that," said Noah. "I'm sending you a diagram." Once members had pulled it off their secure server, he continued. "It's complicated, but here's the gist: We can all but confirm that RussTech is connected to *Der Kreis*. Russia's sending money to an account at the *Banque Cantonarde de Genève*."

"The same Bank that my mother's diary mentioned," murmured Hélène.

"Exactly. It gets more interesting. Not only did RussTech transfer money to an account at this bank in Geneva, but nine million Euros were also sent from that same account to one in Albania. Sofie overheard the German confirming such a transfer to her uncle. We have the bank account numbers at the *Cantonarde* and the bank in Tirana, Albania, but nothing more. So, we need some help from our banking expert, a.k.a. Max, to find out who holds these accounts in Geneva and Albania."

"Agreed," said Max.

"Another strange item: RussTech has been communicating on a frequent basis over the years with one Decorative Arts International, a company also based in Geneva. I have a hunch this DAI may be a front for something, may have some connection to *Der Kreis*. We need more information on it."

"This is a great lead. Thank our Swedish friends," said Rik.

"I'm not finished. According to the transcripts of what Sofie overheard her uncle to say, funds were transferred `in the usual way' to `the Arab'. I've found confirmation. Five million Euros were sent from the same *Banque Cantonarde* account to one in Dubai on the same date that she was at Fitch."

"Talk about burying the lead, Noah," exclaimed Rik. "If that transfer was to `the Arab', then we're getting closer to identifying the terrorist group that *Der Kreis* must be using. Can we identify who holds the bank account at the *Cantonarde* and in Dubai?"

"Hold on, everyone," interrupted Max. "From a banker's perspective, these large transfers would draw the attention of authorities trying to identify money laundering scams. The Cantonarde would, at least, have to report whose account it was transferring money to and why. What may be happening, and this is just my first thought, is that *Der Kreis* is using DAI as a cover to make money transfers to nefarious characters. Maybe this Decorative Arts International has a branch in Dubai. If that's the case, then, at the Dubai end, you could expect there'd be yet another transfer of funds from the DAI account to a third party. Dubai doesn't have the best record for identifying third party recipients, which makes it an ideal spot for money laundering. But who's the Arab in Dubai?" he asked rhetorically.

Adina, her voice infused with intensity, took over. "Please, follow me for a minute. We know that the woman who assassinated our mole and `saved' Sofie in D.C. went into Gaza for over a month beginning this February. *Hamas* runs Gaza." She paused because the stitches in her mouth were hurting. "The Prime Minister of *Hamas*, Bashir Fakhoury, spends more time in Dubai than he does in Gaza. In fact, his family lives in Dubai. What if *Der Kreis'* Arab is the head of *Hamas*?"

Noah scoffed. "That's pretty far-fetched, isn't it? *Hamas'* target has been you guys, as far as I've heard."

"A year or two ago I'd have agreed with you, Noah. But, since then, Gaza's situation has changed dramatically. The heads of Gaza and the West Bank are at war with each other. The Prime Minister of the Palestinian Authority, which controls the West Bank, has cut salaries of Gazans and payments for electricity and other necessities hoping to force *Hamas* to give up control of Gaza. It's a power struggle. And people think with their pocketbook, so *Hamas* is worried. Then there's Egypt. It's isolated Gaza over the past decade because of Gaza's support for the Muslim Brotherhood. Qatar, a strong ally of Gaza, can no longer get supplies through as a result of the blockade by Saudi Arabia. With *Hamas* hurting, it's very possible that Der Kreis made Fakhoury an offer he couldn't refuse. Maybe this Greta woman, this assassin, went into Gaza to make a deal with the Palestinians."

"What Adina is saying makes sense. We need to figure out whether it's *Hamas* or not. If not, then who? And what the hell was this woman doing for more than a month in Gaza?" Max's voice was tight with frustration.

"Max," said Rik, "do whatever you need to, with discretion, to identify the account holders in Dubai and at the *Cantonarde*. We can deal with Albania as a lower priority. Adina and Hélène, be very cautious but let us know quickly what you can glean about both the *Cantonarde* and this Decorative Arts company, their history of directorship and employees, their reputations and anything else that will either confirm or eliminate their connection to *Der Kreis*. What's the ETA on other info from our Swedish friends, Noah?"

"It looks as if results are going to dribble in. They're working hard on our file. I'll be on top of it and keep you informed."

"Hélène, can you continue your search into Richthoven and those early pictures that your mother took of *Der Kreis* members?"

"*Oui*," she replied.

"Aslan, if things go the way I think they are, we may need you to make a trip into Gaza for us," said Rik.

Evening, April 24, 2019, London, England

Miriam was seething. Not one word had been said to her over the course of the call. She might as well be invisible. Fuck them for treating her like a glorified secretary.

Without consulting Rik or Neal, she flew back to her home in The Hague to spend the night and the next day. She'd given up a lot to move herself to London, including a hot relationship that she'd had to put on hold.

Ummm. Her mouth watered as she imagined another bout of rough sex. She was feeling reckless. He'd wanted to do some things, but she'd said no. Maybe she'd made a mistake. Let's see what he had in mind, she thought.

CHAPTER 17

April 25, 2019, Morning, The Gaza Strip

Bashir Fakhoury's cell vibrated.

"Your next mission is on. It must happen immediately."

He made the call to Albania. Despite the confidence he held in his plan, the consequences of failure were unbearable to contemplate.

April 25, 2019, Evening, Durres, Albania

Once a week over the past month, four trucks had driven early harvest cabbage crops to Austrian and German markets, encountering no problems along the way. This time, their cargo was not only cabbages. Farid felt sweat drip off his forehead onto the vinyl seat between his legs.

Four hours into the trip, the convoy reached the entry point to Kosovo where the guard asked them to open the back. After receiving the usual care package for his family, including some of the most reachable cabbages, the guard let the trucks pass.

Tonight they'd sleep in their cabs. At dawn, they'd pass through the western border of Kosovo into Serbia. There, they'd make a quick switch of their license plates from Albanian to Serbian, no one the wiser. After that, eight hours to get to Hungary and another twelve to reach Austria. And then, the payment that would help him buy the papers needed to get him and his family into England.

Evening, April 25, 2019, Geneva, Switzerland

Manfred Friedl made the call. All was going as planned.

Early Morning, April 26, 2019, Sarajevo, Bosnia

Rik groped for the mobile beside his bed and looked at the clock. It was 3:00 a.m.

"Wakey, wakey, my boy," said Neal with obvious relish. "Rik, are you there?"

"What the fuck?"

"Eloquent as always, I see. Wake up, now," Neal said firmly. "I just received a tip that a load of arms is about to head northwards through Serbia. Guess where the trucks started."

Rik, groggy and grumpy, said, "What? When?"

"Yesterday in Albania and today in Serbia," responded Neal. "Isn't it interesting that Swedish intelligence suggests an Albanian connection with this *Der Kreis*, including a recent payment to the Albanians? Rik, are you there?"

"Okay. I'm up." Rik turned on the light and went into action. "Is there a plan to intercept?" he asked sharply.

"Serbia's a mess. No one's in charge until the election's done. Interpol's the brains, but the Serbs' counter-terrorism battalion will do the heavy lifting. Interpol's using satellite Intel to track the movement of the four trucks. They may try to take back roads up to Belgrade but after that they'll have to use the main highway through Vojvodina in the north. I want you there. Interpol's expecting you in Belgrade at 9:00 a.m."

"Got it. Any idea of where the tip-off came from?"

"A colleague of mine in Lyon's Interpol office received a call from one of his contacts who was apparently tipped off by someone yesterday. All very vague, unfortunately."

"Will you or I have any say in how the Serbs proceed?" asked Rik thinking of the carnage he'd witnessed two short weeks ago in Moldova.

"Unfortunately, no. But once the intercept is complete, you'll have full access to the cargo and the crew."

"I hope the Serbs know we need to take the drivers alive."

"I made that clear, but they aren't the best listeners. Call me if you have any issues," Neal instructed.

"Roger that."

Morning, April 26, 2019, Novi Sad, Serbia

Rik hurtled north from Belgrade with the Serb commander. Little was said until they reached Novi Sad, where they met up with the interdiction troops.

"The trucks are an hour south. Once the terrorists are within ten minutes of our intercept point, southbound traffic will be diverted. The tollbooth guards here have been replaced by our people, who will let the convoy through. Then, they'll prevent any other traffic from proceeding."

Rik put on the bulletproof vest as instructed. After ten minutes of tense silence, a small plume appeared as a distant truck belched diesel. Rik counted them. Four. Although he didn't move, he became hyper-aware of his surroundings.

The first truck approached the barrier. He saw passports and cargo papers being exchanged through the window. He counted the seconds until they were handed back. The truck was waved through. Then the next. And then the one after that. Finally, all four trucks were through. He heard the grind of gears as the last one went from first to second, and watched as it accelerated down the highway.

Any time now, Rik thought. Come on come on come on.

Six army transports inched onto the tarmac and formed a barrier just as the lead truck moved into third gear.

It accelerated and rammed into the first battalion vehicle square on, crushing in its front and grinding its wheels forward at full throttle, metal screaming on metal until its engine stalled.

As the Serbian soldiers leaped from their vehicles, gunfire broke out. Rik could see that three of the four drivers were still in the fight. He ran to his Serb counterpart who understood English. "We must keep these guys alive!" shouted Rik over the din. "Please tell your men to hold their fire."

The leader looked disdainfully at Rik and shouted back, "Two of our men have been killed." A shot rang out. As the leader fell, Rik hit the ground and grabbed the dead man's SIG 552 Commando carbine. Fuck. He shimmied his way over to the closest battalion member. "Someone's firing at us from over there," he yelled, gesturing to the left shoulder of the road and then using his arm to point to the dead leader. "Who's in command now?"

The other man pointed and started firing again.

Rik zigzagged reaching the new Serb in charge. "We need to make sure we take at least one man alive!" Just as he crouched at the tail end of one of the battalion cars, he saw two combatants jump out of the back of a truck, running south.

Rik raced around the corner of the tollbooth. He took aim. One went down, screaming in pain. The other stopped and whirled around. He was wearing a vest with explosives. For an instant, they held eye contact. The youth appeared resigned, then serene.

Rik dove to the ground. Then, a stark white quiet. "I'm dead," he realized, feeling...stillness...peace.

"Mr. Whitford? Mr. Whitford!" A jarring sound pierced him.

"Wha...?"

"Stay still, please."

He came to consciousness with the searing burn that went up through his arm.

"Can you hear me?" asked a white-haired man above him, his hand on Rik's brow.

"Yes," he said, his voice reedy.

"You're extremely lucky. You've lost no…"

Rik drifted again and then felt a hand touching his throat.

"Open your eyes, please," he heard from afar. "I'm a doctor. You're in a hospital. The vest you wore saved your life, though you've sustained an injury to your arm."

The face of a gangly youth appeared. Rik tried to lift his arm to cover his eyes to erase the images that kept coming. With no warning, a cascade of the last few days' events contorted him into panic. "How long have I been here? I need to get to Sarajevo, now!" He groaned as he tried to sit up.

"Just rest. You're being taken there tomorrow morning."

Night, April 26, 2019, Sarajevo, Bosnia and Herzegovina

At 6:00 pm. Sofie, who'd been at the office for the day, got a call from Neal Havers in London.

"Sofie, give me a call back when you're on a different telephone please?"

Ten minutes later, Sofie returned the call from her apartment. "I'm here."

"I need your help. Rik went to Serbia early this morning to respond to news of a terrorist convoy passing weapons from Albania up to Austria or Germany. The bloody idiot got caught in the fire fight."

Sofie gasped and grabbed for the window frame.

"Is…is he all right?"

"He's just had shrapnel removed from his arm, the stupid fool, and he's banged up. It's just like him to put himself in the centre of things."

She breathed in again. "What can I do? I can go to Belgrade."

"No. Wait for him to arrive back tomorrow. I'll let you know his ETA. He's in a lot of pain at the moment, and when I get a chance to give him a piece of my mind, he'll be in even more."

Sofie tried to regain her balance. "Will he go to the hospital here, then?"

"No. Under normal circumstances, we'd have had him stay in Belgrade. However, he's not going to have that luxury. According to the doctors, he's functional, and that's what we need from him right now."

"I don't understand. Why Serbia?"

"We had a hunch that *Der Kreis* was involved. Max is on his way to handle the interrogation there. In the meantime, your job is to get Rik on his feet."

Absently, Sofie made tea and sat on the sofa looking off into the starlit hills above the darkening city. Her breath caught. In that infinitesimal second when I didn't know if he was alive...

She closed her eyes.

Morning, April 27, 2019, Geneva, Switzerland

Manfred Friedl was elated. One convoy driver at least had survived. Brilliant.

Afternoon, August 27, 2019, Belgrade, Serbia

As Max looked on from outside the room, the Serb interrogator drilled the surviving driver. "Who are you?"

"Farid Roweis."

"Your passport says you're Palestinian. Is this true?"

"Yes, I was born in Gaza."

"A terrorist."

"No, no, no! I'm not a terrorist. I swear."

"Stop lying to me."

"I swear I'm telling the truth. I was paid money to do this."

"Who hired you?" asked the Serb interrogator.

"I do not know."

"If you don't start talking, you'll be thrown into a cell and never see the light of day again."

"There was no work in Gaza. I had a relative in Albania. I came there to look for a job as a driver. I thought it was a good job, until I saw the weapons."

"Then why did you not leave?"

"If I didn't do the job, they said they would harm my family."

"Where were you taking the arms?"

"Our instructions were to get them to a truck stop in Vienna where other drivers would take over."

"So, you don't know the final destination?"

"No."

"Where did you pick up the weapons?"

"In Durres."

"Is that where you trained? Lived?"

"No. We all met for the first time at a place in Tirana two months ago and then they brought us to Durres. They gave us instructions. We drove this route many times, carrying vegetables."

"Who instructed you?"

"I don't know his name."

"Was he Palestinian?"

"Yes."

"How did he communicate with you when you weren't together."

"No one did. Each meeting he told us what we needed to know

and when to show up again."

"How were you paid?"

"With Euros."

"Why were you all resisting arrest, willing to give up your lives, if you weren't involved in any actual terrorist event?"

"We were all doing it for the money. If we were caught, we were told our families would get nothing. That is why we fought. I am the unlucky one who survived."

Max's gut was telling him something was off.

Afternoon, August 27, 2019, Sarajevo, Bosnia,

Mercifully, the flight from Belgrade to Sarajevo was under an hour. All Rik could think of was to take a couple more painkillers and sleep.

He made his way through the gate, protecting his arm from those rushing past him and using his good arm to pull his small overnight case. He walked blindly on, mindless with exhaustion.

"And the conquering hero returns," he heard a voice.

He looked to his left and there she was with her dishevelled black hair. She was in her usual black and white uniform, a red and black scarf hanging around her neck. She looked sardonic as she said, "Neal gave me the gist and suggested I make sure you get home safely considering your accident-prone nature."

"Accident? Is that what he called it," he gritted out as he allowed her to take hold of his bag. They laboured through the terminal to where she had a taxi waiting.

"Did they give you any medications?"

He nodded.

"Okay, good." An awkward silence ensued. "I've bought some Tylenol Extra Strength, some tea, milk and a few fast food goodies. Do you need anything else? Want to stop along the route?"

"Thanks," he said, unconsciously moving his arm. "Just need to get home and crash."

"I'll drop you off. You can tell me what happened tomorrow. Or, do you think you'll take tomorrow off?"

"No. There's too much to do."

"Right. If there's anything you need, you have my number."

He struggled out of the car at the front of his apartment building, unable to contain a groan.

"Lean on me. Enough with the heroics. I'm going up with you."

He waved her off with his good hand.

Seeing his efforts to conceal his pain, she said, "No arguments I'll just help you to get settled in."

Rik wasn't used to having anyone look after him, wasn't sure he wanted it. "Maybe for a few minutes. Hold the taxi driver."

Ignoring his order, she pulled his bag into his flat. The first impression was that it didn't look lived in. There were no personal effects. The living room was pretty neat, if a bit dusty. She found the kitchen, unloaded the groceries and put on the kettle. Grabbing a tray, she set out a full plate of food on the dining room table.

As she knocked on his bedroom door and peeked in, he was trying to lift his bag. "Just stop," she said and moved him out of the way. She placed it on a low table and undid the zipper. "I've laid some food out in the dining room. Would you like some tea? Something stronger?"

"Tea. Thanks."

When he didn't appear, she became worried and knocked on his bedroom door, which was partially ajar. Rik was having trouble with the buttons of his shirt.

"Oh, for god's sake." She pushed his hand aside and swiftly undid the buttons and helped him take it off. Dark hair covered his muscled chest. She blushed deep red. "Get into bed," she ordered, plumping up the two pillows against the headboard. "I'll bring you a tray."

She worked quickly, afraid that he'd fall asleep before he could get nourishment. When she re-entered the bedroom, his eyes were closed. "Rik. Rik," she said in a louder voice.

He opened his eyes and his stomach growled. She put the tray down and helped him to sit up. He wolfed down the generous portions of bread and goat's cheese. Five minutes later, when he was finished, she took the tray to the kitchen.

"Okay. Well," she called, feeling awkward and almost motherly. "I guess I'll get going, unless you can think of anything else." No answer. He'd fallen into a deep sleep. He looked so defenceless. Damn it, she thought, annoyed with herself. I'm a sucker. There's no way I can leave him to fend for himself.

Finding his keys, she headed for the office to collect her computer, and then to her apartment to pack an overnight bag. On the way back to Rik's, she picked up more fresh bread and the makings of a salad and soup.

Around 8:00 pm., she heard the rustling of sheets and a soft moan. Should I wake him up? She looked at the prescription bottle and saw that he was due for another dose.

"Rik, it's Sofie. It's time to take your pain pill." He opened his eyes. In this light, they looked as dark blue as the ocean.

He tried to sit up. "What time is it? Why're you still here?"

She ignored him. "Why don't you freshen up while I get you some dinner? Then I'll answer your questions. Do you need me to help you to get to the loo?"

He shook his head and lay back as if gathering his strength for the short walk.

She returned ten minutes later and watched him pick at the plate. "Take your pill."

"So senseless," he murmured, his eyes closed.

She watched as he grimaced.

"Do you want to talk about it?" She received no response. "Let me get your painkiller."

"He was just a sad kid."

She waited. He's forgotten I'm here. "Rik, just rest now." She took his hand and placed the pill in it, guiding it to his mouth, helping him take a sip of water. She walked out into his living room, sat down and stared unseeingly into the dark. He was important. Her heart ached, at first for him and his vulnerability and then, for hers. She found blankets, washed her face, brushed her teeth and applied her moisturizer. To fend off her growing anxiety, Sofie sat cross-legged on the floor to do her meditational breathing exercises, then lay down on the dark leather sofa.

Night, April 27, 2019, Gaza

Bashir Fakhoury paced his little office. "Fuck!" His Palestinians had paid the ultimate price for this disaster. Given the amount of money he was being paid, he had no leverage to object to the shabby outcome of the mission. He hunched back into his chair, staring blankly out the tiny window, afraid he'd made the biggest miscalculation of his life.

CHAPTER 18

April 27, 2019, London, England

Hana and Fatima had just begun to share a small flat in a housing estate in Tower Hamlets, a predominantly Muslim part of eastern inner London. They prepared tea and sat at a small round table near the window that looked out over the rest of the depressingly colourless housing estate.

"Perhaps we should get to know each other better, now that we'll spend these special weeks of our lives together," said Hana shyly. Fatima nodded.

"I'll start," offered Hana. "I beg that you do not judge me."

Fatima nodded, looking curious.

"I have just turned twenty-two years old. I grew up near Manchester. My family is very traditional. We speak only Arabic at home. When I turned fifteen, I met a girl, Elizabeth, at my school. We fell in love."

Fatima couldn't hide her shock and revulsion.

"Until then, I did not know that such feelings could exist or that a woman could feel this way about another woman." Hana looked down, feeling shame. "We hid it from everyone, but I felt so guilty and knew, somehow, it must be forbidden. Eventually, she started to make fun of my Arab heritage in front of me to her friends. It was very hurtful. We drew apart. And then, a year ago, my new lover, Agnes and I had a big fight. She came out and told everyone about me. My parents were so angry. My father tried to match me with a forty-five year-old man, who found out and would not marry me. It was so unbearable that they sent me to Gaza, to my father's family, hoping that, hoping that…I am not exactly sure what they were hoping."

Fatima broke the long silence. "Was this your first time in Gaza?"

"No. My second. The first time I arrived there, I was desperate to do something to remove the shame. If I hadn't left when I did, I think my brother or father would have killed me. Three days after I arrived, bombs from Israel fell all around us. I was so scared. The deaths, the grief, they were beyond anything I could have imagined. Because of a shortage of medical assistance, I helped. From that moment, I knew I must do something greater than myself."

"I know exactly how you felt."

Hana continued, "Two weeks later, I was invited by a friend who was a nurse to hear an inspirational speaker from *Hamas* talk about the infidel, the ultimate sacrifice and the reward in the afterlife for heroic deeds. One of the leaders of the group spoke to me after the meeting and asked why I was there. He listened to my confusion and then told me to trust my intelligence. I felt someone really saw me. I wanted to become more involved. I studied the *Qur'an* as I had never done before. I prayed for hours each day. And I realized that my life in England had no meaning, no value."

"Were you cured?"

Hana looked offended and then defeated. "Yes, of course. My life became much bigger than myself. It was a miracle from *Allah* that at one of our meetings, a representative of the Government of Gaza approached me. She said there was a mission to punish the infidel. Though she gave me some days to consider my answer, I would have happily said yes at that very moment. The woman said I must return to England and wait to hear from a contact. After one month, they came to me and told me money would come to my family when I completed my mission. She gave me a ticket to return to Gaza for a month of training. Now that I'm committed, there's no going back. So it must be. *Allahu Akbar.*"

"*As-salaamu aleikum,*" murmured Fatima.

"Now it's your turn."

"As it was for you, it is very hard for me to tell my story. I was…" She looked off into the distance. "I was completing my German and Italian studies in February of last year in Manchester." Her voice clogged with emotion. "One evening on my way home, three men attacked me. I…I… I was raped, many times."

Hana, with tears in her eyes, reached for her hand and held it tightly.

"One of them was arrested, but then released. The police asked why I was walking home at night, as if it was my fault. I hate the English. I was so afraid, I wanted to die. Even my parents blamed me. Fatima, they told me, they were repulsed. My father would not look at me. After two weeks, they sent me to stay with distant family members in Gaza. And then…and then, I found out I was pregnant."

"*Ya Allah!*"

"I was in shock. During that time, I studied the *Qur'an* hoping for some comfort, some understanding. At one moment, I would feel rage, and at the next, I would cry uncontrollably. I had the cursed baby in Gaza. One day, my cousin invited me to hear a speaker, and every word he said spoke to me. Our oppression is our own responsibility, he said. It is only we who can change our lives, to give them the ultimate meaning, to do the work of *Allah*. The enemy is evil in his many forms. He robs us, rapes our women, kills our people and pretends holiness. If we wish to experience the glory of the afterlife, we must answer with our own war. Hana, it was as if I was the only person in the room and he was talking directly to me. I stayed at the end. I told him what had happened to me. He asked how he could contact me in the future, so I gave him my mobile number. A couple of days later, I met with him and another. They told me what they wanted from me and said the Infidel's child, my child, could be a useful tool. I had to return to England, they said, and then I would be re-contacted."

"The child will be brought to us here?"

"Yes, I think so," replied Fatima. "I cannot stand to look at it. It reminds me of... But soon, it will be here."

"I'll be with you and look after you. For me," Hana said, "the days in Gaza were the best of my life, although Greta was such a bitch, if you forgive my language!"

Fatima laughed, releasing tension. "You're right. There is no other word for her. Did you not wonder why an infidel woman was training us?"

"Yes," responded Hana. "I just think she wants revenge for something. Or perhaps she's the best trainer for such things. Or perhaps it's for money. Whatever the reason is, it gives us a chance to fulfil our destinies. That is all I care about."

"For me, too, the training was wonderful - to know how to drive cars and even motorcycles. I did not like the weapon training, perhaps because I was afraid and not very good at it."

"I loved praying to *Allah*. I know that, when our time comes, we will have an afterlife beyond anything we can imagine. But that last week was a nightmare. To think that of the twenty women it was we who lasted."

"We should leave if we want to be on time, shouldn't we?" asked Fatima.

An hour later, they reached a large apartment building, walked up a flight of stairs and knocked on the door as instructed.

"Come in. Take a seat."

Today, Greta looked particularly hard. Her dark hair was straight and cut bluntly. "Have you been practicing the skills we taught you?"

"Yes, ma'am."

"Today, I'll test you. For security purposes, I cannot tell you the exact date of your mission, but it will be soon."

"Is the baby still a part of this?"

"Yes. Do you have a problem?"

"No, ma'am," said Fatima.

"Has anyone suspicious been watching you? Is there anything out of the ordinary? If so, we must know."

Fatima and Hana looked at each other. They shook their heads.

"Here are new burner phones for you both. They will only be used to text you about meeting times and places. All right. Let's get started."

April 27, 2019, Manchester, England

Marwa and Rania met at the appointed site and awaited the arrival of Greta. Marwa, at twenty-six, still lived with her family in a suburb of Oldham, while Rania, twenty-three, lived in Manchester with her husband's family while her husband was fighting for ISIL in Syria.

Several months before, Marwa's beloved brother had been arrested in Manchester for alleged violence against a synagogue. He was innocent and yet they charged him with other offenses so that they could keep him imprisoned. The last time she'd seen him, he had been so badly beaten that she was sure that he could not survive. Her family was devastated, as was she. As she tried to continue on with her life, she was constantly harassed for wearing the hijab. And then, her brother was attacked by an inmate and died in jail. She was invited to attend a gathering of Muslim women near her home once each week. These were powerful and glorious moments stolen from an otherwise useless existence. Marwa was outspoken and articulate. She was a leader among her friends, perhaps because of the anger that drove her. One of the participants invited her to Gaza, where she had family. She'd accepted without hesitation. She would find a way to avenge her brother's death and to show the infidel who was righteous. Marwa was grateful for all of the special skills that she'd been taught in Gaza. She appreciated the trust that was being placed in her to do a very important job.

Rania lived in extreme poverty with almost no support. Without her husband, the factory-cleaning job she'd found exposed her to constant harassment by men who were inferior pigs. Her husband had told her he had to fight the infidel to cleanse his conscience and to assure a glorious afterlife.

Before Greta's arrival, the two women made desultory small talk. They did not know each other well. Contact among the women had been discouraged, except during team-building exercises.

Greta arrived and gave them their instructions. Rania wondered what Greta's interest was in this fight, though, in the end, it didn't matter. She'd been given an opportunity to make her life worthwhile. She was anxious to complete her mission. She only wished it could be tomorrow.

CHAPTER 19

April 28, 2019, London, England

Karl Mueller awaited the arrival of the primary drivers of *Recht und Macht*.

Manfred Friedl entered the eastern side of the compound. "Where's my daughter?" he asked.

"She'll be here. For security's sake, she's taking the train and we're having her picked up."

Oswald Outerridge, publisher of fifty-three newspapers, owner of several extremist websites and two popular television networks in the United Kingdom, entered with his usual panache. Starting with nothing but smooth talk, he'd built his empire with the bricks of resentment and anger at the Labour Party. He was achieving impressive results through the targeted infiltration of print and social media with stories that were tailored to *Der Kreis'* aims.

Dieter Graf, head of the *Banque Cantonarde*, was next to arrive. He shook hands with Karl and wandered over to the coffee urn.

A few minutes later, Wilhelm Hertz, Commander of Germany's armed forces, entered the house accompanied by his close counterpart and friend, Ernst Graf, head of the *Grenzschutzgruppe 9 der Bundespolizei*, Germany's federal counterintelligence force. Ernst embraced his cousin, Dieter, before shaking hands with Karl.

The final participants came in together, Air Chief Marshal and Chief of the Defence Staff, Marvin Axworthy, Clive Gordon, head of the Metropolitan Police Force and Rupert Gage, Governor of the Bank of England.

"The meeting shall come to order. We will, as always, begin with our pledge to the cause of *Der Kreis Im Quadrat.*"

> *"We are the secret covenant of the most superior of skill and intellect. We devote our lives to the achievement of an Aryan, racially pure society here in Europe and in other civilized countries. We will do all that is necessary to attain ultimate political and economic power to ensure that inferiors are eradicated from Western society. We agree to a lifelong pursuit until we achieve this glorious goal."*

"And now, Manfred, will you please provide our *bruders* with an update of our progress."

"Very well." He looked around the room. "I'm sure you all want a report on our *Hochmeister's* apparent demise. We deemed it necessary to take this extraordinary measure when our Israeli source discovered a data search for Werner Richthoven and *Der Kreis*. That this should happen so close to the moment we have all been working towards these many years was of concern. We had no choice but to evacuate our *Hochmeister* and terminate our Israeli runt. The sanction was performed without incident."

"How did the Israelis discover our existence?" demanded Clive Gordon, wiping his brow with a stained handkerchief.

Friedl sent a repressive glare at the interruption. "Unfortunately, our effort to capture and interrogate the Israeli researcher failed. Our man was killed in the process. The woman was hurt and has disappeared. Under the circumstances, the *Hochmeister* deemed it wise to take the measures that he did."

Karl received nods from around the room.

"In the highly unlikely event that the Israelis could make a link between Richthoven and our *Hochmeister*, his apparent death enables us to move forward, confident that there will be no worry of pursuit."

Hertz shook his head as if in doubt.

"A couple of days ago, we launched our diversion in Albania," continued Friedl. "It went as planned. One of the drivers was caught alive but would have nothing to tell his interrogators. If someone does have knowledge of Der Kreis, they'll believe that their seizure of our weapons and personnel has severely damaged our operations."

"An expensive diversion, don't you think? How much were the arms worth?" asked Graf, always the banker.

"We agreed that a diversion was prudent. The cost is immaterial," said Karl, brooking no further dissent.

"Let's get back to the main question," said Hertz. "How did the Israelis discover Der Kreis? In all these years, no one has known of us. This is disastrous." God damn it, he thought. He could be the first casualty should the goals of *Der Kreis* be discovered and linked in any way to Germany, or to him.

"Of course it's a concern to all of us," conceded Friedl with impatience. "As I've explained, we're not sure whether anything came of the Israeli's search. You may believe that we're looking at all possible sources of a leak, including everyone within *Der Kreis*."

"To eliminate the fallout of this unfortunate occurrence, we must accelerate our plans. Once we're victorious, it will not matter what anyone did, or did not, know about us," stressed Karl. "Manfred, let's move on. Report to us on the status here in Britain."

"Very well. Let's turn to just that. *Recht und Macht* is working just as we'd anticipated. Our initiatives to deepen and exploit the fractures here, especially the population's fear of the inundation of Islamic immigrants, are well into its final stages. Our largest investment to fund Islamic terrorism and increase the level of fear is creating fruitful conditions for our takeover. We must also acknowledge our success here in Britain with our expansion of membership in alt-right groups and our key role in the realization of Brexit. Membership in these groups continues to grow every day, in no small part due to the initiative of

Bruder Oswald."

To Manfred's disgust, Outerridge puffed and preened, never one to deflect a compliment. Manfred continued. "The terrorist acts we've funded have exponentially increased fear among the broader European population, even the so-called middle-class liberals," the last word spoken with venomous derision. "As a result of our efforts we're seeing an exponential rise in calls for extreme measures against immigrants."

"But are our efforts enough for us to accomplish the *putsch* here?" asked Gordon.

"We've managed what others thought was impossible," Friedl continued. "We've induced many moderates to move their allegiance to our nationalist parties. Hungary, Poland, the United Kingdom, and, of course, the U.S., are successes of which we can be proud. We continue to till the populist soil for the rise of authoritarian governments in Germany, France, Netherlands, Italy and the Nordic countries. And, yes, Gordon, the time has arrived to take power to rid this country of the mongrels that have polluted it for so long. And after that, the rest of Europe."

"But we must be cautious," Gordon challenged. "Here, in Britain, despite all of the incidents we've funded and the negative stories we've disseminated, anti-immigrant sentiments seem to have plateaued. Shouldn't the masses be begging for a takeover by our military by now?" He looked around and saw a few cautious nods. "We must face facts. We haven't generated the panic we had foreseen. Without it, how can our plan work?"

"May we conclude that you've lost confidence in *Recht und Macht*?" asked Mueller in a mild tone that fooled no one and sent a chill throughout the room.

"No. No, *Hochmeister*. It's just that my countrymen seem to be less responsive than we'd anticipated," he trailed off.

"Clive, I fear you may not be up to the task at hand. Your comprehension of all that we've planned is less than adequate," Karl said. "I suggest you listen closely. Oswald, Marvin and Rupert, please remind *Bruder* Clive and any others who are suffering from a lack of spine of what is coming, lest they have forgotten."

Outerridge nodded. "As my reports to you have shown, our papers, social media, radio and television have been running images of immigrants beating whites. Over the past two years, we've accelerated our stories of rapes of white women and have broadcast transcripts, both real and concocted, of hate talk in the mosques. The Lithuanian has planted evidence that the crimes he committed were done by immigrants. He continues to provide weapons and funding to both sides. We've also sent funds through indirect channels to an array of anti-immigrant groups. This was one of our most successful strategies with Brexit."

Karl nodded approvingly waving his hand for Oswald to continue.

"In no small part attributable to our multi-media campaign, the latest poll shows that residents believe one in every four people in the United Kingdom is Muslim. In actual fact, the correct number is one in twenty. We've been seeing panic even in places where the Muslim populations are not concentrated. Residents perceive they're being occupied. Alt-right groups are springing up in local towns across the country. Increases in violent hate crimes initiated by both the alt-right and Muslim groups are occurring more and more as a result of the conflicts we've created between the two extremes."

"You don't share the fears of failure that one of our members has raised?" Karl asked, glancing at Clive.

Oswald hesitated for a moment and said, "While I believe we are nearing the conditions necessary for our overthrow, we're not there yet. White Brits may or may not be turning anti-immigrant to the extent we require to achieve our ultimate goal."

"Marvin, perhaps you can assuage the concerns of our *bruders*."

Marvin Axworthy stood up and strode to the wall where a map of the United Kingdom was projected, his eagle eyes peering down at them over a hooked nose. From his earliest childhood years in Switzerland, his father, a founding member, had ingrained in his son the enduring values of *Der Kreis*. Marvin and Manfred, whose father had also been part of the original group, knew, more than even Mueller, what *Der Kreis* was meant to be, what it must achieve. *Recht und Macht* will succeed, no thanks to the overgrown ego of Karl Mueller, thought Marvin derisively. As he caught Rupert Gage's glance, he nodded, almost imperceptibly. Here was a man who could be counted on, who, despite his unfortunate pedigree, was executing his essential component of *Recht und Macht* to perfection. "Notwithstanding cowardly claims to the contrary," as he cast his gaze at Gordon, "the plan is proceeding precisely as intended."

"Quite so," stated Oswald Outerridge, as he ran his hand down his gaudy tie and jiggled his double chin.

Pointing at the map, Marvin continued. "I've deployed troops to the streets of Oldham, Brighton, Liverpool, Bradford, Hampstead, Birmingham, Swansea, Belfast and Glasgow for weeks now, in response to the unrest and violence we've sown. Curfews have been set in parts of downtown Manchester. I've worked with Gordon, here, to enable my troops to guard the main sights in London, just as we had planned. Our first step towards martial law has been executed impeccably." He scanned the table seeming to dare anyone to challenge him. "The team I've hand-picked from the larger military force will, without question on the day, follow specific orders I give them. With Oswald's help, I've finalized our plan to seize the communications infrastructure on the day of the *putsch*. We'll control and guide the information that is disseminated."

Karl looked around the table, tension and impatience showing in his voice. "There's no time for weakness or doubt. *Recht und Macht* foresaw the possibility that extreme measures would be required to turn the tide of opinion in a definitive way. Rupert, please update us on your activities which, I trust, will allay some of our jitters," he said infusing the last word with sarcasm.

Rupert Gage exuded power and assurance as he smiled at the *Hochmeister*, his mentor and the author of his life's path. As a gifted student born of a working class family, he'd been accepted to attend the London School of Economics. Within four short months of arriving, he'd met Axworthy and Outerridge, both on the LSE Student Union debating team, both already young members of *Der Kreis*. At that precise moment, his future was set. His impoverished background would never again be used against him. He'd divorced himself from his past, even changing his name to evoke an aristocratic family tree. With the help of *Der Kreis* as he found out later, he was engaged by the United Kingdom Financial Investments Ltd., U.K.F.I., the agency managing all government investments. Shortly thereafter, he was introduced to Karl, who recognized his potential. Their plan had worked perfectly. As *Der Kreis* manufactured financial crises, Rupert `foresaw' them. So impressed were his bosses that he rose like a rocket, becoming Deputy CEO within ten years of his hiring. Thereafter, he moved to Her Majesty's Treasury where he became the youngest-ever Head of Government Economic Service. From there, Karl and *Der Kreis* orchestrated his appointment as Deputy Governor of the Bank of England. *Der Kreis'* blackmail-worthy material forced the Governor to resign leaving Rupert with a direct path to his current post, which he'd held for the last four years. Only forty-eight years of age, he'd become the youngest-ever Governor of the Bank of England, his powers equalling any other Central Banker in the world.

Rupert began. "Those of you who have shown fear today seem to have forgotten the crowning role that the banking component of *Recht und Macht* has in creating the level of panic needed to invoke martial law."

Karl nodded approval at his protégé who was one of the most productive and creative members of *Der Kreis*.

"The investment of thought, time and money over the last ten years will now pay dividends, if you'll pardon my banker language," he smiled, exuding charm. "The banking component of *Recht und Macht* the *Hochmeister* and we conceived so many years ago has worked brilliantly."

"Perhaps," Dieter Graf said," you should review for those who are not bankers, what we've done together."

"Very well. As you're all aware, our aim is to create panic in the streets across the country by causing the four banks that hold the vast majority of residents' assets to fail, or appear to fail. Our back-door attack on these four banks began years ago and is multi-pronged. Dieter and I, and our hacker who unfortunately could not be here today, created many thousands of fake accounts in those banks, seeding each of them with considerable funds amounting to a significant proportion of the capital cushion these banks rely on."

"Capital cushion?" asked Clive.

"Each bank is required to maintain a percentage of its assets at all times. The remainder of their assets can be lent out or borrowed against by the banks. Most banks are overextended these days. They have the minimum capital assets required, leaving them vulnerable. One aspect of our attack will be the abrupt withdrawal of all the funds from these fake accounts. But this alone will not cause bankruptcy. To further erode these four banks' solvency, over the past few years, we have caused the failure of many banks around Europe. How, may you wonder?" he asked rhetorically. "It's complicated, but every one of these banks, when they failed, caused an impact on British banks that just happened to be their largest creditors."

"How did you cause all of these failures without someone noticing what was happening?" asked Clive.

"Now, that is a good question. We used several different methods to bring them down. In some cases, we induced greedy bank managers into massive money laundering and then made sure they were caught. Soon after, those banks closed. Our Russian President and his oligarchs were a great help with this aspect, providing the laundered money. Also, in tandem, the high value of securities we bought left other banks vulnerable if we decided to divest our holdings. Allied with this, we identified and purchased securities in companies that were the main customers of the banks, and in whom these banks had invested. All very incestuous. These companies failed when the sale of our shares caused a crash in their stock values, a loss of confidence and their demise. In turn, the banks that had lent to these banks saw their capital cushions dramatically decline."

"How do these failures help our work here? Is there any chance the banks here know that they're being attacked?" Outerridge asked.

"Quite simply, the impact of the European bank closures on the British banks has been enormous, in the billions. And when we decide to empty our fake accounts, the combined effect will be to bring bank reserves to dangerous lows, so dangerous that you, Oswald, will use your multi-media approach to suggest that the banks are in peril of collapsing. Even the perception of failure will cause mass panic and run on them. As to whether the banks realize what's happening to them, the answer is no. They would have discovered our fake accounts long ago if they were going to, and the bank failures appear so random it would be impossible to perceive a pattern." He smiled in a self-congratulatory way.

"Wouldn't the Bank of England rescue the banks, just like the Americans did in 2008?"

"Have you, perchance, forgotten who is the head of the Bank of England? Of course, there'll be frantic calls for action to be taken by me. I'll ensure that my Deputy and I `study' the situation. Our inaction will allow extreme panic to spread sufficient to justify Marvin's imposition of martial law. Any more questions?" he asked rhetorically. "Not to worry. The *Hochmeister*, Marvin and I are working closely to coordinate the timing of our joint operations. And, by the way, we've taken a similar banking approach in Germany, but now is not the time to discuss that."

Just then, Marta entered. She nodded respectfully to the group and sat down, waiting to be addressed.

"Thank you, Rupert. I trust we're all confident in our plan." Turning to Marta, Karl said, "It's unfortunate you were unavailable to hear our update. Please provide us with your report."

"The women are excellent. There are no second thoughts. They actually believe in all this reward-in-the-afterlife nonsense. They've arrived at their appointed sites where they're waiting to receive their final instructions from me."

Karl nodded approvingly and turned to Ernst Graf and Wilhelm Hertz. "Wilhelm, for Phase Two of *Recht Und Macht* to work in Germany we need you to apply the same strategy at your end over the next six months. Once we've secured control here, you'll have our full attention and support. It's time to conclude. Marvin and Oswald," Karl said, "you will ensure that the Lithuanian completes his final tasks. Is that clear? With only days to the launch of the *putsch*, I count on each of you to do your parts."

There was a profound silence around the room. After their efforts over so many years, the moment was upon them.

He continued. "From this moment forward, we must be extremely careful not to communicate unless absolutely necessary. Whoever is investigating *Der Kreis*, we must not, will not, give them any target. If any one of you senses you're being watched, you will alert Manfred or me immediately. Rupert and Oswald, stay after, please."

April 28, 2019, The Hague, Netherlands

Her eyes blinded by the mask, Miriam smiled savouring her soreness and the thought of her next round with him. She'd welcomed the exquisite pain that he'd imposed unmercifully but carefully, so as not to leave a mark.

"Time to face reality," his voice said laced with contempt, as he held and shook her hard.

Now fully awake, she struggled with her bindings, sensing that the game was over. "Let me loose!"

"As you wish." He cut the ties, tore off the mask and pulled her to a sitting position. "It's been a pleasure in all respects," the man who had seemed so attractive said with an evil that turned him ugly in the blink of an eye.

"Take a look at your investment portfolio."

"What do you mean? Why? This is crazy."

"You made the unfortunate decision to borrow from me against your flat. Do you remember?"

Yes, she'd borrowed from him. He'd said the investment was a sure thing and would give her a huge return.

"The investment didn't turn out so well for you. You now owe me a lot of money, or your flat."

"But I…"

"I've enjoyed you thoroughly, in bed and out. And your flat. Now I'm going to enjoy it even more."

She scrambled, naked, to her computer and fumbled to type in her password. No! She was going to lose everything if she couldn't come up with over 400,000 Euros to pay him back.

She was going to kill him. She ran after him, tried to block him, but he held her by the throat until she fell.

Two hours later, she'd come up with only one option.

CHAPTER 20

Morning, April 28, 2019, Jerusalem, Israel

Pain pills, no matter what brand, made her feel groggy and unproductive. Adina, her face and shoulders aching, pored over documents from the archives. She turned to her computer. She wondered if her enquiries were being monitored by a new mole and whether she would be targeted again. She hadn't seen Max for three days. She wasn't sure what he was doing and felt unsettled by his absence. Fickle! You can't stand him when he's here, and you miss him when he's not. She went back to work.

Four hours later, Adina shouted, *Metzuyan!*"

Hélène looked up in surprise and saw Adina's smile, made crooked by the pain in her mouth. "What is this, *Metzuyan?*"

"How would you say `excellent' or `fantastic' in French?"

"For me, I would say `*formidable*'. Tell me! I need some happy news."

"Your mother said the manager of the *Banque Cantonarde* was at the first Der Kreis meeting in 1945. I found him, finally! The bank opened its doors in the late 1920s. That much is on its website. But there's no record of past managers there. I asked Max, but he said that it would require him to make calls that might alert someone if he sought out his bank contacts. So, after hours and hours focused on the bank, I gave up and decided to look at Decorative Arts International."

Hélène, visibly impatient, said, "Adina, *si'l te plais*! Tell me what you've found."

"Listen to this! The owner of Decorative Arts International is named Manfred Friedl."

"And so?"

"The company's biography of Manfred Friedl says that he's the son of the founder of the company, Heinrich Friedl who left the *Banque Cantonarde de Genève* in 1948, three years after your mother saw him, to create Decorative Arts International. So, I looked into our records to see if there was a photo or any record of Heinrich Friedl. There was nothing, but maybe the photos your mother took may include him."

"Mon Dieu."

Adina took a moment to collect her thoughts and resumed. "We know Decorative Arts International held numerous calls with RussTech and that, as Sofie overheard her uncle to say, RussTech is sending money to Albania. We also know now that RussTech and Decorative Arts International are parts of *Der Kreis*. I think it is likely that it was Manfred Friedl on the call with Mueller. Friedl is the German or rather, the Swiss. The fact that Manfred's father was at the *Banque Cantonarde* when *Der Kreis* was formed and then created DAI leads us directly to present-day Friedl."

"You have discovered someone besides Mueller who is *Der Kreis, n'est pas?*"

"Yes. And Manfred Friedl's bio says he attended Yale University. It will be easy enough to see if Karl Mueller and Manfred Friedl attended at the same time. How many Swiss attend Yale each year? It cannot be an innocent coincidence. This may be the way in which Karl Mueller was introduced to *Der Kreis* in the first place. By Manfred Friedl!"

Hélène was silent for a moment. "Adina, *Der Kreis*, and before it, Richthoven, needed a bank and a trusted banker to keep their illicitly acquired wealth. It's logical that the *Cantonarde* was its bank. But who is now running the *Cantonarde*? Heinrich Friedl left the Bank in 1948 to create the Decorative Arts company. Mighten, in fact, mustn't, the manager of the Bank be *Der Kreis*?"

"Perhaps, perhaps not. I have a name, but no more than that at this point. I suppose it's possible he's not involved but just carries out the work of the bank. Before we notify the team, I want to look into a couple of ideas. Let's take two hours and then we'll bring everyone in on what we've found."

They worked quietly for an hour and a half, at which point Adina was satisfied she'd done what she could. "Hélène, according to what I see, Manfred Friedl was born in 1938. He'd be two years older than Mueller. I haven't been able to access the Yale alumni records yet to see if Mueller and Friedl overlap. I've just completed a general search on Friedl. There are no photographs, which is surprising considering he runs a big company. He must have taken measures to avoid having his picture taken. I also found out that he has a daughter who'd be in her thirties now. I wonder if she's part of the family enterprise."

"For my part," Hélène said, "it appears that Rosenberg's *Einsatzstab Reichsleiter Rosenberg* gave Richthoven/Haas a powerful vehicle to steal art and money from holocaust victims. He was in France, Czechoslovakia, Poland and Moldova when the roundups of the Jews were happening. His main job at *ERR* was to plunder as much as possible. I think it's reasonable to assume that at some point during the war, he went to Switzerland where he must have met Friedl Sr., and arranged to set aside some of what he'd stolen for himself for after the war."

"The Raphael painting that's been missing since the war, the one that your mother wrote about, would seem to confirm what you're saying about his plunder. Keep digging."

"Digging?" Hélène smiled.

"Sorry. Keep searching. See if you can track down those in the photos your mother took. Also, Anna mentioned a Nuremberg judge, the German foreign minister and people from France and the United States. I know it's tedious, but perhaps you could see if you can match the faces in the pictures your mother took with war film."

"*D'accord.*"

Afternoon, April 28, 2019, Jerusalem, Israel

Max was tired and discouraged. He had little to show for his efforts to identify the holders of accounts in the Albanian and Dubai-based banks that had received funds from RussTech's account at the *Cantonarde* in Geneva. Part of the problem was that he dare not risk alerting *Der Kreis*, which, Anna had written, had a founding member embedded at the *Cantonarde*. Even if he could bribe someone in Albania or Dubai, the danger was too great. He'd decided that the best chance would be to accompany Noah back to Sweden. For hours, they'd sat with the analysts at FRA.

The money transfer he was focused on went to an account at the *Banque Commerciale Suisse* (BCS) in Dubai. The FRA indicated that significant funds were then sent from the BCS account to another at a smaller Dubai bank. The account was numbered, so there was no way to identify its holder. There might be one possible bright spot. Considerable and frequent transfers of funds had occurred over several years back and forth between an unknown account holder at the *Banque Cantonarde* in Geneva and an account previously identified as RussTech's. Given the frequency of voice communications between RussTech and this elusive Decorative Arts International (DAI), perhaps the unknown account holder was DAI.

At moments like these, when he was exhausted and disheartened, Max couldn't manage to fend off painful self-examination. When Dini and he had been together, he'd felt supported in a way that no one else had ever achieved. She acted as if he was her hero. His mistake of excluding her from the Op had cost him his world, because he'd cared too much for her and had wanted to protect her. At least, he thought, she was still alive. If she'd gone on the mission with him and had died, he would have lost her forever. But every day now, he faced life alone. His bluster and his immature behaviour at times were deflections to prevent people from seeing the raw person inside. He summoned that bluster as he entered the room.

"Hello, girls!" he grinned airily as he threw himself into one of the office chairs. His legs outstretched, his arms stretching over his head, he gave an exaggerated yawn. "What have you ladies been up to while I've been away? You're looking a lot better than the last time I saw you, Dini, and Hélène, you're looking beautiful as always."

Both women looked at each other and rolled their eyes. Dini was annoyed at herself. All he had to do is enter the room and she was helpless to stop the *frisson* of excitement.

She said harshly, "What have you found out wherever you've been hiding?" Hélène and he both looked taken aback.

"Adina is a terrible slave driver, Maximillian," she said in her fluid French accent. "I needed you to save me, but you were nowhere to be found."

"I know exactly how you feel, Hélène. Before I tell you my news, I'm anxious to hear if you've had any success."

"*Metzuyan!*" chirped Hélène.

One black eyebrow raised, Max looked at Adina. "I see you've been giving Hélène some Hebrew lessons."

Hélène nodded. "Adina made very important progress. We were just about to contact the group to share it. Let's let Miriam know that we need a conference call right away."

Adina took a moment to contact her in London.

"Sorry," said Miriam. "Rik had to go on a trip. He's expected back tonight. Until then, he cannot be reached, I'm afraid. Is there anything you need? Anything I can do?"

"No, thanks Miriam. Can you please just let him know that we'll need to have another team discussion tomorrow morning? It's pretty urgent."

Can't you tell me what it's about?" Miriam asked.

"Unfortunately, no, not at the moment. We'll talk tomorrow then? Thanks, bye."

"Let me in on your secret," begged Max. "I hate to admit it, but my past two days feel like they were a waste of time. I was with Noah in Sweden, trying to get some Intel on the bank accounts. Unfortunately, what we learned was quite limited."

Adina told Max what she'd discovered.

CHAPTER 21

April 29, 2019, Sarajevo, Bosnia and Herzegovina

Half awake, Rik struggled out of bed and staggered to the living room. "Ow," he yelped. "What are you still doing here?"

Sofie squinted, the morning light temporarily blinding her. Damn it. She covered herself and then saw that he'd come out in his briefs. Umm, her body thrummed.

"What do you think I'm doing?" she asked, reddening. She covered her eyes with her arm and groaned with exhaustion. "Take your pill," she yelled as he walked back to the bedroom. Rik had been out of commission all day yesterday, but had seemed to be improving. She gathered her belongings and left.

Rik reached the OSCE office by 8:00 a.m., angry with her for leaving and at himself for his ingratitude, and, he admitted, intrigued by the lust he'd felt surge through him at the sight of her half-naked on his chesterfield. With decaf in hand, he sat down at his desk just as the secure line rang.

"I heard what happened. Are you okay?" asked Miriam.

"It wasn't the best of days, but I'll survive. Is Neal in?"

"Yes," said Miriam. "He's not in a good mood."

"Any idea why?"

"I think his exact words were, 'the idiot got himself hurt'. In any event, I'm calling because Adina and Max need to have a group call urgently. Shall I arrange it now?"

"Let me check if Sofie's in yet." He walked out of his office and across the hall. "Ah. So you're here."

Without looking up, she replied, "So you see."

"Sorry about earlier."

He sounded sufficiently contrite. She nodded.

"Look, I have Miriam on the phone. We'll be on a group call in a few minutes. Why don't you come into my office and we'll listen to whatever it is that Adina and Max want to tell us."

Ten minutes later, the phone rang. "Sofie," boomed Max. "Tell us how Rik looks."

"Even uglier than usual." Laughter erupted across the line.

"Rik," interjected Neal curtailing further humour, "I thought I ordered you to stay out of the action. Was it worth it?"

"We took one of the participants alive. So, yes, I think it was," he said defensively. "Max can tell us what he heard from him."

"Right. The trucks were carrying an arsenal of Russian-made weapons, apparently pilfered from Syria. According to the guy we captured, the convoy started in Durres and was headed for Vienna. It feels like a set-up to me. The participants were Palestinian workers with no interest in terrorism. They were told to die fighting, if they were caught. Otherwise, their families would suffer and receive no money. If this were a serious terrorism plot, why would the trucks travel in a convoy? It was just too easy to stop them all at once. And who tipped us off? Too convenient if you ask me. Also, the types of weapons they were carrying are easily obtained in northern Europe. So why go to the bother of transporting them all the way there? Maybe I'm wrong. I'm still wrestling with what *Der Kreis'* game is, if this was its operation. Whatever is going on, the Palestinians are in the middle of it."

"I'll call my Interpol contact and dig further into who the source was that put us onto the operation," said Neal.

"We've had a breakthrough here. Adina and Hélène, why don't you tell us all what you discovered," said Max sounding like a proud parent.

"Thanks to Noah's work in Sweden, we're in a position to go after *Der Kreis* immediately," said Adina, her quivering voice betraying her excitement. "We discovered that one Heinrich Friedl was the *Cantonarde* banker Anna saw in 1945 and that he then created Decorative Arts International in 1948. We also now know that he has a son, Manfred, who happens to be in charge of DAI today."

There was a moment of silence as everyone absorbed the news. "So," Max bellowed, "We can conclude that this Manfred Friedl followed in his father's footsteps and is part of *Der Kreis.*"

"Shhh," said Adina, annoyed at the interruption. "We also discovered that Manfred, the son, went to Yale during the same years as Karl Mueller. It seems reasonable to surmise that Manfred, like Sofie's uncle, was part of the same secret society there, and that he brought Karl to the attention of his father, Heinrich. At some point, Karl must have been introduced to Richthoven and *Der Kreis*. If Noah hadn't identified Decorative Arts International as a *Der Kreis* front, we wouldn't have made the connection between the *Cantonarde*, DAI and the Friedls, or between them and Mueller."

Sofie was watching Rik. He was gritting his teeth and his brow was knit with frustration. She frowned. Either he's taken too many pills or not enough. Now he was fiddling with the sling and rubbing his eyes. She saw the moment when his mind caught up with what Adina had said.

Neal took over, his voice exuding calm and gravity. "This makes our next move critical. As I see it, we either pick this Manfred Friedl up and interrogate him or track him to Mueller and the rest of *Der Kreis.*"

"We have no real evidence or legal grounds to arrest him. If we do, we risk tipping off the rest of the organization," argued Adina.

"If we *don't* grab him and he disappears, then we have nothing," Max countered.

"Can we track him or trace his calls without him knowing?" asked Hélène.

"That's the key question. And how much more tracing of phone calls and emails can we do without alerting someone or there being a leak?" added Adina, rhetorically.

Rik hadn't said a word.

After a long silence, Neal, realizing Rik wasn't going to step in, took over. "All right, people. Noah, can you ask the FRA to continue to monitor the calls between RussTech, DAI and the *Banque* Cantonarde? Find out if there are other cyber interventions we can use. Also, ask FRA if we can tap Vice-President Sumner Hayes. Do whatever you can, *carefully,* to monitor money transfers and calls. Adina and Aslan, I believe we need to get you into Gaza."

"Adina's still recovering from the attack," objected Max.

"I'm fine," Adina replied.

"Someone's got to go," Neal continued. "We know that our *Der Kreis* woman assassin spent over a month there, and that the Palestinians are deeply involved in whatever `events' *Der Kreis* is planning. Svi, can you use satellite imagery for the period she was in Gaza? If there is something out of the norm, we'll need to nose around to see what they were doing. Svi, I assume your people can get a team in there."

"*Ken,*" he said in Hebrew.

"That's very high risk," argued Max. "If she goes, I should go with her."

"Max, you'd stick out like a sore thumb. Aslan is perfect," said Adina. "We can play husband and wife."

Max's scowling silence was so loud it could almost be heard over the line.

"Rik, if you're able, I think you and Sofie should open an account at the Cantonarde. We'll deposit a hefty amount there to solidify your credibility. We need to know who the current manager is and how the *Banque* operates. Max, you need to do a reconnaissance on Friedl. Oh, and Sofie, Rik will help you to develop a disguise with the help of our experts, in case Friedl knows what you look like as the niece of Mueller."

Sofie raised her eyebrows at Rik and whispered, "Are you up for this?" He seemed to consider and then nodded, slowly.

"I know it's tedious work, Hélène, but please continue hunting down the names of the people in those photos your mother took of *Der Kreis* members. It seems to be a family business. Who are the offspring of those your mother identified? There are more *Der Kreis* out there and we need to know who they are." Neal concluded. "We have a short time to stop whatever is planned. Keep pressing forward. Any questions?"

Everyone murmured his or her agreement. Rik remained silent. As the call ended, he looked up and saw Sofie shake her head. He stood up. "I'm going to work from home for the rest of the day. I'll arrange for the disguise. Make travel plans for Geneva please." With that, he motioned her to leave his office.

For a moment, she fumed. Then, she realized that he must be in far more pain than he had let on and was covering it up. She watched his office until he exited, trying to carry his laptop and bag of files with one arm. She intercepted him at the elevator. "Give me a break," she said, grabbing the bag from his shoulder.

He hit the down button.

"The way you are now, I have no reality around us going to Geneva in tomorrow. So, we're going to get a doctor to look at your wound and then you'll rest the remainder of today. No work."

"Not a chance."

"If you don't, you're useless to us. Wait here," she said firmly, obtaining his promise. Three minutes later, backpack and purse in hand, she returned to Rik and pushed the elevator button again. "I walked. Do you have a car here?"

"No, I took a taxi."

"Okay. We're going to a Dr. Khalbad, and then you'll go home and rest."

After the appointment, Rik was wincing with pain. He fell into the taxi with Sofie's assistance.

"Get into bed. I'll bring you something to eat in a few minutes." Not waiting for a reply, she grabbed his keys and left for the corner market.

"A sandwich first, then the prescription. I promise you, Rik, if you're not better by tomorrow morning, we'll have to put off the trip to Switzerland. So, do what you're told."

Once again, she collected supplies from her apartment and returned. She opened her laptop and started to work. Five hours later, she woke Rik up. He wouldn't sleep the night if he didn't eat.

"Have you moved in?" he demanded groggily but without attitude.

"I'll give you a few minutes to freshen up, and then you'll eat," her voice brooking no disagreement. She realized she rather liked this feeling of being needed.

She brought him her famous spiced tomato soup and soft Sarajevo bread along with cold meats, which he consumed with one hand. When she brought in his tea, she found him asleep. Two days' beard and the harsh worry lines across his forehead warred with gently slackened features, a slightly open mouth and the beginnings of a soft snore. Not buying your adorable act, or at least she hoped she wasn't.

CHAPTER 22

Morning, April 30, 2019, Jerusalem, Israel

Svi Bikovsky had put in twenty-four straight hours working out how to get Adina and Aslan into Gaza. "Our satellite surveillance shows some suspicious movements along the Gaza coastline during the five-week period the assassin was there. That's where you'll head. You'll cross with scarcely any money. Once inside, you'll go to a drop spot where funds and a motor scooter will be waiting for you, along with instructions as to where you will be staying. Your story to any border officials is being worked out as we speak, but it will involve agriculture."

"Agriculture?" asked Adina.

"The imagery we have shows that the area where we've identified suspicious activity is near the Wadi Gaza and Dayr al Balah, the location you can claim as your relations' farming property."

"Okay," said Adina, looking closely at Aslan, wondering whether she could put her life in his hands.

"We're working on an exit strategy. It may be by boat at night, or we may pass you back through a different border crossing with a story that you are returning to the West Bank."

"How can we communicate with you?" asked Adina.

"Burner phones will be left at the drop but must only be used for emergencies. Our contact will let you know the exit timing and plan by passing information to you. Instructions will be in the first drop regarding where the next drop site will be. If our contact has any concerns he'll reach you on the burner phone with instructions to avoid capture. Clear?"

Both Aslan and Adina were silent. There were many uncertainties in the plan. "Let's set a secure exit time now. If we feel we have to change it, we can use the burner. But it's important, I feel, for us to have some clarity regarding when we're coming out," Adina said. She was feeling uncharacteristically jumpy. God knew she'd been in many difficult situations, but it had been a while and she didn't know Aslan.

"Right. Let's agree on how much time you need."

Aslan, silent until now, offered, "I think we must have three days. No more, no less. The first day we must hope that all goes as planned, but that day will be mostly travel and reconnaissance. The second day we'll separate and find out what we can. The third day we can either try to get confirmation of what we've heard, or continue our investigations if nothing has turned up. If we need a fourth day, we can use the burner."

Svi nodded. "You'll go in tomorrow morning, *beseder*?"

"Beseder."

As Adina and Aslan left the room, it struck her as strange that Max hadn't tried to interfere, or at least have his say. She poked her head back into Svi's office, gesturing Aslan to leave her alone for a few minutes. Svi looked up, raising his eyebrows.

"Um. Has Max had his input on this?"

Svi's lips lifted almost imperceptibly, his eyes twinkling. "Frankly, I thought Max's time would be better spent following up a lead in Switzerland. I sent him to Geneva to see if they can trace the ownership of the car in the photo that Anna took of the first *Der Kreis* members back in 1946. He wasn't pleased, and that is an understatement. I've asked him not to be in touch with you today because any unnecessary communication we cannot afford."

Adina, who didn't know Svi very well walked over to his desk and took a seat. "I'm glad you're keeping Max out of this. But I wanted to ask you something on another note. Usually, when we're trying to stop something as dangerous as what we suspect this *Der Kreis* is up to, we look to the Americans for backup. At least that has been my experience.

It feels odd not to read them in on this."

"With all the leaks coming out of Washington, we can't afford it. But god help us if our efforts to stop this group fail. The U.S. will be all over us, as will our esteemed Prime Minister who seems to have a blind spot as far as the U.S. President is concerned. Given that this *Der Kreis* appears to have contacts at the highest levels, we're extremely limited in whom we can trust and that includes the Americans."

"Even in Gaza, there'll be American agents. We'll need to make sure we don't raise their antennae either."

Svi nodded and stood up, a polite indication that the conversation was over. However, they were both glad to have made a connection of sorts. She reached out her hand and he took it.

Afternoon, April 30, 2019, Jerusalem, Israel

Hélène had not wanted to alert anyone until she was sure that she had something. Her decades of work to combat anti-Semitism had put her together with many committed researchers. Since arriving in Jerusalem, she'd contacted two, one in Germany and another here in Israel. She'd also asked Svi how to link a post-war photograph to identify someone who may have been tied to the Nazis. Enormous databases existed. The challenge was to narrow it. Facial recognition was going to be important too, although the photos her mother had taken were grainy and might not be sufficient.

This morning, one of her Israeli contacts that said they might have something for her, based on archival newspaper photos. Would she like to come over?

She'd taken a taxi, impatient as it waded through the noisy traffic. It seemed even worse than usual. She arrived and climbed the four flights of stairs to reach a dingy nameless office where she was ushered into a large room that was impressively messy. File folders littered all surfaces, including the floor. Ancient filing cabinets lined the walls. The people working in the room seemed as antiquated as their office. Her contact, seeing her, waved her into another room where there was room to sit.

"Here's what we're looking at," he said, laying out Anna's photo and another that appeared to be from a Swiss newspaper from 1947. She scanned the two images and then looked up with a fierce expression. "Who is he?"

Her contact pulled out a thin file that appeared to contain several other papers. "We think he's Edward Axworthy, a British-born subject who spent World War II in Zurich."

"Why would he be of interest to you?" asked Hélène, disappointed. "Why would you have a file on a British person? It hardly seems likely he was a criminal."

"There, you would be wrong. Edward Axworthy was a British consul stationed in Bern. He was in charge of either enabling or refusing refugee status for Jews fleeing occupied countries. He was singularly responsible for the deaths of hundreds of people to whom he improperly refused status. Even at the time, the British received many complaints but did nothing."

Hélène became animated. "What happened to him after the war? Was he arrested?"

"No, quite the opposite. He eventually returned to England, none the worse for his war experience. Somehow, he entered the aircraft-building industry and made his fortune. His reputation was never tarnished. May I ask why you have an interest in him?"

"At this point, I can't. Perhaps I'll be able to share more in the future. What's in the rest of the file you have there?"

"For characters such as Axworthy, we always recorded anything that arose about him, just in case we could prosecute. Most articles pertain to his family. In fact, Edward Axworthy's son is the top professional in Britain's military. The elder Axworthy died back in

2002 at the age of 90."

"*Mon Dieu*. May I take this file with me?"

"Yes. All of its contents are copies, not originals."

"Do you have any reason to believe that the son is also anti-Semitic?"

"Hard to say. You'll see from the file that he's not well liked. It seems like he rose through the military by leapfrogging over more qualified individuals. Even his combat experience is light. It's quite conceivable that he had help from his father and others in positions of influence. He didn't get to where he is today because of a distinguished military career, that much is clear. Beyond that, he is reputed to be ruthless in his orders related to the treatment of Muslims, whether in Afghanistan, Iraq or at home."

"Thank you! Thank you so much!" exclaimed Hélène surprising the man by embracing him tightly.

Afternoon, April 30, 2019, Bern, Switzerland

It was Neal who'd smoothed the way for Max to be taken seriously at the central police offices for Switzerland located in its capital city of Bern. He met with the chief of archives.

"Good afternoon, Monsieur Duhamel. I believe you're expecting me," said Max who'd arranged with Neal to use a fake name for the purposes of this meeting.

"It was a very interesting request that your colleague extended to us. I was sure it would be a great challenge. However, we in Switzerland are famous for running our affairs like, as they say, clockwork. The record of ownership for the license plate you provided dates back to 1945. It was attached to a Mercedes owned by a Monsieur Wilhelm Hertz." The archivist gave Max the registration, which included an address in Geneva.

"I'm grateful for your Swiss commitment to good record keeping!" boomed Max, slapping the neat little man hard on his back. Max left the building at 4:00 pm. Rik wasn't answering his phone. He called Israel hoping to reach Adina but got Hélène instead. She was clearly animated.

Max cut her off before she could share her information. "Hélène, I've discovered the owner of one of the cars in your mother's photo. He's Wilhelm Hertz. I'll send you the information. Can you hunt down anything on this man and his family?"

"*Oui*, I'll try. And I've just found out the name of another one of the men in my mother's photos. I think we must have a joint call to share this information. In the interim, I'll do more research on this Hertz. How grateful I am that my mother's photograph was useful!"

"Yes. I must get off the phone, but am wondering if you know where Adina is at the moment?"

"She's on a mission."

He gritted his teeth and said a quick goodbye.

Afternoon, April 30, 2019, Geneva, Switzerland

Sofie looked at herself in the mirror of the opulent hotel room they'd booked near the *Banque Cantonarde*. I look hideous, she thought. God preserve me if this is going to be me in twenty-five years. She heard a knock on the door, opened it, and burst out laughing. There stood Rik sporting grey hair, a moustache and full beard and frameless glasses. Was he wearing eyeliner? "Aren't you pretty! Are you sure you want to be seen with a frump like me?"

Rik peered at her myopically. "You look vaguely familiar, but I can't be positive. Have I ever seen these legs before?"

"Ha, ha," she said dryly. "I lost the argument to wear pants."

He walked to the sofa, his injured arm hanging loosely by his side, and sat down, He surveyed her from head to toe. "I have something for you."

"What? A corsage to complete my ensemble? Perhaps a seeing-eye dog? With these thick glasses, I can't see a thing. And all this expensive jewellery. My uncle would never recognize me, even at my own age, decked out like this." They'd chosen a navy blue skirt and jacket with a white blouse, a Balenciaga bag, and diamond earrings.

"Your outfit, Mrs. Anderson, is missing an important item or two. I'd get down on one knee, but I'm afraid to tip over."

She was suddenly embarrassed. She cupped her left hand and held it out. He extracted a gold wedding band and an opulent, diamond-studded ring from his pocket, turned her hand, palms down, and gently placed them, one by one, on her finger.

Self-consciously, she raised her hand to the light. The room felt charged and awkward. "At least you're not cheap," she said, and breathed to centre herself again.

He cleared his throat and said, gruffly, "We'd better get going. Have you got the files?"

The *Banque Cantonarde* was a stately institution, lined with mahogany walls and priceless paintings, one, a Van Gogh. There was an immobilizing silence about the place that disturbed Sofie so much that she felt panic coming on. Oh, no. Not now. She looked at Rik. He was pale, in pain. Her nerves settled as she focused on him.

They were ushered into a plush private room. Though she wasn't close enough to read the signature, she was sure she was looking at a series of Albrecht Dürer paintings. Gingerly, Sofie lowered herself to an Eighteenth Century antique French sofa. Rik sat beside her.

Five minutes later, a man in his forties entered the room. "I am Dieter Graf," he said in clipped English. He extended his hand to Rik, who shook it. "How may I help?"

Rik began in English, "My wife and I wish to set up an account here, subject to the clarification of certain matters."

"Of course," smiled Graf. "Please, tell me of your needs."

Sofie said, "My aunt recounted her days here during and after the war. As she became infirm, her affairs were handled by, and then transferred to some cousin whose name I cannot remember. Nevertheless, the cousin mentioned my Aunt's use of your bank and her satisfaction with the service she received. Before we consider other options, we thought we would come to you. I have been struggling to recall the name of the manager my cousin mentioned. It was so long ago, perhaps 1947 or 1948."

"Ah. That would either have been Mr. Friedl who was here until 1946, or Mr. Hertz who took over from him."

Sofie jerked, but recovered quickly and smiled, "That was it, Hertz." She turned to Rik. "Dear, I'm sure it was this Mr. Hertz who managed my Aunt's accounts."

Rik nodded, affecting boredom and impatience, as he pulled out papers. "No matter. We propose to start with a deposit of five million Euros and then we'll see. We wish it to be a numbered account. We may need to transfer funds to other countries from time to time, and will expect discretion."

The manager scanned the paperwork Rik handed him. "We can begin the paperwork immediately, unless you wish to consider other banks?"

Sofie and Rik looked at each other, as if weighing their options. They nodded to each other. "Let's proceed. We have one hour before another appointment. Does that give us sufficient time?"

"I will have my assistant come in. He'll be happy to complete the paperwork with you." He left, leaving Sofie and Rik staring at each other hard, afraid to say anything until they could leave.

Max was waiting for them when they arrived back at the hotel.

"Give us a few minutes to get rid of these disguises. Find a quiet place in the bar and we'll meet you there."

An hour later, Sofie took a full gulp of her martini, mentally raising a glass to herself on this, her thirty-fifth birthday. She hated a fuss and was glad that no one knew.

Rik nursed a Perrier and wished he weren't on medication.

Max ordered a beer and then called Hélène. "I asked you to research Wilhelm Hertz, owner of one of the cars your mother photographed. Based on Sofie and Rik's investigations it turns out he was the head of the Banque Cantonarde. Can you keep looking into his past? Find out whether he had any offspring?"

"*Mon Dieu*. Yes, of course. Should I make this my priority?"

"Yes, please."

"I've let Neal know we need to know as much as possible about Marvin Axworthy, without raising his suspicions," said Rik.

"We can't wait much longer to address what we're going to do about Manfred Friedl. He's our best lead, now that my uncle has disappeared," said Sofie.

Rik nodded. "I don't think we can afford to wait."

CHAPTER 23

May 1, 2019, Gaza

Adina wondered how women of the Arab world coped. On this scorching day, she was dressed in a long heavy black dress and a headscarf. She slowed down so that she walked behind Aslan, who looked cool in his blue jeans and a dirty cotton shirt.

They approached an Israeli soldier stationed in a pillbox at the Erez border crossing.

"Open your bag," he barked. "Now, your papers."

They were directed to enter a large hanger where another Israeli carefully went through the documentation to which he finally applied an Israeli stamp.

She schooled her face to hide her fear as they entered no man's land, the gap between Israel and Gaza. They passed through a depressing concrete tunnel and walked along a fenced-in corridor for two kilometres. At the first Palestinian stop, they passed through quickly as the process was operated in a lacklustre way by the guards. Now the worrying part, the checkpoint run by *Hamas*. Aslan muttered something unintelligible in Arabic to Adina, transmitting the tension they both felt.

The *Hamas* officials were treating the man in front of them roughly. Now, it was their turn. "Documents," demanded the official dressed in blue pants and a blue top that was devoid of any insignias. Aslan complied, looking meekly at the officer who was scrutinizing Adina's bruised face.

"What happened to your wife?"

"She was disobedient," replied Aslan, which drew a smirk from the other man.

"What is your purpose in Gaza?"

"Sir, our family's home was bombed by the Israelis several months ago. I went to Ramallah for temporary construction work. Now, we're coming home to stay with family members and work with them in their fields."

The *Hamas* officer briefly patted down Aslan and gave Adina a thorough body search, enraging her, and then looked through their bags and returned their papers, waving them through.

Relieved, they found a taxi and headed for the drop area, a fruit stall in a bazaar.

Adina resumed her role as Aslan's wife. "What kind of fruit shall I buy?" she asked as she surveyed the lowest-priced items.

"Only three oranges. Nothing more." Aslan held out his coins and asked the woman to place the oranges in his backpack, ensuring that the placement of an additional package would go unobserved.

"Let's get to our scooter. It should only take us an hour to reach Dayr al Balah," said Adina as she looked at the material provided at the drop.

In fact, it took them two hours to reach their destination, so poor was the quality of the roads. They were hot and gritty with dust.

"What I wouldn't do for a bath," said Aslan. "Too bad there's no public bathhouse here. That would have been the ideal gossip centre."

Once they'd deposited their bag at the tiny room that had been arranged for them, they took a walk through the town to orient themselves. Motioning to a shop, she left Aslan outside. "*As-salaamu aleikum*. I have been away in Ramallah. Now, I must find work to help support my family. With respect, could you help me?"

"Why are you asking me?" she asked. "You must use your contacts and family members. That's the only way. Most of the time even I have no work."

"I heard," said Adina, casually, "that some women found work near the sea a couple of months ago. Perhaps there is still work there."

The woman shrugged and had no comment.

Giving up, Adina left.

They filled the scooter with petrol and drove by barely habitable shacks, small stores and shanties where fishing nets were laid out to dry.

As she smelled the salt of the Mediterranean, Adina was saddened by the difference that a one-hour sea journey northward from here could make, from this ravaged, derelict tragedy to the hustle and bustle of Tel Aviv. Jews and Arabs had begun their history in the same lands, had lived and struggled together, had come from the same roots until religion got in the way. She could enjoy traditional religious celebrations but, as far as she was concerned, religions were the cause of war, not peace.

Aslan slowed the scooter to a halt as they reached a fenced area. They looked around and decided to head left as they thought they saw a small entrance and a guard shack. "*As-salaamu aleikum,*" ventured Aslan to the clearly bored uniformed guard who was sitting on a chair.

"What is your business? Are you lost?"

"Our family has land on the other side of this wired area. This fence makes it hard for us to reach it. We are worried. It wasn't here when we left for Ramallah a few months ago."

Adina shyly added, "Sir, we are looking for work and heard, upon our return from Ramallah, that there was some kind of activity here. We wish to apply."

"Who told you such things?" the guard demanded.

"It's common knowledge. People in our village mentioned it. We heard many were hired."

The guard said, disgusted, "Such an exaggeration. Villagers know nothing. There were just some women here for a few weeks. Now they're gone."

"Women!" both Aslan and Adina exclaimed. "If only I had been here and not Ramallah," she scolded Aslan, "I could have gotten work here."

"No! The women were foreign. You would not have been permitted here."

"Foreign! When so many of us are unemployed! Why should they hire foreigners? What skills do they have that we, who live here and know the land, do not? And likely they couldn't even speak our language," scoffed Adina.

"Of course they could. They were Palestinian, but also British. You are impertinent to challenge our leader's decisions."

What leader, wondered Adina.

"Even the trainer was a foreigner, such a bitch," he said waving his hands up to Allah for guidance.

She handed him some fruit and a can of cola. "What kind of training or work was it that they should need so many foreigners?" asked Adina, wondering if she was pushing too far.

"It was not for us to know. Only a few finished their trainings. You should forget this place. I hear I'll be moved soon. Likely, they'll take the fence away and your problem will be solved," he said more kindly.

"Thank you, sir, for your time."

By late afternoon, the heat was abating. Adina and Aslan considered their exit strategy. "We're close to the sea. It will be too suspicious to go back out through Erez," worried Aslan.

"But *Hamas* has patrols. They're shooting, even at their own boats. They seem to be obsessively preoccupied with entries and exits from the water. I think it's too risky." Adina thought for a moment. "The drop gave us a different set of identification papers. I'll disguise my bruises as best I can. Let's go back out over the next three hours. We either make it or we don't."

Aslan agreed, knowing that Adina knew the Gaza situation better than he did.

"Svi," Adina called on the secure mobile, "we're leaving. Can you have Israeli border officials at Erez ready to rush us through? All being well, we'll arrive at the office, by 10:30 tonight."

They walked up the *Hamas* customs post and were directed to a shack. The door closed behind them. There were no handles or knobs on the two doors at each end of the small room. They were there until *Hamas* let them go. Aslan, Adina saw, was perspiring profusely.

"You are Israelis, aren't you?" yelled the official. "Your big nose and shifty eyes give you away." He pointed at Aslan.

Damn. Was Aslan equipped to brazen his way out of the interrogation? Had this terrorist organization somehow intercepted her call? Adina's heart was pounding hard.

Aslan replied, his voice ringing with conviction. "I am from Ramallah and pray to *Allah* for guidance all my days. Even to speak of me as a Jew is to send me to the worst hell, *Allah* forgive you. The Jews forced my mother and her family into the Zarqa refugee camp in Jordan in 1948. Eventually, she escaped to her family in Ramallah and met my father. I am no dirty Jew." He spat on the ground.

Not satisfied, the guard asked, "How long were you in Gaza, and for what purpose?"

"My wife's cousin was having a child and they asked us to come to help look after the rest of the children since her husband is away, fighting in Syria. I took leave from my job in Ramallah to come with her. We've been here for three weeks."

The guard glared and left the room. Aslan looked at Adina, fear visible in his eyes.

Her lips firmed and tilted upward. He'd earned her respect over the last couple of minutes.

When the guard returned, he waved them to the door. "Go, and be glad I'm in a good mood tonight."

Two hours later, they arrived at Svi's office. Hélène was still there and greeted them both with kisses and hugs, surprising a smile from Adina.

When he'd heard their findings, Svi's expression became grave. "I think it's becoming clear that the target of the so-called *putsch* Sofie overheard is planned for Great Britain." He added under his breath, "As preposterous as that sounds."

"But Britain is the most stable democracy in the world," objected Aslan.

"Let's consider," countered Svi. "The head of the military there is likely part of *Der Kreis*. This Axworthy has already used recent local conflicts to justify sending troops into the streets in recent months. That alone is unprecedented. There's also the assassin, Geist, who was directed to head for England. And now, these women. We must also conclude that our dear *Hamas* leader is working with *Der Kreis* and providing them with women jihadists."

"But why would Fakhoury risk attacking Britain? That's crazy." Adina shook her head.

Hélène interjected. "We mustn't exclude the possibility that Germany could be the target. Max has just discovered that a Wilhelm Hertz owned the Mercedes in one of my mother's photographs. Sofie and Rik found out that this same Wilhelm Hertz replaced Friedl senior as manager of the *Banque Cantonarde* in 1948. Unfortunately, it appears his son, also Wilhelm, is now a top official in Germany's military. *Der Kreis* has people in high places in England, America and Germany."

"We must be absolutely sure that the United Kingdom is the target. If we're wrong..." Adina's voice tailed off.

PART III

*My whole life has been pledged
to this meeting with you...*

Alexander Pushkin, Eugene Onegin
Friedrich Nietzsche

CHAPTER 24

Afternoon, May 1, 2019, Amsterdam, Netherlands

Miriam's choice was either death or betrayal. Death is a fool's choice, she comforted herself.

She arrived at Schiphol Airport and passed through customs using an alias and disguise she hadn't used for years. Finding a location where noises of the airport would not be heard, she dialled the number and took a deep breath. "I must speak to Manfred Friedl, wherever he may be. Now!"

"What's your name? I'll see if he is here."

"My name's not important. Tell him I have information that he needs if he wants to survive." She was put on hold, and felt her hands sweat as she waited.

"This is Manfred Friedl," said a menacing voice.

"Prepare to put ten million Euros in the following account while we're talking." She gave him the account data.

"Why would I do respond to such an outrageous demand? In any event, it's impossible to make a transfer so quickly."

"Your membership in a particular organization is now known. That information alone will cost you the first million, which I'm waiting to see. You will then have two minutes to ask three other questions, each of which will cost you three million."

"How do I know that what you tell me is true?"

"Is that one of your questions? No delays or I'll hang up in ten seconds."

"I need at least five minutes to make arrangements."

"You have three." She hung up.

Manfred picked up one of his mobiles equipped with the latest encryption software created by a *Der Kreis* member. He reached Karl immediately. "Someone's blackmailing us for ten million Euros, claiming our organization has been discovered. We may not be able to afford refusal, considering Fitch."

"Call Dieter. Make any transfers as slowly as possible. Get him to use our tracking technology. We need to grab them. Male or female?"

"I can't tell. They've masked their voice."

Friedl hung up and dialled Graf. "Dieter, we have a problem. Here's what I need you to do."

Dieter took a moment. "Right. I'm concerned. You might as well wave a red flag with that kind of transfer."

"Someone knows about us, and we need to know who they are and how much they've discovered. If the authorities look into the transfer, you'll have left the Cantonarde by then. We protect out own."

"I'll wire one million now. Text me exact amounts of any additional transfers. We'll attempt to track the account."

Friedl resumed the call with his blackmailer. "You're playing a very dangerous game. I have done nothing wrong. How do I know that you're not Interpol or some other law enforcement trying to extract information of some type?"

"Ten seconds and I hang up."

"Who's discovered this organization as you call it?"

"Israeli intelligence."

"But who in Israeli intelligence?"

"Is that your second question? I don't see three million Euros."

"I won't pay even one more Euro unless I know the precise identity."

Miriam thought. "You already know who this person is. You attacked her. If I don't see three million Euros in fifteen seconds I'm hanging up." It appeared.

"How did they identify this organization, even supposing it exists?"

"From an old photograph that identified Werner Richthoven as Werner Haas. Someone who knew Richthoven took the photograph. It included your father, by the way."

"But how would they know about such an organization from a photograph?"

"You get a free answer. I'll simply say that the person who took the photograph also included notes of meetings that were held by Richthoven and the organization's founders. These notes recently became known and led to you. Now, another three million or you don't get your last question." The transfer was completed.

"What do they know of the organization today?"

"That you're a part of it and that some terrorist event will occur within the next few weeks. Now, I expect to see the final three million in thirty seconds. If it appears, I'll give you a bonus question. If not, I hang up in eleven seconds. She began to count down, aloud. The ten million was now in her account. Abruptly, she ended the call.

The normally unflappable Friedl rushed to his feet, grabbing for the mobile.

"How bad is it?" asked Karl.

"My identity's known. I must leave immediately. I'll use the emergency plan. Any files that can hurt us are being destroyed. Warn Marta and put out the alert. I've got to leave, now," Manfred shouted.

"Calm yourself. Is my identity known?" asked Karl, ignoring Friedl's distress.

"No, I don't think so, and anyway, as far as the world's concerned, you're dead. I have to get out of here. They could arrive at any time to seize me."

"Who?"

"The Israelis, for Christ sake. Warn Dieter," he shouted and hung up.

Confident in the voice encryption technology she'd used, Miriam boarded the flight that would take her to her new life on the other side of the world.

Afternoon, May 1, 2019, Geneva, Switzerland

It was past 5:00 pm. and Max was getting hungry. He'd long ago graduated from stakeouts. But Manfred Friedl was of immediate importance. Miriam, the obvious choice for watch duty, hadn't been reachable.

At 8:00 a.m., he'd seen Friedl arrive alone in his black Mercedes. Max had texted the license plate number to Rik. DAI was unimpressive, nondescript. Nine hours later, he yawned and decided to call Rik.

"Anything?" Rik asked.

"He's still at the office. Where the hell is Miriam? She's the obvious one to take over from me."

"She's become a big problem. She's not in London. I asked a contact in The Hague to go over to her place and she's not there."

"Hold on," Max's voice dropped with tension. "There's a helicopter landing on the roof of the building. Fuck. We're losing him."

"God damn it. Give me a few minutes. If he's trying to escape, he'd likely head for a private airstrip. And that's if he's trying to escape. He could just be using the helicopter for a scheduled meeting, couldn't he?"

Max considered. "Who knows? I think we have to consider the worst case that someone has tipped him off. I'm heading back to you."

"I'll alert Neal to what's going on and ask Noah if the Swedes can see if there's been any call that came from DAI over the last couple of hours."

The Neal that Rik had always counted on showed up now. "I'll see if we can track flights of small aircraft from private fields around

Geneva. That's what I'd do if I were Friedl. I'll get back to you. I expect you back here tonight. I'll let you know the arrangements I make."

It took Max forty-five minutes to arrive back at the hotel where he, Sofie and Rik met up in a second room he'd booked under an assumed name. "Noah says FRA's checking and might get back to us in minutes. Neal's doing what he can to trace Miriam's whereabouts."

Two hours later, an email from an unrecognizable name arrived in Rik's inbox, entitled, Sorry.

"Rik, I got myself into some serious trouble. I've had to disappear to a place no one can find me. All I told them was that someone knows about them. That's all. They don't know anything else, except they think it's the Israelis. I know you won't forgive me. I can't forgive myself."

Noah contacted the group at 8:00 pm. "A call from a burner phone came in to DAI from a location near Amsterdam. Within one minute, another call went out, this time from DAI to an area outside of London. Fifteen minutes later, from what you've told me, Friedl left on the helicopter. Why is he calling London unless that's where Mueller is?"

"I just received an email from Miriam. She's betrayed us. Why, we're not sure. I'll have Neal monitor ports and airports in England in case that's where Friedl's headed. Miriam is in our crosshairs too. The three of us here are formulating our next move now that they know we're on to them. I'll get back to you." Rik put down the phone and gritted his teeth. "This one is on me," he said, furious at himself. "Bad judgment. I never imagined Miriam would do something like this, that she wouldn't feel she could come to me for help. What the hell are we going to do now?"

Sofie had been quiet and increasingly depressed as she heard Rik's half of the conversation with Noah. "Oh, shut up!"

Rik looked up surprised and insulted.

"You're not clairvoyant. You're not superman either."

Max smirked.

She glared at them both. "I don't know how you stand it, to have someone you trust with your life do something like this. It makes me sick. Wherever Miriam is, she should be shot. She's betrayed every one of her family members who either died or survived the holocaust, not to mention all of us. I hope that we're going to go after her."

"Yes. You can be sure of that." Rik frowned and then swore. "God damn it, Sofie. Miriam knows your connection to Mueller. We have to pray she didn't say anything about you to Friedl."

Sofie paled as a nightmarish scenario played out before her: If her uncle did know about her, she'd never be able to live free of fear until he and Der Kreis were out of the way.

"If it's the last thing I do, we'll get Miriam, and your uncle," swore Rik. "In the meantime, we're going to have to take a leap of faith and decide that Britain is Der Kreis' target. It's time to focus our limited resources there. We know the Palestinian women are from England. We have Axworthy and the Lithuanian assassin in London. The fact that Friedl phoned to some location near London is another indication. Neal's making travel arrangements for us all to go there tonight. Now that Der Kreis knows we're on to them, they may try to move up whatever they have in store. The sooner we get there the better."

Just then, Rik's phone rang. It was Noah again.

"Can you get the team on? It's important."

Ten minutes later, the team was assembled.

"The Swedes just called," said Noah. "They've been monitoring our Russians, including Evgeny Sokolov, Sofie's RussTech oligarch. In light of his dealings with the Friedls and DAI, and his funding of Der Kreis' account in Albania, Sokolov must know something about Der Kreis. We have an exact location for him based on a communication he just made to Russia. I'm proposing we extract him while we can. He's even more important now that we've lost Friedl."

Sofie couldn't restrain herself. "Where is he? In Transnistria?"

"You got it. You've spent time there, right?"

"Yes, and I have my undercover guy there who helped me identify Sokolov and who can help us get in, at a price."

"I assume our oligarch is well guarded," said Rik.

Sofie thought for a moment. "For sure. However, according to my source, Transnistria is where he acts as if he's untouchable. He believes he's `the king' and that if any strangers enter, he'll know. The big challenge, apart from seizing him, is getting the team in to Transnistria at such short notice. Since it's an outlaw principality of Moldova, how do we get a clean visa to get in there? Plus, we're also going to need a fluent Russian speaker to communicate better than I can."

Neal, silent until now, said, "We're up against time, people. Is this a worthwhile venture? Can we pull it off with our team as it is? If we believe that the action is going to take place in England, should we be haring off to Moldova at this critical point?"

Noah intervened. "I've seen the records and they're pretty convincing. Given the sheer number of transactions and calls by Sokolov to DAI and to the Russian President over the last three years, I have to think he's part of Der Kreis. If there's even the slightest chance of grabbing him, it's worth a shot. With the disappearance of Friedl, he may be our best option."

"Agreed," said Rik. "I think Max and Adina with Aslan might be the logical combination. Max and Aslan speak Russian and they have the extraction skills."

"You'll need my help with my informer. He won't work with you without me present," argued Sofie.

"No. I think you should go to London to follow up on leads," said Rik.

She looked at him in surprise. "I know more about Sokolov than anyone here. My informant won't trust anyone but me. The team needs me there. Besides, if my uncle does know about me, the only way I'm ever going to feel safe again is if we catch him. And right now,

Sokolov's our best bet to get to him. I'm going."

Rik shook his head.

Neal intervened. "Sofie, stay on the line with Adina, Aslan, Max and Noah. Figure out a plan. Run it by me and Svi in Israel so that we can make a final decision. Assuming you can grab him, I'd like to bring him to London for safe storage. We'll provide a house for interrogation purposes. That's assuming you can come up with a viable plan that can be implemented within the next twenty-four hours."

"Wait a moment." There was a pause and Neal came back on the line. "I'm just getting news here that a small craft took off from what looks like a private airstrip outside of Campagnole off the F5 an hour northeast of Geneva. It headed north and then turned west across Belgium. We lost her for about one hour and then we think it was the same plane that headed over the channel. We need to pay that airstrip a visit."

"I'll follow up on that," said Rik. I'll see you tomorrow. To maintain my usual pattern of behaviour, I'm going to stay at my parents when I get back to London. Can you put a surreptitious watch on the house for me?"

"Yes."

"Did you talk to your Interpol contact? Any word on where he got his tip about Der Kreie' diversion, the weapons passing through Serbia?"

"All he knew was that he received it from a colleague from the OSCE."

The OSCE. Fuck!" Rik didn't like the picture that was coming together in his mind.

"Now, on spec," Neal was saying, "I'm going to arrange private transport for the team to arrive in Moldova. Let's discuss visas and cover stories."

Rik pulled Sofie aside. "I'm not happy with you going on this mission. It's high-risk. You haven't been trained to execute Ops like this one."

He could see her colour rise and rushed to avoid a blow-up between them. He rubbed the back of his neck. "I should be going with you. Damn this bloody arm!"

"You're stuck with me," she said, mollified. "If we can grab Sokolov, we not only get closer to Der Kreis. We also get to seize the monster I've been chasing for over five years. You can't begin to know what that means to me."

"I know it's unlikely, but if anyone at the OSCE should contact you, don't talk to them. Let me know right away."

"Even Marc?"

"At this point, I'm thinking especially Marc, even though there's no proof of his complicity or involvement with Der Kreis. While you're in Transnistria, I'll begin to take a closer look into his background." Rik drew her around the corner. It seemed the most natural thing in the world to put his good arm around her and hold her tightly to him.

After a brief moment, she pulled away, shocked at her own charged response to his embrace.

"Be safe," he said gruffly and left the room.

CHAPTER 25

May 2, 2019, Chisinau and Transnistria, Moldova

Ruslan Chertov ground his foul Russian cigarette into the ground, relieved to see Sofie exit Chisinau's airport. For thirty years, since the fall of the USSR and the creation of Moldova's breakaway state, Transnistria, he'd eked out a living as a taxi driver catering to adventurous tourists willing to visit there. At fifty-three, he'd do whatever was needed to get out of the monotonous dead-end life that he'd been doomed to live. His dream was to live with his wife in Varna, Bulgaria. There he could savour the Black Sea's faintly salty smell, its beautiful pastoral scenes, its wine and freedom. He'd visited there once when he was young, before 1989, when one could travel anywhere in the Soviet Union.

His children had long since escaped to Spain and Portugal where they were doing well. From time to time, they'd send some money to him through a friend of his in Chisinau, enough to help him and his wife fend off abject poverty. Sofie McAdam was offering to get him and his wife out today. He knew what she asked was dangerous. But he would do anything, anything, to fulfil his dream of seeing his children and his grandchildren for the first time in his paradise.

"*Zdrastvuy*," said Sofie, choosing a personal greeting that she would offer to an old friend. "These are my colleagues." She offered a gentle smile intended to put Ruslan at ease.

The team had not been happy about having to bring Ruslan and his wife out as part of the bargain. In the end, however, they'd had little choice but to embrace this desperate man as part of their team. Israel's experts had manufactured tourist visas for Moldova sufficient to get all four team members into Transnistria. Aslan and Sofie, Adina and Max would be two married couples travelling together.

The full magnitude of fear at what they were about to do settled on her. Maybe Rik was right. She *was* an amateur. Would she be able to control her fear? She looked over at her teammates and wondered if, behind the scenes, they'd argued against her presence. Rik! Last night, when he held her, she'd felt long-dormant emotions. For now, she'd focus on Sokolov and on getting her team and herself back safely. And then, she promised to herself, she'd let herself explore her feelings.

According to Ruslan, Sokolov's days in Transnistria consisted of business meetings in his Tirasapol nightclub, dubbed the Casa Nostra by locals. At lunch, surrounded by bodyguards, he might go across the street to the restaurant. Or he might have food brought in. Almost invariably, at 7:30 pm., he'd be driven to a bar he owned on the other side of town for drinks with his comrades. Most, though not all of the time, around 10:00 pm., two bodyguards drove him to his ostentatious, castle-like mansion, a gaudy obscene display of his wealth in the midst of poverty. It was believed, although this rumour was yet to be confirmed, that his wife, who had never deigned to set foot in Transnistria, lived in an enormous home on the outskirts of Moscow.

Communications were a problem. Sokolov and his thugs almost certainly monitored any in- or out-going calls that caught their attention. The plan would have to work perfectly.

Ruslan carried them along in his taxi van. When they arrived at the border just beyond Bender, an official, likely FSB, perused Ruslan, whom they were accustomed to seeing, and the tired-looking, sloppily dressed tourists. He barked something at Ruslan.

"Show your passports," Ruslan instructed.

The guard took the documentation inside a small office. Sofie swallowed hard. She couldn't have a panic attack now. She began to control her breathing. If this mission went wrong, it would not, she vowed, be because of her.

The guard returned, looked with a suspicious frown at them all. "How long are you staying?"

Ruslan relayed the question in English.

"Just overnight."

"Where are you staying? "

"At the Tirasapol Hotel," Ruslan replied.

"Get out of the car." The guard roughly searched them, feeling up Adina who could scarcely contain her fury. Twice in one week. Sofie was looking appalled, like some tourist who wished her husband had never decided to come to this godforsaken hellhole.

"Open your bags," he ordered. Ruslan paled. He looked imploringly at Sofie who gave him a slight nod, though she looked like she was going to faint.

The small travel bags were taken out of the vehicle and items strewn on the concrete. Apparently disappointed, the guard left the piles on the ground.

Ruslan managed to get them back into the trunk, slipping the guard the obligatory bribe.

Once they'd driven across the bridge into Transnistria, Sofie allowed herself to be distracted by the dreary scene as they jolted along the bumpy road into Tirasapol. Small, poorly maintained homes and businesses made for a haphazard, ugly jumble. Most people seemed to be elderly, the women wearing babushka scarves hobbling alongside old men.

They arrived at Ruslan's home at 2:00 p.m. An hour later, Ruslan and Max left. They must complete two essential and potentially dangerous tasks. For the most part, the others waited in silence. Adina knew that, apart from the extraction itself, the biggest danger was happening as she sat at this house. She felt helpless and worried.

Ruslan's plump wife always enjoyed meeting her husband's clients. Typically, she would cook a big meal in anticipation of their arrival. It was a way for her and her husband to make a little extra money and break the monotony of their existence. She insisted that they taste her homemade vodka.

Ruslan had been instructed to tell his wife nothing about their imminent escape. He was to pack one small bag without her noticing. There was no fear that she would resist leaving her home. She was unhappier than he was and yearned to meet her grandchildren. To ensure that she had no chance to divulge her departure to anyone, everyone agreed, even Ruslan, that she should not be told until one hour before departure.

It was getting too late. Adina could barely swallow with fear. Where the hell were they? Had Ruslan been detained? And Max! She'd wanted to say something to him before he left. With everyone milling around, she had only been able to send him a worried glance.

By 7:00 pm., Sofie and Adina felt compelled to discuss a Plan B. They should have been back two hours ago.

Mercifully, at 7:30 pm., the van pulled up in front of Ruslan's little house and Ruslan jumped out. The deal had been done. In exchange for two thousand Euros, three Kalashnikovs with optics platforms, two pistols with silencers, ammunition and two smoke bombs were purchased with the cash they'd stuffed into the van's seats on which Sofie, Max and Adina had sat. Ruslan entered the house, fear etching his features. He nodded without speaking.

Ruslan's wife became animated when she was told they were leaving now, for good. The bags brought in by the team were burned. They all entered the van and drove to within a block of the bar where they picked up Max who had been staking out Sokolov.

By 9:00 pm., it had become pitch black. Max was jumpy but relieved that Sokolov was, so far, following his usual practice.

Let the oligarch's hubris, his belief in his untouchability, be his downfall, Sofie prayed.

At 9:45 pm., Sokolov exited the bar and got into his car. Max quickly made the one call that their plans allowed. Now, they had no more than twenty minutes to execute the extraction.

The moment Sokolov stepped out of the bar, Ruslan started the van and sped ahead. He was going as fast as he could along the main road trying to avoid car-eating potholes. Finally, he turned right onto the long, unpaved path that led to Sokolov's house. He turned around a bend and sequestered the van to the side of the road.

Max, Adina and Aslan, wearing black balaclavas leapt out of the vehicle, weapons in hand. They stationed themselves on each side of the road.

Max peered through the optic he'd mounted on the Kalashnikov and saw the lights of the car as it turned. He aimed at its tires. As the driver struggled for control, the black Mercedes skidded sideways to a halt. One of the bodyguards was already out of the front door. Adina shot him, twice. Almost simultaneously, Max killed the driver. Only Sokolov remained in the car. Just as he was reaching into a side pocket of the car, Adina climbed into the front seat and put a gun to his head while Max unlocked the back door. Aslan ignited the coloured smoke bomb in the middle of road.

Sofie and her two companions sat transfixed and frozen with terror. Within two minutes, the team had Sokolov tied up and blindfolded. Never in her whole life had she been more grateful than when she heard the `thwack thwack' of a helicopter descending. They piled in. Within one minute of landing on the road, it lifted off and then zigzagged to avoid gunfire erupting from the oligarch's house.

Twenty minutes later, in Chisinau, they transferred to a private plane that flew them to Sofia, Bulgaria. Sokolov was sedated and would remain tied up until they reached their final destination.

Sofie and Adina joined the Chertovs as they were introduced to two Bulgarian handlers who were Israeli plants in the country. "You will be kept in hiding for the next three months for your own safety. Assuming we have determined that no one is looking for you, we will bring you to your new home, a farm with an orchard outside of Varna.

You will receive a monthly payment for your services to us for as long as you live. You will also be given a van, similar to the one you left behind."

Ruslan and his wife hugged each other.

Adina, always the worrier, cautioned, "You must not contact your children or anyone who knows you until we're sure you're safe. They must think you're missing or dead. Do you understand? Do not underestimate your situation. By helping us take down an oligarch and friend of the Russian President, you've put yourselves in the most dangerous situation."

"But we want to see our children!"

"We'll be inventing a story to explain your disappearance from Transnistria designed to get the Russians to stop their investigations. Until then, your lives and those of your children will depend on you. If you choose to break our rules, we will no longer be able to protect you. I advise you to enjoy your new freedom and well-being."

"What if we need to be in touch with you?"

"Our two colleagues will explain everything."

After goodbyes were exchanged, a private plan flew the team to Vienna where they then boarded a military plane to London.

CHAPTER 26

Morning, May 3, 2019, London, England

Sofie arrived in London at 6:00 a.m. and was brought to MI6's Vauxhall Cross headquarters, better known as the River. She scarcely took in the bizarre post-modern building as she entered and passed through tight security. She was, she thought, quite possibly in shock. Down the elevator she went.

As she walked along the dark corridor to Neal's office, fury surged through her at Rik and Neal for insisting she'd be staying with Rik at his family's house. "I desperately need rest and down time to function. I can't do that if I have to pretend to be polite to strangers. I'll stay in any hotel or any other house you can provide. Surely, you owe me this," she'd pleaded with Neal by phone just an hour ago.

"Sofie, dear girl, I'm delighted to finally meet you. Felicitations on Sokolov," said Neal, smiling and reaching for her hand while taking her measure. A beautiful, lithe tigress, he thought, tall, strong and fragile. At this moment, her hazel eyes were boring through him.

"Ahh. You're upset."

Silence.

He had the grace to express his regret. "I've limited resources to protect you. In light of your connection with your uncle, you're particularly vulnerable. For those reasons, the most efficient option is to have you and Rik stay at his home where I've arranged security. Dear boy," he glared at Rik, "haven't you anything to say?"

Rik did his best to mollify her. "Sofie, my mother will welcome you with open arms. If you want to be alone, it's a big house. We'll arrange it so you can keep to yourself."

Sofie banked down the panic building within her. "I need air," she said, walking out of the room.

"Go after her. Damn it!"

Rik was already out the door. Grabbing her arm he stopped her from entering the elevator. "Sof, you're knackered. Can you just please come back and tell us what happened? Then, we'll make sure you get some down time, as you call it."

She felt herself tilt towards the wall and thought, no one, since her best friend in university, had called her Sof. When he took her arm she had no energy to resist.

He drew her back to the office.

"There, now. Nothing like a good cup of tea to restore one's spirits," said Neal, forcing her to accept a stained mug that featured a young Queen's face. "The only good thing the Portuguese ever did for us."

"The Portuguese?" Rik rolled his eyes.

"Yes, dear boy, the Portuguese. Our merry monarch, Charles II, allowed tea to be imported around 1660, just after Cromwell, when our country needed it most."

She took a sip and almost choked on the sugar. She was incredulous. He was right. Tea was better than a drug. As her eyes became focused, she looked around. Neal and his office were stunningly messy.

"Where are my glasses?" Neal's hands fumbled on his desk.

Unable to remain surly, she laughed aloud and pointed at his head. He responded with a beatific smile.

Rik was agitated, whether from the pain, worry, or relief at Sofie's return, he didn't know. "Let's get started," he said gruffly, drawing a questioning look from Neal. "Before you debrief us, Sofie, let me give you both a quick update. I got the registration of the plane Friedl escaped in. DAI owns it. According to the flight plan, it was headed for Brussels. Our tracking suggests it refuelled there and then headed on to

England. Unfortunately, we lost it over the Channel." Unbidden, Rik's face contorted in pain as he grabbed his arm. He ground out, "Your turn to give us the full story."

"Yes, Sofie, please do," said Neal, who added, "My boy, I've our doctor coming in a few minutes to take a good British look at your arm."

Rik shot Sofie a look. "What are the chances that *Der Kreis* can trace Sokolov's extraction to us?"

So we begin, thought Sofie. "Obviously that was one of our worries from the outset. Thankfully, the guard didn't take the time necessary to photocopy or scan the pictures in our passports either. Of course, if we're wrong, if he copied just one or two, we might be in trouble." She provided a concise summary of the operation and added, "When the final extraction happened, no one could possibly see us. We're hoping that the dead bodyguards," she took a laboured breath, "and a message that we left in the car convince authorities that a rival Russian mafia gang nabbed him. When the helicopter took off, we headed north towards Ukraine and Russia for a couple of minutes to help reinforce that perception."

"What about Ruslan's disappearance? Mightn't it draw attention to you?"

"Under normal circumstances, yes. The guard could report the four tourists that he permitted to cross into Transnistria. But if he values his future, he'll deny any knowledge of our crossing for fear of appearing incompetent to his bosses and, more importantly, to the thugs at RussTech who will be trying to recover Sokolov."

"Our dear President of Russia will surely have been informed of his kidnapping. I wonder how long it will take for him to contact *Der Kreis* to let them know that a key member was captured. That should make this group very nervous," speculated Neal.

"Let's hope so. Sofie, I had a surprising call yesterday. It was Marc Jansen."

"Weren't you going to be looking into him while I was in Moldova? What was his reason for contacting you? Did he ask about me?" Sofie could feel herself become agitated.

"Weird coincidence, isn't it? He called because he was `worried' about me, had heard that I'd been involved in the Serbia intercept. I asked how he knew. He gave some evasive non-answer. He did ask about you. I said I'd given you a temporary position in my Sarajevo office. He cut the conversation short, saying a call was coming in."

"If I thought I was scared before, now I'm terrified." It had been only three weeks ago that life had felt safe and normal. Exhausted, she felt tears threatening.

"We're going to keep you safe, whatever it takes," Rik vowed.

"Sofie, dear girl, would you like to freshen up while Rik's being attended to? We have a workout space here where there are showers."

She turned her eyes to Neal and nodded.

An hour later, the three entered the back seat of an unremarkable grey sedan bound for the safe house where Sokolov was sleeping off his sedation. They found the whole team sitting around a large table in a windowless room.

Max greeted Neal like a long lost friend. It was Noah and Neal's first encounter. The two eyed each other with respect borne of their knowledge of each other's careers. Svi, who'd encountered Neal on previous Ops involving Max and Rik, walked over and shook hands. "Good to see you again, my friend."

Hélène looked elegant and younger, vibrant and pretty. Surprising. Adina and Max were sitting next to each other. Had the Transnistria mission created a détente?

The entire team stared at a sixty-ish bookish individual who'd just entered the room.

"I'd like you all to meet Terry Johnson, a colleague I've worked with for over thirty years, and someone, I believe you will all agree, we need at this time," said Neal.

Adina, Max and Svi frowned, perturbed by the insertion of a new team member.

"I took the liberty of reading him into our project because we're urgently going to need what he can bring us." Neal's elfish demeanour disappeared as he looked around the room anticipating objections.

Rik intervened. "Neal disclosed Terry's addition to our team late last night and I'm fully on board."

Neal continued, "I'll ask Terry to say a few words, and then I'd like you to introduce yourselves."

"I've worked for what we now call GCHQ, Government Communications Headquarters, my entire career. It was our organization that broke the enigma code at Bletchley Park. I'm with the National Cyber Security Centre which is the part of GCHQ that's responsible for making sure our communications are secure here."

"Terry's being modest. He's the head of the NCSC, which makes him third in command within GCHQ. It's become abundantly clear to me that our team needs to track down *Der Kreis* here in England, something that the FRA in Sweden cannot do as easily. I didn't bring Terry in lightly. I'm asking you all to trust my judgement on this." Neal looked apologetically at Terry. "We've discovered that some highly respected, high-profile people are members of this evil organization. Everyone here will be wondering if you are among them."

Terry nodded and looked at each person in turn. "I'll do whatever you ask of me, whatever I can, to defeat this enemy."

Max was the first to end the silence. "We can use all the help we can get." He looked at Neal. "Have you made him aware of the consequences of telling anyone about us?"

"Neal has, and I fully understand that no one outside this room can be trusted," Terry responded.

Neal turned to Rik. "Let's get to it."

"Two days ago, we had a major setback, losing Friedl and our only live connection to *Der Kreis*. Thanks to the team, we've compensated by seizing Sokolov. But before we talk next steps, Hélène, you indicated to me that you made an important discovery last night?"

She nodded, animated. "You asked me to find out what I could about Manfred Friedl. He is, how would you say, a shadowy figure, despite the prominence of DAI. What I was able to uncover was a daughter, Marta Friedl. I found this photograph last night." Hélène pulled several sheets out of her smart black leather portfolio and passed them around.

There was a moment of silence, then a hubbub of comment.

"It's all making sense!" exclaimed Adina.

Sofie paled. Had it been just days before that she'd been touched by this killer?

Rik placed his hand next to hers without thinking. "Quiet down. So, in the midst of what seems to be a male-dominated *Der Kreis*, our assassin and trainer of terrorists turns out to be Manfred Friedl's daughter?"

"*Oui*," said Hélène. "*Justement*."

"Our best guess is that the *coup* discussed between her uncle and Manfred Friedl is going to take place here in Britain," continued Rik. "We have considerable evidence to point to our country, and little that directs us elsewhere."

Noah added, "According to the FRA, Friedl received what we can only think was a warning call from Miriam, minutes before he escaped. He then made a call to a location in the London area, unfortunately untraceable to an exact spot. It seems logical to conclude that it was *Der Kreis* Friedl called. If we're right, then Mueller is likely here in London. If we're all in agreement, we'll proceed to concentrate our efforts here as an urgent matter, starting with the interrogation of Sokolov," concluded Rik.

Svi nodded. "And with the capture of the terrorists. We had some of our technicians go through customs videos of those exiting Gaza a couple of days before and after we saw Marta Friedl leave there. Four women came out in two groups of two, each with British passports and all reporting they had stayed for about five weeks. We have what we believe are their real names. Two are from Manchester, and two from London. Our advantage may lie in the fact that there's no reason for *Der Kreis* to suspect that anyone was watching these women come or go from Gaza. They didn't bother to hide their real identities. If we can seize them, we may be able to stop whatever is planned."

"If a *coup* is their goal, how can this little group stop them?" asked Aslan.

Tension filled the room.

"*If* it's about to happen!" said Noah, still in wilful disbelief. Fuck, he thought. I can't even bring the U.S. in to help, knowing that my Vice-President is quite possibly Der Kreis. He put it to the team. "It would be a catastrophe, not just for Europe but also for the U.S., if Britain were destabilized. There must be some way for our country to help."

"No," Neal said. "If we reach out beyond ourselves, we risk being eliminated. We know *Der Kreis* has spent seventy-five years recruiting people in high places, not the least of which includes your country."

"There must be someone we can enlist, given what we know," said Sofie.

"The Queen, ninja warrior," said Max, drawing sour looks.

"I assure you, you have Israel," pointed out Svi, "although we mustn't include Mossad as *Der Kreis* would logically target it for infiltration."

"Can we get to Axworthy?" Rik looked at Neal.

"He's been invisible for the last several days."

"Invisible, just like Dieter Graf, the head of the *Banque Cantonarde*. When he escaped, Friedl must have instructed members of Der Kreis to make themselves scarce," said Max.

"We need to interrogate Sokolov," Rik said flatly. "If we can break him we may be able to stop *Der Kreis*' entire operation in its tracks.

How much time do we have before whatever they have planned begins? If it were I, I'd be moving up my schedule. We need to get something definitive out of him right away."

Noah nodded. "I think our other obvious move is to intercept the women in Manchester and London. If we do that, their terrorists are dismantled, or at least we hope so."

"We find them," said Sofie quietly, arousing surprise and particular focus as she rarely said a word. "Then we likely find Marta. Just as she trained them in Gaza, wouldn't she be preparing them here?"

"We'll start with the addresses Svi found. I think we should follow the women until they lead us to Marta and she, in turn, to the leaders. Arresting the women alone is like seizing the weapon without the shooter," said Max.

"How do we know there weren't other women beyond these four?" asked Neal.

"The guard in Gaza told us about the training camp. He was from the area and said it hadn't been there more than three months. We can't know for sure, but I don't think there are others given what the guard said," replied Aslan.

Adina added, "And, as far as we know, Marta/Greta never entered or exited Gaza other than the one time we identified her."

Sofie ventured, "Can we investigate Axworthy without him knowing we're on to him? God, there's so much to do, and so few of us."

Again, there was a long heavy silence. "We have to assume that *Der Kreis* has someone within GCHQ. If their aim is to pull off a *coup*, then control over communications is going to be a tool they use," Terry responded. "If I try anything related to Axworthy, it'll be a one-time thing."

"Let's face it," Max said. "It all comes back to Sokolov. He's worked with DAI for years. Given the amount of money he's siphoned off from RussTech to give to DAI I've got to believe he knows who he's funding, and for what purpose."

Adina nodded. "We need to get something out of him today, not tomorrow or the next day. I've been thinking about him. He's going to require an incentive to cooperate right away. I think I know what our leverage is. The one person he seems to love is his only son, Sasha. If Sokolov doesn't tell us what we need to know, we paint the picture of what will happen to his family when the Russian President hears how he has revealed secrets to the Israelis and the British."

"Makes sense, but I'm not sure it's going to be enough to get him talking right away. What else?" asked Neal.

"We could strike a bargain with him," returned Adina. "We'll extract his son and his wife if he wants, and let Sokolov live with them under our care if and only if he reveals everything he has about RussTech's criminal operations. He must also reveal any links between the Russian government and *Der Kreis*. We lure him with the thought of a limited but safe life in return for giving us what he knows. Refusal means he dies in prison, having condemned his family to hell. He'll have nothing to gain by refusing to cooperate with us. If we have him under our watch, we might also be able to find a use for him later."

"He's the worst kind of animal," Sofie objected. "He's caused incalculable pain to so many families whose loved ones have been trafficked. He was responsible for those young girls dying in front of Rik, and for Philippe's death. He doesn't deserve any special treatment. When I think what he's done, what a monster he is..."

There was a brief silence until Svi spoke. "We'll threaten his own death in a very painful manner today. We'll tell him the Russian President has already ordered his family, including his wife and Sokolov's mother to be killed if Sokolov is not returned to Moscow immediately. We have to be willing to follow through as far as his death is concerned," looking at Max, whose face had tightened and eyes flattened, as if he were steeling himself for what he would be asked to do.

Afternoon, May 3, 2019, London, England

The interrogation began in the basement, in a small windowless room that was cut off from the rest of the house by an impenetrable steel door. The location had long ago been designed for this very purpose. Sophisticated recording equipment would allow those outside the room to see, listen and convey questions without Sokolov being aware of who his captors were.

"Aslan, you'll be in the room with the prisoner. Max will be the point person who feeds you questions through your mike."

As Aslan entered the room, a shackled Sokolov, sitting on a metal chair, turned his head from side to side, as if trying to see through the blindfold. "Who are you and what is this about? What craziness is this? I can't tell you nothing. You've wasted your time."

Max spoke and Aslan translated. "We are your best friends, the people who will keep you and your family alive, *if* you tell us within the next hour what we need to know. Even one lie and you die today."

"Friends?" he scoffed. "I do not have friends, only enemies."

"Whether we are friends or enemies, this is that one moment in time when you must choose either to cooperate or, well, must I state the obvious?"

"What do you want?"

"Everything you know about *Der Kreis* and RussTech's activities, including your funding of terrorism and *Der Kreis'* dealings with the President of Russia."

"*Der Kreis*? What is this *Der Kreis*?"

"Time is ticking away. The Russian will soon know that you're in our hands. And what do you think he'll do to your family?"

Sokolov paled. "How can I trust that you will, as you say, save me or my family?"

"If you provide us with information that we need, you will live a simple life with your family and perform little favours. The more favours you provide, and the longer you provide them, the happier you and your family will be. If, on the other hand, you do not tell us what we need to know, you'll die today, and your family, tomorrow."

"How can I be sure that you will not kill me immediately after I tell you what you want to know?"

"Good question. It's all about timing and your value to us. We'll know if you're lying to us. You tell us all you know about *Der Kreis*. Everything. The rest of what you know about other matters can come later. Time is passing. Start talking. If you omit even one detail…"

"I want to see my son!" Sokolov ground out. "Until I see him, I will say nothing."

"Your son! I want to spend more time with my son!" Max lied. "If, and listen hard, if, *Der Kreis* succeeds with its plans, you, with or without your son, will have no bargaining position and your lives will end. You're wasting valuable seconds."

Sokolov felt someone tighten his bonds. Why had he not been informed that someone knew about *Der Kreis* after all these years? If he could figure out who these people were, he could make a deal. First, he would assert his authority. "I am not some peon, some pawn. I know things of value that are beyond your questions. Until I see my son, I will say nothing."

Adina looked at Max who had paled at the prospect of having to use his special skills. She said into the microphone to Aslan for translation. "Very well. Prepare the camera. The Russian will get the first picture. Might he wonder what you told us before you died? I wonder what revenge he'll take on your family."

Sokolov thought hard. "If you can bring me my son, I will talk."

"How would we do that?"

"He is in Odessa. I will order him to drive to Chisinau. It will take five hours at most. You can bring him to me. Only when you get him here will I talk."

"Give us something valuable to prove your worth now, or you and your family die."

"*Nyet*. Until I embrace my son, you will get nothing from me."

"We need him to answer at least one question about Der Kreis before we give in to any of his demands. And we must get his son here. Svi, can we do that?" asked Adina.

"Yes." Svi looked at Neal and knew that his comrade would need every ounce of strength to face whatever Der Kreis was about to unleash on British soil. Maybe now Britain would know what it felt like to be country confronted by those who hated and wanted to eliminate you. Success would be a boon to Israel, Svi knew, if its mission succeeded. Neal and Great Britain would owe his country an enormous favour for what he had done in Transnistria and Gaza and now what he, and Israel, were about to take on.

"I think we should force him to give us answers to more than just one question," said Sofie who was sickened by this evil man whom she'd tracked for so long.

"Where are *Der Kreis'* targets and when will they attack?"

"I can't answer until I see my son."

"Where is *Der Kreis'* centre in England?"

"Same."

At Neal's direction, Aslan slapped his cheek viciously evoking a bleat from Sokolov.

"Who are the members of *Der Kreis*?"

No response.

Neal and Svi left the room to deliberate and returned fifteen minutes later. Neal said, "Adina, you'll take over for Aslan as far as translation is concerned. Sofie, we're going to ask you to go to a bedroom and have a rest for an hour or two."

"Are you kidding? No one here would ever have heard of RussTech or *Der Kreis* were it not for me." Sofie scowled at them all. They were underestimating her. "I stay."

Rik shook his head, fearing that what was ahead would jade her forever. But she had a point. She'd earned the right to be here.

The interrogation continued. "If you give something useful to us right now, you'll see your son tomorrow. If not…"

"No. Bring him here and only then I will tell you something."

Adina suddenly had a thought and whispered to Rik who immediately signalled his intention to ask the next question. In a calm and reasonable voice, Rik intervened, Aslan translating. "Something? Let me tell you something! The next five minutes will determine whether you live out the next hour. You're not our only source of information. We have *Der Kreis'* favourite woman assassin in the room next to us who just happens to be the daughter of an important member of *Der Kreis*, as you well know. Very interesting details she's been sharing, about the Albania-Serbia caper, the training of the Gaza women and your money transfers to DAI for terrorism purposes."

Sokolov's belligerent stance wilted. He struggled with his restraints.

"You must see that your value to us is diminishing minute by minute. Your expiry date is drawing near. You want to see your son? You won't, ever again, unless you tell us something useful now. Do you understand?"

"I will tell you how to bring my son to me without any trouble to you, but only if we make a deal to save us both, first. Believe me. I have information that you need."

Rik's voice was broadcast into the room so that Sokolov could hear it. "Here is what is going to happen. You will give us answers to two of our questions this very afternoon, and you will see your son tomorrow. Give him tea and five minutes to consider his options."

After two minutes, a subdued Sokolov said, "I will answer one question. And then, I know the ideal place to bring my son to me."

"No, you will answer two questions. Ah, it seems you have four minutes left to reconsider."

"What is your first question?"

"What is or are the events planned by Der Kreis?"

"I do not know."

"Where is the centre of Der Kreis in England? Where are its leaders right now?"

Sokolov became even more agitated. "I don't know! Please!"

"You have one more chance and then you're useless to us. Where are its leaders holed up?"

"Stop! I don't know."

"We don't believe you. You've met its members and you've met them here in England."

Sokolov shook his head but remained silent.

"Very well. Bargaining time is over in 10, 9, 8 ..."

Sokolov heard the door open, gloves applied and sounds of metal implements being prepared. How many times had he been on the other side of this process? He knew these were professionals. He would not be able to hold out.

Sofie felt her entire, exhausted body sag. For god's sake, what had she expected? But to see her colleagues, her friends, Rik, like this. She should have left as they'd demanded. When she tried to push herself up, she fell back, weak and mesmerized.

"Stop. There is someone located in northern England. I only know his code name, Tango. He's in the media. I think he owns a big newspaper company. He has spread false stories to inflame the British and create chaos. He has become an increasingly powerful person within the organization."

"What organization?"

"*Der Kreis.*" Sokolov looked confused.

Adina knew her Latin. She said, through the microphone to her colleagues, "Tango is not only a dance. It's a Latin word for speech. He's probably telling the truth."

"Very well," continued Max, Aslan translating. "Tell us about the Lithuanian who killed the Russian Energy Minister."

"I will give you this and then I will speak not one word until my son is with me."

"Go ahead."

"His code name is name is Ghost, *Geist* in German, but his real name is Yuri Kozlov. He's not Lithuanian. He's from Kaliningrad."

"What does *Der Kreis* do when you need to reach them?" demanded Max.

"This is a third question."

"Answer it and you'll see your son."

Sokolov was tiring. "There may be a way for me to contact them, but only after I see my son."

"Your son will be here by daylight tomorrow, assuming he is where you say he is. I suggest you enjoy our hospitality and consider the advantages of remembering everything you know about *Der Kreis*."

CHAPTER 27

Evening, May 3, 2019, London, England

As the taxi turned onto a street in fashionable Fulham, Sofie's nervousness at the prospect of having to function with strangers overrode her exhaustion. After everything she'd gone through the past six months, the past three weeks, the last twenty-four hours, she was indignant that Neal had forced her into the situation she now found herself. Absently, she fumbled in her purse and applied her lip balm.

What am I going to say about my family when the inevitable question comes up? That I come from alcoholic parents and a master criminal uncle who's a Nazi sympathizer bent on taking over the United Kingdom, for God's sake?

She looked up at an imposing, four-storey, white stucco house that consisted of a central section with wings on either side. Columns rose from the second floor to a triangular Grecian pediment. It appeared Rik was part of the English aristocracy. They walked a few steps to the elegant black door.

"Rik, darling, and Sofie, is it? Welcome! Come in, come in! Roger, your son and his friend have arrived," Rik's mother called merrily as she kissed her son, took Sofie's hand, and shifted to let them enter.

She might be royalty, thought Sofie, but here was a woman who was, above all, a doting mother. She withstood the not-so-discreet scrutiny coming her way. No sign of the father.

Rik kissed his mother with great warmth.

"How do you do, Mrs. Whitford. It's very kind of you to let me stay with you," ventured Sofie.

"Sofie, my dear, please call me Margaret. Why don't I show you to your room? It's so rare that Rik brings us a visitor," she said, taking her arm in hers. "Rik told us you'd be very tired and would want a little nap. Let's get you settled. Your room is on the quiet side of the house."

As they climbed up the elegant spiral staircase, Margaret told herself to stop babbling. Rik's friend was in need of the care of a mother. That was clear for anyone to see! Such a beautiful girl, such stunning, soulful eyes! And no putting on of airs, thank God.

"Here are your towels, dear. The loo and shower are in there. Now you just take a rest and we'll wake you in a couple of hours for tea."

Tea? Oh, dinner. "Yes, thank you. You're very kind."

Two hours later, she woke up to a quiet but persistent knock on the door. She'd been out cold. "Sofie, dear. Why don't you come down for some food when you're ready? Or," and Sofie detected a faint whiff of censure, "would you prefer it if we bring up a tray?"

Her lifelong habit of being accommodating had her responding, "I'll be down in a few minutes." A rare moment it was that she found herself wishing she had something more fancy to wear than her austere black and white wardrobe. She took extra care to make herself as presentable as possible, adding a long multi-coloured scarf. She forced herself to look in the bathroom mirror and was unsurprised to see dark shadows under her eyes. She granted herself an exception and applied mascara and lipstick and revaluated. She'd do.

As she walked down the stairs, she could hear a blur of quiet voices. She turned left into a bright room lit by windows facing the front of the house. Fresh spring air was coming from screen sliding doors that gave access to what looked like a backyard.

Rik held a little girl in his good arm. He was tickling her with his stubbled cheeks.

She shrieked with laughter, wriggling to escape.

"No! I won't put you down until you give me a kiss."

She took Rik's face in her little hands and blew a bubble on his cheek, drawing a wide smile from him.

Her complexion, Rik thought, held that special rosy colour that suggested recent sleep. Her beauty is…is…he struggled to find the word…luminous. He took a breath. He approached, still carrying the little girl. "Sofie, over there is my sister, Sigrid, and this pretty little squiggler is my niece, Annie, who just turned three a couple of days ago."

"Nice to meet you, Sigrid. And happy birthday, Annie!" Sofie smiled at the little girl, bright in her navy tights, tartan skirt and a yellow wool sweater.

Annie said nothing, though her blue eyes shone with curiosity at the newcomer.

Sigrid stood up and extended her hand. "Welcome."

"Why don't we sit outside and enjoy our unusually warm weather," suggested Margaret. "Sofie, dear. Would you care for a glass of sherry? Wine? Something else?"

"I haven't had sherry in years."

"Then sherry it shall be."

Six wicker chairs were scattered around a large round plexiglass table on the stone patio. To one side was a square wooden table covered with crayons and drawing paper. Two tiny chairs were tucked into it. Beyond the deck was a small patch of grass edged by a neat garden and high fence.

Rik sat beside Sofie and leaned toward her. "Did you get some sleep?" he asked quietly.

"Yes. Thanks. Your parents have a beautiful home. Did you grow up here?"

"I did, until I went away to school."

"Any news?"

"No. In any event," he said under his breath, "we mustn't speak of work here."

Sofie was watching Annie who was busy drawing.

"I should tell you. Annie isn't talking yet. It's a worry."

Margaret came out of another door along the back and walked to the table with a sherry for Sofie and juice for Annie.

"Mrs. Whitford, Margaret," she corrected herself. "Are Sigrid and Friderik Norwegian names?"

"You're close. My parents were Danish. Rik has the same name as his grandfather."

Sofie smiled and nodded.

"You work with Rik?" Sigrid asked.

"Yes. I…"

Annie thrust a piece of paper onto Sofie's lap.

"Oh, what's this? Look at the colours! Did you draw this all by yourself?"

Annie nodded solemnly.

"It's so pretty. May I keep it?"

The little girl nodded again.

Sofie stood and walked over to the little table and lowered herself onto the miniature chair, wondering how she'd get back up.

Annie tiptoed nearer.

"You know what my favourite colour in the whole wide world is?"

Annie shook her head, her eyebrows raised in rapt anticipation. She came closer.

"Purple," said Sofie. "Is there purple here?"

Annie's head bobbed up and down. She stepped forward and picked up the purple crayon.

"What's your favourite?" asked Sofie.

The little girl gravely considered the question and finally chose a well-used teal blue stick.

"Oh. I like that one too. It reminds me of a lake. We could draw something with your favourite and mine, couldn't we? Do you like flowers? Maybe, we could do a garden, by a pond."

Annie sat and bent her head to her work as Sofie watched.

Margaret looked over at her son who was staring at Sofie. She dare not let herself hope.

After a couple of minutes, Annie finished her drawing and showed Sofie her results.

"Isn't that lovely. May I take this one with me, too? I'll put it on my wall." Sofie took another paper and drew an inverted V and then, a horizontal line to complete the A. Can you sign it, `A' for Annie?"

Annie set her face close to the table and laboriously copied Sofie's example, using the purple crayon.

"Thank you. Every time I look at it, I'll think of you."

Annie beamed, stood up and began to run around the garden.

Sofie walked back to her chair and took a sip of sherry. "You're so lucky to have her," she said to Sigrid. She leaned back and closed her eyes to enjoy the warmth of late afternoon sunshine. For the first time in months, she was bordering on light-hearted, or was it lightheaded? Minutes later, she felt a little hand tapping on her arm. She opened her eyes to see Annie signalling she wanted up.

Sofie looked over at Sigrid who was smiling at her daughter, and then at Rik, deep in discussion with his mother. She pushed her chair back and lifted Annie onto her lap, her arms encircling the little girl's waist.

Annie bobbed up and down, playing with Sofie's scarf. After a time, she yawned and turned sideways to nestle against Sofie's breasts.

At peace, Sofie closed her eyes. Later, she'd wonder if she'd fallen asleep.

"Oh, here's Roger! Roger, I'd like you to meet a friend of Rik's and our guest for a few days." Margaret's voice sounded brittle.

With Annie still in her arms, Sofie couldn't stand. She smiled up at a distinguished, older version of Rik. "How do you do Mr. Whitford."

Roger nodded and then turned and shook hands with his son, a greeting that struck Sofie as formal and cold, although he did acknowledge his daughter and granddaughter.

Sigrid picked up her sleepy daughter. "It's time for us to be on our way. Bye!"

Margaret stood. "Bring your drinks in. I'll just finish up in the kitchen."

"May I help?"asked Sofie.

"Yes, thank you. Will you toss the salad?" A few minutes later, the two women brought a piping hot lamb dish, a vegetable casserole and the salad to the table.

"Roger, can you open the wine?"

They sat around the formally set dinner table.

"Sofie, tell us a little about yourself."

The dreaded question. She took a breath. "Well, as you can tell from my accent no doubt, I'm Canadian, although I have tried to eliminate `eh' from my vocabulary." This elicited chuckles from Rik and Margaret and a faint smile from Mr. Whitford. "I grew up in Quebec. When I was twenty, my parents both passed away."

"Oh!" Margaret gasped. "How terribly sad. Do you have brothers and sisters, other family?" she asked, hopefully.

"No, none," lied Sofie, forcing herself not to look at Rik. "After… After, I left to go to university in Sweden and then the Netherlands. I loved Europe and found a job with the United Nations Development Programme."

"How did you come to meet Rik?"

At this point, Rik intervened, "Sofie, let me explain so you can get a bite in edgewise. Sofie was working for the UNDP in Moldova. Through some very good research, she discovered a group involved with human trafficking. She brought this to the attention of the OSCE, at which point a number of my colleagues and I became involved. When our mission related to Moldova ended, I offered Sofie a job with the OSCE in Sarajevo."

"My goodness. Trafficking. How frightening. And Sarajevo! Sofie, dear, is that any place for a young woman to live these days? Isn't it dangerous and isolating for you?"

Roger interrupted. "Yes, why bury yourself in a backwater like Sarajevo?" His forehead furled, he continued, "Rik has been wasting his time and his career in obscure places when," he turned to his son, "you could be doing something useful here at home."

"Roger, I don't th–"

"Margaret, don't interrupt me. I've earned the right to speak as I wish in my own home."

Apparently, Margaret hadn't, fumed Sofie.

"I don't know if you've been paying attention to the news." Roger scowled at his son. "You do realize that England is in danger of being taken over by Muslim extremists. For god's sake, we've even elected an Islamic mayor in London!"

"Rog–," Margaret pleaded, her face reddening.

Roger extended his arm, his palm towards her, shaking his head back and forth.

Sofie's exhaustion warred with anger. She watched as Rik placed his hand over his mother's. "Here we go again," she thought she heard him mutter under his breath.

Roger continued on. "No! We're all grown-ups. Every day there's a new story about acts of violence against our people by immigrants who hate us, and are determined to destroy our way of life. If that's the way they feel, they should be deported. Good riddance. My father and his generation fought and died to preserve our freedom and democracy. Every one of us, including you," he pointed his finger at Rik, "need to do our part before it's too late."

Rik dropped his fork on his plate with a bang and gripped the table tightly as his mother stroked his hand. She looked helplessly at her husband.

There was nothing that pissed off, no, *enraged* Sofie more than a bully. "With all due respect, sir, I'm alarmed by that point of view. I think of Yeats' poem, The Second Coming. I can't remember it all, but part of it has always stayed with me:

Things fall apart; the centre cannot hold;
Mere anarchy is loosed upon the world,
The best lack all conviction, while the worst
Are full of passionate intensity..."

She continued. "Have you noticed how we're always being forced to take sides, these days, how our thoughts are being drowned out by the loudest, most extreme voices on both sides? It scares me. Civility and kindness have given way to sheer vitriol. We hear it so often that we think it's acceptable. I think that the hate talk, as I call it, is bringing out a mob mentality. We may not know it, but we're being forced to choose an extreme. It feels like history's repeating itself and we're not noticing."

"I don't see how this relates to anything I just said," huffed Rik's father.

Sofie took a sip of her wine, glad that her hand was steady. "My dread, Mr. Whitford, is that moderate voices are being drowned out by radical elements. Do we really want them to define our future?"

Sofie's face felt hot. It was she who'd been uncivil, lecturing her host.

Roger was frowning his displeasure. "England, you may or may not know, defended itself bravely and at great cost during the war. We came this close," and he held up his thumb and index finger an inch apart, "to being defeated. Now, we're facing a different, invisible war against people who want to destroy us, who show no respect for the very values that are the pillars of our culture. I live here. You don't. And I'm telling you, we're losing. Post-Brexit, we have no one coming to our defence. We're in a war and my son is missing in action."

If Sofie weren't here, I'd pick my father up and throw him against the wall, thought Rik, mortified at his father's dismissal of him in front of Sofie and furious at his treatment of his mother. It took everything he had to restrain himself. Affecting a cynical smile, he said, "It's so nice to be home." Turning to his mother, he asked, "What's for dessert?"

After dinner, Sofie excused herself, exhausted and disturbed by the hostility that underlay what seemed to be a happy family. Roger had real reason to be concerned about his country. It wasn't his fault that he didn't know Rik was fighting to protect Britain's future at this very moment. Rik, for his part, showed contempt for his father. Margaret seemed caught in the middle.

Worst of all, Rik's father was saying the words that fed right into Der Kreis' extremist, racist beliefs. Depression set in. Has Der Kreis already won? If their coup succeeds, will men like Roger be the first to jump on board?

Sofie got into her pyjamas, lay on her bed and fell asleep within seconds.

At 1:00 a.m., she jolted wide-awake. Damn. She put on a robe and crept downstairs hoping to find a book to read. En route, she passed the music room on the other side of the house, paused and entered. She closed the glass doors. Earlier, when Sofie had run her hand along the keys of a beautiful baby grand piano, Margaret had encouraged her to play whenever she liked. If she played quietly, no one would be disturbed.

Rik woke up from a light sleep, wondering for a moment if he was hallucinating and then realized he really was hearing music coming from below. It wasn't his parents, who didn't play at all. He was the only one who did, except, apparently, Sofie, who, he now remembered, was a musician.

Impulsively, he threw on sweatpants and padded downstairs. Once through the living room, he peeked through the glass doors. She was playing Chopin in the dark. Passion, he thought, sheer passion. So intimate was her expression as she played that he turned away. When he sensed that she was finishing, he tiptoed up the staircase, his throat constricted.

CHAPTER 28

Morning, May 4, 2019, Sevenoaks, England

"Stand easy," ordered Marvin Axworthy as he surveyed the covert group he'd trained over the past eleven months. "The day we've been preparing for has arrived. As every one of you is aware, there are unsavoury forces at work whose primary purpose is to undermine our country. It will be your job to provide safety to all of our countrymen. Brigadiers, hand out the orders," he barked at the twenty-five brigade leaders, each of whom assembled their assigned soldiers together in specified parts of the enormous room.

Wilhelm Hertz, Commander of Germany's Armed Forces, sat with Axworthy and looked on. "I must learn everything I can. I should like to begin with my questions."

"Proceed." Axworthy crossed his arms and stared at Hertz, as if trying to intimidate him.

"How did you choose these men?"

Axworthy thought back to those early days of planning that had begun five years ago. "First, I found two men whom I could trust to do whatever I asked. One of my first instructions to them was to oversee the development and application of a sophisticated test across the ranks."

"A written test?" Hertz's eyebrows rose and his head jerked back, scepticism clear in his face.

"Yes, a written test, to start. You may scoff. But this was how we identified those who favour authoritarian rule, subscribe to radical paramilitary publications, value loyalty and are loners. They must also be keen for promotion. Most important, they must follow orders without question. Of course, we needed to exclude those who showed signs of independent thinking. And geography played a part. We've ensured that we have soldiers from all the main communities that we will occupy."

"And after the written tests?"

"Interviews. The test produced five hundred candidates. My two men and I interviewed every one of them. It was a time-consuming but requisite task. I have total confidence that the three hundred that we have here will perform as we need."

"Surely, they must have many questions. What did you tell them you want them to do?"

Axworthy pursed his lips in displeasure. "Those who would question orders were eliminated early. We told most of the men you see here today that they were handpicked for a top-secret, special mission to impose martial law, should it be needed. They were instructed that they must train to quell resistance, even from mainstream troops or the police, should such a situation arise. We made it clear that their lives would be in jeopardy should they reveal anything to anyone about this special battalion."

"*Most* were told? Do you infer that others were told something else?"

"Our plan will not work unless we have a handful of the troops, *primaries* as I call them, who are prepared to take extraordinary measures. My test and the interviews revealed a select group who hold high levels of anger and will undertake violent tasks, legal or illegal, without question. As you will soon see, my *primaries* are vital to our creation of the conditions that will justify my imposition of martial law. Some have been trained to perform special tasks."

Hertz grilled Axworthy regarding what, exactly, would be expected of the primaries. He paused, and then asked, "How did you determine the number of brigades you'd need?"

"We calculated that we'd need twenty-five to cover the country, including five in London, and others in Manchester, Liverpool, Bristol, Birmingham, Glasgow, Belfast, Edinburgh, and so on. Every major population will be under our control."

"What guarantees are there that the majority of troops, who are unaware of our plan, will perform their duties?"

"We promoted all three hundred of the troops you see here so that they outrank the troops that we'll deploy to the streets. They'll have no option but to obey the orders they are given."

"What about the police?"

"Clive will ensure that the Metropolitan Police force here in London follow his orders, which will be to cooperate with the armed forces. The regional police in other parts of the country will be far outnumbered by the troops we deploy. We do not consider them a problem."

"How will these secret brigade members know who are part of the group and who aren't?"

Axworthy smiled. "Come with me. I'll show you."

Morning, May 4, 2019, London, England

"One more time. Tell me your orders. Leave nothing out," instructed Marta.

Fatima frowned, but obeyed.

"Now, you, Hana."

Marta was jittery. She admitted it. Might the women lose their nerve as their final day drew closer? No, she assured herself. These women showed not the slightest hint of hesitation.

She'd just returned from up north, having re-situated Rania and Marwa to where their chosen targets would be. Since Karl had decided to move up the operation, the two original targets were no longer viable.

It had not been easy. She'd had to identify entirely different sights. If she'd had any worry, it was that last-minute changes might cause the women to balk. They hadn't.

"We must have proof that our martyrdom will benefit our families, as you promised."

"I will fulfil my commitment. Your families will be informed of the heroic acts of their daughters. You've both been excellent students. Good luck." With that, she left.

"What a relief that we will not have to see her again. Let us prepare our favourite foods for each other. And then, let us read the *Qur'an* together, my sister."

Morning, May 4, 2019, London England

"God damn it, Karl," huffed Manfred, slamming his fist down on the marble counter.

"This isn't helping. Focus. Every second you get emotional is a second you're not devoting to our mission."

"I loathe that we're trapped here. If it weren't for the goddamn Israelis, we'd be in central London, watching our life's work unfold. As it is, we're useless." Manfred began to pace.

"Calm yourself. Our most important job must be to eliminate whoever is aware of *Der Kreis* the moment we've seized power. Imagine the consequences if we're exposed."

"Who's going to believe whatever the Israelis might say about us? We're invisible."

The secure mobile buzzed. "Shit!" grimaced Karl. "It's Sokolov texting that he needs to call us, urgently. If there's anyone who could do us harm, it's that fucking asshole."

"Now *you* need to calm yourself." Manfred gritted his teeth and sat down.

Karl quickly regained his placid demeanour. "Let's reason this out," he said, his hand cupping his chin. "Why isn't he dead or in captivity if some Russian gang got hold of him? How could he get a call out?" He thought for a moment.

"Our Russian should have taken measures to rescue him. Sokolov knows too much about us, about where the bodies are buried."

"Figuratively and literally," said Karl absently as he considered *Der Kreis'* options."

"I think we need to talk to our Russian. See if he knows anything about Sokolov." Manfred resumed his pacing.

"Sit down. Before we do anything, we review our options. What could Sokolov know that can change our plan here at this point?" A quiet descended on the room, as the repercussions sank in.

Mueller made the call and was immediately transferred. "Mr. President, thank you. A certain person is missing from one of your –"

"I am aware."

"Do you know who was responsible?"

"*Nyet.*"

"Sokolov's texted us, demanding to speak to us. We assume his captors have initiated this contact."

"He has many enemies here in Russia who want him out of their businesses. Do not worry about him. We will find him." The Russian hung up abruptly.

"Where does that leave us?" said Manfred as he stood up again and hit the counter.

"Let's pray that it was one of the oligarchs. If it was the Israelis, we could be in trouble."

Afternoon, May 4, 2019, London, England

Rupert Gage and Oswald Outerridge huddled together at Gage's palatial home.

"Are we certain the withdrawals have happened?" asked Outerridge.

"Yes. Precisely one hour ago, I sat with our hacker and saw the accounts emptied." Gage smiled to himself, imagining the sheer terror that was being felt this very moment by those arrogant sons of bitches in the City and Canary Wharf. "I need to review and approve your social media and news releases before you're authorized to proceed."

Gage took his time perusing them and made a few changes. "If this doesn't get them out on the streets, nothing will."

CHAPTER 29

Early Morning, May 4, 2019, London, England

Sofie crept downstairs at 5:15 a.m., and was surprised to find Margaret preparing tea.

"Good morning, dear. I hope you slept well."

"I did, thank you. But you didn't have to get up for us."

"It's not every day that I have Rik and a friend here to spoil. For me, it's a special occasion." She smiled at her son who entered the kitchen and kissed his mother's cheek.

"Just what I needed," he said as he accepted the steaming cup. "We may or may not be back this evening. Please, Mum, don't wait up for us or cook anything,"

"Sofie, dear, if you're going to be staying with us, do you have a favourite food?"

Taken aback, Sofie replied, "Well, ah…No one has ever asked me that. Um…Rik's right. It's going to be a long day. Please don't go to any trouble."

"Trouble. No, dear, it's what would make me happy." Margaret took her hand and squeezed it.

Sofie's fingers twitched and then relaxed into the warmth. "I used to love oxtail stew, but it's so messy to eat," she babbled. "As Rik says, our work means that fast food will probably do for us tonight, that is, if we even make it back at a reasonable time." Sofie smiled.

"I understand." Margaret patted and let go of her hand.

Her son was stunned. Sofie had passed through his family's dysfunctional looking glass unscathed, it appeared.

"The car's here. Ready?" he ventured.

"Yes. Let's go."

By 6:15, the team was assembled in the boardroom of the safe house.

"Permit me to convey our gratitude, Svi," said Neal. Looking around the table, he explained. "Sokolov's son was brought here about two hours ago and had a brief reunion with his father. Our subject's ready to talk. Aslan, let's get you into the interrogation room."

"Evgeny, what does *Der Kreis* have planned?"

"I do not know the exact plan, but something big will occur here."

"Here in London? Here in England?"

"The United Kingdom."

"When?"

"Something was supposed to happen in the middle of, or late May. But I believe the plan has already started."

"How do you know this?"

"Because part of the plan involves the banks here. We deposited a lot of money in them over the years, and I was told two days ago that the money would be coming back to us within a couple of days."

In the boardroom, Max held up his hand to silence Neal, who had been relaying the questions to Aslan.

"Which banks?"

"Lloyds, Barron's, Royal Bank of Scotland and another one. I cannot remember its name."

"What is *Der Kreis*' aim with the banks?"

"I do not know."

Max walked to a corner of the room and dialled a number. "Henry?"

"Yes, Max! I need to talk to you. I've been at the Bank all night. Something's happened that could bring us down."

"Let me speak to the most senior person you can find."

"No one listens to me."

"They'll talk to me," Max said.

A moment later, a harried voice shouted, "Parkinson, here."

"I'm Max Becker."

"I know who you are."

"I believe I know what your bank is facing. Let me help."

"We may not be able to wait. Doors open in a couple of hours."

"I'll be there before that," he said and hung up.

"Fuck. My banker here confirms a catastrophic event has happened that could bring his bank down. Sokolov's telling the truth. I may have to leave before you finish with him."

"If you can, stay for a few minutes. Let's get on with it, quickly."

"Who's the leader of *Der Kreis*?"

"His name is Mueller."

"Who else is in the organization?"

"I do not know everyone. Speaking of banking, though, *Der Kreis* has a very senior British banker. Also, I know they have people in the United States and Germany, but I don't know exactly who."

"You will tell us about your funding of terrorism later."

Sokolov became agitated. "I am not funding terrorism."

"We'll see."

"Your boss in Russia, is he a member?"

Sokolov looked sick. "I can say that he has dealings with the organization. I am not sure."

"Who tipped you off when you were transferring girls out of Moldova?"

"Someone in The Hague."

"Someone?"

"I don't know who he is or what he does."

Rik looked at Sofie. "That rules out any thought of Miriam being the mole."

"It must be Jansen." She felt ill at the thought that the man she and Philippe had brought her information to, the man she'd worked for six months had betrayed them and caused the deaths of Philippe and those young women.

"Neal, who do we have who can pick him up? If he's one of them, we need him here."

"I'm afraid we don't have the time or resources to get to him right now without exposing ourselves," responded Neal. "Especially if Sokolov is correct and *Der Kreis'* plan has already started. The bank crisis seems to indicate it has." He spoke to Aslan. "Tell him that his future and that of his family depends on him getting us to Mueller."

Terry turned to Neal, animated. "Last night, I looked back at the VPN calls by Friedl to London that Noah mentioned the FRA couldn't trace the day he escaped. I think with what I have now I can triangulate, *if* we can get them to answer one more call."

"Would this triangulation give us a precise location, or a just range?" asked Sofie, wondering how close her uncle was to her at this very moment.

"An exact address, with any luck."

"You'll help us prepare an urgent message to *Der Kreis* now, Sokolov. Fail and you'll be of no use to us."

Sokolov appeared relieved and happy, thought Rik. Was he so delusional that he believed his future was going to be a comfortable one because he and his son were now united?

"What will I say?"

"Very simple. The group that seized you has information that will bring Der Kreis down unless they get paid." Neal turned to Terry. "That should buy you the time you need to do the trace. Right?"

Terry showed crossed fingers.

Neal's mobile rang. "What? You're positive?" He hung up. "We've got facial recognition on one of the terrorist women. Two days ago, Rania Hadid took the ferry to Belfast."

"Two days ago. What's in Belfast? Christ!" asked Terry.

Rik began a frantic search in his limited-access database. There was a tense silence. "Our Prime Minister is addressing the Northern Ireland Assembly at 11:00 a.m. this morning. That's only four hours from now."

Neal dialled a number and explained who he was. "I need to speak to the Prime Minister, urgently." After a pause, he continued, "I have intelligence that indicates an imminent attack on him this morning." Neal was becoming agitated. "No, the source did not reveal himself. We need to evacuate him and the entire building, now!"

"Give me a moment please, while I talk to my superior."

"No. Please put me through to the Prime Minister or his guard duty immediately."

"One moment."

Neal waited, frantic at the delay.

"I've relayed the message to my superior who has promised he will address the matter. I have been instructed to inform you, sir, that we have the matter in hand."

Neal heard voices across the line, and then a dial tone. Incredulous, he called an aide. "Book me a helicopter, now. Rik, Adina and Aslan will come with me. I may be able to talk my way to the PM. He knows me. Failing that, we'll do what we can to identify and apprehend the woman."

"Can you get to your Prime Minister using other channels?" asked Svi.

"We can try." Just as Neal began to issue orders his mobile rang. He listened and hung up. "They're saying two to three hours to get us there. Weather over the Irish Sea could be a problem."

Max took Adina by the arm and said quietly, "You know more than any of them about suicide bombers and you're the best shot on the team if it comes to that. Your only chance is to take her out, but from a distance for god's sake." He shook his head. "Shit. You don't have any status here. The British forces could turn on you. Neal," Max gestured, "Adina and Aslan need some kind of British papers. If they're in the action, they could get taken out by your own people."

"He's right," said Rik. "And we need to get someone from the armed forces to be with us."

"There's no time at this end. I'll use my credentials to get the troops on side over there. Though, who knows if we can even trust them?" Sofie thought Neal's voice shook with what sounded like panic.

"Max. Keep us updated about the banking issue. Sofie, you, Noah and Terry need to work with Sokolov before we get him to call Mueller again."

Sofie held her breath. Her hands began to feel numb, a sign that she might be hyperventilating. She began to breathe through her nose. When her panic rose further, she took part of a clanazopam. She managed to grit out, "Rik, your arm. You're not ready to be in a gun battle. Wouldn't you be more useful dealing with whatever comes up here?"

He whirled around and glared at her.

Neal intervened. "She's right. You need to be here, coordinating our activities. You'll function as central command. If those women are out there, we could have several attacks today. Focus on getting a bead on Mueller's location, and on sending an anonymous bomb threat through to Belfast. Do anything you can think of to stop the Prime Minister's speech, as will I."

Rik shook his head in frustration at Sofie, who was pulling lip balm out of her purse.

Neal and members of the team departed.

"I can get a bomb threat through to Belfast using a covert communication," said Terry to Noah and Sofie. "Let's craft the wording and figure out where to send it. Probably, multiple people. The Prime Minister's wife, if we have to."

Max took the tube, the fastest route at this time of day, to Barron's Bank and was rushed up to the top floor by security. It was 8:15 a.m.

Henry Maplethorpe met him at the elevator. "The President's

waiting." He pulled Max into George Parkinson's opulent office, which stretched across the long rectangular side of the building. Six men and one woman were arguing with each other at a round table to the far right of the room. After terse introductions, Max was asked to assure total confidentiality in writing. He did so knowing he could not acknowledge that a covert team was already aware of the assault on the Royal Barron and its main competitors.

For Max's sake, Parkinson quickly summarized the size of the withdrawals overnight. "What are our options?"

"We must conclude that you're under deliberate attack. At this point, identification of the source must be set aside so that we can focus all of our efforts on mitigation."

"If it's one of our competitors who's responsible, we do need to know."

"As you may or may not be aware," said Max, turning the rest of the group, "Henry Maplethorpe asked me to look into some odd occurrences. I had a breakthrough a few hours ago," Max lied. "I have some level of certainty that your competitors are not the perpetrators but very possibly, fellow victims."

As Max's statement sunk in, the President urged him to continue.

"To state the obvious, this sudden depletion of assets means that your reserves may be insufficient to cover any additional withdrawals. Should these facts become known, and were there a run on your bank you would be facing default, insolvency and bankruptcy."

This simple statement of fact caused one senior executive to run to the loo, another to wipe copious sweat from his brow, and the woman to unleash an impressive chain of epithets.

"We are *not* insolvent," said Parkinson. "Yes, we're depleted, but we can stagger through this."

"We must prepare for the worst, however," argued Max. "Should word get out, and it may well if the attacker wants it to, panic will set in. Each of you knows what happens if there's even the perception that you're not viable. Public panic based on false rumours has brought many a bank down."

If ever a silence were deafening, it was now. "You must be ready within the next hour, by the time the doors open, to refute any claims of insolvency should they come. Someone within your inner circle needs to pull together a smart series of communications for the media. That needs to happen now. You," Max turned to the President, "will need to be calm and convincing that the Bank will go on for years. Branch managers across the country will need to be given statements to release. In addition, you must use back channels to discuss the problem with Rupert Gage at the Bank of England. The last thing he can want is for panic to set in across the United Kingdom and abroad."

"Rupert Gage is an arrogant son of a bitch. I wouldn't count on him for any favours."

"He is obliged, however, to do his job, which is to stabilize a situation such as this," countered Max. "Let me posit to you again, that, if you're under attack, your competitors may also be. One or two of you should use whatever pretence to meet up this morning. Are they available? Do they appear to be under stress? If so, the problem becomes one well beyond that of your bank. It becomes a crime at which point MI5 would need to be brought in on, among others."

"You, Jack, and Irene, do what Max suggests with Lloyds and RBS," instructed the President.

Max nodded. "The next item. For now, come up with a limit on how much cash can be withdrawn by any one client. At some point, you may have to discontinue withdrawals entirely while you're doing what you can to obtain support from the Bank of England or other sources. Given the panic that could ensue, we need to devise a plan immediately for security if there is a run. Under those circumstances, you would need to close the doors of your branches across the country and abroad. Do you have a contingency plan for an occurrence such as this?"

The President looked down the table. "Not one this bad."

"Right Let's identify two people here who will identify a top-flight security firm with reach throughout the country and, ideally, abroad, who can be prepared to dispatch its people at a moment's notice. You'll also need to be prepared to bring the Met and police around the U.K. into the picture. The last thing you want is for violence to erupt. If it does, you need to have alerted the police to the possibility of issues, even without telling the exact reason."

"What can you do to help us while we're implementing your recommendations?" asked Parkinson.

"Let me assure you that I'm going to track whoever is instigating this assault. I will be trying to identify them and halt their progress. I must warn you that we cannot rule out the possibility that someone within the Bank of England may be complicit. So, tread carefully there. Let's hope it isn't Gage. If he doesn't respond immediately and appropriately, as he should, you must let me know. I will also need to be informed if your sources at other banks are revealing a similar plight to the one you are facing."

"Turn on the BBC 1," yelled the woman at the end of the table who'd been looking at her phone.

The BBC has received an unconfirmed report that Britain's four major banks have depleted their reserves to unprecedented, dangerous lows. Normally, it would be our policy to withhold this report until we could obtain an independent confirmation. However, under the circumstances, we cannot ignore the fact that this report has spread across the nation and throughout the world on social media. RBS, Lloyds, Barron's and Barclay's may be in a dire financial situation. We bring in our financial expert to consider the fallout of..."

"I don't care how you do it, but get security to all of your branches, now. Inform the police of what is about to happen." Turning to the President, Max said, "Call your competitors and come up with a statement of solidarity that these claims are false. Get Gage involved. All of this has to happen immediately. Use me, if necessary, as a banking expert, to refute the claims. I need to return to my office here to do what I can to help you."

Mid-Morning, May 4, 2019, Belfast, Northern Ireland

Rania stood in the line to go through security along with others who wanted to be in the Parliamentary gallery. She looked around her at those who would soon be dead, the three young women, probably sisters, a middle-aged couple and a large school group, all wearing their plaid uniforms. Unfortunate timing for them, she thought remotely. When she reached the long bench, she placed her loose-fitting coat and purse on it, and showed her identification papers.

"Why are you here? What is your interest?" asked the official.

"I am doing a university course in the law, and I thought it would be helpful to have an authentic experience of parliament at work."

She passed through the x-ray machine and waited for her scant possessions. A military man on the other side waved his head signalling her to follow him. Good. Just as Marta had said would happen. He led her up into a small room and unlocked the door to a storage closet. She now had what she would need. She saw him staring down at her and she nodded back at him. She was ready. Her coat finally closed over the package she was carrying. He led her to the gallery, where a person in the front row stood up and left the seat for her. Thirty minutes to pray. She closed her eyes.

Neal, Adina and Aslan rushed to the entrance of the Parliament building. It was 11:05 a.m. Showing his credentials, Neal indicated the urgency of his concern to the guard, who waved over a military guard.

"We have every reason to believe that the Prime Minister is going to be attacked at any moment," Neal said, desperation ringing in his voice.

"Stay here," instructed the military officer, leaving Neal and the team fuming.

While Neal became increasingly agitated, Adina scanned the area. "Neal," she said pointing, "Whatever happens, we need to get the feed from those cameras." There was nothing she could do except observe events as they unfolded. Two minutes, and no sign of the officer.

Just as she thought Neal was going to be arrested for trying to barge through the barriers, the building shook and glass shattered. Everyone in the anteroom was thrown to the ground. Seconds, perhaps minutes, passed.

Neal's ears were ringing as he tried to stand. He saw both Aslan and Adina stir and move towards him. "Are you all right?" he asked and received tentative nods.

"The Prime Minister. He's dead!" shouted a man who staggered out of the gaping hole created by the blast.

"This is a fucking cock-up. How did she get through security?"

Adina knew immediately. "They had someone on the inside."

"How? Who?" Neal was struggling to collect his thoughts.

"We've seen it over and over again in Israel. The military or security can bring in weapons if it appears to be part of the protection plan."

"Axworthy made it happen," Neal said flatly.

"Yes."

Aslan had his phone out and was taking video of the scene.

"Let's get back to the 'copter'," shouted Neal amid the chaos. "We could be targets if the guard who saw my credentials was part of Der Kreis and decides to find out how much we know."

"We must obtain the camera feed, if it survived," reiterated Adina.

"I'll arrange to get it."

Late Morning, May 4, 2019, London, England

Hana made her way through security, accepting that she must have a photograph taken in order to enter the Houses of Parliament in the Palace of Westminster. She rejoiced that her last moments as a martyr on this earth would be seen by Agnes and her family.

She recognized the officer immediately from the insignia he wore. She looked at the special watch she'd been given. Twenty to thirty minutes.

Late Morning, May 4, 2019, Edinburgh, Scotland

She'd hated leaving Manchester. She wished that her mission were more important. She spat as she passed by Holyrood Park and the Palace, which, apparently, was the official residence of the Queen while she was in Scotland. She reached the Scottish Parliament and accepted the brisk search of her possessions and her body.

Once seated, she thought of her brother and the glorious reunion that they would have in mere moments.

Late Morning, May 4, 2019, London, England

Fatima arrived at the Tower Hill Underground Station and carried her cursed baby up the stairs. She made her way to the Tower of London entrance. The baby was sedated, thanks be to *Allah*. As she had prayed, the security check caused no delays. One of the Yeoman Warders brought her to a military officer who led her to her final destination.

Mid-Afternoon, May 4, 2019, London, England

Sofie fought the urge to take another half a clonazepam as she watched the scenes of horror unfold. They've won, she thought.

> *What we are witnessing is unprecedented in the recorded history of our country. In the space of four hours, our Prime Minister, Deputy Prime Minister and one of the Queen's most beloved great nephews have been killed along with hundreds of others in strikes on the most sacred bastions of our democracy, the Parliaments of England, Scotland and Ireland. The Crown Jewels, profound symbols of our monarchy, have also been obliterated for all time. Preliminary reports indicate that these attacks were coordinated by Islamic terrorists. The rumours of bank insolvencies we reported this morning have caused mass panic on the streets. We're awaiting a statement from the Bank of England. We take you to our correspondents around the country."*

The feed from the Belfast disaster had just come in. Rik, Svi, Max and Noah were scanning it.

"Did you see that? The woman walks through security clean!" exclaimed Noah.

"Zoom in!" instructed Rik.

"On what?" demanded Noah.

"Those two in uniform."

"You're wasting time. Your goddamn country is imploding while we twiddle our thumbs," Noah almost shouted. He'd seen his own men die in combat but at least he'd been a part of the fight. He wanted to punch his fist through the walls.

Hélène placed her elbows on the table and her hands over her eyes, feeling the full weight of condemnation of her mother, who had transferred to her the responsibility of exposing this hateful enterprise, so many years ago.

"Zoom in on the left arm of the sergeant who escorted our bomber," Rik repeated.

"I see it," Sofie exclaimed. "The orange patch. Oh my god. It's the Der Kreis insignia."

"Shhh. Listen."

> *In the wake of the panic that has rocked the country, troops have been dispatched by our top military official. Air transport in and out of the country has been suspended until further notice. There is no spokesperson for government in the aftermath of the assassination of our leaders. We expect an announcement shortly. Please, hold for a moment. Air Chief Marshall Axworthy is about to make a statement.*

At that moment, Neal, Adina and Aslan, dishevelled and in pain, entered the room and motioned others to remain in their seats as they stared at the monitor.

> *We are invoking martial law. Every citizen or visitor is asked to return to your domicile so that we can restore order. A curfew will be established such that anyone who is on the street between 8:00 pm. and 8:00 a.m. without authorization will be arrested and brought before a military tribunal. Resistance will be met with force. We will now assume control over all communications to our citizens until further notice. Stay calm. The country is safe. Please listen for further instructions.*

CHAPTER 30

Night, May 4, 2019, London, England

They'd failed, miserably. *Der Kreis* held power over the entire United Kingdom. Rik held his head in his hands. The crimes, the carnage, the betrayal. He steeled himself. They must never give up, must be prepared to fight to the death. "The next twenty-four hours are going to be critical. They may have power, but it's not solidified or codified. We must think, focus, as never before."

Neal nodded. "We should concentrate on finding the location of Mueller using Sokolov as bait. If we can capture him…"

"Yes. But Mueller and *Der Kreis* have control now. What other options?"

"We take out Axworthy, if we can find him," said Max, disconsolately. "But the streets are clogged with troops and military vehicles. How do we do that?"

Rik threw out his hand, demanding quiet. "Neal," he said tensely, you revealed who you were to the soldier in Belfast. *Der Kreis* is going to come after you. The first place they'll come is here. We need to get you out." He paled as he realized that the entire team, and Sofie in particular, were also in grave danger of being seized by *Der Kreis*.

Rik looked at Neal. "We need to find somewhere we can hide while we work out what to do next."

Is this dark office in the basement of MI6 what I will remember as where I gave up the last vestige of hope, wondered Sofie. She fell into a deep depression that she knew was shared by all in the room. Heavy silence permeated the room.

All of a sudden, Sofie blurted out a question.

Rik and Neal looked at each other and then back at Sofie. Confusion slowly turned to clarity. "That's it. That's it!"

The team gave themselves thirty minutes to work out the complex plan.

Early morning, May 5, 2019, London, England

Max and Adina went up the lift to the ground floor of MI6 and found what they were looking for. "Captain?" They motioned to a military officer posted by the front door who was wearing an orange patch on his left arm. "We have a security problem in the basement. We urgently need help."

Heavily armed, the officer moved in front of them and descended the stairs. Max exerted all of his force to disarm him while Adina applied a chokehold that brought the soldier to the floor, unconscious. They dragged him to Neal's office where members of the team secured him. Again, Max and Adina reached the ground floor and walked, this time, to a second entrance that was being guarded and repeated the process.

While Rik and Max donned the uniforms and the submachine guns, Sofie procured from Hélène the precious cargo she would be responsible for.

"Let's go," said Rik to Neal, Max and Sofie. It was 1:30 a.m.

Adina touched Max's arm and he looked down at her. "Be careful. Be smart," she said.

Years of animosity dissolved. "*Ken*. You, too."

Rik, in his soldier's garb, held Sofie, while Max was rough with Neal. They exited the main door and descended the steps, passed through a gate out into a temporary parking area. It was dark and eerily silent. "Lieutenant," barked Rik. "We'll need the vehicle to transport these two."

"Yes, sir." They saluted.

As they crossed the Chelsea Street Bridge and headed west along the Chelsea Embankment, Sofie became increasingly frightened at the heavy military scene. *One wrong move and we could be dead.* She shivered.

Fifteen minutes later, they arrived at Rik's parents' home. Max and Rik alighted and again took Neal and Sofie by the arm, frog-marching them to the door. It opened and they quickly entered.

"It's time to tell me what this is all about," ordered Roger Whitford. Margaret paled and looked appalled to see her son armed and in uniform.

"We have urgent need for your help," said Neal. "I'm terribly sorry but what we have to say is classified. Is there a place we can speak privately, Mr. Whitford?"

"Who are you?"

"Mum, Dad, this is Neal Havers, the head of MI6. And this is Max Becker, a colleague of mine over the years. We've had to wear this gear to get here when the city's under a curfew."

"Sofie. Are you a part of all of this?" asked Margaret, her hand shaking as she touched Sofie's arm.

"I'm afraid so."

"We haven't much time, Mr. Whitford. Where can we talk in confidence?"

"I'll make tea," said Margaret drawing a grateful acknowledgement for her decorum under pressure from Sofie, as the four followed Rik's father into his study.

"Again, we haven't much time, Mr. Whitford, so I'm going to begin. Everything I have to say cannot be repeated. Is that understood?"

He nodded. "Call me Roger," he ordered, belligerently. "Who are you to my son?"

"Neal recruited me out of university. I've been working for MI6 ever since then. Dad, It's been hell not to be able to tell you and Mum the truth. It's a huge relief to let you finally know." Rik stopped and realized how enormous a moment this was. Tears threatened. He couldn't speak.

"MI6. You? My god."

"Mr. Whitford. Roger. Please. We haven't a minute to waste. Here's the situation. Roughly three weeks ago, Sofie, here, overhead the discussion of a plot to undertake a coup somewhere in Europe. She brought this information to us. The perpetrators of the plot are members of a secret organization formed at the end of World War II, called *Der Kreis Im Quadrat*. We've determined that the United Kingdom is their target."

"This is preposterous," Roger scoffed.

Max intervened, impatience showing in his voice. "Mr. Whitford. I'm with a foreign intelligence service. We became involved because, among others, we have papers in our archives that confirm the existence of this powerful organization. And because we discovered recently that they have infiltrated us."

"I…" Roger looked at his son in a military uniform and paused.

Neal continued. "We've identified several members of the organization, not without difficulty and danger. What we've been able to determine is that Marvin Axworthy, the head of our country's military, is one of its members. He is now in charge. The *coup* has already taken place, as you can see out your window. Look at the orange patch on this uniform." Neal poked at Rik's shoulder. "That is *Der Kreis'* insignia. We think that those wearing it are a secret military force of *Der Kreis* within our army."

Roger looked at it in horrified fascination. "But the assassinations and the banks' collapse warranted - no, it demanded - martial law."

"Except that it was *Der Kreis* that funded and planned these very assassinations and engineered the bank crises. Again, we have unquestionable proof."

"Good god. If that's true, then…"

"We're out of options, Mr. Whitford. Roger. Here is what we need from you." As Neal talked, his father steeled and, before his eyes, became more alive than Rik had seen him in years.

Margaret knocked on the door.

Sofie took the tray from her with thanks. Alone, after serving the men she retreated to the corner. Panic. Oh, no. She closed her eyes. In, out, calmer, deeper, calmer, deeper, she repeated over and over to herself. And then she thought of Rik, solid, devoted, heroic.

It took Roger over two hours to accomplish what had been asked of him. He was gratified that his distinguished career as a lawyer, parliamentarian and ultimately, cabinet minister, meant he had friends in hallowed circles.

Three hours later, the team, now expanded to include Rik's father, departed. A worried Margaret hugged her husband at the door and made a helpless gesture towards her heavily armed son.

"We're going to have to brazen this out if we get any questions," Rik instructed Max as they drove.

They pulled up to the imposing gate. A guard wearing the orange insignia squinted into the vehicle. "You have not been granted a pass. Take one move forward and you will be detained."

"Stand down. We have urgent business. We've been ordered to bring these two here for a meeting of some kind. They're expecting us."

He made a quick call, appeared satisfied and let them pass.

Sofie stared in wonder as she was escorted through the Quadrangle and the front entrance into the alternative reality that was Buckingham Palace. Roger Whitford had come through. He was that important? Whatever he'd said, whoever he'd called, they'd listened. And here they were.

They were led up the Grand staircase into a green drawing room.

"Mr Whitford and Mr. Havers. You are to come with me," said an armed member of the Palace guard. "The Queen will see Mr. Whitford, who requested this Audience. She will also require the presence of Mr. Havers."

As Sofie, Rik and Max stood by, the remaining guards, three in number, gestured that Rik and Max should surrender their weapons. They did so with the greatest of reluctance. A tense silence began.

What could be happening? Why was it taking so long? Could the Queen be part of *Der Kreis*? Or perhaps she supported martial law? Surely not. Sofie eyed the rifle trained at them. She began to shift her weight from side to side, felt her agitation rising to alarm.

Suddenly, the door opened. The Queen entered, followed by Neal and Roger. Rik and Max bowed, while Sofie gave her awkward impression of a curtsy. The Duke appeared behind the Queen.

Even at this early hour, she looked perfectly elegant, looked like the Queen.

She addressed the entire group. "Mr. Havers has just explained to me the reason for Mr. Whitford's extraordinary request for this Audience. Now, Mr. Havers, please introduce me to your colleagues."

Rik intervened. "I am Rik Whitford. Your Majesty, may I approach?" He leaned over her. "We have concern for your safety, Ma'am. We need to be sure that your guard has not been infiltrated. At the very least, could you instruct all but two of them to leave, and ask the others to return our rifles? My colleagues and I must be able to protect you."

Not for a moment did she lose her composure marvelled Rik as he watched her consider his request.

"Very well," she said quietly.

Rik walked over to Max and they conferred. Max moved slightly towards one of the guards, as Rik moved towards another.

The tension continued to mount within Sofie.

The Queen turned to the guards. "Two of you, please stand outside the door." She gestured to the remaining guards. "Please return the weapons to these two men, immediately."

They did so without question. Rik and Max exchanged relieved glances.

"Now, you may introduce me, Mr. Havers, to all those present."

A moment later, the Queen beckoned Sofie to approach. "You may show me the papers Mr. Havers described to me."

Shaking, Sofie pulled out the timeworn pages that Anna had written so many years ago.

The Queen put on her glasses and read for two minutes. She looked up. "I understand from Mr. Havers that it is your uncle who is the so-called *Hochmeister* of this *Der Kreis*?"

"I'm afraid so, Your Majesty," replied Sofie, closing her eyes.

"I further understand that it was you who knew who the Commander-in-Chief of the armed forces is here in Britain."

Sofie lifted her head and nodded. "Yes, Your Majesty. I must have learned it in school in Canada."

"Very well," she said smartly. She looked at Neal. "You've prepared something for me?"

"I have, Your Majesty. May I first make a call to GCHQ? We'll need them to support us."

"Yes. Do so. I will look after the matters we've discussed."

The Queen left the room. Five minutes later she returned. "My Private Secretary is making the call. While we wait for a response, let me review what you've prepared."

Sofie marvelled at the calm the Queen exuded despite the terrible burden she would need to carry over the next several hours. She shifted from one foot to the other just as the Queen looked at her.

"You must all sit. Let me see if we can get some tea and coffee in here."

Ten minutes later, the Queen received a call. "He'll be here in one hour."

"Your Majesty. May we summon the most trusted among Palace Guard now? We must ensure our success and, above all, your safety."

Morning, May 5, 2019, London, England

Marvin Axworthy was elated. Neal Havers, a very important loose end, had apparently been led out of the River House handcuffed. Once he was finished here, he'd see to the interrogation himself.

He was now in charge of the Empire. As he strode across the Quadrangle at Buckingham Palace receiving the salutes of his soldiers, he thought of his hero, Napoleon. No bowing and scraping to this obsolete institution, as they would soon know.

When he reached the top of the stairs, he was instructed to enter a room on the right. "Your soldiers must wait out here. This is a private Audience with the Queen."

Even better, he thought. "Very well."

The doors were opened for him. Immediately, he was overtaken by the opulence, the splendour and the utter solemnity of the occasion. He stepped in and heard the doors close behind him. The Queen and the Prince stood some forty paces in front of him. Involuntarily Axworthy bowed his head down. Suddenly, he was grabbed from behind. A handkerchief covered his mouth.

"Get him to the chair." Rik and Max watched as two of the Palace Guard bound him up and gagged him with a cloth.

Sofie put her hands over her mouth.

The Queen looked on dispassionately. "He deserves, and will receive much worse for his treason."

"Your Majesty, may I ask that these members of the Guard remain?" asked Rik.

"Why?"

"May I approach?"

The Queen nodded.

Rik approached. "We cannot afford to take the chance that one word of what has happened escapes this room. The Realm, and your safety, hang in the balance," he whispered.

"Very well," she said quietly. "Is GCHQ ready?"

Rik made a call. "Terry? Did you manage it?"

"Yes, though it wasn't easy and I don't know how long we have. Count on one or two minutes only."

"It will have to do. We'll be sending you the feed as soon as it's complete, but don't broadcast it until Neal or I give permission to proceed. One more thing. You're going to have to multi-task. We have Axworthy's mobile. We're hoping he and Mueller have communicated at some point over the last few days. If we call these numbers, can you trace them?"

There was a brief silence as Terry considered his answer. "Give me ten minutes. So we're to do the trace and then the broadcast?"

"Correct," said Rik. "We have to locate Mueller before he knows what's happened to Axworthy. It's our only chance of ending this nightmare."

"Right," said Terry. When you're ready, call the number I'm going to give you. Use Axworthy's mobile. Wait until I answer. Once you've done that, wait a few minutes."

Rik did as instructed and then asked, "Your Majesty. While you record your message, may we use another room here to see if we can locate Mueller?"

"Take two of the Palace Guard with you, and ask the other two to come back in," she instructed.

Roger had remained sitting quietly, away from the action, studying the son he'd never understood. He remembered what he'd said a couple nights ago at the dining room table and felt tears well in his eyes. He wiped them away quickly.

"Axworthy brought a couple of soldiers with him. They're out in the corridor waiting for him to exit, Your Majesty."

"I think we may need to put them alongside Mueller. We can show him and them wearing the orange insignia," blurted Max, ignoring any protocol.

Max looked at Neal and then the Queen who stared at Max and then nodded. "Try not to break anything," she said wryly, immediately allaying the tension in the room.

Sofie found a corner and shivered. One of the Palace Guards stood behind the doors along with Max and Rik. Another guard opened the door and gestured for Axworthy's two soldiers to enter. As soon as they crossed the threshold, Rik pointed his weapon and said with lethal intent. "Place your weapons on the floor. Do it slowly."

The two soldiers looked at each other, as if considering the command.

"Do it now, or I'll shoot out your kneecaps."

Sofie watched wide-eyed as this violent version of Rik took charge.

As Max picked up the weapons, Rik waved his rifle.

"Put your hands behind your back." Once their hands were bound, he instructed them to sit on the floor against the wall, alongside Axworthy.

"How long have you been with *Der Kreis*?" spat out Rik.

"*Der Kreis*?"

"When were you told to wear that insignia?"

"When we received special training."

"Special training for what?"

"For martial law."

Max drew Rik aside. "Let's not forget that some of these guys armed those women terrorists. I don't buy the innocent act."

"How many are there of you?"

"I'm not sure."

"Sit tight. Soon, you're going to be famous."

Rik looked at Sofie who was at her lip balm again. He walked over to her and she seemed to shrink before him.

He shifted his rifle away from her as best he could. "I guess you're not going to forget this day any time soon."

She stared back mutely.

"Do you want to come into the next room with us while we see if we can raise your uncle?"

Her spine straightened. She stood up and followed him, ensuring that she bowed slightly to the Queen, who didn't notice the courtesy so intent was she on reading and revising the text before her.

Axworthy had two mobiles, one that he used to communicate to his military and defence contacts. The other showed repeated calls to only four different numbers.

Rik called Terry using Axworthy's mobile. "How do we know if these are VPN numbers?"

"Read them to me. Hmm... They may all be encrypted. But we've come a long way here at GCHQ."

How are we going to do this, wondered Rik. "Let's get Noah on the line. While we're calling from Axworthy's mobile, he can get Sokolov to call whatever number he has for Mueller. That doubles our chances of Mueller picking up and you getting his position."

"You and Noah call the numbers now, Rik," said Terry.

"Here goes," muttered Rik.

Morning, May 5, 2019, Periphery of London, England

"I think this occasion calls for champagne." Karl Mueller hadn't slept at all, so excited was he with the outcome of years of planning.

As he poured three glasses, he looked fondly at Marta and Manfred. "To *Der Kreis*, to *Recht und Macht* and to Axworthy. He executed perfectly. And I just received confirmation that Russia has invaded Lithuania, as planned. With everyone's attention focused on what's happening to Britain, the EU and NATO will be slow to act if it does at all. The Russian is impressed with our success. He's promised us his on-going support for our future actions."

"I'm so happy for you, for all of us. What will we do today?" asked Marta, as she sipped the *Veuve Cliquot*. "We should be able to go into London to see everything for ourselves, shouldn't we?"

"We can and we will. We'll take a drive and then meet with Marvin and Rupert. The second order of business will be to find out what Havers knows about us."

Karl's mobile rang. "Ah, speak of the devil. Marvin, where are you? We were just raising a toast to you."

There was a crackling sound and a far-away voice saying, "Damn...hold on. I dropped the phone..." Loud noise and interference continued.

"Hello? Hello! Marvin. I can't hear you."

Then the line went dead. Karl held it out from him with a frown. "That was odd. We got cut off."

His other mobile rang. Karl picked it up. Damn it. It wasn't Marvin. It was fucking Sokolov. "Get off this line you fool," shouted Karl, and hung up, annoyed that that cretin should interrupt this special day. He'd deal with him later.

The three of them watched the live shots of London and other cities across the United Kingdom. Few people were on the streets.

After ten minutes, Karl called Marvin's number. It rang repeatedly. What was he doing?

"Let's be ready to go into London when Marvin calls back."

Morning, May 5, 2019, London, England

"We've got him! He's in Meadvale, near Gatwick. I'm texting you the address," shouted Terry over the line to Rik.

He glanced at Sofie who no longer looked timid. Rather she stood up and put her hands on her hips.

As he identified the location on his mobile, Rik looked at Neal. "There's a private airfield at Redhill within a few kilometres of his location. I suspect that if he needed to do a runner he'd head there."

The three of them rushed back into the room. The Queen sat looking out the window. It was now light. She turned.

"We know where he is, Your Majesty." Rik's mind was racing. "We need armed troops, perhaps a dozen or more. I can use this uniform and my rank to gather a collection of troops together who aren't wearing the insignia." He looked out the window. "I'll grab them from down there, whether or not they're trained for this sort of thing," he pondered aloud. "To get him, we're going to need a helicopter as soon as possible."

She picked up the elegant telephone. "I need one, no, two of the larger helicopters here within the next thirty minutes." She hung up. "Will that do?"

"Very much so. Thank you," said Neal.

"What about transportation from Redhill?" asked Max.

Again, the Queen picked up the telephone. "Arrange for eight private cars to be at Redhill Aerodrome within the hour."

Rik turned to Max. "Let's get Adina and Noah here. They're trained for combat. Your Majesty, could you write two identical notes so that Max and I can show the soldiers we're empowered by you?"

Without responding, she walked to a small table and pulled out a pen. "Here they are. I'm going to record my broadcast now. You may all go to the next room now to complete your plans."

"Yes, Your Majesty. I suggest that we broadcast your message the moment we're in place at Meadvale. May I also ask that the four Palace Guards remain here to guard you? Is there a secure place within the Palace that you could remain while we see what the fallout of your broadcast is?"

"Leave those matters to me. God speed, Mr. Whitford."

The team was ushered out of the Palace to the helicopters. There, waiting, were Noah and Adina. Rik, still wearing the orange insignia that conferred him with power over the troops, hustled fourteen soldiers without badges over to the helicopters. "We'll be giving you your orders once we're in the air," he shouted.

When Sofie moved towards the door, Rik stopped her. "No way. You're a civilian. It's too dangerous. And you could get in the way."

"I can't believe you just said that. After all we've been through! Let me point out that I'm the only one here who can instantly recognize my uncle. I'm the only one here who introduced you to *Der Kreis*. I put my life on the line to get Sokolov. Finally, might I add that I can shoot, if necessary?"

The fate of his country lay heavy on his shoulders. "You're going to have to wear a vest, and we'll get you a pistol. Damn it, Sofie. I just want you safe." He felt a tap on his shoulder and turned around.

It was Roger. "Son, get this job done and come home." He held out his hand and Rik took it.

"Thanks, Dad. We couldn't have pulled off any of this mission without you. Give my love to Mum." Once in the cockpit, he pulled the Der Kreis badge off. He motioned with his hands over at Max to do the same.

Forty-five minutes later, they were in Meadvale.

"Adina and Noah. Get a look at the house and report back," instructed Rik.

"Soldiers, attention!"

"We are under orders from the Queen, your Commander-in-Chief, to apprehend a group of people who are hiding in a house nearby. Each one of these people has committed crimes against this country, including the murder of our Prime Minister and Deputy Prime Minister. They'll put up a fight. Are you up to this task?"

"Yes, sir," was the resounding response.

Adina and Max returned. "It's an ordinary-looking bungalow. There's some kind of park or forest behind it. A Mercedes is sitting out front. No guards. I guess they don't want to draw attention to themselves."

Max, Noah, Adina and he talked over the plan. Sofie stayed quiet.

Rik made the call to Terry. "Broadcast the Queen's message in exactly ten minutes."

Six of the troops followed Max and Adina and stationed themselves across the street from the house. Six others went with Rik and Noah to the forest, at the back of the house. Sofie trailed behind them. The rest of the soldiers were left to ensure that neighbours stayed out of the action.

"Those of you with mobiles, tune into BBC, immediately!"

> *"Today, I speak to you, not only as your Queen, but as the Commander-in-Chief of the Armed Forces across our United Kingdom. These days have seen the loss of our Prime Minister and Deputy Prime Minister, of a beloved family member of mine, as well as numerous citizens. It's caused many of you to worry about the status of our banks and your future. What you could not know is that these crises were brought about deliberately by a secret group attempting a coup d'etat. One of its chief members has been apprehended. As you can see, he is sitting here with me and is the former Chief Air Marshall of our forces, Marvin Axworthy.*
>
> *Now, I am speaking directly to my troops, as your Commander-in Chief. Notice the orange insignia on Axworthy's uniform and on those of his guards. That is the symbol of this secret society. As your Commander in Chief, I am ordering all troops who are wearing this insignia, whether in Ireland, Scotland, Wales or England, to surrender, to lay down your arms,*

immediately. You will be held until we can determine your futures. You who are not wearing this insignia are ordered to arrest these men or women immediately. Should they resist, you will use force to bring them to justice. In the meantime, I'm instructing all citizens to stay indoors while our troops are apprehending the criminals who have attempted to take over our democracy. There will be other arrests coming shortly. One last and very important matter. There is no bank crisis. It was a false rumour spread by this group that took hold and caused sufficient panic to enable Axworthy and his group to justify martial law, to seize power. The Bank of England will affirm the stability of our banks shortly. Please, be safe. And be proud of our troops who are protecting us in our time of need. God bless you all.

The troops looked at Rik's shoulder, confusion in their eyes.

"Ah. Yes. I had to wear the red insignia in order to have the power to order you to take part in this mission. It was my colleagues and I who met with the Queen and who drew Axworthy to Buckingham Palace, where we disarmed and bound him." Rik held out the authorization letter. "Her Majesty arranged the helicopters for us from the Palace as you well know. I've taken that detestable insignia off now so that we can all act as one to capture the people who planned this *coup*. Are we ready?"

"Yes, sir."

Rik used his mobile. "Any sign of them leaving?"

"Nothing. We can't afford for another fucking helicopter to arrive and take them away. Let's give them three minutes and then we'll attack from the front. That'll force them out towards you."

"Right. Don't get any holes in you, or Adina."

Precisely three minutes later, Max and his group began their assault, yelling and spraying gunfire. "Surrender, now, Mueller. We know you're in there."

They rammed down the door. "No one's here! Can you see them going out the back?"

"No! Keep looking in there."

Max raced to the basement. "Fuck. There's some kind of tunnel they've built. It's been blocked off. It looks like it's going right under where you are."

Rik turned to look back to the forest. It was thick and leafy. The tunnel could open up anywhere and he simply didn't have the manpower to cover every bush. Off in the distance, he heard a thwack thwack thwack sound growing louder. "Run!" He pointed. "They're trying to get to a helicopter." And then a horrific thought struck him. "Max, Adina! Get out of there, now. They're not going to leave the house intact." Thirty seconds later, he saw Max all but carry Adina out, hurtling to the other side of a small berm.

Moments later, a deafening explosion shook the ground. Metal and burning wood showered down.

Rik threw himself onto Sofie, shielding her. Thirty seconds might have passed. "Are you all right?" he shouted into her ear.

"Yes. Let me up. Hurry. They're getting away." Sofie had never felt more desperate. "We need to get him."

He pulled her up. The rest of the troops were slowly standing, though two appeared to be labouring.

Rik swore. Sofie was sprinting ahead of the troops who were weighed down by their equipment.

Faster, faster, she chanted to herself, her long legs reaching, part panic, part drive. She darted through the trees, aiming for the sound of the helicopter. Suddenly, out of the corner of her eye, she spotted movement. It was her uncle. She was sure. Further off to the left Marta was in a flat out sprint followed by what must be her father, Manfred, who was falling behind. They hadn't seen her yet. Instinctively, she planted herself, took aim and fired off three rounds. She slid behind a tree. The soldiers were running by her now. Was Rik one of them?

Rik raced past Mueller who was on the ground, writhing in pain. "Stay with him," he yelled to two of the troops.

Marta had never run faster. She must leave behind her beloved Karl. He would demand that she escape. Bullets passed all around her. She began to weave back and forth. More bullets. Where was her father? Five more metres. She dove into the hold of the helicopter and turned around. Her father reached up, terror in his eyes.

He fell to the ground, killed before her very eyes. Survival was paramount. She felt stings in her left arm and leg. "Get us out of here," she screeched in agony.

The team sprayed the skies but the helicopter stayed up and disappeared into the distance.

Rik called Neal. "Can you track the helo? I need to get back to Mueller."

Sofie bent over her uncle, out of breath.

"You! You bitch," he bleated, blood pouring from his mouth.

Rik ran and pulled Sofie aside. "Treat him! He needs to be kept alive," he screamed at one of the troops.

"I was aiming for his legs," cried Sofie.

"He got hit multiple times. It wasn't you."

"We won." Mueller's mouth twisted in a macabre smile that froze as he died.

"What did he say? Did you hear what I heard?" demanded Rik.

"He said *he* won. But I'd say we've had a pretty good day." A humming noise sounded in her head and she wondered if she was going to faint. Her only relative in the world was now dead. She stooped and sat on the hard ground.

Relieved and exhausted Rik let himself fall beside her. "This time yesterday..." He looked over at Sofie. "If you hadn't had your brainwave about the Queen, I'm not sure where we'd be." His blue eyes turned to steel. He grabbed her by the shoulders and pulled her towards him. He stared straight into her hazel eyes. "When you shot Karl, did Marta see you?"

"Umm. I...Let me think. I took the shots and...I'm sure I didn't even see him go down. I jumped behind a tree. So, no, I don't think she could have seen me. She was running away with her back to me."

"For as long as she's out there, we need to make sure no one is aware of the part we played in this *Der Kreis* saga. Who knows how many are still out there, who'll want revenge for what we've managed to do."

Sofie chilled at the thought of Marta coming after her. "I wonder if the Queen is aware that our roles must be kept confidential."

"We'll make sure."

Tears began to down her cheeks.

"Are you hurt?" Rik demanded as he gently took off her helmet and inspected her.

"No. At least I don't think so." She felt numb, relieved, shaken and grateful to be alive. If ever she'd earned the right to have a meltdown it was now. But she felt no panic. Wasn't that amazing? She smiled through her tears. "I just fine. What about the others?"

"Let's find out." He pulled her back up and looked around. Max and Adina were sparring. Something normal, he smiled to himself.

Afternoon, May 5, 2019, London, England

Marvin Axworthy never left anything to chance. When allowed to go to the toilet under armed guard, he quickly raised his handcuffed arm to his mouth and used his teeth to take the capsule from the inside of the cuff on his right arm. He died within seconds.

Rupert Gage didn't know whether to run or brazen it out. The moment he heard the Queen's message, he donned his disguise and ran, or, to be more accurate, walked to a little basement flat, six blocks away from his tony townhouse. He could live there on the cache he'd stocked for well over a year. "Mr. Gordon (for Gordon Gekko, of course) Smith" (for Adam Smith, again, of course) would live a quiet life for some time. If his past had taught him anything, it was that he could reinvent himself, better than anyone else he knew could. He had a face that people recognized, now. Curious how money talks, wasn't it?

Afternoon, May 5, 2019, Manchester, England

Six hours ago, Oswald Outerridge had dressed for celebration. His red, white and black bow tie still adorned his corpulent chin. The Queen, of all things. Could there be a worse outcome than being beaten by someone who was over ninety, for god's sake? Sweat stained the front and back of his shirt. Could they identify him? How could he know for sure? Bloody Mueller had regaled him with his glorious future once they'd succeeded. Where was the god damn Hochmeister now?

He packed his most precious possessions and headed for the sea. Nice to have a younger half-sister who happened to be a star sailor – and the only person he'd ever loved.

CHAPTER 31

Morning, May 6, 2019, London, England

Sofie shifted in the sumptuous sheets and slowly rose to consciousness. What time is it? She sat up in a panic, and then, as the memories flooded back in a jumble, she let herself fall back. It was 6:30. She'd slept for twelve hours.

Forty minutes later, dressed in her black-and-white attire, she tiptoed down the staircase. She was ravenous.

"Oomph," she yelped as she ploughed into Mr. Whitfield and felt something hot spill over her right hand.

"Sofie."

"Sorry."

"No worries," he said as he put down his mug, dried his hands and handed her the towel he'd grabbed from the stove. "We thought you wouldn't be up for hours."

We? She peeked behind him and saw both Rik and Margaret sitting around the table, eating what looked like fresh muffins.

All is right with the world, smiled Margaret as she looked at her son and then at a reddening Sofie. Goodness, that poor girl could be awkward, couldn't hide an emotion if her life depended on it. Her smile faded as she recognized the true import of those words. She never wanted to feel the utter helplessness of yesterday when her husband, her son and Sofie had walked out into that hostile war scene.

"You must be hungry. Try one of these! Fresh out of the oven." She forced a happy trill into her voice.

"Thank you, Margaret. They smell wonderful." She walked over to the table, grabbed one and sat down. She tried, unsuccessfully, to bank down her embarrassment as the recollections of last night rushed back to her. After a quick debrief at MI6, they'd been given a military escort to Fulham. Margaret had grabbed her son and hugged him fiercely, and then, her. "Sofie, dear, what you need is a sherry and a long hot bath. Come, dear." In response to that small gesture of kindness, Sofie had surprised herself with a flood of tears. Rik and his father had stared at her, helpless.

"There, there now," Margaret had embraced her as the men had disappeared, letting the rest of her meltdown occur in private. After that, Sofie couldn't remember a thing. She looked down at the table. Bloody hell.

"Ahh, Sofie," ventured Mr. Whitford, "did you know that the Queen wants to meet you again? It isn't every day that someone has an Audience with her two days in a row!"

Rik's throat constricted. He would never, ever, forget last night. When he'd reached the front door, his father had grabbed him before his mother could and had hugged him long and hard. He'd felt like a little child, had let the entire weight of his exhausted body rest. The only thing that had saved him from embarrassing himself had been Sofie's emotional outburst.

"Neal and the team are meeting us whenever we say we're ready." Rik raised his eyebrows in question.

Sofie nodded, noting the sombre look that passed between Margaret and her husband.

Mid-Morning, May 6, 2019, London, England

"First, my government, namely the Queen, would like to meet with you all, later this afternoon."

"I won't bow or curtsy," exclaimed Adina.

"I'm afraid it's a necessary expression of respect, Adina," said

Neal. "Don't forget the courageous role she played…"

"Oh, if I must. I'll think of her as Golda Meir…"

"Now, people, it's time to discuss whether our work as a group is complete." Neal gazed around the table.

Rik began. "We know that we've disrupted *Der Kreis*, but that its membership is wide and deep. Its aim to rid Europe of immigrants may only gain strength as refugees continue to pour in, and terrorist attacks continue. Karl Mueller's chilling last words were `we won'. It's forcing me to question whether *Der Kreis* is planning another attack here."

"We also know that *Der Kreis* has members in Germany's military as well as high up in my government," said Noah. "I'm not comfortable with the thought of waiting until Der Kreis resurfaces there. We need to keep after them."

"I agree," said Sofie. "If we look across Europe, I wonder if *Der Kreis* has been doing the same there as it did here, funding both Islamic terrorists and the far right to cause destabilization and fear."

Rik nodded. "Just look at what happened to Marić in Serbia. And isn't it interesting that Russia invaded Lithuania the moment the coup attempt began here? Yet another country being run by autocrats. What I'm wondering is how we can take on *Der Kreis* by ourselves."

"That's the real question," agreed Max. "All of us have our own jobs, and pretty important ones, at that. If we let others know about the existence of *Der Kreis*, we put ourselves into direct danger and risk sending their members underground."

"Let's table the question as to whether we continue as a group for the moment," said Neal. "There are several actions that we urgently need to undertake to complete our operation. Let's begin with Rupert Gage. He's disappeared, affirming that he's part of Der Kreis and was a key player in the plot to create chaos among our banks. We need to find and interrogate him. We also need to hunt down Tango, the purveyor of false news stories. If we can get hold of these two, we'll be deep into *Der Kreis*."

"The world is soon going to know that the women terrorists were trained in Gaza and that Bashir Fakhoury was complicit. He needs to be arrested and tried for murder," said Svi. "However, I fear such an action will cause further unrest in our part of the world. Will it be up to your country to bring him to justice? If not, who?"

"As the head of MI6, I will make sure that we take the lead, working closely with Israel," Neal responded. "We must also consider what to do with Sokolov. We may be able to use him to infiltrate *Der Kreis*, or, at the very least, bring down some of the Russian trafficking rings. I could run him through MI6 proper, but to do so would mean revealing what we know of *Der Kreis*."

"The manager of the *Banque Cantonarde* must also be part of *Der Kreis*. We must consider him as a target of our interrogation, *n'est pas?*" asked Hélène.

"Yes. I hate to pile on with more loose ends," said Rik. "Jansen. He's undermined several ops and was indirectly responsible for the death of Philippe Lapointe. The moment he finds out that Mueller is dead, he may disappear. Hell. He may already have. I want him arrested and brought here for interrogation. And Milan Marić. We have enough leverage now to demand his release and the restoration of his good name. Then, there's *Geist*, and our own traitor, Miriam. Hell. We can't do all of this."

"I have a meeting in thirty minutes. Let's adjourn for now. Can you all come back here tomorrow morning?" Seeing nods around the table, Neal motioned to Svi and Noah. "Since it is we three who arranged the resources for our little group, it may be useful for us to talk in advance of tomorrow's meeting. Are you free for drinks after Buckingham Palace?" he asked quietly.

Afternoon, May 6, 2019, London, England

"If you're meeting the Queen, you'll wear a skirt or a dress," Margaret said firmly.

"But she's already seen me in–"

"Shhh. Try this on." She handed her the sleeveless black dress and soft bolero-style over jacket she'd asked Sigrid to bring over.

"Margaret, you're pushing me."

"Try it on," she repeated firmly.

"Oh, for heaven's sake. I'll look ridiculous."

"See if these shoes fit," ordered Margaret. This helpless girl was the angel sent to her, one who needed her love.

Two hours later, the entire team entered Buckingham Palace in three blackened vehicles.

"Your Majesty, may I present –" began the Private Secretary.

"Give us privacy," commanded the Queen peremptorily. Once the door was closed, she held out her hand to each person in front of her. "Sit down, please. There have been difficult times during my reign, but none that compare to what we've experienced these past few days. I understand that our Kingdom's debt to you all cannot be acknowledged publicly. However," she said in her clipped manner, "the events of the past several days have been recorded and stored in a safe place for the sake of our history. Your commitment and bravery will not be forgotten."

Rik felt the unreality of this moment, remembered his abject despair less than thirty-six hours ago. Involuntarily, he turned his gaze to Sofie. She looked awkward and uncomfortable. He smiled to himself. She was also stunning in the black dress and some sort of green jewellery that accentuated her eyes. Let her take in this moment. If it hadn't been for her…

"Mr. Bikovsky, Mr. Becker and Miss Kagan, I thank you and Israel on behalf of Great Britain for your extraordinary efforts to help us. Madame Lévy, I read your mother's words, heard of her brave actions and yours. You have my sincere gratitude. Mr. Aliyev and Mr.

Sindegard, thank you for volunteering your assistance. And your role, Mr. Johnson, was critical to the positive outcome of our efforts. I fear we will need to rely on you even more heavily as time passes. Miss McAdam and young Mr. Whitford. We would not have defeated this vile conspiracy but for your discovery of the plot, your formation of this team, and," she smiled, "the enlisting of my involvement."

Rik returned her smile. Sofie nodded solemnly.

"Roger and Neal," she said with fondness.

"You've each worked for decades, contributing to our United Kingdom. Over these recent days, you've saved us from a horrendous fate. For this service, you will be made Knight Commanders. Henceforth, you shall be Sir Roger Whitford and Sir Neal Havers."

The voice of the Queen receded from his hearing and Rik wondered if he was experiencing PTSD. He struggled to return his attention to the room.

It should have been Rik, thought Sofie, fiercely.

He must have felt her gaze, for his head turned and their eyes met. Is she upset with me? No. What he felt was an intense, unnamed emotion emanating from her. He held her gaze, steadily.

Margaret swelled with pride at her son, her husband and this girl who was, who was…who was someone worthy of a great deal more love than the world had offered until now.

Evening, May 6, 2019, London, England

Sigrid and Annie dropped by. Thank god, martial law had ended. "Let's go out to the back garden," Margaret suggested and led the way.

"What a terrible time to be visiting our country, Sofie. You must have an absolutely detestable impression of us. But let me tell you, despite the Queen and her declarations, we need someone strong to get us out of the mess we're in."

"Sigrid," Rik groaned.

Ignoring him, she continued. "It was terribly tragic, all the loss of life. Still. Now we know we've been infiltrated by people who hate us. I'm tired of it and so are my friends." Sigrid looked at her dad for approbation. He looked away.

Sofie could understand Sigrid's point of view. After all the distortions of truth, outright falsehoods and fear mongering amid some very real terrorist acts, had the window of time for understanding and rapprochement disappeared? Perhaps her uncle had won. She picked up a couple of cookies and walked out to the middle of the grass where Annie was holding a small flower to her nose.

"Come, tell me what you smell."

Annie turned and saw inviting hands.

She pointed at Sofie.

"You smell me?" Sofie fleetingly wondered if she was rank.

Annie reached for one of the cookies.

Tickling her, Sofie cried, "Someone's trying to take away my cookie."

Beaming, Rik knelt down, grabbed the cookie from Sofie's hand and teased his niece. "You want this?"

She swayed, reached and scrambled.

He evaded her, holding it up.

Annie jumped around him, at last wrestling the sweet from him.

Time might not erase darkness entirely but it could, for a moment, heal.

When Annie had played herself out, Sigrid announced it was time to go home.

Annie resisted as her mother scooped her up and walked her back into the house to the front of the house.

Looking resigned and helpless, Sigrid strode to the front door amid the wordless wails of her daughter.

"Let me take her," Rik said, holding out his arms.

Sofie watched the warm exchange of glances between brother and sister.

Sigrid let Annie fall with total trust into her uncle's arms.

"Give me a butterfly kiss," demand Rik.

Annie leaned towards him and blinked her eyelids rapidly over his stubbled cheek.

He laughed uproariously and jiggled her. "Stop! Stop! I'm too ticklish!"

Margaret approached, gave her granddaughter a gentle kiss and went to open the front door.

With dramatic effect, Rik thrust Annie back to his sister.

Sigrid looked sad but resigned as she gathered her daughter into her arms.

Without warning, Annie leaned out of her mother's arms and threw herself outward.

Sofie caught her in mid-air. Overwhelmed by an unnamed emotion, she felt herself redden. Her grip tightened. "And who may pretty little girl in my arms be," she asked as she stared directly into the midnight blue eyes of her charge.

Annie beamed.

Rik didn't. He'd just seen the future he wanted for himself.

As they left, Margaret called, "Tea's ready. Please come to the table." She had prepared Sofie's favourite, oxtail stew. Sofie shook her head and silently smiled her gratitude to Rik's mother. She was touched. They enjoyed blessedly ordinary conversation along with their wine and were now settling into dessert and brandy.

"Sofie, dear, what will you do now?"

Sofie flushed. "I, umm. It's a little bit up in the air."

"Oh, dear. Are you, like our son, limited in what you can say?" Margaret looked frightened.

She glanced at Rik and then shook her head. "I'm not sure what's next for me. I do know that I want to rebuild the cottage my uncle destroyed as soon as I can. I'd like to spend some vacation time each year there. When it's ready, I hope to return the hospitality you've both shown me. Have you been to Canada?"

Margaret shook her head but smiled, pleased with the invitation.

"As far as work is concerned what I know most about is the trafficking of women from Eastern Europe. It's barbaric. It's also tied, unfortunately, to economic necessity and, as we found out, it's linked to the funding of terrorism. I could continue to work in that field. However, I'm also thinking about finding some way to combat the wave of complacency and polarization I see passing across Europe."

Roger's eyebrows rose in question.

"I'm afraid that people, especially young people, who've enjoyed the benefits of democracy have either forgotten, or are ignorant of, the millions who died to give them this gift. They're becoming more used to the idea of accepting authoritarian rule as an answer to what they perceive as danger."

"When you say danger…"

"Let's face it. People who don't look like us or don't agree with us are feared. How often are we being told," Sofie looked at Margaret apologetically, "pardon my language…that we're being screwed over by immigrants, by government institutions, by the media, etc.? Someone's called it `otherization'. That's exactly what it is. It's demoralizing. Life-long government employees or anyone who's an expert who doesn't happen to agree with us is being denigrated, demonized by our leaders. I'm sick of it. We're being brainwashed, or brain-bashed as I think of it. If you hear something often enough, it's hard to resist it from infiltrating our psyche."

Rik shook his head, not in disagreement, but in disbelief. Who was this assertive, confident woman? And how, of all things, did she feel free to talk to his parents? He knew what he felt, had never felt before.

Deep in thought she continued. "Think of it. Most young people are obtaining their news, much of it false or distorted, through Facebook, Twitter or other platforms I don't even know the names of." She took a sip of wine. "I think what I feel most disappointed in is the ease with which forces can manipulate people so that we behave like sheep."

"We?" asked Rik.

"Yes. Sure. I think we're all in danger of going along with the crowd." She was silent for a moment. "Very much so. I'm not sure what I might do, what my role might be, but I'm going to think about it. If we don't start fighting against the forces that are appealing to our fears, we may find ourselves, sooner than we can even imagine, losing our freedom and living under dictators. That's what almost happened here. I'm not sure what one little person like me can do, but I want to find others who're raising similar concerns."

"One little person like you has already done a lot!" said Roger. "But I still think that we've accepted too many immigrants. They stay together and form ghettos. They don't integrate. And they don't speak out against the terrorists enough. If you live here, you should be required to adopt and follow our values," he argued quietly.

Rik felt relief and lightness wash over him. When was the last time we had a civil discussion about important matters at this dinner table?

"Yes, I agree with you," Sofie responded. "Governments had better start thinking about immigration policies and programmes that not just promote, but achieve integration and that demand respect for our fundamental values."

"Will you continue to be in Sarajevo? Or, could you do whatever it is that you want, from England?" asked Margaret.

Sofie was taken aback. "I've never considered that possibility." "We want to see you, dear, and not just once in awhile," Margaret said firmly, looking over at Roger, who solemnly nodded his head.

Tears threatened to erupt. "Thank you for a delicious meal and a happy night. Please excuse me." She stood abruptly, turned and made her way to the staircase.

CHAPTER 32

Early Morning, May 7, 2019, London, England

Wanda Pierce, leader of the Opposition, sat in her parliamentary office mourning the passing of Karl Mueller. Such a great visionary. "Even if our Plan were to fail," he'd said to her, "it would only slightly delay our ultimate success." As he had predicted, the terrorist acts alone were going to cement her alt-right party's victory in the national election that would come soon enough. The Russian would help ensure a positive outcome. And if Oswald and Rupert were going underground, she would have the shadow team come to the fore when it was time.

Her first act, she thought vindictively, would be to put the Queen in her proper place: the ground. If the Queen hadn't ruined the Plan, Wanda would have been appointed by Axworthy as the acting head of government under martial law. It might or might not have been constitutional, but who was going to fight the troops on the street?

Her biggest concern now was who would become the next *Hochmeister*. Such a silly word. But traditions must have their place. Likely, Sumner and the Russian would make a play for the leadership. Not a happy eventuality.

She was grateful that she had been instructed not to communicate with any other members over the last year. If Karl's cover had been blown, she had to believe that hers was still intact. She knew he would have gone to his death without revealing even one detail of *Der Kreis*.

She limped over to the sideboard to prepare another cup of coffee. While she may not be photogenic, her past as a victim of a terrorist act was a rallying point for her base of support. It was also what drove her, every day of her life, to rid her country of the filth that her weak successors had permitted to infiltrate Great Britain. Karl had understood her trauma, and she would miss him.

Sumner Hayes wanted a conference later this afternoon. Should she break the silence she'd kept over this past year? Perhaps not. Let the dust settle, as the Americans were wont to say.

Morning, May 7, 2019, London, England

"Good morning, *Sir* Neal."

"Stuff and nonsense," he waved his hand. "Grab yourself one of your wastes of time in a cup, you cretin," he glared at Rik. "My dear, get yourself a cup of real coffee and find a place to sit."

"Terry, glad you could make it. Now that we're all here, let's move to the conference room."

They sat around the table.

Neal began. "Good morning. The Queen has commanded that our enemy be defeated. She expects to be kept informed of our progress. Last night, Svi, Noah Max and I met and decided that our little clandestine group must continue. Britain will fund the fight, for now. We have the most at stake. If the interests of the United States or Israel become more obvious, they will increase their contribution beyond information sharing."

Svi interrupted. "We needed a name that would be a benign, an innocent line item name for our budgets. Since we seem to produce our best work in the early morning, we propose to call ourselves the Breakfast Club, like the American movie."

Rik stood up slowly. "If you'll excuse me." He exited the room in shock. God damn it. He'd hardly slept last night thinking of next steps. Apparently, they'd already been decided for him by people he'd thought of as his peers, not his superiors.

Neal looked back at the door in mute surprise.

"You, you, you..." Sofie was beyond furious. "*Sir* Neal," she said sarcastically. "Did you put your life on the line several times? Did you save your country? Rik is the heart and soul of your so-called Club and you excluded him?"

"*Ken*," said Adina, swearing under her breath.

Neal shook his head in wilful denial. "Rik's an adult. That's the way our organizations have to work. We had to agree on money. He knows that."

"A lot of good your money will do without him. Frankly, you have your heads in a very dark place."

Neal, Svi and Noah were silent, apparently unused to such overt disrespect being shown by a subordinate.

Sofie glared as she walked out the door.

"I couldn't agree with her more," said Adina, her voice dripping with disgust. "I have no idea how you're going to make it right with Rik. You'd better pray that Sofie can bring him back. Without him, there is no Club."

This was his warrior at her best thought Max. The situation might have been humorous if he'd been sure Rik would return.

Noah interjected. "Look. We were all tired. We made a mistake. Let's make it right."

"It isn't going to be easy," said Max. "He's going to feel we bought him off if we offer him a promotion. Let's just apologize for a stupid-fuck move."

"Rik, slow down. We need you." Sofie placed her hand on his.

He used one arm to brush her off. He felt humiliated. He looked away from her. How she must see him now, diminished by his boss, by his colleagues.

"Please."

He shook his head. "It's time I moved on."

"No. You may want that. But until we stop them, it can't be time.

What will it take for you to stay? What do you want? Tell them. Demand it. But please don't quit. You'll regret it for the rest of your life. And," she said quietly, "So will I." She turned and walked slowly back to the room, feeling as if she was moving through molasses, as if her whole life might just have been altered.

When she returned to the room and sat down, no one spoke.

Suddenly, the door opened. Rik towered above them, spoke quietly. "You met without consulting me. That was your prerogative. It reflects your reality. Here's mine. If you wish me to continue, you'll place me in charge of this group. I'll develop the budget. I'll develop the plan in consultation with each of you. I'll mobilize the people. If this scenario is unacceptable to you, I'm out. Believe me, leaving the Service is a very attractive option right now. Decide, and let me know."

Neal caught his arm as Rik turned towards the door again. "We bloody messed up. We're all overtired. For Christ sake, sit down." Turning to the room, he said, "Get the man his decaf!"

Max laughed, deliberately. Others followed.

Noah stood and waved Rik to his chair. "Rik, my man. You've just been promoted to be Acting Director of whatever you want to call this benighted group. We'll negotiate terms later."

Afternoon, May 7, 2019, The Hague, Netherlands

Marc Jansen's hands shook as he drank the cup of coffee his secretary had brought in for him. No one ever told him anything. He'd tried to get through to his cousins in Germany and Switzerland. What had gone wrong? Was he in danger?

Thirty seconds later, he fell to the carpet.

Geist exited the building. The dragon that kept him fed had a new head. Job security was important to everyone, even him. He smiled. For a while, he could rest at home in Kaliningrad with his wife.

Late Morning, May 7, 2019, Moscow, Russia

The President waved his translator out of the room. The idiots, he screamed to himself. New sanctions, credible threats of escalation into a war that Russia couldn't afford and didn't want, all because of Mueller and his incompetents.

He picked up the phone. "Withdraw."

"Mr. President?"

"I said, get us out of Lithuania, now."

Late Morning, May 7, 2019, Washington, D.C.

That shit, Mueller, so full of himself, had died a shameful death, the Vice-President thought contemptuously. It was long past time that he became Hochmeister. He'd all but bankrolled it. Now, he'd run it, and soon, an entire country.

Afternoon, May 7, 2019, London, England

"Stay here. Work with Rik. You can't go back to Israel, Dini. Whoever's in charge of Der Kreis will come after you. As far as they know, you were the one who blew their entire operation."

"I can't imagine not living in my home, my neighbourhood, my country."

"Dini, we need to destroy this group. Until we do, you can't live there."

"What do mean `we'? You can't quit being a banking guru. Israel needs you to keep tracking terrorist money."

"I know what I want, and that's to finish this job we've started. And I need us to do it together."

"Svi will never let you go," said Adina.

"He will, once he acknowledges that, if Der Kreis' next target is either Germany or the U.S., neither is in the interests of Israel. I think Neal is working on him, as we speak. Dini, come with me to Berlin. I'll show you where I've been holed up these last years. Maybe, we can take a week and go somewhere warm. Just give me a chance to make up for my mistake."

Adina looked up at him, sensed his vulnerability and saw something she had always wanted to see in his eyes.

"Come to dinner with me tonight. I know this great little place that will remind you of home. Please."

It was the hardest thing in the world for her to trust. He'd betrayed that sacred bond and had broken her heart.

He stood, helpless, unable to move.

Finally, she stepped forward, wrapped her arms around his body and held him as if her life depended on it.

Night, May 7, 2019, London, England

Margaret would be up tomorrow to prepare breakfast before their early flight back to Sarajevo. Sofie just knew it, though they'd just said their goodbyes. Margaret had hugged her long and hard, and she'd responded in kind.

She turned down the covers of her bed, and climbed in. A quiet knock sounded. "Are you still awake?"

"Yes. Come in." She sat up.

Rik entered and pulled up a chair to sit close by the bed. He leaned forward.

He looks uncertain, she thought, and adorable, his long lashes framing his eyes. Tonight, they were midnight blue.

He slid his hand towards hers, grasped them in his hands. "Tell me you're up for what's next."

ACKNOWLEDGEMENTS

I profoundly thank the following people, who, through their on-going encouragement, critiques and technical inputs, have made this book possible:

My family members, John Lamb, Alison Lee, Ron Lamb, Nicolien Lamb and Max Lamb, who had the patience to listen to preliminary ideas, read early versions of the book and who provided their honest and invaluable feedback.

My Aunt, Phyllis Agnew, who was largely responsible for fostering my love for languages, proper grammar and writing.

Many friends and colleagues who took the time to read through early drafts and offer their inputs, including: Bev and Lou Nettleton; Paula Gretsinger and Ben Gasman; Anne Richards; Rikki Durbin; Andrée Shore; Shoshana Fine; Margaret King; Judie Fraser; and Georgia Watterson.

My cousin, Heather, whose love, generosity of spirit and support were so appreciated.

Kim Echlin, a Canadian author and teacher, who stressed that, the more you develop your characters, the more they'll take you on an exhilarating narrative ride you could never, otherwise, have imagined.

Katie Isbester of Clapham Press in London, England, who provided her editing expertise.

Robert Hughes, who patiently took over the production of all graphics and who formatted and printed my book.

Phillippa Baran, whose unfailing encouragement, positivity, love and support kept me going through the good times and bad times over the course of writing *PERIL*.

Dan Baran, whose enthusiasm for, and knowledge of the ideas I was developing, spurred me on.

Maida Rogerson and Martin Rutte, who shared their experience of writing and publishing and who exhorted me to keep at it.

Rik Kristjansson, who put me in contact with an important source of technical information that I required for my story.

Sally Davidson, my friend and business partner, who, through a comment she made, sparked the idea for this book in the first place.

Made in the USA
Las Vegas, NV
11 October 2021